MW00479772

PRAISE FOR THE NOVELS OF KATIE MacALISTER

Memoirs of a Dragon Hunter
"Bursting with the author's trademark zany humor and spicy romance...
this quick tale will delight paranormal romance fans."
—*Publishers Weekly*

Sparks Fly
"Balanced by a well-organized plot and MacAlister's trademark humor."
—*Publishers Weekly*

It's All Greek to Me
"A fun and sexy read."
—The Season for Romance
"A wonderful lighthearted romantic romp as a kick-butt American Amazon
and a hunky Greek find love. Filled with humor, fans will laugh with the
zaniness of Harry meets Yacky."
—*Midwest Book Review*

Much Ado About Vampires
"A humorous take on the dark and demonic."
—*USA Today*

"Once again this author has done a wonderful job. I was sucked into the
world of Dark Ones right from the start and was taken on a fantastic ride.
This book is full of witty dialogue and great romance, making it one that
should not be missed."
—Fresh Fiction

The Unbearable Lightness of Dragons

"Had me laughing out loud...This book is full of humor and romance, keeping the reader entertained all the way through...a wondrous story full of magic...I cannot wait to see what happens next in the lives of the dragons."
—Fresh Fiction

Also by Katie MacAlister

Fireborn

Starborn

A Born Prophecy

Katie MacAlister

REBEL BASE BOOKS
Kensington Publishing Corp.
www.kensingtonbooks.com

Rebel Base Books are published by
Kensington Publishing Corp. 119 West 40th Street New York, NY 10018

Copyright © 2019 by Katie MacAlister

All rights reserved. No part of this book may be reproduced in any form or by any means without the prior written consent of the Publisher, excepting brief quotes used in reviews.

All Kensington titles, imprints, and distributed lines are available at special quantity discounts for bulk purchases for sales promotion, premiums, fundraising, and educational or institutional use.

To the extent that the image or images on the cover of this book depict a person or persons, such person or persons are merely models, and are not intended to portray any character or characters featured in the book.

Special book excerpts or customized printings can also be created to fit specific needs. For details, write or phone the office of the Kensington Special Sales Manager:
Kensington Publishing Corp.
119 West 40th Street
New York, NY 10018
Attn. Special Sales Department. Phone: 1-800-221-2647.

Kensington Reg. U.S. Pat. & TM Off
Rebel Base and the RB logo Reg. U.S. Pat. & TM Off.

First Electronic Edition: December 2019
ISBN-13: 978-1-63573-075-3 (ebook)
ISBN-10: 1-63573-075-9 (ebook)

First Print Edition: December 2019
ISBN-13: 978-1-63573-076-0
ISBN-10: 1-63573-076-7

Printed in the United States of America

Prologue

"Who would like to read their poem?"

The room was stifling hot, so hot that the faint sheen of reddish-brown dust blown in through the glassless window seemed to dance on every surface in the schoolroom. Lala, apprentice in the Temple of Kiriah Sunbringer, ignored the heat and dust to focus every ounce of energy, every iota of power in her being to will Peebles to see her wildly waving arm.

It seemed as if the priestess must be blind, because as she cast her gaze over the class of approximately six young apprentices, all between five and ten summers old, only Lala's arm was in the air. After a moment's consideration, Lala raised her second arm, feeling it greatly increased the odds that Peebles would call on her to read her epic poem.

And epic it was. She had worked for many a long hour on the poem, and she was not going to have the bad eyesight of her teacher snatch away the praise that was sure to be heaped upon her head after everyone heard her work.

A gentle cough, really more a clearing of the throat, came from the rear of the room, where Lady Sandor, head of the order of priests, sat. Lala waved her arms with even more vigor, thrilled to the tips of her sandals at the thought of Lady Sandor hearing her poem.

Visions of honors danced in her head. Sandor might be so overcome with her handling of the poem that she would make Lala a full priest right then and there, eight years sooner than usual.

The cough repeated itself, and Peebles, with a sigh, said, "Yes, Lala? You have a poem you wish to share with us?"

Lala didn't waste time explaining that she did. She didn't even stand at her desk as the other, more reluctant, apprentices did. She grasped her much scribbled-over pages, and marched to the front of the room, little eddies of dust swirling behind her.

With another sigh, Peebles moved aside and gestured to her. "You may begin, Lala. But mind you, speak clearly and concisely. Lady Sandor is a busy woman, and she has only a few minutes to spend with us."

Lala ignored Peebles, filled as she was with confidence. This was her moment, her time to shine before the goddess Kiriah and Sandor together. With a business like throat clearing that mimicked Lady Sandor, she picked up the first sheet, and began to read. "The Saga of Allegria Hopebringer, by Lala Smalls, apprentice priest."

"Allegria? I'm not sure that's a fitting subject for our class," Peebles said, casting Sandor a questioning glance. The latter said nothing.

Lala gave the two youngest apprentices in the front row, who had burst into nervous giggles, a quelling glance before returning her attention to her paper.

"'Twas a year ago, on this very day
That Allegria, warrior priestess, rode away.
To join Lord Deosin, she did plan,
and fight the dread invading Harborym!"

"Plan and Harborym don't rhyme," Peebles interrupted.

"I couldn't very well say Harborham," Lala replied, frowning. "You said that poets sometimes varied their rhyming scheme, and that to do so was allowed."

"Yes, but those are poets who have much experience—" Peebles, with another glance at Lady Sandor, heaved a third sigh, and said, "We will leave that discussion for another time. Proceed."

Lala shook her papers in a meaningful manner. Really, to be interrupted was most vexing. She had to count on Lady Sandor recognizing genius even if Peebles didn't.

"For Deo had taken the invader's own magic,
and used it to create his army most tragic!
Banes of Eris were they, dire and dreadful to be seen,
They sailed to Genora, land of Deo's mama, the queen."

"Your timing, my child," Peebles murmured, shaking her head. "We must have a talk about meter later."

"But brave Deo's father, Lord Israel of Abet.
Raced to Genora, and there he met
A handsome young arcanist, one named Hallow
Lost in a strange land, master-less, his fields were fallow."

"Er...his fields were fallow?" Lady Sandor asked, soundly faintly puzzled.

Lala stifled her irritation at being interrupted again, and with a little frown, said, "It's a metaphor. It means he didn't have a plan."

"Ah. Indeed." Lady Sandor passed a hand over her mouth as if she had to cough. "Pray continue, child."

"Allegria and Hallow met and fell in love,
And with them came Thorn, a wooden bird, but not a dove.
Hallow was given Kelos, land of spirits and fierce ghosts,
While Allegria wielded the light of Kiriah's blessed sun motes."

"This really isn't very good," one of the two youngest apprentices whispered.

"Shhh! She's looking at us!" the other answered.

Lala sharpened her glare for a moment, then returned to her epic saga.

"Lord Deo, Allegria, Hallow, and Thorn, too
To Starfall city they all but flew.
Queen Dasa was prisoner of a heinous brute,
Wielder of chaos, the captain Racoot."

"Racin," came the correction from the back of the small room. "The captain's name was Racin."

Lala paid no mind to the comment, too caught up in the beauty of her vision. Besides, she was getting to the good part. She stood on a chair, and with one arm lifted high, continued in as a ringing tone as she could muster given the heat and dust.

"Deo's sword sang with blood of the vile Harborym,
While Allegria and Hallow hacked them limb from limb.
But the captain was canny, and through his portal he took the queen,
Leaving Lord Israel behind, to face the Council's spleen."

"Really, Lala," Peebles protested. "Spleen is definitely not a metaphor."

Lady Sandor gave another one of her odd coughs.

"The Council of Four Armies was very, very mad.
They did not like Deo. They thought he was bad.
So Lord Israel used the queen's own precious moonstones,
To send Deo far away, to a rocky outcast home.
And when Racin returned, intent on grinding us all to sand,
Allegria and Hallow and Deo cast him from the land.
Through the very portal he came in, and which Allegria destroyed,
but not before Deo, fearing for the Queen, a hasty plan employed."

Lala paused, giving them all a look she felt was most potent. Every eye was on her, the room as hushed as a tomb. She dropped her voice until it was almost a whisper.

"Now. Deo is gone, and Lord Israel is most grave.

Allegria and Hallow seek the three moonstones to save.
Their friend, and the queen, who are captive on Eris,
Find them they must, else surely they will perish."

Faint noises of everyday life at the temple wafted in through the window; the distant chatter of priests as they went about their chores, the gentle hum of bees on the honeysuckle that climbed along the corner of the schoolroom, and the soft lowing of cattle as they were herded in for afternoon milking.

But in the room itself, all was silent. Lala smiled to herself. Content that she had held her audience captive in the palm of her hand, and while returning to her seat, adopted a modest expression, as befitted one who was an apprentice priest.

"Er...yes. Very...imaginative." Peebles seemed to have some sort of trouble speaking, and Lala focused her attention on Lady Sandor when the latter rose and made her way to the front of the room. She paused as she passed by Lala, her lips twitching a little when she looked down at Lala's hopeful—yet modest expression. Then she was gone, the door closing quietly behind her.

Lala glared at the door, annoyance mingling with anger for a moment until she realized what had happened. Obviously Lady Sandor didn't want to show favoritism by promoting Lala on the spot. It might make for hard feelings in the older girls. No doubt that's why Sandor had to appear indifferent.

Thus it was that while Peebles called on one of the other apprentices to recite, Lala planned just how she'd make a fair copy of the poem and present it to Lady Sandor later, so it could be framed and hung in the head priestess's bedchamber. Perhaps she might slip away from Peebles's attention long enough to run into town and give a copy over to the local weekly newspaper. Yes. That was a satisfactory thought. A very satisfactory thought, indeed.

Chapter 1

"You do not belong here, Allegria Hopebringer. Begone before the Eidolon make you one of their own!"

A face materialized in the almost complete darkness of the crypt, the eyes appearing black and hostile as they considered me. Little tendrils of ghostly light surrounding the face evaporated just as if bits of him were turning to dust before my eyes.

"Blessings of Kiriah, my lord," I said politely, digging through my admittedly scant knowledge of history. This particular spirit had to be one of the Eidolon thanes, long-forgotten kings who had ruled the seven lands of Alba well before the coming of the modern races. It was rumored that the tunnels honeycombing the area under Kelos were home to beings who had been dead longer than the memory of man, and evidently the rumors were correct. "I mean you no harm, although I wonder how you know me."

The face seemed to fade into the blackness, only to suddenly appear again, parts of his visage drifting off into nothing as he spoke in a slow, ponderous tone. "You bear the grace of the sun goddess as well as the stink of mortals. Who else would you be?" He faded again, then materialized immediately in front of me, his ethereal face thrust into mine, his voice carrying the heavy rumble of thunder. "Your kind is not welcome to walk our paths! Begone, I say again!"

I held my swords easily, one in each hand, the runes on the blades dulled by the fact that we were deep underground, out of the reach of Bellias Starsong, goddess of the night sky. "I mean you no harm, lord thane, but pass I must. I have been charged by Hallow, the Master of Kelos to search the crypt." That was not wholly the truth, since said master, who also happened to be the man I loved, believed there was nothing in the crypt but spirits best left to them selves. But I had a bet with the captain of the guard in charge of protecting the ancient center of magic, and I wasn't going to let him best me.

"Search for what?" For a few moments, curiosity lit the black eyes of the thane.

"Three moonstones hidden by the previous Master. Do you know of them?"

The face faded, remnants of the ghostly halo around it remaining for a few seconds before dissolving. "Mortal concerns mean little to the Eidolon. Leave now." His voice echoed off the stone arches that lined the crypt.

The fact that he knew who I was made me wonder if we weren't too quick to dismiss the spirits here as being of no help to us. If he knew me, he might well know the whereabouts of Queen Dasa's moonstones, scattered after they were last used. "That's not really an answer. I don't want to be annoying, but a yes or no would be helpful," I said, mindful of the way the hairs on my arms rose, warning me of unseen movement around me. "I'm afraid I'm going to have to insist on an answer. A proper answer, that is, not one that is nothing but confusing."

A hissing noise followed, as if the thane was sucking in all the air of the already airless crypt. Although I'd placed a lit torch in one of the brackets on the wall, the glow of its golden light didn't penetrate very far into the cloying darkness. I could make out large rectangular shapes that I knew were sarcophagi of the arcanists who had once resided in Kelos, but beyond the tombs…another shiver rippled down my back. The inky black beyond the pool of light cast by the torch seemed to move and shift, little flickers of shadow visible only in my peripheral vision.

"You challenge the Eidolon?" The words seemed to roll around me like the growl of a cave bear.

"I do not challenge. I simply seek information. If you won't answer my question, then I must search the crypt." I gripped my swords and sent a little query to my patron goddess Kiriah. There was no answering warmth, just a claustrophic sense of being buried deep in the earth. I held onto the panic that wanted to rise at the knowledge that somehow I'd displeased the sun goddess, and she was withholding her blessings from me, and instead reminded myself that I had fought deadlier enemies than a single spirit.

But then I'd had Hallow and our friend Deo at my side.

The rush of air behind me gave me less than a second to respond, but it was enough to send me whirling to the side, both of my swords flashing. The thane emerged from the shadows fully formed, his body encased in ghostly armor from at least two millennia in the past, and his translucent white hair flowing around him as if it had a life of its own. But it was the sword he raised that held my attention, and I barely had one of my own narrow blades up in time to block the blow that would have sundered me in twain.

I leaped to the side, clambering onto one of the sarcophagi as he swung his sword low; the visible section of his near-translucent face was frozen in a snarl, his eyes all but spitting black ire at me. I didn't attack him, using my weapons only to defend myself, but my breath came short when I spoke.

"I know you're annoyed at being disturbed—" I dove off the stone structure when he leaped up, his sword held high overhead, only to stumble backward when he lunged after me, my swords dancing in the air to parry the lightning-fast blows that seemed to rain down on me. "Goddesses above, how is it that spirits are able to move so quickly? I just want to know if you've seen the moonstones! Ow! Oh, now you're in for it!"

That last was in response to the tip of his blade scratching across my upper arm when I swung both of my swords upwards, crossed in order to stop another of his two-handed blows. He snarled something, but I hadn't survived the battle of the Fourth Age for nothing. I dove downward, my blades slashing as I rolled past him, only to leap to my feet and watch with satisfaction as one of his legs collapsed. Although I couldn't kill a spirit, I could attack the energy he used to become corporeal, and I had just weakened the stream of energy that flowed up the thane's left leg.

He collapsed with another snarl, kneeling on his good leg to glare at me.

"I'd say I'm sorry for hurting you, but we both know that you'll be fine just as soon as you rally enough energy to restore your leg," I said, panting a little. "Now, perhaps you'll answer my question—"

A faint breeze behind me stirred my hair. To my horror, the fallen thane smiled, then stood up, his damaged leg apparently whole again.

Fear gripped me good and hard then, along with the awareness that I had done something extremely foolish, and if I didn't get out of there, I might well join him in the spirit world.

"It is too late," was all he said before he melted away into nothing. I turned and gazed down a long hallway made up of graceful white stone arches, receding as far as I could see. The fact that I could see them sent another wave of fear through me, gripping my belly with a cold hand; from the light that illuminated the length of the crypt came the slowly emerging Eidolon, members of the thane's company. Men and women who had fought two thousand years before, arcanists and soldiers and wielders of magic long since lost to our kind, all formed wispy grey figures. The stone ribs of the crypt were visible through their bodies as they started forward.

Toward me.

"Kiriah's ten toes," I swore under my breath, and spun around to run for my life.

A war cry rose from behind me, echoing down the long hallway and catching me as I was partway up the thirty-nine steps that led to the cellar under the tower of Kelos. I didn't dare glance behind me to see how close the spirits were, having had ample proof from my brief skirmish with the thane to know that spirits can move very quickly when they choose to do so. But a cold breath seemed to touch the back of my neck when I reached the door. I sheathed my swords and yanked open the portal, then slid through the opening, slamming it shut just as the nearest spirit swung his sword.

Panting so loudly that I couldn't hear anything but the beat of my own heart, I clutched the circular iron link that served as an anchor for a chain that normally stretched across the door, holding tight in case the spirits tried to follow. The runes that had been engraved into the iron bands that crisscrossed the door flared to life with a dull white glow, then faded. I tried to catch my breath, well aware that my hands were shaking. After taking a moment to control myself, I wound the chain through the anchor, and locked it into place.

The captain of the guard was waiting when I turned around, his arms crossed, a slight smile on his lips. I relaxed at the sight of him, one part of me marveling that I had grown so comfortable with the spirits—the captain included—who resided above ground in Kelos, although they were often a trial to Hallow, they had given me no problems.

Except for the captain, who took offense over the fact that the first time we'd met I had separated his ghostly head from the rest of his body. It had taken him a good hour to generate enough power to become corporeal again; a fact that almost a year later, he still held against me, often setting me difficult challenges to overcome.

Like the Eidolon. With the memory of just how close my escape had been, I glared at the captain.

His smiled broadened.

"If Hallow wasn't busy trying to find those blasted moonstones, I'd *so* tell him you set me up," I informed the captain, handing him the key to the locks.

His eyebrows rose. "I take it that you had no luck?"

"No, I didn't. Why didn't you tell me that the spirits down there were Eidolon?"

His smile became even bigger. "You said you wished for more practice with your swords than my soldiers offer you. Who better to hone your skills that the most feared warriors of Alba?"

"The thane I could handle…mostly…but there were hundreds more of them that came pouring out of their resting places," I said, with a glance back at the door. I hesitated before climbing the second set of stairs. "Er… you're sure that's going to hold them? They were more than a little annoyed when I fought their king."

"Oh, the door isn't scribed to protect us from the Eidolon," the captain said blithely as he preceded me up the stairs. "It's to keep other spirits from bothering them."

"It just keeps the spirits out?" I shook my head. "That makes no sense. If they wanted to remain solitary, why wouldn't the protection extend to keeping everyone out?"

He paused and cocked an eyebrow at me, a gleam of amusement in his faded eyes. "No mortal would be foolish enough to annoy an Eidolon. I assumed you knew that."

"Oh, you did not…gah!" I said rude things under my breath as the captain marched upward, but at the same time, I felt twitchy until we emerged into the open, climbing out of the cellar of an outbuilding next to the master's tower. I turned my face up to the sun, and sent a query up to the goddess, but other than a slight warmth that was my awareness of her, Kiriah seemed to keep her blessings from me.

My heart fell. It seemed that every day since the battle that ended with my channeling Kiriah herself, I had been more and more removed from her. *One day,* the paranoid part of my mind whispered, *one day, she will refuse you altogether. And then where will you be?* "Useless. Wholly and utterly useless…" I answered the insidious whisper.

"You think so?" The captain paused and made a show of turning back toward the stairs. "I can have the lock and chain removed from the door if you wish to confront the Eidolon again, although I can't say I recommend such an action."

"No, I wasn't talking about the Eidolon. I meant…oh, never mind." I pushed my misery down into a small ball of worry and walked past the captain. "Although, you could have told me that the thane himself was down there. Yes, I know I said I wanted practice fighting more adept opponents, but next time, let me know that I will be fighting against a king and his entire company."

The captain shrugged and strode next to me when I went to the stable yard, where there was a pump. My throat was parched from the airless, dusty environment of the crypt. "It does little good talking when the Master won't listen to what I have to say."

"Hallow is very busy trying to locate the moonstones. The two he hasn't found, that is." I splashed my face with water from the pump, then took a long drink, washing away not just the dust, but the panic that had filled me in the crypt when faced with the knowledge that I was in over my head.

"So he repeatedly tells me, when he deigns to notice me, that is."

I frowned down at my hands holding the metal drinking cup that hung on the pump. If I'd had my lightweaving abilities in the crypt...if Kiriah had not turned deaf ears to my pleas...if I had been more adept with my swords, then I wouldn't have run from the Eidolon.

"Which isn't very often. 'You are naught but a spirit bound to this place,' he said to me the other day, just as if the captain of the guard of Kelos has no power of his own! I have served seven masters, and I will serve seven more before I pass into the region beyond this world."

"Mmhmm," I said absently, then filled a bucket and hauled it over to where my mule Buttercup dozed in a small paddock. She rolled an eye toward me to see if I had any treats, looking disappointed when I merely filled her water tub.

"He treats me as if I am nothing but an annoyance, and yet I have done my best to serve him." The captain's voice was filled with pique.

I was well aware that he disapproved of Hallow almost as much as he did me, but there wasn't much I could do about that even if I had the time to act as peacemaker. "I'm sure he's very grateful you keep the spirits here in order," I murmured, wondering how best to tell Hallow that my expedition to the crypt had been useless. Not that he had truly believed Exodius, the former Master of Kelos, had hidden the precious moonstones there, but still, it was one more setback. If we didn't get those stones, we couldn't rescue our friend Deo and his mother, Dasa.

And the guilt that plucked at me over Deo's plunge through the portal to the shadowland of Eris made it imperative that we find a way to save both of them.

"I do more than simply keep the denizens of Kelos in order," the captain said with a snort. "I am a guardian, protector of the knowledge of Kelos. To me, the Masters impart their most valuable secrets, knowing I would protect and keep them until such time as they are needed. And that time is now."

He followed when I headed toward the tower that was one of the few standing structures in Kelos. Once the famed center of learning for arcanists all over Alba, it had fallen into ruin; most of the buildings having collapsed into piles of rubble and stained bricks. Of the beautiful silver domes, pierced with the shapes of stars, planets, and other heavenly bodies, nothing remained but tales of glory days in the books found in Hallow's library. Now, the same grey dust that made up the ground seemed to gently envelop everything from the scrubby plants that grew through the broken walls and foundations, down to Buttercup, and Hallow's horse Penn. At least once a day I had to dust them both off.

"I wish I could have seen Kelos when it was in its prime," I said, distracted for a few moments. "Hallow says it was famed across Genora and Aryia both and was second only to Starfall City for beauty. I would love to have seen that."

"It was far more beautiful than the city of the queen," the captain said, his voice full of pride as he walked next to me. "The white stone of the towers glowed at night, and the domes shone almost as bright as Bellias Starsong herself. And of course, we had many more arcanists than those who served at Starfall. It has ever been an honor to serve the Master directly, and the arcanists who lived here were the most powerful Alba had ever seen."

"Hallow's pretty powerful in his own right," I said, feeling defensive on his behalf. I didn't mind the captain chaffing Hallow a little, but it was quite obvious to me just how learned Hallow had become since Exodius had gone into the spirit realm, leaving Hallow to wrangle the arcanists who made up their order. "Without his help, Lord Deo and I would never have been able to close the rifts that the Harborym used to invade us. I will admit that I don't know the extent of Exodius's power, but I have seen Hallow in battle, and it was awe inspiring."

The captain eyed me. "So sayeth the priest who has channeled Kiriah Sunbringer herself."

I couldn't help but glance down at my hands. Fine scars ran from my elbows to my fingertips, fanning out like flames, the result of our last battle with the Harborym. "I am ever blessed by the goddess," I murmured modestly, knowing just how much I owed to my lightweaving abilities.

If only Kiriah would grant me the full extent of my powers again, rather than the brief little sips that came with decreasing frequency...

"Which is why the Master needs to think twice about spurning my offer of help. Without it, you will not succeed."

I opened the door to the tower where Hallow and I resided, the runes on the door keeping the spirits from being able to enter, including the captain of the guard. He glowed with a faint bluish white light, his face set in its usual impassive expression, but I felt a sense of frustration in him that was different from his normal impatience with Hallow and me. I hesitated, biting my lip for a moment, knowing that I didn't have time to try to resolve whatever problems the captain had with Hallow's leadership.

"We would never spurn your assistance," I told him in a soothing tone, deciding a few seconds spent smoothing his ruffled feathers might give us a little peace and quiet. "But unless Exodius told you where he hid Queen Dasa's moonstones, then I doubt if you can help us much. Hallow is doing everything he can to locate the two moonstones that are hidden, which is why it's important to let him conduct his search without disruption. The spells he casts to look through the veils that obscure the stones' location take much concentration—"

"Bah," the captain said with a snort. "All he has to do is take the talisman."

"What talisman?" I asked, wanting to go in and report my lack of findings, and more importantly, check how Hallow was doing. I hadn't seen him since early evening the night before, when he had climbed to the upper floor of the tower, where he joined five other arcanists scattered across Aryia and Genora to commune via arcany.

A coy expression crossed the captain's face, translucent as it was. "I cannot give it to anyone but the Master of Kelos. It is he who must seek my aid. Thus it has been, and thus it ever will be."

"Doesn't it normally work the other way around?" I asked, confused. "Shouldn't you serve the Master?"

"I do!" he said, looking outraged. "But I am the captain of the guard! It is for the Master to ask for my service."

I opened my mouth to say that didn't make any sense, then shook my head, and murmured something about letting Hallow know what he'd said. By the time I made it to our living quarters halfway up the tower, I had mentally drafted a speech in which I pointed out to Hallow how important rest was, and that he hadn't slept in over twenty-four hours; thus, he needed to let me put him to bed. And if I joined him, making sure he was well loved before he rested, well, who was to complain?

Our living area showed no sign of a blond-haired, blue-eyed arcanist, which made me tsk to myself in irritation. I glanced upward and tried to decide if it was worth interrupting Hallow to tell him about the Eidolon, then decided that he'd had long enough to commune. "It's time we do something," I said aloud, climbing a short ladder that was used to reach the upper levels of the tall bookshelves that lined the tower before clambering onto a small landing, and proceeding through a narrow door to an even narrower stone passage that wound upward to the top level of the tower. I eased the door open, worried I would interrupt Hallow in the middle of a spell or incantation, but although the scent of smoke and incense wafted through the open door to me, there was no noise from within.

I poked my head through the opening. Sunlight flowed through crescent shaped windows, making motes of dust dance in the air, and leaving warm, golden pools shimmering across the stone floor. Unlike our living quarters, this room was bare of all except a small table, a plethora of candles that had burned themselves out, and one prone arcanist, lying in the center of the circle of candles, a sheaf of papers on his chest.

"Hallow?"

His body lay still. Too still, without movement or breath.

Fear dug into me with sharp little claws of despair, sending me forward with a sob caught in my throat. "Blessed Kiriah, no! Hallow, my love!" What had happened? Had his magic gone awry? Had the other arcanists done something to harm him?

I was across the floor before the last word left my lips, kneeling beside the prone form of the man who had so wholly captured my heart the year before, tears pricking painfully at my eyes when I reached a shaking hand out to him. He lay so still, his beautiful burnished hair splayed on the floor, a similar golden stubble covering his jaw and chin. "I can't...Hallow, I can't do this without you...goddesses of day and night, help me!"

"Hrmph?" To my utter stupefaction—followed immediately by joy, and a few seconds after that, anger—Hallow gave a little snort, rubbed his nose, then turned his head to peer at me with sleepy eyes. "What did you say?"

"You...you..." I wanted to laugh and cry and yell. I wanted to shake him, and kiss him, and strip the blue arcanist's robes he'd donned for the communion from his body, and show him just how much I'd missed him. Instead, I grabbed the papers on his chest, and smacked them onto the top of his head. "I thought you were dead, you great oaf! Don't you ever scare me like that again!"

"Dead? Me?" He sat up, rubbing first the top of his head, then his face. He yawned, the rat, his eyes warm despite the rich blue hue that characterized all users of arcane magic. "What made you think that?"

"You weren't breathing." I put my hand on his chest, over his heart, just to reassure myself. "Your chest wasn't moving at all."

"Of course it was. You just didn't see it because you were too busy ogling my manly form." He smiled, making me feel as if I had been lying out in a summer field receiving Kiriah's warmth. Then, with a hand on the back of my neck, he pulled me forward to kiss me, murmuring against my lips, "My heart, I can't promise that we will leave the mortal plane together, but I can swear that we will not be long parted in this world or the next."

I allowed myself to be mollified, and would have given in to the temptation that he posed but just as I slid my hand inside the neck of his robe to stroke his chest, he leaped up, saying, "Bellias blast me to the stars and back. It's morning?"

"Yes, and if I were any other sort of woman, I'd take umbrage with the fact that you clearly don't want me to do more than ogle your manly form."

He laughed and pulled me to my feet, giving me a swift kiss as well as pinching my behind. "You know full well there is nothing I would rather do than dally with you in bed…and on the green couch…and that rug with the white fur that you said tickles your legs…but there is much we need to do before the day is gone. I must have fallen asleep after dispersing the arcany that built up during the communion."

His eyes were lit with a glint that I had once thought was him laughing at the world, but now knew was simply his joy of life. I stopped him as he headed through the door, my gaze searching the face I loved so dearly. There was an air of suppressed excitement that didn't fool me. "You found the two stones?" I asked.

"I didn't, but Avas located one." He smiled again, his hands on my arms as he gave me a little squeeze. "He was passing through Ilam, and he sensed the presence of one of the stones close by."

"Ilam?" I asked, confused. "But that's in the High Lands of Poronne, isn't it?"

"Aye." His eyes positively danced with mirth. He waited, clearly expecting me to piece together the clue he'd just given me with what I knew about Exodius.

"Why would Exodius send a stone to the lands held by the Tribe of Jalas…Kiriah's nostrils, tell me he didn't give it to the ice queen?"

His smile turned into a cheeky grin. "One of these days, you're going to have to get your jealousy of Lady Idril under control. And no, Exodius didn't give it to her."

"I'm not in any way jealous of Idril. Her life choices are not mine. The fact that she threw over Deo to marry his father is neither here nor there. If I had wanted Deo, I could have had him."

"Yes, I'm perfectly aware that your boyfriend claimed kisses from you before I did," Hallow said with a pointed look that was softened by the twitch of his lips.

"He was never my boyfriend," I said automatically, then clicked my tongue in disgust. "Exodius must have given the stone to Idril's murderous father."

"I'm not going to comment about the methods a man must use to control as many fractious tribesmen as Jalas controls," he said evenly, taking my hand and pulling me after him down to our tower room. "But you are correct—Avas felt a stone's presence in Jalas's keep."

"That means we just have one to find if Avas retrieved Jalas's stone." Silence met my statement.

"Avas *did* get the stone, didn't he?" I asked, watching when Hallow, having released my hand, pulled out two stiffened leather packs from under our bed, hauling them around the screen that gave us a modicum of privacy.

"No." The humor in his eyes faded a little when he went to the shelves that held baskets containing our clothing. "Jalas would not admit he had the stone, and when Avas tried to locate it, there was an incident with a bear."

"A what?" I gawked at him, absently pulling out a few garments I used when we traveled: my old Bane of Eris tunic and leggings, a robe designating me as a priestess of the temple of Kiriah Sunbringer, and my one nice gown of a rich, very soft garnet velvet that Hallow had given me on the day we were wed. I had only worn it once—on the night of our wedding, and then only for a few minutes before he stripped it from me, saying it made him mad with lust—but I felt strongly that if we were going to the court of Jalas and his perfect, never ruffled daughter Idril, then by the twin goddesses, I was going to look the picture of elegance.

"Evidently Jalas has a pet bear." Hallow stopped tossing clothing into one of the leather packs, rubbing his stubbly chin. "Avas was a bit hesitant to give details, but I gather that when he found out there was a bear guarding Jalas's bedchamber, he shaped arcany to fool the bear, and there was…an incident."

I stared at him, the soft folds of my velvet gown in my hands. "You can shapeshift?"

"Me? No." He shook his head, gathering up a couple of journals and the sword that Deo's father, Israel Langton, had given him. He strapped it to the top of the pack. "Master Wix never taught me such things. I doubt if he knew the way of it, himself. But Avas has spent much time in isolation, perfecting his abilities to shape arcany, and evidently he can don the appearance of other beings for a short time."

I carefully folded my gown and tucked it away in my leather pack. "So he went into Jalas's bedchamber disguised as a bear, and the other bear attacked him?"

Hallow made a choking noise, his face averted as he tucked the journals into his pack. "In a manner of speaking."

"But…" I thought about that for a minute. "Did he disguise himself as a female bear?"

"No." Hallow's face was a mixture of amusement and what I assumed was sympathy for the arcanist who was helping him.

"But what did Jalas's bear do to him if not attacking or attempting to mate?"

"Er...I didn't actually say the latter."

My eyes widened. "Oh. You mean...oh! I see."

"I fervently hope you don't, my heart," Hallow answered, laughing now. "You are a priestess, after all."

"Pshaw," I said, gathering my bow and quiver. "I'm not as innocent as you think, arcanist. We have men in Temple's Vale who prefer the company of other men to those of women. Sandor said that all were blessed in Kiriah's eyes, although she didn't care much for those who rutted with the temple's sheep."

"The goddess said that?" Hallow asked, his eyes round with surprise.

"No, Sandor did." I added a metal girdle that was set with silver links that Sandor had given me upon leaving the temple, feeling it would go well with the velvet gown, then closed the pack, and buckled the straps. "She said it made the sheep overly skittish around the shearers."

"I should imagine so," Hallow said, his lips twitching again.

Silence fell for a few minutes while he finished packing, then slid into the scabbard on his back the straight black wooden staff that contained the spirit of Thorn, a previous Master.

"Mind you, she threatened to shut the sheep buggerers into a shed with one of the rams just so they could see how traumatizing it was for the ewes, but I don't know that she ever did so. The older priests were reticent to answer my questions about that."

"Allegria!" he said with a shout of laughter, taking me into his arms to kiss me on the nose.

"What?" I asked, wiggling against him, wondering if we had time for a little dalliance before we had to be on our way.

"You are a priestess. You shouldn't know of such things such as men preferring sheep over women, let alone terms like 'sheep buggerers.' You, my love, are incorrigible."

"I like to think of it as being curious. And that same curiosity is prodding me to ask if we're leaving immediately to sail to Aryia, or if we have time for me to make sure that your exposure to intensive arcany last night hasn't caused you any bodily harm." I waggled my eyebrows at him.

He glanced behind me toward the screen and bed. "I had intended for us to be on our way as soon as Kiriah graced us with light, but perhaps I should have you check. So long as you let me check you over, as well."

His hands were roaming as he spoke, sliding the bow and quiver from me and unbuckling the scabbard I wore on my back.

"I would appreciate that," I told him, my breath catching in my throat when the warmth of his hands seeped through my linen tunic.

His head bent toward mine, his breath hot on my mouth when all of a sudden he swore and jerked backward, spinning around to glare at the window. "Kiriah's bane on him!"

"No," I said on a whimper. "Don't tell me."

"I'm sorry, my heart," he said, handing me my scabbard before pulling the straight black staff from his back and holding it out.

A little breeze ruffled my hair when a small black swallow darted through the window, circled us both three times, then landed on the top of the staff. The bird—like the staff itself—was made of wood.

Thorn had returned.

I sighed, wondering how long it would take Hallow to find some other mission upon which he could send Thorn. Although the former Master of Kelos meant well, he drove Hallow nigh on to madness with his inane chatter, demands, and orders about how to run both Kelos, and the arcanists themselves.

"Yes, I heard you." Hallow slid the staff into place on his back before turning an apologetic glance to me. I shrugged, knowing that Thorn was chattering away at Hallow, even if only he could hear the spirit's voice. "Yes, she does look annoyed, but it wasn't I who annoyed her. Thorn offers you greetings, Allegria."

"Hello, Thorn," I said, trying to look less sexually frustrated than I felt.

Hallow heaved up one of the packs onto his shoulder and reached for mine. I let him take it, collecting my bow and quiver, as well as gathering up some bread and fruit in a clean cloth. I followed him down the stairs, and out of the tower, smiling to myself despite the way the morning had turned out. It always amused me to listen to Hallow deal with Thorn's excited chatter.

"No, I'm not going to take down in writing what you have to report. We don't need to have a permanent record of your words. If that happens, and I find it difficult to believe that vast herds of arcanists down through the ages will be lusting for a record of your every word as you think they will, then I will take responsibility for their anger. No, I am not going to employ a scribe so that I can dictate your words to him. It's not about the coin that it would cost…Thorn, Allegria is a priestess, a lightweaver, and a former Bane of Eris. She is not going to become your scribe either. For the love of the goddesses, just tell me what you found in Starfall."

As we hauled the packs out to a small cart, Hallow murmured to me to tether Buttercup to the back while he fetched Penn, his gelding, all the while dealing with Thorn's obviously non-stop liturgy of demands, comments, and information.

"Right. I will. No, she isn't mad at you; she would simply like to be able to talk to me, and she can't do that if you're talking. Yes, well, she doesn't know how lucky she is that she can't hear you. That wasn't a slur... for the love of the stars and moons above, go! I don't care where you go, just go before my mind snaps!" Hallow, who had tied his hair back in a leather thong, had run his hands through it so many times in the last fifteen minutes that tendrils flickered in the slight breeze. Thorn rose off the staff, plopped onto his head, making a rude gesture with his wooden hindquarters, then flew off to the north.

"I'm sorry," Hallow said, turning to me. "He was worse than usual."

"He just gets excited about things," I said with a little shrug, deftly avoiding Buttercup's teeth when I tossed a couple of water skins into the back of the cart. She liked to nip at things whenever she felt she was being taken advantage of, which was basically any time that did not include a meal. "Did he have any news from Darius?"

"Yes." Hallow's expression darkened as he backed Penn up into the cart shafts. Penn usually objected to such demeaning work as pulling a cart, but he had clearly been bored by his enforced inactivity and suffered himself to be harnessed. "He's reforming the Starborn army."

"That's a good thing, isn't it?" I wondered about the little frown between Hallow's brows.

He hesitated, absently stroking Penn's neck. "Under normal circumstances, yes, it would be good."

"What's not normal?" I asked, confused. "You weren't happy when he let the army of Starborn—an army that you, yourself, rounded up and organized—scatter to the winds earlier this year. So why are you frowning now?"

His gaze held mine, the shiny blue of his eyes now pale, just as if they were frosted over. "Thorn says the army he's building isn't in service of the Starborn, or of the queen. It's his own army. He's declared the queen dead, and himself king in her place."

Chapter 2

Hallow was worried.

"I don't see that we have much to fear," Allegria said, climbing into the cart. "Darius is weak. He can declare himself king of all of Alba, but that doesn't mean he actually *is* king. After all, he couldn't even keep the army of Starborn from disbanding."

Hallow checked that the supplies were secured in the back of the cart, avoided Buttercup's attempt to snap off his arm, and moved around the captain of the guard when the latter suddenly materialized in front of him. "Perhaps not, but Thorn said that Darius had help from a magister who seemed to have much more backbone."

"Going somewhere?" the captain asked, popping up in front of him again as he double-checked the harness. Penn hated drawing a cart, but it was easier than finding another horse to do the same.

He gave Penn a consolatory pat on the neck before answering the captain. "Yes. We go to Aryia. I am placing you in charge of Kelos while we're gone."

The captain pursed his lips. "All the way across the sea? Isn't that a little premature?"

"No. Two of the three moonstones are there." Hallow tried not to allow his irritation with the ghostly captain to show. Although they'd worked out a mostly peaceful relationship since Hallow had taken over as head of the arcanists—and Master of Kelos—the captain seemed to delight in challenging him at every opportunity, throwing obstacles in his path whenever possible.

"But what of the third?" the captain asked in what Hallow would have deemed a coy voice had it been anyone else.

"A magister?" Allegria asked at the same time, clearly chewing over the idea of Darius's treachery. "What is a Fireborn doing helping the steward of the Starborn?"

"Undoubtedly claiming some power." Hallow turned to get into the cart, but once again the captain stood in his way.

"You do not answer me?" the captain demanded, now looking insulted. "Do I no longer matter to your grandiose plans now that you are Master?"

Hallow only just managed to keep from rolling his eyes, reminding himself that patience was his most valuable tool when dealing with the deceased. "I don't know where the third stone is, but there are twelve arcanists besides me hunting for it, so I'm sure we'll find it. Now if you don't mind, we would like to get underway before Kiriah sends the moon into the sky."

The captain pursed his lips and cast a pointed glance at Allegria. She didn't see it, frowning as she stared at nothing, obviously thinking about Darius. Hallow got into the cart next to her, and started Penn moving forward.

The captain disappeared, then materialized directly in front of Penn. The horse was used to the spirits of Kelos by now, and simply swished his tail in irritation as he marched through the translucent figure.

Hallow had a glimpse of outrage on the captain's face before his insubstantial form dissolved.

"I don't see what benefit this magister hopes to gain from helping Darius. For one, magisters fall under the domain of Lord Israel, and we both know that the lord of the Fireborn isn't going to take kindly to one of his own defecting to Darius. Especially since the latter let us all down when it came to clearing out the Harborym last year." Allegria's face always gave Hallow pleasure, but now, with her abstracted expression, he had an almost overwhelming urge to take her into his arms and kiss every inch of her lightly freckled skin. He particularly liked to kiss the circlet of black dots that crossed her forehead, a relic of her time as a Bane of Eris.

"Lord Israel is more than a little unhappy with Darius since he has refused to attend any of the councils of the four armies, but I don't know that he would be overly upset by a magister working with the Starborn. It might very well be that the man is there on his orders," he pointed out.

The captain of the guard's form shimmered into view again in front of Penn. This time, he held out one hand, commanding, "Halt!"

Both Hallow and Penn ignored him as his form was dispersed again. Hallow's thoughts were turned toward the arguments he would lay before the guardians of the two moonstones he and his arcanists had located, which left him little time to worry about placating the irate captain.

"A spy, you mean?" Allegria asked. "I suppose he could be acting in that role, although wouldn't Darius be suspicious of him, and suspect that he might be working for Lord Israel?"

"You give Darius more credit than perhaps he deserves," Hallow said judiciously. His own opinion of Darius was that the man was weak-minded, and weaker still of spirit, taking the easy path whenever it was presented to him rather than considering what was best for his fellow Starborn. He seemed to have little regard for anything but his own comfort, leaving the restructuring of Starborn society to individuals who weren't equipped for such responsibilities.

"Oh, I have no doubt that the man is an idiot," Allegria said with a disgusted snort that delighted Hallow. "He wanted Deo and me killed, after all. Only someone lacking in even the most basic levels of common sense would want to eliminate the very people who saved his wretched hide."

The captain appeared in the road again, this time with his sword in hand, striding toward them with a purposeful look on his face. Penn, sensing that this time the captain had donned a corporeal form, stopped, and tossed his head in warning.

"For the love of Bellias, you will not treat me as if I am a mere lackey, one who is unimportant in the functioning of Kelos and Genora!" The captain's voice echoed off the broken buildings, stirring little swirls of the grey dust that covered everything around them. "You *will* heed me!"

Hallow pulled his thoughts from the concerns that plagued him and turned his attention to the irate spirit. "What is it you want? I left you in charge—you can have no complaint that I have usurped your position by placing another spirit, perhaps one who doesn't wave his sword in my horse's face, in charge of Kelos."

"Ask the priest!" the captain said, crossing his arms despite the fact that he still held his sword. "She swore she would tell you after I allowed her access to the crypt so she could hone her skills, which naturally stirred up the Eidolon. I expect the thane will be speaking to you of her scurrilous actions."

Hallow raised an eyebrow at Allegria. "You went into the crypt to stir up the spirits?"

She spoke a very un-priestly word under her breath, glared for a few seconds at the captain, then turned a smile on him. "Of course not."

"You didn't go into the crypt?" he asked.

"Well…yes, I did, but not to stir up the thane and his followers. In fact, the captain didn't bother to tell me the ghosts down there were Eidolon. He just said that if I wanted more of a challenge than what his people provided, I could find seasoned warriors sleeping in the crypt. And since we'd talked about searching there—and decided against it, because Thorn said Exodius gave the crypt a wide berth, having no wish to deal with the powerful spirits who resided within."

She cleared her throat and cast another quick glare at the captain, whom Hallow couldn't help but note was looking smug.

"Since we talked about searching there, I thought I'd combine two tasks into one, and get in a little sword practice while also making sure that the moonstone wasn't there."

The captain sniffed. "And after you woke up the thane's entire contingent of soldiers and enraged them by attacking their king before their eyes, you escaped and swore you would relate to the Master our conversation."

Hallow went so far as to raise his other eyebrow at Allegria.

"My heart, I assure you that you are more than proficient with both your swords and bow. Challenging the spirits who sleep beneath Kelos will only end with the thane and his people seeking to avenge themselves upon us."

"It wasn't like that at all—oh, never mind. It doesn't matter now that we're leaving for Aryia."

Hallow sent up a little prayer to Bellias Starsong for more patience than he seemed to have of late.

"The captain wants you to beg him for his help," Allegria added with a little sniff of her own.

"Does he, indeed," Hallow said mildly, and turned his gaze back to the captain.

"What is it you want?"

"You need my aid," the captain said, a stubborn set to his jaw.

Hallow sighed to himself. He wished to be on his way. He had spent long months locating two of the three moonstones, and now that the time had come to act, he was anxious to be underway. "For what?"

"That I cannot tell you until you seek my assistance."

"I think we should run him down," Allegria told him. "He keeps saying things like that, and it's extremely annoying. Or I could lop off his head. It'll take him a good hour to recover enough energy to put it back on, and we should be a long way away from Kelos by then."

Hallow's shoulders shook but he managed to stifle the laughter that he knew from experience would only enrage the captain.

"I was addressing the Master, not you," the spirit said with injured dignity.

"Captain," Hallow said with as much composure as he could muster, "your assistance in maintaining Kelos is vital—"

"Not Kelos," the captain interrupted. "I serve the Master, not just Kelos."

Hallow frowned at him, for once wishing that Thorn was present so he could ask him what it was the captain wanted.

"As the Master, I appreciate your assistance, but we are hours later starting than I wish, and—"

"It's the stone, you insane arcanist!" the captain bellowed, waving his hands—including the one bearing the sword—around wildly. Penn tossed his head again, backing up a few steps. "I'm talking about the stone you seek! The third moonstone! You ask me for aid, and I will tell you how to locate the third moonstone."

"You know where it is?" Hallow asked in disbelief. "How?"

"Exodius told me. *He* had no qualms asking me for my help."

Hallow turned his gaze to Allegria. She looked as astonished as he felt.

"I had no idea that's what he was yammering on about," she told him. "He said something about a talisman, but nothing about the moonstone."

They both looked back at the captain. "Where is it?" Hallow asked.

The captain stared back at them.

Hallow sighed again, then handed Allegria the reins and climbed down from the cart before making a bow that his former master had told him would charm even the hardest heart. He said in a voice that belied his growing sense of frustration, "Please, captain, take pity on this poor Master, and lend me your aid in locating the third of the moonstones that Exodius hid."

The spirit smiled and reached inside his armor to pull out a small metal object. It was covered in strange runes and consisted of a gently curved narrow pipe strung on a hide thong. He offered the object to Hallow. "Find the one known as Quinn the Mad. He lives on the Cape of Despair, in the town of Aldmarsh."

"Does he have the stone?" Hallow asked, thinking that although Exodius hadn't been the most mentally stable of individuals—all arcanists had a touch of madness about them—the old man wasn't flat out crazy. Hallow doubted if he'd entrust anything so powerful as a moonstone to someone who wasn't worthy of such an honor.

"Find him. He is a traveler, one who has seen more battles than you can conceive of. He will guide you to what you seek," the captain told him with cryptic finality.

"That means he has the stone? Or does he know where it is?"

The captain's form shimmered as he returned to an incorporeal state. "Find him, and he will guide you to all you seek."

"What interesting runes it has," Allegria said, taking the thong bearing the strange whistle from Hallow as he climbed into the cart again. She traced a finger along the delicate silver pipe. "I don't know some of them, but this is a rune of clarity, and the one here is of understanding."

"The others aren't exactly runes as you know them. They are sigils, a type of symbol used by ancient arcanists to reach beyond the mortal world," Hallow said, glancing at it when she slipped the thong over her head so that the whistle hung between her breasts.

"It's a ghost whistle?" she asked, looking at it askance.

"It is a talisman," the captain said abruptly. "A most important one that—no!"

He lunged at Allegria when she raised the whistle to her lips, clearly about to sound it, but in his incorporeal form, he simply dissolved into nothing when he ran through Penn, causing the horse to rear up.

"The only one who may use it is Quinn the Mad!" the captain's voice came from nowhere. "For anyone else to do so is to court disaster. Heed me well, Master of Kelos—it won't be easy to convince Quinn to help you. Do not waste your time offering the talisman to lesser beings."

And with that, the captain took himself off to wherever he went when he wasn't busy patrolling Kelos and ensuring that the spirit citizens who dwelt there abided in peace. Hallow eyed the pipe, and took the reins from Allegria, telling Penn to walk on. "Why do I have the feeling that the captain's talisman is going to give us endless grief, rather than resulting in locating the third moonstone?"

Allegria smiled and pressed a kiss to his jaw. "Because you're not only the most brilliant of men, but you're also well aware that everyone who lives in Kelos is a bit twisted."

He pursed his lips.

She laughed and patted him on the leg. "Yes, that includes us, although we're not nearly so bad as the captain. I assume we'll go find Quinn the Mad once we have the other stones?"

Hallow hesitated a few seconds before answering.

"I think perhaps we'll head south rather than west."

She frowned. "To this Cape of Despair place?"

"Yes."

"But you don't know for certain that the talisman will lead us to the third stone. The captain didn't come right out and say Quinn had it—which is just like him, speaking in riddles instead of answering the question put to him. Hallow, I want to find that third stone just as badly as you do, but at least we know the locations of the other two. I'm not saying it's going to be easy to convince Sandor to give up the stone she holds, but I'd much rather have the two stones we can set our hands on than chase after the third, which may or may not be in the possession of Quinn."

"Exodius told the captain where the stone was," Hallow argued. "Or at least he left a clue that I could follow, although I really wish the captain had seen fit to tell me that three months ago when we started the search in earnest. Still, he told me, and handed over what is obviously an ancient talisman. I believe we must tackle Quinn first. It's only a few days' ride to the coast, and with luck, we can find a ship sailing to Aryia from a nearby port."

"You're putting a lot of faith in the captain," Allegria warned him.

"No." His lips twisted into a wry smile. "I'm putting my faith in Exodius. Which is far, far more worrisome, my heart. Now, do you think if I was to wrap the reins around the brake, you and I could go into the back of the cart, and indulge ourselves in a little sport celebrating the fact that we've been wed almost six months?"

She laughed, her dark eyes lighting so that the little gold flecks in them glittered like sunlight. She pressed her lips to his, the warmth in them instantly lighting little fires of desire.

"I think that would be an extremely ill-planned idea, although I appreciate the thought. Perhaps later, at night—Hallow! You can't possibly mean to—anyone who rode up could see us!"

He lay back on the soft furs and blankets that lined the bed of the cart, his heart singing a little song of happiness while Allegria sat astride him. He had no idea whether or not the captain was sending them on a chase that would end in success or sorrow, but he was content to face whatever befell him with Allegria at his side.

He just really hoped for a success. Sorrow they'd had in abundance.

Chapter 3

Deosin Langton was bored almost to the point of insensibility. Racin's yammering didn't help matters.

"Your death will mean nothing to me. Nothing to my queen. It will be completely trivial."

Not a man who was at all comfortable with inactivity, Deo yawned, and idly scratched a spot on his left pectoral. He wondered if something had bitten him under the silver harness that crossed his torso, tried to remember if he had seen signs of fleas on the rat that rode on the shoulder of the guard who delivered his meals, but decided that of the two, the rat was likely the cleaner.

"I grow tired of asking you questions. Give me one reason why I should not gut you where you stand. Er...lie."

Now there was an itch on his back. He shifted a little on the cot, making a mental note to ask the woman who brought him water and took out his chamber pot to arrange for his bedding to be washed. No doubt the guard was the one with fleas.

"You think your silence will save you, but it will not!" The man who stood at the door raised his voice until it echoed around the stone cell in which Deo had lived for almost an entire year. Deo paused at that thought, distracted, and glanced over to the opposite wall, where he'd used a sharp piece of flint to scratch out a tally of weeks spent imprisoned. He counted. "Kiriah blast it, I forgot last week!"

"Nothing can save you, not your silence, not my queen's pleas, not even your beloved twin goddesses," ranted Racin, the captain of the Harborym, watching him with black eyes that were now tinted red, a color that almost perfectly matched his skin. "You will die as surely as the rest of your kind."

Deo made a neat mark next to a row that closed out that month and decided that his boredom warranted a little reward. He turned and gave Racin a long look. Nothing had changed about Racin in the last almost-year. He stood a good two heads taller than Deo; his body bound by leather and steel, his face twisted with anger. Long black hair slithered across shoulders bulging with muscles that were grotesque, a parody of mankind. Deo knew well how the use of chaos magic changed the body—he, himself, showed the signs of consuming chaos—but the changes wrought to Racin were extreme to the point of making him an abomination.

He certainly had the personality of a body louse. Deo opted for a raised eyebrow to express his disdain. "Ah. Was that you speaking? I wasn't paying attention."

Racin's lips drew back in a snarl, giving Deo much satisfaction. There were few things he liked more than baiting Racin, although his mother had begged him to cease doing so after the last time.

The last time was delicious. And look what it got you! A new domicile, new attendants, and the respect of the Speaker.

Deo frowned to himself even as Racin ranted in front of him.

Speaker? What did that mean? It was on the tip of his tongue to ask the chaos magic that spoke in his mind just what it meant, but in time he remembered his promise to Dasa. There would be no more deaths of innocents. Not at his hands, anyway.

He eyed Racin, who was now gesticulating with one hand, little flecks of spittle flying as the monstrous man heaped verbal abuse upon Deo's head. "Who is the Speaker?" he asked.

"—just as soon as I learn how it is you have mastered that which eludes me—what?" For the time it took to count to six Racin stared at Deo, his eyes glowing hot with ire as he narrowed them. "I am the Speaker!"

"Of what?" Deo thought for a moment; then, aware of the scars on his back from numerous whippings made by countless tutors who believed the only way to teach was to beat facts into him, he made a face and corrected himself. "Rather, to whom?"

Racin seemed to swell. His chest puffed out until Deo was concerned the leather bands crossing it might snap, sending the steel rivets ricocheting around his small cell. "I am the Speaker of the Unseen Shadow, the Master of the Dark."

"I have not heard of this," Deo said, frowning. He disliked it when people had knowledge that they withheld from him. "Who is this master?"

Nezu, the chaos magic whispered in his mind.

The name told him nothing. He was about to ask Racin who Nezu was when the captain did something he hadn't done since the last time Deo had taunted him. He stepped into the cell. Just one foot crossed the threshold, but it was enough.

The magic roared to life within Deo; the runes etched into the harness across his chest and bound on silver bands around his wrists and ankles lit up with a pale golden light. Rage boiled inside him that quickly narrowed into one bright, glittering intention: destruction of all things.

Kill, the magic said, and with that one word, power flowed through his blood, making him burn from the inside. *Kill the Speaker. Kill them all. Destroy this place, and become stronger, become what you are meant to be.*

The fire in his veins grew until it felt as if he was going to explode into a million white-hot embers.

Embrace it. Use it. Kill the Speaker. Kill the unworthy. Cleanse the world and take your rightful place as master of it all.

With a snarl of pain, Deo fought to control the urge that almost maddened him…and that threatened to consume him body and soul.

The stone walls around him began to smoke and tremble, and Deo, desperate to avoid a repetition of the destruction of twenty-seven innocent Shadowborn, spun around and allowed the chaos power to burst out of him, blowing out the wall of the cell with a percussive blast that momentarily deafened him.

The power in him rejoiced, flooding every iota of his being with a delirious sense of invincibility.

As the noise of the crumbled wall and cries of people outside the wall faded, the air shifted behind him, and before Deo could leash the magic that claimed him, he was at the door, Racin's throat in his hand. His fingers dug deep into the red flesh, but he felt no satisfaction. Rather than showing fear, Racin laughed, and slammed a red wave of pain into Deo, sending him flying backward into the rubble of what had once been a foot-thick wall.

"Do you think to try your puny powers on me, savior of the Fourth Age?" Racin asked, his voice as rough as the sharp mortar and stone that pierced Deo's back. "I am the Speaker of the Unseen. I walk in shadows, with death at my side. There is nothing you can do to me, as by now I would have thought you would know. This attempt proves once again that you are an insignificant insect, as worthless as the dirt beneath my feet."

Deo snarled an oath. He *hated* it when people referred to him by the savior title. Moving with care in order to determine how badly he was injured, he got to his feet, his movements slowed by the tendrils of red chaos power that all but shackled his arms and legs.

End this now, the power said to him, filling him again with the heat of a thousand suns.

"I will," he ground out, but rather than directing the power outward, he lifted his head and held Racin's gaze while he allowed the power to slip just enough to encase him in a pale golden-red glow. It burned through the chaos bonds, then faded, the murderous rage once again controlled by the runes bound upon him. He made a mental note to add a few more, since he hadn't liked how close he'd come to giving in to the voice in his mind.

Always you fight me. And we could be so successful together...

The smirk that curled Racin's lips slipped as he beheld Deo marching toward him, free of the bondage of red chaos. He went so far as to step back, wariness tinging his black eyes when Deo brushed past him, heading to the cell across the narrow passageway.

Deo looked around the cell. It had a view that looked out onto a valley in the distance. He nodded twice and said in a voice filled with the arrogance natural to him, "This will do. Have a servant fetch my things."

Racin spat out an invective, and before Deo registered that the larger man had moved, was confronted by his captor, chaos snapping in waves down Racin's body. "You think to dictate to me?" he roared, making Deo's ears ring.

Pain laced his body, flaying him as no whip ever could, the magic that Racin poured over Deo cutting through flesh and muscle until it threatened to break his very bones.

His own version of that magic, sensing the threat, came to life a second time, and gratefully, Deo pulled on it to buffer him from the worst of the assault.

One corner of his mind absently wondered how and why his chaos had changed into something unique, but Deo had little patience for pondering the unknown, preferring instead to deal with whatever was in front of him.

He ignored the chanting voice in his head urging him to do the most heinous acts, added another prayer to Kiriah and Bellias that his mastery over the power wouldn't fade in the face of Racin's attack, and gritted his teeth, bowing his head as he focused.

Dimly he heard a voice calling his name; then Racin and the waves of red, pulsing pain were gone.

"Stop! You will bring the whole temple down upon us. Already the rocks at the base of the temple are cracking. Deo, control yourself. My lord Racin, there are surely more important matters claiming your time than chastising my son." Dasa's words, spoken with a lightness that was belied by the anger in her eyes, did their work nonetheless, for Racin gave in to the restraining hand on his arm, and took a step back.

"Your whelp thought to challenge me," Racin snarled, his eyes narrowing on her. "*Again.*"

"He does it simply because he knows it bothers you," Dasa told him, her gaze locked on the monster.

Deo, who once again had control of himself, felt his lip curl with disgust. The fact that his mother, the greatest warrior of the third age, and queen of the Starborn, could consort with such an abomination as Racin turned his stomach.

"He goes too far." Racin all but spat the words at Dasa.

She didn't react. Deo had to give her credit for that, although it bespoke a familiarity that did nothing to calm his unhappy belly. He wondered for a moment what his father would do when he heard of the queen's perfidy and decided that he wanted to be there when Israel Langton was told.

"I will speak to him," Dasa said, her voice weary with exasperation. She urged Racin from the cell. "My time will not be wasted as yours would be should you wish to lesson him. Again."

Deo smiled. The only other time Racin had thought to teach him his place in Eris, Deo had destroyed not just the citadel within which he'd been imprisoned, but half the mountaintop city as well.

With that act came the deaths of innocents, though. His smiled faded at that memory.

The magic within him stirred, but remained quiet.

Racin continued protesting, throwing threats at Deo, but at last the queen had him out of the temple and on his way back to Skystead. Deo stood gazing out of the small window, his eyes on the valley spread out below him.

"Did you have to do that?"

Deo stiffened at the censure in his mother's voice, then forced himself to relax. "As a matter of fact, I kept myself from killing him. Do you not wish to thank me for that?"

"Thank you?" Dasa strode into the small cell, grabbed his arm and spun him around to confront her ire. "For almost ruining everything we've worked for? I ought to smite you where you stand. It would cause me considerably less aggravation than trying to teach you to heed the common sense that you were evidently born without."

"You would know," he said, allowing an ironic little smile to play about his lips.

She looked as if she wanted to strike him, but managed to get her temper under control. "The issue of your upbringing under your father's care aside, what did you hope to gain by challenging Racin? You know full well you can't destroy him on your own. Are you as mad as the priests say you are?"

He was distracted by that thought. "I haven't been mad since I left the Isle of Enoch. Not *truly* mad."

"The priests report that you speak when no one is in your cell. You draw runes in the air that glow with the light of Kiriah Sunbringer, something no one has seen since the coming of the Harborym. They say you pace the cell endlessly for days, casting spells and summoning minions of death."

"If I had the ability to summon minions, do you think I'd be here now?"

"What I think is that you have frightened the priests of this temple until there are only a handful remaining. Should those leave, Racin will be forced to take action."

Deo rolled his eyes. "He could imprison me in Skystead again."

"After what you did to the keep?" Dasa glared at him. "Deo, I know this inactivity is hard on you. Bellias knows I find it almost unendurable to have to pretend interest in a thousand mundane activities when I would much rather fetch a sword and smite our enemies, but your father and I had long ago determined that we could not let Racin follow the path of destruction he started upon, or all of Alba would be enslaved, crying out helplessly under his yoke. You agreed to our plan. So why do you now cast all that aside in order to satisfy your need for revenge?"

Deo sighed. He wanted to be angry with his mother, but he couldn't. "It wasn't me. It was the magic."

She eyed the runes on his harness, touching one of them with the tip of a finger, immediately snatching her hand back and shaking it. "Blessed Bellias, how can you bear such heat?"

He shrugged. "It is part of me. Just as the maddening urge to kill Racin is also in me."

"Well, tell that part to be quiet," Dasa snapped.

"Do you bring me any news?" he asked, changing the subject. He knew from experience of the last eleven months that arguing with his mother would only leave them irritated and annoyed to the point where one or both of them might be driven to violence.

"No." Dasa breathed heavily for a minute, then laid her hand on Deo's chest, on a spot not covered by the harness. To his surprise, she tipped her head back and smiled up at him. "You enrage me with your wild ways, Deo, but there is pleasure in the knowledge that my blood clearly rules you. You are indeed a fitting warrior of my house, and a fine reflection of your Starborn ancestors."

He was momentarily silenced by the words of praise, having seldom heard them. He felt an unwelcome desire to preen in front of her and stifled it immediately. Although she might think he took after her, he had too much of his father's sagacity to believe he was anything but what he was—a man tormented, one who had sacrificed much in order to fulfill the role to which he had been born. "Your words are pleasant, but they would be pleasanter still if you had something to tell me of Racin's studies."

She sighed and made a face before turning to the window. "The people dragged before him are subjected to his…studies…as you call them. The lucky ones die instantly. Those who survive the transformation usually die within days, most by their own hands, but some go berserk and attack the others."

Deo was silent considering this. "I don't understand."

"Why he is decimating the population of Eris?" Dasa asked.

"No." Absently, he rubbed his thumb along the line of runes on the wrist band of his other hand. "Why, he has so little control over his magic. Once I had mastered the magic, it took me a relatively short time to find a dosage that my Banes of Eris could take without killing—or consuming them, and yet he's been attempting to do the same since we drove him back to Eris. Why?"

Dasa shrugged, turning back toward him, leaning against the wall. "It's magic. It is unstable."

Deo mused that *his* magic was unstable…but the chaos magic that he had first used was not. Powerful, yes, at times fighting for control, but it was only since he'd traveled to Eris that his magic had become unstable and uncontrolled. "It makes little sense. He seeks to duplicate the creation of my Banes, and yet he has an army of Harborym at his disposal."

"Made up of soldiers who are easily defeated by you," Dasa said smoothly, moving to stand next to him. "He fears you, my son. He doesn't want to admit it even to himself, but he knows that you have done something to his magic that leaves him vulnerable. You pose a threat to him that he can't tolerate, one that drives him to experiment upon the Shadowborn to find out just what you have done, so that he can find a way to best it…or unmake it completely. That fear drives him to the point where soon there will be no Shadowborn left untainted in all of Eris."

"Since when do you have a fondness for the Shadowborn?" Deo asked, momentarily amused by her apparent concern. He was under no illusion

that his mother put her people's welfare first and foremost in her life...
even above that of her son.

"I have never condoned the slaughter of innocents," she murmured.

He glanced at her, the words echoing with his own oath. "So I must
continue to fester here?" He made an aborted gesture of frustration, wanting
to vent his anger and impatience, but knew it would stir the chaos within
him. "I remain an impotent prisoner, unable even to defend myself against
the monster's attacks?"

"You defended yourself to the point where you almost brought the
temple down upon your head," Dasa replied acidly, giving his arm a pat
as she moved past him to the door. Outside it, the Priests of the Blood
Hand stood at silent attention, their pale flesh and luminous, large eyes
reminding Deo of frightened rabbits. *Dangerous* frightened rabbits. "Have
patience, Deo. The moment Racin reveals a weakness that we can exploit,
we will destroy him, and make all of Alba safe."

"That could take decades," Deo growled, his hands fisted. "Or centuries.
I will go mad if I have to stay captive here."

"Then return to Aryia," Dasa said in a similar growl, clearly having
had enough of Deo's attitude. "I did not ask you to come here."

"But you knew it was inevitable," he stated, rounding on her.

She was silent a moment, her gaze on his face before it dropped to her
hands. "No. I thought someone else—oh, it matters not. Do nothing that
will endanger my plans, Deo, or I will have you removed to Aryia myself."

She strode out of the cell before Deo could respond that he'd like to
see her try that, but the mocking laughter that filled his head did little to
soothe his frustration.

"My lord, if you please..." The soft voice came from one of the serving
women who attended to the temple and its priests...and prisoners. This one
had coppery red hair, and the bronzed skin that told Deo she had been born
since the coming of the Harborym. The woman placed fresh bedding on
the cot that sat in the corner of the cell before bringing in a jug of water,
and a small, cracked bowl. She hesitated, her gaze moving from Deo to
the door. Two priests stood outside, their heads together as they spoke so
softly Deo could not hear them.

"My lord, you will forgive me, but I must speak. I can stand your
suffering no longer."

Deo, who was deep in abstracted thought about ways to force Racin to
show his weaknesses—assuming he had them—frowned at the woman
who plucked at his arm.

"What is it?" he asked, unable to keep the irritation from his voice.

She turned so that her back was to the door and smoothed out the bedlinens. "Today is a holy day for the priests. They will hold a great feast tonight to celebrate. There will only be one guard, and with my help, you can escape—"

"Why would I do that?" he asked, his frown deepening.

The woman—he remembered her name was Mayam—looked momentarily startled, her dark eyes flashing confusion at him before her gaze dropped to the floor. "You must—you are a prisoner here."

"So?"

Irritation flickered across her expression. "You are a great warrior. The priests say you defeated the Speaker and his Harborym. Such a man as you cannot wish to stay here, trapped in a small cell."

Deo smiled a grim smile, one that he felt said it all. But just in case the maidservant didn't appreciate the grimness of his gesture, he said, as he gently pushed her out the door, "You have no idea what sort of a man I really am."

Chapter 4

"By Kiriah's breath, will this blizzard never end?"

Israel Langton, lord of the Fireborn, slid a glance toward the man who rode next to him, one so covered in furs and thick woolen garments that if he didn't know better, he'd assume it was a bear instead of his faithful Marston. He fervently hoped that the snow upon the steep cliffs that seemed to choke out the sullen white sky didn't give way and collapse, because given the four layers of clothing that he'd donned in order to resist the bite of the cold, he doubted if he could even dismount from his horse, let alone flee an avalanche. "Ilam is not far ahead, old friend. We will have respite from the snow and winds there," he answered, his voice muffled behind the thick woolen cloth wound around the lower part of his face.

His horse stumbled, the droop of the beast's head showing just how hard the journey to the High Lands had been. Israel cursed the need to come at this time of year, when the pass between the home of the Tribe of Jalas and the rest of Aryia was beset by snow and high winds, but there was no help for it—the journey would be twice as long if he had come by sea. And he had little time to waste.

He needed to do what Hallow could not.

The horse stumbled again, almost going down on one knee. Israel raised his hand, pulling down the wool cloth to call out an order to halt. He dismounted awkwardly, looking back at the score of men who traveled with him. They all looked as numbly miserable as he felt. "We will rest as best we can," he ordered, leading his horse over to a sharp overhang of rock. The narrow neck of land that connected Poronne to Aryia was infamous for its rock slides and avalanches, but at that moment, Israel cared little about its reputation. He had pushed his men and horses to the breaking point and knew he would lose both to the cold if he didn't give them some respite.

There wasn't much they could do other than kick drifts of snow and use hands numb and red despite many layers of leather and wool to carve out a spot for the horses to rest away from the wind. He covered his horse with his own blanket, strapping on a feed bag with fingers that felt as if they belonged to someone else.

There was not enough shelter to even start a fire, so the men huddled together, snow-covered effigies that pressed themselves to the black stone wall beneath the overhang. A few men slumped against the wall, all but their eyes hidden beneath layers of clothing.

"My lord..." Marston, Israel's friend and lieutenant, approached, his eyelashes and eyebrows coated with ice and snow.

"I know," Israel said, feeling more tired than he had in all the long centuries of his life. Part of him wanted to rouse the men and continue on, but another part, a deep, primal part, reacted to the insidious creeping fingers of cold that slowed his brain, and lured him into the desire to just sit down for a little bit, so he could rest...and sleep...

A vision rose in his mind's eye, one that seemed to waver along with the flurries of snow. He had a presentiment of danger, of a dark, sliding threat coiled around something most dear to him, leaving it...*her*...at the risk of being destroyed...and then a fresh blast of frosty wind hit him dead in the face, and he was shocked back to reality.

"Dasa." The word was out through his bloodless lips before the name had even formed in his mind. She was in danger. He knew that just as he knew that unless he did something, he and his men would die there. And what would happen to Dasa and Deo if he died so needlessly? He shook his head, pushing down the desire for the peace that sleep would bring. With an effort, he peeled off the protective layers of wool and fur covering his frozen hands and reached into the saddlebag for a small tapestry bag. He stroked a finger over the embroidery worked on the thick cloth, tracing out the star and moons of Bellias that Dasa had stitched as part of a present to him.

His lips were too stiff and frozen to smile at the memory of just how inappropriate she knew the gift was, since it was intended to store the tools he used to practice the grace of Kiriah.

It took him three tries before he was able to bring from the bag the two small shards of polished antler, a collection of dried herbs, and a piece of bark the size of a man's hand which he had plucked from an obliging willow before setting out on the journey. He laid the items onto the bark and set it on the snow before him, which rose almost to his knees. His arms and hands pricked painfully in the wind, the bite of it sufficiently stinging to pull his attention from where it should be. It took a few moments of concentration before he could focus, but at last he did, casting wide his arms and tipping his head back to look up into the angry white sky, speaking the invocation to Kiriah that would bring him either her grace...or her rejection. If he was to die there, at least he would have done everything possible.

"Stone, earth, bone, and tree.
Sunbringer, shed your light upon me.
Your songs I have sung,
Your light I have shone,
Your grace I have shared,
But your children are cold and alone."

The snow and wind whipped around him with a violence that almost toppled him, but that was nothing compared to the despair that gripped him with the painful knowledge that he had failed. He'd failed his son just as he'd failed Dasa, not to mention all the people of Aryia who looked to him for protection. But the vision he'd had of Dasa in dire peril drove him back onto his feet. He pulled on the dregs of his strength in order to conduct one last invocation.

As the last words were spoken, he held his breath, waiting to see if the goddess would hear his plea...or if she would doom him and the ones he loved the most. His shoulders slumped when there was no answering rush of power, no sense of the goddess blessing him...until he became aware of a dull sensation of warmth bathing his frozen head. The wind dropped suddenly, taking with it the snow. His skin tingled, chapped by the harsh weather, but Israel welcomed the pain as he looked upward. The dull whiteness that was the sky had started to change; hints of pale blue peeping between the dense clouds, as slowly, they began to tear apart and evaporate. He sent up a humble prayer of thanks to Kiriah for blessing the Fireborn with the grace of Alba, then turned to Marston. "Are there any spirits left?"

"Aye," the lieutenant answered, and actually smiled when he, too, looked upward. Pale rays of sunlight pricked through the remaining clouds, the warmth of Kiriah's touch bringing new life to the company.

The men stirred themselves when Marston passed amongst them with a couple of skins bearing the fiery alcohol known colloquially as Kiriah's Essence. Even the horses perked up when Israel ordered their saddles and wet blankets removed, so that they could feel the warmth of the sun on their hard-worked bodies. Snow melted around them, not completely, but enough that a couple of fires could be started on some exposed rock, and water heated.

And that was how Idril, Jewel of the High Lands, found them—seated in patches of melting snow, the horses dozing in the sun, and the men sitting around drinking cups of broth made with dried meat, joking, laughing, and all singing the praises of Kiriah.

"Lord Israel," Idril said when he helped her off the grey stallion that her father normally rode. She glanced around with the very faintest of frowns between her delicate silver-blond brows. "I come in answer to the message of your arrival. I suspected you might try the pass rather than the sea. I brought extra horses, assuming you had been caught in the storm, and would have need of them, but I see I underestimated your resourcefulness."

"I would have been desperately glad of your horses and aid a short while ago had not Kiriah heard my plea."

Idril gave him one of the same cool smiles she had bestowed upon him during the short time they had been wed. It was wholly impersonal, and he wondered if love for anyone or anything had ever truly touched her heart. His son claimed she was heart-sworn to him, but Israel saw no signs on Idril's lovely countenance of any emotion other than mild interest. "It doesn't surprise me that Kiriah would listen when you beseeched her for help. You have long been in her favor. Do you need food? We brought supplies as well as horses."

"What I would like is a hot bath and dry clothing," he said with his usual straightforwardness. Israel didn't suffer fools gladly and believed in saying what he thought without playing any of the verbal games that were common to other members of the Council of Four Armies. "If you can provide that, my men and I will be most appreciative."

She inclined her head and allowed him to assist her into the saddle. "Ilam is but an hour's journey from here. If your horses are too tired to travel now, my men can remain with them—"

"They have had a rest. We will push on together," Israel said firmly. Although he had a long history with the Tribe of Jalas, not all of it was as amiable as in recent years, and he was loath to splinter his company, small as it was.

It took closer to two hours for their tired mounts to wind their way through the mountain pass to Ilam, the city that sat pressed at the base of a craggy, snow-mantled peak, which was home to Jalas. Kiriah had seen fit to melt away all the clouds between the pass and Ilam, making their travel less fraught with peril, although Israel noted the clouds had begun to gather again behind them just as they approached the tall black iron gates.

"And how does your father do?" Israel asked as they entered the keep.

"The last I heard from him, he declared himself at death's door."

Idril allowed three of her handmaidens to remove her long white woolen cloak, gloves, and the assorted outer garments that were intended to keep the cold from her fair skin. "He does like to believe himself mere seconds away from departing this world, but in truth, he seems well enough. He refuses to leave the keep, however, saying his limbs are weak and give him great pain. The doctors can find nothing wrong with him, but I can't help think…" Her words trailed off as she looked across the great hall.

A figure stood shadowed in an alcove, barely visible in the dim light of the hall. For a moment, Israel thought it was a statue, but as the flame from a lamp on a nearby table flickered, he saw the glint of eyes.

Eyes that for a moment, he could have sworn regarded him with hostility so intense, it sent a pang of concern through him.

Then the figure was in motion, and Israel dismissed his impression as a figment of his tired brain.

"Lord Israel! My daughter did not tell me you were expected." Jalas limped forward using a great hawthorn stick, his face gaunt and grey, with two red spots on his cheeks beneath the bristles of his braided copper-colored beard. "What madness has brought you out during this storm? Idril, my chair. No, I have changed my mind; the hall is too cold for my thin blood. Come to my chambers, my lord, and you shall tell me news of the world. Idril is too busy to spend time with her failing father."

Idril said nothing at the chastisement, but Israel noted the way her lips tightened. It was a telling point in a woman who had such extreme control over her emotions.

A short while later, after seeing that his men and horses had been accommodated, Israel found himself in a large wooden chair pulled up to a fire that was almost uncomfortably hot. Across from him, Jalas allowed Idril to get him seated, several pillows having to be adjusted just so, in order to pamper his aching joints, before she poured out a huge flagon of ale for him, and a smaller one for Israel.

"Now then, I believe I can bear sitting up long enough to hear why you've come to the High Lands," Jalas said after taking a long pull on the ale, wiping his mouth with one hand before he leaned back, giving Israel a piercing look.

"Do you wish me to remain or leave, Father?" Idril asked in her soft, placid voice.

"Eh? You might as well stay," Jalas said, then grimaced and added to Israel, "She will have control over the Tribe soon enough. Much good may she get from it when I am gone, since the clans are even now fighting amongst themselves, something Idril seems to be unable to stop."

Idril dismissed her handmaids, and sat in a chair next to the window, picking up an embroidery tambour, apparently uninterested in what her father was saying.

Israel didn't want to get into the politics of the Tribe members, but he didn't care for the way Jalas so easily cast blame upon his daughter. Idril might be many things, but he knew from experience the lengths to which she was prepared to go in order to keep the peace. "The clans of the High Lands are known for their fierceness. I have no doubt they have tempers to match," Israel said in what he hoped was a noncommittal tone. "It must be difficult to lead them without a good deal of experience. I'm sure Lady Idril does her best."

Jalas grunted, and drained half the flagon, belched, wiped the foam from his moustache, and asked again, "What news have you?"

"Little enough that would interest you," Israel said. "Hallow sent me a message saying that he is concerned about Darius, the Starborn steward."

"Hallow? Oh, the mad arcanist who was in your company?" Jalas finished his ale. "I heard a nasty rumor about him, that he tied himself to that pox-marked female who was tainted by your son."

"I doubt if even Deo could have tainted Allegria," Israel said drily, but was aware of an uncomfortable feeling in his belly. Jalas hadn't taken it well when he'd been told that rather than destroy his son, Israel had only banished him...for a second time. He didn't want to get onto that subject again, so offered up information that would hopefully serve as a distraction. "And you are correct in that Hallow and Allegria were wed in late summer, at the temple where she'd served. Lady Sandorillan insisted they perform the ceremony there."

Jalas grunted and gestured for more ale. Idril rose, and without glancing at Israel, refilled their flagons before returning silently to her seat. "More fool he for binding himself to one who will likely try to kill him one of these days. What was it about Darius that concerned the arcanist?"

"Evidently there are signs Darius feels he no longer needs to abide by the rules the Council has set down."

"The Council of Four Armies is disbanded," Jalas said, and for a fleeting second, his expression was sly.

Israel frowned. Perhaps Jalas was merely feeling the strain of his illness. "I wouldn't use the term *disbanded* when 'at peace' is more appropriate."

"Oh?" Jalas's eyes narrowed on him. "Do you maintain the army you had summoned for the battle with the Harborym?"

"Not the full force," Israel answered, a sense of something in the air—suspicion? Resentment?—making him wary. "But I always have need of a standing army. The Fireborn are, on the whole, a reasonable people, but it does not mean they are willing to live in complete harmony. You must know how important it is to remind your people of the repercussions should they cross you."

Jalas murmured it was so, drinking from the flagon as he did so.

The next half hour left Israel with a definite idea that something was very wrong with Jalas. Although he expressed interest in Darius, he appeared distracted and didn't once inquire what Hallow and his fellow arcanists were doing.

It wasn't until later that evening, when Idril had escorted him from her father's chambers that he gave voice to the concern that most bothered him. "Your father is a changed man."

"Yes." Idril stood in front of the fire in the great hall, her demeanor as mild as ever, although her shoulders rose in a slight shrug. "He did not take our divorce well."

"Considering he knew our marriage was one in name only, it was unrealistic of him to expect us to continue it."

"My father has ever been a man who follows his own counsel," she said evenly, her gaze still on the fire. "Even when he knows he is in the wrong."

Israel frowned, remembering the thinly veiled barbs that the older man had cast at his daughter. "Does he maintain no control over the Tribe any longer?"

"No. He claims he is too weak for it." She turned to him, her gaze as steady as her seemingly unruffled emotions. "The clans are threatening to form their own leadership. He blames me for that, but will not allow me to do anything to assert my dominance, much though I would like to. A more ungrateful, obstinate group of men I have yet to meet."

"Your father?" Israel asked in confusion.

"The Tribesmen." She clicked her tongue and corrected herself. "And yes, my father, too."

He searched her face, looking for signs of distress, but despite her bitter tone, her expression was as placid as ever. "Is there no other way of rallying the Tribe to your banner without your father's blessing?"

"Of course there is. It's simply a matter of whether I wish to fight my father at the same time I bring the Tribe to heel, which is what will happen if I try to claim control."

"Idril..." He stopped, not sure what he could say to her. He had not wished to marry Idril, but had agreed when it became clear that Jalas would remove himself and his people from the Council if he did not do so. Neither Idril or he had ever believed the marriage was anything but a temporary legality, one that would allow Jalas to save face, and Israel to keep from having a contentious neighbor to the north.

He picked his words carefully now. "I don't know why your father has changed so much since the Battle of the Fourth Age, or what estrangement is between you and him beyond the dissolution of our marriage, but I feel obligated to offer you sanctuary should you require it."

"Sanctuary?" Surprise flickered through her eyes. "From what?"

"The Tribe. Your father has ruled your people for many centuries, but it has not been an easy rule, and if you find yourself unable to keep them in control—"

"It is not the Tribe from whom I need protection," she answered.

"What do you mean by that?"

Her gaze went past him, causing Israel to turn to see who had entered the hall.

It was Marston, who gestured a question that clearly asked if he was needed. Israel shook his head, and the other man left the room as silently as he'd come.

Idril turned and fetched the wine from where it had been mulling on the hearth, pouring him a goblet of the steaming liquid. "You did not endure the hardships of snow and travel just to see how I was faring leading my father's people. Yet you spent two hours with Father and did not ask him anything. It makes me wonder why you would go to so much trouble to be here at Ilam."

Israel smiled and sipped at the spiced wine. Although he'd changed into dry clothing earlier, the memories of the cold passage to Ilam were all too fresh in his mind, and he relished the warm burn of the wine. "I see the six months we've spent apart have done nothing to dull your astuteness."

She raised an eyebrow a fraction of an inch. "Did you think I would fade away to a colorless drab in your absence?"

"No," he said, turning his mind back to the question of Jalas's behavior. "I assumed you would fare as you always do. Since you have guessed as much, I will admit that I am here for a specific reason. You took note of what I said about Hallow?"

She seated herself in a wooden chair that seemed to be made up of elegant curves. "That he is concerned about Darius? Yes. What I found puzzling was what you did not say: exactly what it was Hallow did with regard to Darius. You simply mentioned them, and then encouraged my father to be distracted with gossip about the priest."

"You haven't lost any of your shrewdness, either. Tell me, do you really have an interest in Deo, or is that yet another of his wild imaginings?"

"Deo," she said, smoothing the fabric of her gown. Her gaze was averted so that he couldn't look into her eyes, and as usual, her expression told him nothing. "Deo is lost to us."

"He is in Eris," Israel corrected.

"Which we cannot get to." Her fingers traced the golden threads embroidered on the creamy white fabric of her gown. "No one has ever been able to sail to Eris without perishing most violently."

"No one has been able to sail to it, but there is another way to travel there," Israel said.

She slid him an unreadable glance, the single wrinkle back between her brows for a moment before it smoothed out. "Ah. The portals. But those were created by the Harborym."

"Not by them…but their leader." Israel fought the sense of anger that followed whenever the memory of Dasa rose in his mind. "Their captain, Racin, is the one who sacrificed many Harborym in order to generate the power needed to opened the portals, or so the queen told me years ago. I can't imagine that has changed."

"Indeed." Idril appeared to consider this. "I conclude you are not planning on inviting the Harborym leader back to Aryia simply so that you will have access to his portal leading to Eris, and yet, I can see no other method of getting there."

"I assume that if he had the means to open portals here or on Genora, he would have already done so. Regardless of whether or not he has regained the ability to open a portal, I have not spent the last eleven months reassuring the people of Aryia that they are safe only to bring that monster back," Israel said, feeling suddenly weary. It had been a very long time since he had been able to rest without feeling as if he was being smothered by sorrow.

Her pale lips curved into a faint smile. "Like me, you sacrifice much to keep your people content. But that said, neither are you willing to sit back when there is a fight to be had."

"You confuse me with my son," Israel said, setting down the now empty wine goblet and striding to the fire, welcoming the warmth it brought to him. "I do not run off on a whim to join whatever battle is at hand."

"But Deo is, as I have said, lost to us." Idril eyed him with gentle interest. "That returns us to the subject of the portals, which I gather is the purpose of your trip to the High Lands."

"It is. Or rather, the means of accessing them without bringing Racin down upon our heads."

Idril thought for a moment; then both eyebrows rose a smidgen. "Ah, the moonstone."

"Exodius said he planned on safeguarding the stones since they were too powerful to be used by those who did not understand their strength. He did not name Jalas as one of the stones' guardians, but Hallow has learned from his arcanists that the stone is here."

She inclined her head. "It is. I have not seen it, but before he took to his bed, my father sent away all but his most trusted body servant and hid something in the keep. I knew only that it was an artifact of great power that he dared not use. I thought it might be a talisman or token that he... liberated...from the queen's holdings when we were in Starfall City, but if the runeseeker gave him one of the moonstones used to destroy Deo—"

"*Banish* Deo," Israel murmured, and wondered again what was in Idril's heart. "Sending him to the Isles of Enoch was the only way to save him from your father's wrath. I had no idea that Exodius would separate the stones afterward. That turned out to be much more problematic than I imagined it would be."

"If Father had a stone of such immense abilities, it would make sense that he would hide it close to hand. But I'm afraid if you are here to plead for the stone, he will not yield it. He is very much like a magpie in that regard—once he has a treasure, he will not give it up."

"I am here to explain to him that the stone is needed for a purpose that Exodius did not anticipate," Israel said.

She shook her head. "You do not understand; Father will not resist because the runeseeker asked him to guard it—he will not allow it out of his possession because it is now his, and he does not give up what he holds." Her gaze slid to the side, to the stairs that led up to Jalas's chambers. "Unless that possession is his daughter."

"Regardless, I must have the stone." Israel sat, suddenly so tired he felt as if he could sleep for a week solid. "Hallow will gain access to the one that he says Lady Sandor holds, and I have no doubt his arcanists will locate the third one shortly, but he barely knows Jalas, and will have little ability to convince your father to relinquish the stone he guards."

"Whereas he will do so for you?" Idril shook her head again, so that the silver-blond hair that covered her like a shawl of silk shimmered with the movement. "You are mistaken, my lord."

Israel's jaw tightened. "Then I will take it from him, by force if necessary."

Idril watched him for a few moments, then leaned forward and touched him lightly on the knee. "You risk death simply to open a portal to Eris?"

"The queen is a prisoner there," he answered idly, wondering if his score of men would be enough to take the moonstone if Jalas refused to give it up. "I will not suffer her to remain in the company of the captain of the Harborym when it is within my ability to free her."

"You will not get the stone from my father by force," she said, her pale gaze holding his. "He may play at being frail, but he is as strong as the stones of this keep. There is help available, though…for a price."

Israel fought the desire to snap out an irritated response. "What price?" he asked, his voice as grim as his soul.

For the first time in all the years that Israel had known Idril, she smiled, really smiled, an expression that revealed not just mirth, but satisfaction. It lit up her face, and gave him a glimmer of what had ensnared his son. "Me. You must take me with you to Eris."

That was the last thing he had expected her to say. "You? With all due respect, Lady Idril, Eris is not a place for a gently born woman. It is a shadowland, one beset by Harborym, and filled with priests who perform blood magic."

"Nonetheless, that is my price. I will help you acquire the stone, but I must be allowed to travel to Eris."

"Why?" he asked, but knew the answer even as the word left his lips. The light in her face faded when she turned to pour out another goblet of wine.

"The queen is not the only one who suffers in Eris," was all she said, but it was enough.

Israel reluctantly agreed. He had no intention of letting Idril put herself at risk by traveling with him to Eris, but he would address that issue later, once he had the stone in his possession, and Hallow had the other two.

For now, this was enough. It had to be. There was simply no other way to save Dasa and Deo.

Chapter 5

"I can't say that I think much of Cape Despair." The fetid smell of swamp wafted over us via a short-lived breeze. I wrinkled my nose. "I can't imagine that anyone actually *chooses* to live here."

Hallow eyed the trees that dripped with both wetness and long streamers of slimy-looking vines. "It certainly isn't very pre-possessing, but who knows? Perhaps Aldmarsh is as delightful as this area is vile."

A rotund, furry animal the size of a small gourd, piebald copper and white, stumbled across the road, weaved dramatically, then fell over onto its back, the four little feet at the end of its chubby legs waving in a desultory manner.

"Even the bumblepigs are depressed about being here," I said, halting Buttercup to dismount and check on the little creature. We were riding, having left the cart at Peer's Mill, the town half a day's ride to the north. I prodded the bumblepig. It squeaked and waved its feet again. I sighed. "Sorry, little fellow, I'd like to take you out of this miserable place, but we already have a pet, and even if a wooden bird inhabited by a spirit isn't as demanding as a living beast, we are likely going into battle. You're safer here." I righted the bumblepig and guided it off the road and into the shrubs that lined the verge. It waddled off looking morose.

Hallow looked up from a journal where he'd sketched a copy of a map. "Aldmarsh should be just over the rise."

"Good. I don't think I could remain here for long without losing my will to live." I popped Buttercup on the nose when she tried to nip me, quickly remounting before she could raise a ruckus. "What are we going to do if Quinn isn't there?"

"The captain of the guard said he would be." Hallow's face was grimmer than I had seen it in some months.

"Mmhmm. And the mayor of Peer's Mill says he's never heard the name. Ugh. This place makes me feel like I need a hot bath to wash off all the stickiness."

"As pleasant as the mayor was, I am putting my faith in Exodius and the captain of the guard. Neither has any reason to deceive us. What are you doing?"

My hands danced in the air. Although I'd been a priest at the temple of Kiriah Sunbringer since I was three summers old, I had never been the most studious of pupils. Not until I left the priesthood to bind myself to Hallow, that is…and then encouraged by the amount of time he spent studying his inherited library, I'd looked into some of blessings and protections that had fallen into disuse. "That volume you said that Exodius must have stolen from my temple referenced a benison that offered protection against shadow beings."

Hallow didn't look as impressed as I felt he should. "Are we likely to encounter such beings in Aldmarsh?"

"You never know," I said darkly as I finished drawing the symbols of protection on him and began to draw them over myself. "This place is so miserable, it wouldn't surprise me to find Shadowborn, the old ones who walked Alba before man, and a samartxiki or two hanging around waiting to pounce on us. Ugh. This swamp is decidedly not in Kiriah's favor." I shivered despite the cloying air.

"We should know in a few minutes, although I don't believe I've ever heard of samartxiki."

I smiled to myself. Hallow had an insatiable curiosity, and was always pleased to tuck away any random bit of information he happened upon. "Do you not have legends of them in Penhallow? The older priests used to mention them to the initiates when we were young and didn't have the gravity of spirit that they desired. They used to tell us of how the samartxiki were born in the deepest hours of the night and grew up in the shadows of chestnut trees, hiding themselves until an unwary person passed too close. Then they would leap out and bite at them with teeth like those of a saw. They were supposed to be particularly fond of children who shirked their duties in order to do more pleasurable things."

He grinned at me. "Why do I suspect they had a particular initiate in mind when telling that story?"

"Because you're a smart man who has the most adorable eye crinkles, and you've met Sandor, all of which means you know that I spent more time hunting for rabbits and birds than I did on my knees next to Sandor in prayer."

"For which I'm thankful on a daily basis—ah, there, see?" He reined in Penn for a moment when we crested a slight hill. Below us, a small town sprawled drunkenly along the shoreline. There were a few ships bobbing out to sea, no doubt local fisherman, while further out a larger ship was anchored near a sand bar. The houses themselves—more shacks than actual houses—straggled crookedly, and the sound of the surf and sea birds gave the whole place a curiously desolate air. "It's...uh...it's..."

"Horrible. That house on the end is leaning so far over, it looks like it might collapse. And is that a dead samartxiki in the road? This is just the sort of area where I'd expect to find them strewn hither and yon."

Hallow pursed his lips as I pointed to a blob in the path winding down to Aldmarsh. The shape lay on its back, four stiff legs pointing skyward, where high clouds hid Kiriah's light from the land. I had a feeling Kiriah preferred it that way.

"That, my heart, is a dead cow, not a saw-toothed shadow-dwelling monster," he said, pressing his heels to Penn. The horse started forward reluctantly, and Buttercup followed.

"Also the sort of thing I'd expect to find here," I said, glancing around me with suspicion. "Even the animals don't want to be here."

"Cows die of natural causes, Allegria. Houses lean. And foul airs sometime come up from the ground, making a miasma of decay that permeates everything. There is nothing here that suggests a bad omen," he said with a little laugh.

I sniffed and made a face as we approached the town. "What in the name of the twin goddesses is that? The dead cow? It smells like a hundred rotting corpses. And this cow did not die naturally. Just look at its expression."

Hallow glanced down as we skirted the dead animal. He said nothing, but pulled the staff from his back and rested it on the toe of his booted foot as we entered the town of Aldmarsh proper. A couple of women stood together with baskets on their arms, watching us with a despairing sense of acceptance that made the fine hairs on my arms rise.

"Blessings of the goddesses," Hallow greeted the ladies politely.

They didn't respond, but watched us dismount with flat, hopeless eyes.

"We're looking for a man named Quinn," I told the ladies and sketched a couple of general protection runes on them, a normal practice for a priest, but one that felt oddly out of place here. I could feel Kiriah's presence, but it seemed distant, as if the sun was swaddled. "Could you tell us where he lives?"

"There is no one of that name here," one of the women said. Her voice was as lifeless as her eyes.

"Are you sure? Sometimes he's called Quinn the Mad." Both ladies shook their heads. "Ah. Well, may Kiriah's benevolence shine upon you." I drew another rune on them, feeling they needed it.

Hallow said nothing as we turned and led our mounts down the rutted muddy track that was the main street in Aldmarsh. Faint movement of pale faces in glassless windows dissolved into darkness as the inhabitants, having seen us, returned to their cheerless lives. There were no children playing or running around, no animals save for a few scraggly chickens huddled in uncomfortable-looking lumps, and no sound but that of the sea.

"What are we going to do?" I asked Hallow when he stopped in front of one of the shacks. This one had a fishing net swaying gently from the craggy line of broken tile on the roof, pegged out along the side of the house, no doubt to dry. The breeze from the water did little to dissipate the horrible stench that seemed to come from the ground itself.

He nodded toward the house. "We're going to find out who lives here."

"Why here?" I asked, my back itchy with the sensation of unseen watchers.

"Look at the net. Do you see the knife tacking it to the wall of the house?"

"Yes. So?"

"Look closer." I let him take the reins from me so he could tie up his horse and Buttercup, eyeing the knife. It was small, almost as small as an eating knife, the blade scarred, but not rusted. The handle bore a golden tree on a background of white...the symbol of Lord Israel.

"You think this is the man we want?" I asked when Hallow knocked on the door.

"The captain said Quinn the Mad had seen more battles than I could conceive of—clearly, the owner of that knife has served under or with Lord Israel, and just as clearly, he is someone with whom we should speak." He took my hand, his fingers curling around mine in a way that had me wishing we were back home, cuddled up together in bed, with no demands on us but the need to drive each other wild with touches and kisses, and the particular way his whiskers tickled my inner thighs when he—

"Allegria?"

"Hmm?" With an effort, I pulled my mind to the present. While I had been distracted, Hallow had led me around the shack to the back, where we found three chairs positioned next to a small stack of barrels and a couple of broken crates. On one of the chairs a man was seated with a net that spilled out across his lap and down onto the brown sand. Next to him, perched on one of the crates, a girl of about six sat cross legged, a dirty red cloth doll sitting next to her. "Oh. Er...greetings and blessings to you both."

The man had been eyeing Hallow and now turned his attention to me. He appeared to be of middling age, with black hair that brushed his shoulders, a black goatee, and a raised scar on one cheek that looked like the letter T. "Really? That's generous of you, especially since I don't know you. What sort of blessings do you offer? The useless sort flung around by priests and their ilk, or something more substantial involving coin or ale? Preferably both, possibly with a warm, bosomy alewench thrown in as well. I do like a good bosomy alewench."

Hallow bowed, his eyes alight with humor. "Alas, we have neither alewenches, nor coin, although I do have a few skins of a particularly nice wine back in Peer's Mill that I am willing to share with you. I assume you are Quinn?"

"Name's Ramswell. That's Dexia." He waggled his eyebrows at me, his gaze on my breasts until I crossed my arms.

"Hello," the little girl said with obvious diffidence. She was attempting to force a bit of grey cloth onto her doll. She had nondescript brown hair scraped back into two tight pigtails, and slightly protuberant blue eyes that reminded me of a pet bumblepig that used to be kept by one of the senior priests.

"That's a very pretty doll you have," I lied, smiling at her. "Does she have a name?"

"She's not a doll," Dexia said with a scornful curl of her lip. "Her name is Retribution, and she's a device I fashioned from bits of cloth, hair, and fingernails. I'm cursing Grimalka, the butcher's daughter, because she ate our goat, and now we have no milk. I *like* milk. I'm going to curse Grimalka so that her head shrivels up until it's no bigger than a potato, and then all will know about her despicable acts, and men will shun her, and she will be driven from the town and forced to live in the cave to the east where spirits of the unshriven will torment her until she swims out to sea and becomes food for the eels. I *also* like eels."

I stared in mingled horror and surprise at the child for a moment, then slid a glance toward Hallow. He didn't seem to have heard since he was introducing us to Ramswell. "We come from Kelos seeking one named Quinn the Mad. Our business with him is most urgent. Naturally, we will reward those who help us find him, as well as the man himself."

"So, there's no ale?" Ramswell looked crestfallen.

"I'm afraid not, no," Hallow answered.

"And the priest with the big—" He made a gesture with both hands. "She looks like she's worth the time to get to know those breasts."

I rolled my eyes.

"She is not available either," Hallow told him, a corner of his mouth twitching. "Although I will add that her bosom is plentiful and definitely worth your time. Well, my time since she'd probably gut you if you tried to investigate her tunic."

I punched Hallow on the arm.

He cleared his throat. "We seem to have gotten off the subject. We need either Quinn or the precious object he holds."

Ramswell shrugged, and began darning the net again. "Can't help you."

"Are you sure?" Hallow asked, his voice persuasive. "Quinn has knowledge about a moonstone that we have been sent to retrieve by the former master of Kelos, a runeseeker of the name Exodius."

That was stretching the truth a little bit, but I was all for doing whatever it took to get the stone, so we could rescue Deo and the queen.

"Don't know what you're talking about," Ramswell said evenly.

"And yet you have a knife that originated in the company of Lord Israel of Aryia, and you bear the mark of a thief," Hallow said softly. "That coupled with the fact that you are literally at the most distant spot on Genora leads me to believe that perhaps there is something you might tell us."

"I'm a simple alewench-loving fisherman," Ramswell said, his brows pulling together. He continued to mend the net on his lap, but his movements were jerky as he stabbed into the tangled line. "My life is not complicated. I drink. I fish. I buy goats when they get eaten by the butcher's daughter. She has an upper story that is impressive, but it doesn't hold a candle to the priest's. There is nothing more to me, so if you have no ale, and the priest isn't interested in a tumble, then you can be on your way."

"Or you could bring us a goat," Dexia said, sliding off the barrel. She knelt at the cold remains of a fire, and smeared ashy fingers across her doll, leaving behind symbols that made me feel as if I was standing in the deepest part of night, naked, alone, and chilled to the very center of my being. "We could use another goat. Maybe two."

"Two goats are always better than no goats," Ramswell allowed after a moment's thought. Then he grinned, the change of his expression making me want to smile back at him. "But an alewench is better still. Are you sure the priest with the impressive frontage wouldn't like me to show her how I—"

"My *wife* is not available for tumbling by anyone but me," Hallow said, his lips thinning.

I giggled. I couldn't deny that there was a certain roguish attractiveness to Ramswell, but I wasn't going to admit that to Hallow. He would simply add him to the list of men to whom he referred as my boyfriends, and would bring him up with obnoxious frequency, as he so often did with Deo.

"I would be happy to procure a goat for you and your daughter if you would tell me of the moonstone," Hallow continued. "Or where I might locate Quinn."

"I am now done talking with you," Ramswell said, setting aside the net and standing to stretch. "My bladder is making demands on me, and you're doing nothing but repeating yourself. You admit you have no goat or ale, and your *wife*—" he made sure to mimic the emphasis Hallow had put on the word. "—is too well armed for me to attempt to woo her with my boyish charm and devil-may-care attitude without risking life, limb, or both my bollocks, all of which I enjoy, so I will say to you both good day, fare thee well, and get the hell out of my yard."

Ramswell strode away to what looked like a ramshackle privy tucked behind a large oak tree.

"What do you think?" I asked Hallow in a soft voice. I needn't have bothered—Dexia was now on her knees, the doll before her as she chanted what I had a horrible feeling was a potent curse over it, and no doubt was paying scant attention to us.

Hallow sighed and put his hand on my back, gently pushing me toward the privy. "I think we're going to have to do this the hard way."

"There's not a truth spell or something you can cast on him?" I asked.

"Master Nix insisted they were more trouble than they were worth, and never taught them to me," he said with a wry smile.

"Maybe not, but you've spent the last ten months going through Exodius's belongings. You can't tell me there wasn't a truth spell or two documented somewhere in all those moldy journals."

"Perhaps," he said, his smile now warm and filling me with a desire to grab his head and kiss the breath right off his lips. "But about this, I feel Nix was correct. Such spells do not get consistent results and are tricky to pull off without having something go badly awry. I'm afraid, my heart, we shall have to do this by the simple act of force. I wish I hadn't sent Thorn back to Starfall to watch Darius. I could use him here. This place is filled with magic."

"Really? How do you know?"

"I can feel it. Can you not?"

"No. Kiriah is…" I rubbed my arms. "She's still not talking to me, Hallow."

"Patience—" he started to say, but I cut him off.

"I have been patient for eleven months!"

He took my hand and gave my fingers a squeeze. "You have been very patient, and I know it chafes that your connection with Kiriah is currently in a dimmed state, but you've felt bereft of her blessing in the past, and she was there waiting for you when you needed her."

"This is different," I answered, shaking my head. "Ever since I channeled Kiriah in Abet, I can feel her, but it's as if she's holding her power just out of my grasp. I think this is my punishment, and oh, Hallow, what if she never graces me again? What if I am never able to weave light, or call on Kiriah's strength again? What if I'm doomed to nothing more than drawing ineffectual blessings on hopeless people?"

"Kiriah would not have once so blessed you only to spurn you," he said in the same maddeningly reassuring tone. "If I tell you to stop trying so hard, and just let it be, would you cuff me on the head?"

"Maybe," I said with an acid note about which I immediately felt guilty. I cleared my throat and tried to banish the gloom from my voice. "No, of course I wouldn't strike you, but you don't understand just how frustrating this is. You always feel arcany."

"That's because it permeates everything," he said with irritating mildness, although to be fair, everything irritated me at that moment. "Take heart, my love. Kiriah has not turned her back on you. When the time comes for her to grant you her grace, she will do so in a way that will leave you in no doubt that you are favored in her eyes."

There wasn't much more I could say that wasn't whining, so I let the subject drop, and stomped after Hallow as he headed for the privy where Ramswell had gone. "Let's just get this over with. I'm damp, uncomfortable, and my clothes are going to need to be burned once we leave here, because nothing is going to get this stink out of them. Do you want to force Ramswell to tell us where Quinn is, or shall I?"

"I'll start. You can help if necessary." Hallow squared his shoulders and stalked forward to where our target had emerged from the privy. I spent a moment in admiration of Hallow, at the breadth of his shoulders that made me feel feminine (despite the fact that I was what one of the priestesses had referred to as hearty peasant stock); at his long legs, and the magnificent ass that I loved to touch. I was just anticipating the pleasure I found when watching him wield arcane magic, when he confronted Ramswell. Before I could blink, Hallow went flying backward a good twenty yards, slamming up against a tree before sliding down it to the ground into a limp blob.

"Hallow!" I screamed, racing toward him, pulling my swords from the scabbard on my back as I did so.

"I'm all right," he said groggily, shaking his head and trying to get to his knees. He peered up at me, squinting. "Then again, maybe I'm not. There appear to be three of you. I think I'm a bit stunned. What in the name of the goddess's ten toes happened?"

"I said I was done with this conversation," Ramswell announced, marching up to us. "You will leave now, or I will break your bones into a hundred little pieces and scatter them for the gulls."

I spun around, my swords in my hands. "No one makes my husband see triple!" I pulled hard on the distant Kiriah, but all I felt was awareness of the sun, nothing more.

Ramswell raised an eyebrow. "Really? And how do you expect to stop me?"

"Allegria—" Hallow managed to get to his feet, obviously feeling that he needed to defend me, but we both knew that wasn't necessary. I threw myself onto Ramswell, clearly the last thing he expected, because he staggered backward a few feet before falling to the ground.

"It's all right," I told Hallow, getting to my feet quickly as he hurried over to me with a cry. "Everything's fine. Now, you obnoxious Ramswell, I have a few things to say to you. Let's start with an apology for hurting Hallow."

I approached the prone man, but before I could so much as prod him with my toe, his leg kicked out and I was suddenly on my back, my swords skittering out of my hands, while the cold edge of a blade stung my throat.

"Move, and she dies," he told Hallow, who had lifted the staff preparatory to casting a spell. "And that means your fingers, too. Don't think I can't see you trying to draw a spell in the air."

I raised an eyebrow at Hallow and smiled. Ramswell might have seen the movement of Hallow's hands, but he didn't see mine sketching blessings and protections.

"Watch out!" The high, sketchy voice of Dexia reached my ear just as I spread wide my fingers, planning on casting a net of protection over myself when suddenly, Ramswell was gone, and a mad, vicious creature was on me, biting and scratching, sharp, pointed teeth snapping a hairsbreadth from my face.

It was Dexia, but she seemed to have the strength of ten men as her small fingers dug into the flesh of my neck.

Behind her, I could see Hallow casting a spell, but Ramswell tackled him at that moment, and the two men fell to the ground in a confusion or arms, legs, and various oaths.

Black blotchy spots started to obscure my vision, my strength ebbing as the child throttled me. I squawked and pulled desperately on Kiriah's strength, but the goddess only made my hands glow with a feeble imitation of her light. It was enough to make Dexia scream, though, and she leaped off me, dancing around as if she was on fire. I dragged myself over to where Ramswell and Hallow were still struggling, desperately trying to pull the former off Hallow at the same time as I tried to get air into my lungs.

"Hallow, I—" Before the rest of the sentence was out of my mouth, Ramswell held me by the throat with one hand, while the other hand covered Hallow's face, cutting off his air. But what drove me into a panic was the sensation of a great weight pulling me down into the soft earth, one that crushed me, squeezing my lungs flat and compressing my body until my heart could no longer beat.

"No!" I yelled, kicking and struggling even as the black splotches returned. My mind was a mass of confusion and disbelief. How could these two people defeat us when an army of Harborym couldn't?

And yet the proof was there as I gave in to the massive weight that dragged me down, flattening me until I sagged against Hallow's struggling body, my breath rasping almost as loudly as the heartbeat that filled my ears. I fought, pulling on Kiriah for aid, but my body was too weak, and the goddess too distant, leaving me to fall backward, my body limp and unresponsive.

"My..." Hallow's voice came faint and hoarse, the word drifting away on the wind.

I didn't even have the strength to turn to him, but a word slipped out through my lips. "...heart. What the—" There was a pulling sensation on my neck, and suddenly, I was propped up against the tree, the massive weight that had been crushing me into the ground blessedly lifted. I drew in great gasping, shuddering breaths of air, the black haze fading to reveal Ramswell squatting before me, the captain's whistle that had hung around my neck now in his hands.

"Where did you get this?"

I didn't answer him. The still, lifeless form of Hallow lay next to me. Without thinking, I snatched up one of my swords, and sliced off Ramswell's head.

It bounced to the ground next to him. The head, to my absolute and complete horror, was still animated. It donned an unhappy expression, rolled its eyes, and heaved a big sigh. Then Ramswell reached out, picked up his head, and plopped it back onto the stump of his neck. The skin seemed to merge together and become whole again, just as if my sword hadn't cut through bone and sinew a few seconds before.

"Ow." Ram frowned at me. "Don't do that again. It hurts."

"What...how..." I blinked first at him, then down at my sword, but before I could figure out what had happened, Hallow had staggered to his feet, and was gathering up arcany in his hands.

"I am a patient man, but almost killing my wife and me makes me very, very angry. Hand over that damned moonstone before I blast you full of holes."

Ramswell got to his feet, then turned to show the whistle to Dexia, who was wiping her bloody mouth on the rag doll. "They have the talisman," he told her.

She grimaced. "I suppose that means we're going to have to leave Aldmarsh. And me in the middle of a cursing. You know it takes a good week to get a head shrunken down to potato-size. Maybe they will wait until Grimalka's head is down to a cantaloupe?"

"I'll ask them, but judging by the way that priest whacked off my head without so much as a by-your-leave, I'm judging you will have to settle for simply casting the spell. Here, stop doing that. It's almost as painful as having my head lopped off."

The last was in reference to Hallow's casting little balls of pure arcany at Ramswell, who twitched a little as each ball hit him, but didn't fall over and beg for mercy, as we both expected.

I looked at Hallow.

Hallow looked first at Ramswell, then my sword, then met my gaze. "He's more than he appears."

"That was my thought. He's Quinn?"

"I expect so." Hallow turned back to the man who was absently tracing the symbols on the whistle. "Are you Quinn the Mad?"

The man sighed again but didn't deny it. "I knew you were trouble the minute I clapped eyes on the priest's ample breasts."

Hallow's lips thinned. "Why did you almost kill us?"

"You were annoying me," Quinn said simply. "The priest is dripping with weapons, and if you are Master of Kelos, you are one of the most powerful arcanists on Genora. Why didn't you tell me you had the talisman? It would have been much easier, and I wouldn't have had to defend myself."

"We're looking for a man named Quinn the Mad, not Ramswell the Annoying," I couldn't help but snap. "You could have admitted who you were instead of insisting you were a fisherman named Ramswell. One with a particularly creepy daughter."

Dexia bared her pointed teeth at my accusatory look.

"Eh? Dex? She's not my daughter. She's a vanth."

I came up blank and looked my question at Hallow.

"Vanths are reportedly bloodthirsty, vicious beings born from the shadows who are used by unscrupulous people to set curses upon their enemies. I haven't heard of any in existence outside of Eris," he answered, giving Dexia a long look before returning his attention to Quinn. "As much as I'd like to discuss just who and what you are, not to mention why you're pretending to be a fisherman stuck at the arse end of the world—"

"If people called you Quinn the Mad, wouldn't *you* pick another name?" Quinn interrupted.

"I get called mad on an almost daily basis, but I take your point." Hallow took a deep breath, clearly trying to hang on to his patience. "Regardless, we need the moonstone that Exodius put into your keeping. We are short on time, so if you could give it to us, we will leave you in peace."

"I don't have it."

"But...you knew about the whistle," I said, gesturing toward the item. "The captain of the guard said that if we gave you the whistle, you'd hand over the moonstone."

"I can't give you something I don't have," Quinn said, and with wink at me, he slipped the leather thong over his neck.

"But the captain said you would!" I argued, my fingers itching to snatch back the whistle.

"Are your hands glowing?" Quinn asked, then turned to Hallow. "Tell me, if she touches you when her hands are like that—"

"It's something you have to feel to believe," Hallow said with a wolfish grin at me.

"Reeeally," Quinn drawled and eyed me.

"Want to try it?" I asked sweetly, my hopes dashing when I saw that my hands barely glowed with the light of Kiriah Sunbringer. Evidently once again I was only allowed a modicum of the power I once wielded.

Quinn looked surprised, sliding a glance toward Hallow. "Er... is it allowed?"

Hallow just smiled.

"Of course it is," I said, waggling my fingers, which sadly, quickly lost their slight glow. "I'm known far and wide for my ability to geld without touching a blade. Both hands around a pair of testicles, a brief prayer to Kiriah, and boom: two testicles fall to the ground with a minimum of blood and discomfort to the former bearer. I'd be happy to show you just how it's done."

His eyes opened wide, one hand protectively covered his groin. "Bellias's ten silver toes, you're worse than Dex at her most irate. If you so much as look at my bollocks, I'll cast the talisman into the deepest part of the sea. The oath be damned."

"What oath would that be?" Hallow asked.

Quinn let his lip curl a little before gesturing toward us. "You're not going to just go away, are you? I can tell you're not. Very well, if I have to tell this, I'm going to do it over ale. Dex, finish up your curse. We'll be leaving as soon as Bellias gives us her blessing."

The little girl clicked her tongue in annoyance, but hurried off with her doll in hand, squatting next to the cold fire pit to resume her ceremony.

"Do you have any idea what's going on?" I whispered to Hallow when we followed Quinn into his ramshackle house.

"Only a very slight inkling. The runes on the whistle were those of both Bellias and Kiriah."

"What does that mean?" I asked, feeling out of my depth when it came to such things.

"It means, my stabby little priestling, that I owe my existence—such as it is—to the twin goddesses," Quinn answered, taking a jug and splashing ale into three not-very-clean looking cups before shoving two of them at us. I shook my head and he simply drained my cup of ale before stifling a belch, and adding, "The oath is to them. I owe them my life. Lives. All of them."

"You have more than one life?" I asked, confused.

"Not really." He downed another cup of ale. "It seems like it sometimes, but in reality there's just the one."

Hallow had been studying him, and I could feel him thinking hard and fast on the enigma of the man who sat on a three-legged stool in front of us. I took over the second stool, while Hallow stood, absently sipping the ale. "You're immortal?"

Quinn grinned. "Oh, I can be killed," he said with a sudden grin. "As you just saw. Over and over and over again."

"You're lifebound," Hallow said, a note of awe in his voice.

"That I am." He rubbed the now dried blood from his neck. There wasn't even the faintest of marks where my sword had sliced through him.

"Which means...what?" I asked, disliking this feeling of not understanding. Hallow seemed to be faring much better. He'd actually pulled out a small journal and made a few notes.

"It means he's tied to both goddesses and is in effect their servant, obligated to aid those who bear the talisman binding him." Hallow's eyes were alight with interest. "And as such, a fitting person to guard something so valuable as one of the three moonstones."

Quinn poured more ale. "If you're going to insist that this conversation goes around and around, then I'm going to need more ale. And a woman." He glanced at me. I wiggled my fingers at him. He blanched. "Maybe just the ale would do."

"If you don't have the stone, then why did the captain send us to you?" I asked, frustrated, tired, and desirous of a hot bath to wash off the stink of Cape Despair.

"Simon loves to be mysterious," Quinn answered with a little half smile. "He always has been so. When we were young, he used to claim that he was going to be more powerful than the Master himself, but that didn't sit very well, and he spent the next nine years in gaol."

"Simon?"

"The Master?" Hallow asked at the same time.

"The captain of the guard is named Simon?" I turned to Hallow. "I always wondered what his name was, but he told me he'd always been known as the captain. That rat!"

"You're his...brother?" Hallow's gaze suddenly sharpened. "If you were born at Kelos as was the captain of the guard—er—Simon, then you must be an arcanist, too."

Quinn set down his cup, gave us a cheeky grin, and held out his hands, palm up. Resting on each was a ball of pure blue arcane light. "I was apprenticed to the Master at the time, until we had our...accident...which left me lifebound and in service to the goddesses until they see fit to let me rest in the spirit world."

"I'm going to want to hear the story of this accident and your master," Hallow said, making a quick note before slipping his journal away in an inner pocket of his jerkin. "I wish we had time for it now, but we don't. We must have the stone so we can proceed to Aryia to pick up the second stone."

Quinn shook his head while Hallow was still speaking. "I told you that I don't have the stone. No matter how many times you make me repeat myself, it won't change facts."

"Then why did the captain—" I started to say, but he interrupted me.

"What exactly did Simon say to you?"

I thought. "He said that you would give us what we seek."

"And what do you seek? No, not the stone. What is it that you really want? For what purpose do you need the stones?"

I glanced at Hallow. He held my gaze for a few seconds, clearly mulling over Quinn's questions. "The captain said Quinn would lead us to what we sought."

"But no one can take us to Eris," I pointed out. "It is impossible. Everyone knows that the storms surrounding the continent are impossible to pass through without perishing."

We both turned to look at Quinn, who was now peering into the ale jug. "Damn. That went fast. Barely had a taste of it and now it's gone."

"The ship that's sitting out on the sand bar," Hallow said slowly. "I don't suppose that's yours?"

"The *Tempest*? Aye, she's mine." He rocked back in his chair. "Dexia! Do we have any more ale?"

The childlike voice wafted in on a putrid breeze. "You drank it all."

Quinn swore.

"And would that ship—or rather, the captain whose life cannot be removed from his body—be able to sail to Eris?"

"Ah, mate, you have no idea what you ask," Quinn said, shaking his head with obvious regret. "As your bloodthirsty, if delectable, wife said, it's death to cross the waters off the coast of Eris."

"Unless I'm mistaken, vanths come from Eris, and since I doubt if the Harborym brought your little ward with them, that means you must have been there. And returned." Hallow's eyes glittered with a light that I recognized. It didn't bode well to anyone who crossed him.

Quinn was silent for a moment, his eyes on the scarred surface of the table. He traced a shape that had been carved into it, that of a sailing ship. "The talisman makes it impossible to refuse a penitent seeking aid from me. The goddesses ensured that I can't pick and choose jobs, but even though it's true my life cannot be torn from my body, that doesn't give you any such protection."

"Can it be done?" Hallow asked, his blue eyes as pure as a midsummer morning. "Can you get us to Eris without having to use the moonstones? Can we sail there on your ship, with you at the helm?"

Quinn was silent so long, I thought he might not answer the questions, but at last he moved forward, the thump of the front chair legs hitting the floorboards sounding particularly ominous. "I've been to Eris twice. Both times I lost my crew and passengers. The last time, I barely made it through the storms with Dex and me whole. If you demand of me that I sail you to Eris—or try to—then I will have to comply, but I urge you, I *very strongly* urge you to find an alternate method. One that won't end up with everyone save me dead."

"We'd need the stone for that," I said, somewhat grumpily; I'd reached the end of my patience. The captain of the guard—I had a hard time thinking of him as Simon—had promised us that Quinn would help us, and here he was being no assistance whatsoever. I got to my feet with a scrape of the three-legged stool on the floor, and snapped, "And since you say you don't know where it is, then I don't see what good—"

"I never said I don't know where it is," Quinn said calmly, scratching his goatee. "I just said that I didn't have it."

I looked at Hallow. "If I used both swords and chopped him up into little pieces at the same time you blasted him with your magic, and then we roasted the leftover bits in the fire, do you think he'd survive to plague us more?"

Hallow laughed and pulled me against him to give me a swift kiss before releasing me and then pinching my behind. "No, my heart, you may not chop him into pieces."

"But he's so irritating," I said, then stopped myself at the whining tone in my voice.

"He has been difficult, but our goal is within our reach. Don't let frustration ride you so strongly." He turned to Quinn and asked, "Dexia?"

The former nodded.

"I suppose a vanth is as good a guardian as a lifebound captain. How soon can you be ready to sail?"

"To Eris?" Quinn asked, his face a picture of wariness and regret.

"To Aryia." Hallow smiled, filling me with joy. Although I was determined to do whatever was necessary to rescue Deo and the queen, the thought of sailing through impassable storms left me with a feeling of dread. It would be far easier to simply create a portal using the stones and travel that way. "With luck, we should pick up the second stone just about the time Israel gets the first from Lord Jalas. And then, my wife—who would indeed geld any man who tried to lure her away from my side—and I will use them to go to Eris."

"Nothing good can be found in the land of shadows," Quinn intoned in a voice that sent a skitter of worry down my back.

"Do you refuse to help us?" Hallow asked.

I wasn't surprised by the note of steel in his voice, but Quinn evidently was. He gave Hallow an assessing look, then answered, "I couldn't if I wanted. You bore the talisman. I am obligated to help you...not that I would refuse to take you to Aryia. It is a short enough journey, and one that poses no particular danger."

"And then?" I asked.

He shook his head again. "I'm no adventurer despite what my brother may have told you. What you do after I deliver you to Aryia is your own business."

There wasn't much I could say to that, even though I was thinking that it might be handy having a man who couldn't be killed in our company.

He gave Hallow a little nod of the head, and said just before he left the shack, "I will see to the ship and crew if you will handle the supplies. We will leave when Bellias is at her strongest."

"Why do I feel like sailing when the moon is at its highest is a bad omen?" I asked Hallow, rubbing my arms.

He gave me a hug before gently pushing me to the door. "Because you are Kiriah's priestess and thus have an aversion to doing anything by the light of Bellias Starsong. Come, let us get the stone, then we will arrange for the supplies we'll need for the journey."

"Ale?" I asked, following him. "Or the alewench?"

"The former." He thought for a moment, then made a little bob of his head. "Or possibly both. We'll just have to see what this Grimalkin looks like."

I stayed silent while Hallow talked Dexia out of the stone that she had hidden away in some grubby inner pocket. I glanced upward at the high clouds that blotted the sun from view. I had an uneasy feeling that Kiriah was separated from us by more than mere clouds. It was as if a shadow had fallen between her and us…one that was filled with ill omens and an unformed menace.

Chapter 6

Hallow heard the voice before he saw the bird.

—sailed to Aryia without telling me, not that you can talk to me when I'm in Starfall City, and you're Bellias knows where, but still, you should have warned me of the possibility that you would be sailing when I went to look for you. It's just lucky that I'm not a real bird, or I wouldn't have been able to fly for all this time to find you. Did you get the stone? You must have—you don't look annoyed. Why are you riding so hard? Your horses are lathered, and Allegria looks furious.

The shadow of a swallow flickered across the sun-baked ground, circling over Hallow before settling down on the top of the wooden staff strapped to his back.

"Hello, Thorn. Yes, it is lucky you're not real. The stone is safe. Both of them, that is, although we had a little bit of trouble with Lady Sandor not wanting to relinquish the one she held."

"That is the biggest understatement I've ever heard," Allegria said, grimacing. "Blessings of the goddess upon you, Thorn. Is there news of Darius?"

"I suspect he's about to tell me. My heart, does that look like a dust cloud created by the mounts of a number of angry priests riding in formation?"

Allegria glanced back over her shoulder, squinting against the afternoon sun. "Kiriah smite them! I can't believe Sandor would carry out her threat to hunt us down so she can string us up by our toes before she applies honey and stinging ants to our tender flesh. She's changed since I left the temple, Hallow. She never used to threaten people with torture. She's much more...*intense*...now. I blame the Harborym."

He couldn't keep from smiling at her. "Tying Lady Sandor to a chair so that you might steal a valuable object given into her care has no doubt caused her to become a bit testy with us."

"I wouldn't have had to tie her to the chair if she hadn't threatened to strike us down with Kiriah's own power," Allegria answered, a decidedly disgruntled expression on her face. One tinged by self-righteousness, Hallow was amused to note. "This is the Fourth Age, after all! It's supposed to be a time of peace, not a time of priestesses turning into masochists and threatening other priests just because they want to borrow a stone. One she's not even using, I might add. I don't know why she's making such a big fuss about it when she knows the stone will be perfectly safe with us."

He laughed outright, his delight with Allegria the one constant in his life.

Allegria stole the stone from the head priestess of her order? Thorn asked, sounding both awed and aghast.

"Allegria likes to refer to it as *borrowing* the stone, but yes, that is basically what happened. Lady Sandor refused to give the stone into our keeping, and Allegria...well..."

"I wasn't going to take no for an answer," she told Thorn, looking even more righteous.

I like her a lot. I did a good bit of work convincing her to marry you, Thorn said with satisfaction.

Hallow decided not to comment on the fact that it took a few months before Thorn stopped complaining that Allegria was a bad influence on his life. "What news do you have from Starfall?"

Although I would like to have seen her tie up the priest...what? Oh, nothing beyond what you already knew. Darius has taken over the city and claims that no one shall enter Genora without his permission. He states openly that Queen Dasa is dead, and that he will fulfill her destiny and unite Genora to bring glory back to the Starborn.

Hallow quickly repeated the information to Allegria, adding, "It sounds as if he's determined to be king. I wonder if he truly feels the queen is dead, or if he's simply taken advantage of the situation for his own purposes?"

Allegria snorted while Thorn flapped his wooden wings. "Definitely the latter. Such a mealy-mouthed, weak-minded twit. He couldn't organize his way out of a dark room."

Hallow felt his lips twitch. There were many things that enchanted him about Allegria, but one of the most enjoyable was the way she said exactly what she thought. "I agree that he has an inflated opinion of himself, but if he has actually formed an army—"

He hadn't. He had an arcanist named Lyl call up the army.

"An arcanist? I thought it was a magister who was aiding him." Hallow searched his memory of Exodius's less than comprehensive records. "I don't recall mention of an arcanist named Lyl."

Before your time. He slipped away when Exodius had just taken over for me, and that fool apprentice of mine never did bother to chase him down and make him adhere to the rules of the order.

"I think they're catching up to us. How can they move so fast on fat mules that don't get more exercise than it takes to walk from the barn to the paddock?" Allegria grumbled, glancing over her shoulder again.

"We're almost at Deacon's Cross. I'm sure Quinn will be ready to sail as soon as we arrive."

"Assuming we get there before Sandor catches us. I don't suppose you know a slowing spell?"

"I do, but I would need to be closer to cast it, and I don't want to risk being caught by the fat mules or your head priest. Thorn, if you've recovered from your trip, can you fly back and see how many are pursuing us?"

Only if you promise to tell me again how Allegria tied up the head priestess, and how she threatened to hang you by your toes.

The bird was off before Hallow could do more than roll his eyes, and a half hour later, they galloped into Deacon's Cross, a small, but busy, port town.

By the time Hallow had returned the rented horses to the stable and fetched Allegria from where she was watching for the priests, Thorn flew back.

They've turned around, he said with a disgusted note in his voice. *Priests these days don't have the same stamina they had in my time. Who's the man with the goatee who's ogling Allegria? Is that a vanth that's perched on the figurehead? Where are we sailing? I thought you were going to the High Lands to fetch the third stone?*

"We need to leave as soon as possible," Hallow told Quinn, frowning when he noticed that the roguish captain was indeed giving Allegria a look that was far too warm for his liking.

"Lucky then that I spent the last day resupplying the ship. I assume you wish to sail to Abet? That is, if you fetched the moonstone you were after." Quinn dragged his gaze from Allegria, who had, after a few minutes, noticed the attention, and made a fine show of wiggling her fingers in a 'gelding with the light of Kiriah' sort of motion.

"We do, and we have. Quinn the Mad, this is Thorn, former Master of Kelos, and now a valued member of our company."

Thorn detached himself and flew a few circles around Quinn and Dexia before landing back on the top of the staff. *Tell him how I was an integral part of ridding Genora and Aryia of the Harborym, and how I went through the portal for you to Eris and had to go back into the spirit world in order to return. You may also inform him that I was a far greater arcanist that Exodius ever was.*

Hallow duly repeated the outrageous statements, knowing he'd have no peace if he didn't.

"Your staff...talks?" Quinn looked as if he wasn't sure whether he wanted to laugh or be horrified.

"Only to the current Master. How long will it take us to reach Abet?"

It took Quinn a few seconds of eyeing Thorn before he shook his head and answered the question. "Less than a day with favorable winds. Are you in a hurry?"

Tell him that of course we're in a hurry. We have battles to fight, and Harborym to defeat!

"We are if Lord Israel is there with the third stone," Allegria said, moving to Hallow's side and sliding her arm through his in a way that never failed to warm his soul. "The sooner Hallow can use the stones to open up a portal, the better I'll feel."

"My heart, I've told you time and time again that it is not your fault that Dasa and Deo went to Eris." He felt, as he always did, both her pain and guilt that she hadn't been able to close the portal in time to keep Dasa safe and to stop Deo from heedlessly following his mother. "I know you are worried about them both, but the queen is a warrior, and you, yourself, know how strong your boyfriend is. We will find them both hale and hearty."

They'll be fine. Going through the portal is nothing. I did it without ruffling a single feather, Thorn reassured him, regardless of the fact that his feathers were made of wood.

"Boyfriend?" Quinn asked, looking from Hallow to Allegria, speculation rife in his eyes.

"You don't know that," Allegria told Hallow, sighing heavily even as she rallied a weak smile and squeezed his arm. "You're right, of course. The queen is frighteningly brave, and Deo is the strongest person I know—you excluded—but I worry about the change that affected him right before he went into the portal."

"Your wife has a boyfriend? Is that allowed?"

"When his runes altered in appearance?" Hallow remembered that horrible moment when he'd almost been sucked into the portal, and Allegria had channeled Kiriah herself. Deo's runes had changed from the usual red to a blinding gold, the same as Allegria's had once been. "I have a theory about that."

"Is she taking recommendations for qualified applicants? If so, I'm told that I am quite well versed in the art of bed sport, and I have an unparalleled appreciation of a fine bosom. Of which she has one of the most spectacular I've ever seen."

That captain is ogling Allegria again. Shall I shit upon his head?

Allegria gave Hallow a long look. "Because his runes were golden, like mine, not black, as they were when the portal was tainting his magic? Do you think Kiriah gave him her blessing?"

"In a way."

"I'm also told that the ladies enjoy the feeling of my whiskers upon their delicate flesh," Quinn said with a waggle of his eyebrows. "They say it prickles them. In a good way."

It feels good to be doing something again, Thorn told him, still flitting around the deck. *Have you something I should investigate?*

Hallow held Allegria's gaze, his mind sorting through facts and fitting them together in a way that made sense. "I think when you channeled Kiriah Sunbringer, you not only burned the chaos out of yourself, but you did the same to Deo. Or rather, diluted it, changing it from pure chaos to something unique."

"Both upper and lower areas of delicate flesh, if you take my meaning, and I hope you do, because I wouldn't at all mind being one of your wife's boyfriends." Quinn's smile was both hopeful and broad.

"That makes sense, although I don't know how I could affect Deo's magic..." Allegria turned to stare at Quinn at the exact moment that the captain's words sank through Hallow's thoughts.

"No?" Quinn asked, still looking hopeful.

Hallow lit a blue arcane flame under the man's feet at the same time Allegria spread wide her arms, speaking an invocation for Kiriah to bless her with her power.

"A simple 'the position is filled' would suffice," Quinn yelped, dancing up and down until the flames died down.

"I don't have a boyfriend, no matter what Hallow says," Allegria said, stopping her invocation before turning back to Hallow. "Do you think Deo's magic would protect him? Or hinder him?"

He took both her hands and kissed them, disliking the worry evident in her eyes. "You said it yourself—Deo is the strongest person you know. That we *both* know. He will be fine. Instead of worrying about what the chaos magic is doing to him, let us focus on getting to Eris. Assuming Israel is back in Abet, we should be able to open a portal immediately.

What? Oh, Thorn, yes. I have a message to be taken to Lord Israel if you think you can find him."

I am the former master of Kelos, Thorn responded with a snort, snatching up the small folded parchment that Hallow pulled from a pocket. He flew off, adding, *There isn't a being alive that I can't find, given enough time. I will wait to see if he has an answer before returning to you. Don't have fun without me!*

Allegria remained worried despite Hallow's reassurances, even later that evening, when Hallow lay naked on the bunk in their cabin, his hands behind his head while he prepared to enjoy the sight of his wife disrobing. Normally, she made a little show of it for him, but tonight, as she pulled her tunic over her head, and reached behind her to untie the breastband that hid her delicious breasts, she didn't jiggle, waggle her hips, or even pose seductively. She removed her clothes and got into the bunk with him, a frown pulling her brows together.

Hallow looked down at his erection. "Sorry," he told it. "She's not interested tonight."

"I'm not interested in what?" It took her a moment to respond; then she glanced over and noticed his condition. She made a face. "Of course I'm interested in that. I always am, except when my courses are upon me and I want to clamp your stones in a vise so you know just how much monthly courses hurts, but that's not important."

"My stones beg to differ," Hallow said, frowning at his erection when it lost a bit of stamina at the idea of his testicles in a vise. "Are you still worried about Deo, or does something else have you distracted to the point where my poor manhood must go unloved?"

"Your manhood gets more love than most men's," she said with a little smile, rolling onto her side so she could slide a hand down his chest. "I'm surprised I haven't worn it down by now."

"You'll need to try harder for that to happen," he said, his eyes widening when she pushed herself up and straddled his thighs. In her hand was a small blue bottle that he hadn't seen before. "Don't tell me you have some sort of love potion there? You already fill all of my heart and soul and waking thoughts. A love potion would probably push me over into a mindless love slave."

"And that would be bad how, exactly?" she asked, uncorking the bottle. A spicy scent of oranges and lemons filled the close air of the cabin.

He thought for a moment. "Any number of reasons, none of which I can think of right now, but there are some, and once they come to mind, I will be sure to inform you. What is it you have?"

"A lotion I bought from a harlot named Twenty-finger Sal who was in town selling leather phalluses studded with pearls."

"Why twenty-fingers?" Hallow couldn't help but ask.

"Sal said she could grip men with muscles that didn't involve her hands."

Hallow's eyebrows rose.

"The phalluses were beautifully decorated," Allegria allowed. "She swore the pearls would make my eyes cross. I told her I had you, and you were quite adept at making my eyes cross, uncross, and roll back in my head with ecstasy, but she said that even though we were still enamored of each other, the day would come when we would be less easily pleasured, and she had an oil that would put a smile on your face, and a kick to my walk. I told her that you always smile, and she said this was a special smile. I thought that seemed a bit suspicious, not to mention the fact that she wanted three silvers for it—three silvers!—but she said she'd throw in detailed instructions on how best to use it. And that seemed like the sort of bargain I couldn't refuse. So I bought it."

He eyed her as she poured a little scented oil onto one of her hands, tucked the bottle away, then rubbed her hands together. "It all sounds very intriguing, although I am perfectly happy the way we do things now. Er... do I leave you feeling as if you need a kick to your walk?"

She smiled a smile of pure wickedness, delighting Hallow down to his toes. "No, but it will be fun trying out the oil. Now, the first thing Sal said to do was to coat your man parts with it." She suited action to words, an act that Hallow greatly enjoyed until she paused, looking hesitant. "Sal said that men have a special pleasure button, but in order to get to it, you have to venture into an area that Sandor always said only a physician should attend to, and then only in the direst of circumstances, such as if you had inserted a turnip and it got stuck there. Sandor is a very learned physician, so I trust her about that. Especially since the man who brings hay to the temple has had to have many turnips removed."

Hallow blinked a couple of times. "I have many things to say about that, but first and foremost, there is no pleasure button. Not one that I want you to go looking for."

"Good, because in order to do so, I'd have to..." She made a sharp, stabbing motion with her forefinger.

Various groups of muscles tightened at the same time his erection became less thrilled with the turn in the evening's events. Not to mention conversation. "And neither one of us wants that," Hallow agreed. "How about you go back to rubbing that oil into those parts of me that are clamoring for your attention?"

"Sal did say the rubbing in of oil was important," Allegria said with a little nod, and returned to a stroking action that had Hallow's hips bucking. "I think you might be wrong about the pleasure button, though. She said women have one too, only I didn't get to find out any information about it because I saw you heading for the ship."

"My heart, this I swear to you: if you have a pleasure button, I will locate it," he announced with a grandeur that he felt was suitable to the situation.

"All right, but you may need to talk to Sal about just where to find it." She bent to swirl her tongue over the very tip of him, making him see stars and moons and entire galaxies. "Unless it takes a turnip to find. I wouldn't like that anymore than you would, and I would die of embarrassment if I had to go back to Sandor for an extraction and tell her I was one of the turnip people."

Hallow's shout of laughter filled the cabin, and by the time they'd both given in to the pleasure that overtook them whenever they put their minds to it, they were covered in citrus oil, panting and sweaty, and as boneless as Dexia's cursed dolls.

The only thing that could have made Hallow happier would be the knowledge that Lord Israel would be waiting with the third moonstone when they arrived in Abet. To his surprise—and no little amount of dismay—when they arrived the following day, the only person who greeted them was Idril.

"Where's your husband?" Allegria asked, making a show of glancing around the dock.

"My...oh, Lord Israel?" Idril's eyebrows rose a fraction of an inch as she turned her gaze from Allegria to Hallow. "He is in Ilam, trying to keep the tribesmen from declaring war upon him and what remains of the Council of the Four Armies."

"Jalas wishes to declare war on us?" Hallow asked, taken aback.

"Why on earth would he want to do that?" Allegria took Hallow's hand in a blatant show of possession. The fact that she only did so when Idril was around gave him no end of amusement.

Idril glanced at Quinn, who with Dexia at his side, came to stand next to them. She looked pointedly from them to Hallow.

"Ah, yes, my apologies for not introducing you. This is Quinn, our captain, and his...er...ward, Dexia. Lady Idril is the daughter of the leader of the north men, Jalas. He is—or was—a member of the Council of Four Armies, which prompts me into asking what in the twin goddess's names has been going on while we were in Genora?"

"Welcome to our company," Idril said with exquisite manners, holding out one pale and limpid hand for Quinn. He hurriedly bent over it, his eyes alight with pleasure as he pressed his lips to the back of her fingers. "We are naturally delighted to have such a useful member join our forces. Your ward appears to have very sharp, extremely pointed teeth. It's an interesting look. Allegria, I see you are still marked as one of Deo's banesmen despite losing your extremely useful power. I don't suppose you have managed to regain it now that we have need of such ability?"

"Hello, Idril," Allegria said, imparting a boundless amount of scorn into the second word. "How surprising to find you here rather than at your home, where you belong. Didn't you tell Hallow that your father was ill, and you had taken over management of the tribe? Do you think it's prudent to leave warring tribesmen to get up to Kiriah knows what sort of trouble while you can gallivant off to the keep of a man whom you repeatedly act surprised to find is your husband?"

Hallow sighed to himself and said under his breath to his wife, "So it's going to be that sort of a day, is it?"

She growled softly in response.

"And as ever, you have completely misunderstood what is really a quite simple situation." Idril looked thoughtfully at Hallow for a moment before turning to Quinn, and saying, "But such things are better spoken of in privacy. We will go to the keep. You may take my hand and escort me, Quinn. You are very handsome."

"You can change the subject as much as you like, but it doesn't eliminate the fact that you are here while Lord Israel is with your father," Allegria pointed out, but Idril had already turned away. Taking the arm an apparently besotted Quinn held out, she strolled with him toward the great stone building that crowned the town of Abet.

Dexia moved forward until she was next to Hallow, an oddly assessing look in her uncanny black eyes. "That woman is dangerous."

"Idril?" Allegria asked, surprised. "Yes, but only because you're at risk of falling asleep when she starts talking."

"My heart," Hallow remonstrated.

Allegria heaved a big sigh. "All right, that was a bit too much. I apologize for being so sharp, although just once I'd like to see her with her hair less than perfect, and her clothing anything but spotlessly gorgeous, and her whole demeanor something other than coolly ethereal as if we were dung beneath her pristine feet."

"Hmm," Dexia said, her eyes narrowing before she pulled from her somewhat grubby pinafore a small cloth doll that she'd created during the journey from the Genora to Aryia. "I think I might have use for this sooner rather than later."

"I think we'll do without that," Hallow told the small vanth, catching a grin on Allegria's face before she changed it to a placid look of mild interest. "Shall we see what Idril has to tell us that can't be spoken of in public?"

"I am fair panting at the idea of being in close consultation with her," Allegria told him gravely, but there was amusement in her eyes.

He had a feeling it was going to be a much longer day than he'd imagined that dawn.

Chapter 7

"Why exactly is it that you are here, and Lord Israel is in Ilam?" I asked Idril once we arrived at the room in the keep that I had remembered as being Israel's library. It apparently did double duty in times of unrest as a war room, its walls lined with heavy shelves bearing a number of books, scrolls, and almost as many stacks of parchment as Hallow had back in Kelos.

The room was dominated by a massive table, upon which were spread out a variety of maps being held down by silver tankards, metal figurines, and the odd occasional dagger. Chairs were scattered around the room, everything from the hard wooden variety to more comfortable examples bearing cushions covered in rich cloth.

"I have come to Abet because Lord Israel asked me to do so." Idril glided over to a tall, throne-like chair bearing a gold and white striped cushion and sat in an attitude that showed off not only the silvery blondness of her waist-length hair—not a strand of which was out of place—but the apricot and gold of her gown.

By contrast, my hair was filled with sea salt from sitting out on the ship's deck, I hadn't had a bath in more than four days, my tunic had a spot between my breasts from the porridge we'd hastily eaten before landing at Abet, and there was a tear in my dusty black leggings right at the knee. I felt like a half-starved, scruffy stray cat who had wandered into the presence of a highly pampered pet.

"If you don't mind my asking, why did he send you *here*?" Hallow had a puzzled look that I shared. Idril's presence in Abet made little sense if her tribesmen were as unhappy as she'd told Hallow they were.

"My father is being…" She gestured gracefully with a languid hand. "Difficult. He speaks of himself as being near death, but is not ailing physically. And then there are his suspicions."

"What sort of suspicions?" I asked.

An expression that on any other person would have been called a grimace of distaste passed over her lovely face. "He sees conspiracies against him where there are none. Of late, he has been convinced that I seek not only his throne, but his departure from the realm of the living. It is nothing but foolishness, of course, but Israel thought that my presence was causing my father distress, and he hoped to be able to reason with him after I left."

"Which means he didn't get the moonstone," Hallow said, staring down at the table, his gaze turned inward.

I wanted to wrap my arms around him, to ease the burden of responsibility that he had never sought, but which had been thrust upon his shoulders. I wanted to remind him that it was not his problem, and that he didn't need to solve the woes of Alba on his own. But Hallow fought wrongs when he found them, and never hesitated to step up when his help was needed. I moved to his side, but kept my hands to myself, wanting to provide him with support without distraction. "How strong is Jalas?" I asked him softly.

"By himself?" Hallow shrugged. "Strong enough. You've seen him."

I had. I had a brief memory of a large man, one who was quick to jump to conclusions.

"The tribesmen of Poronne are known for their fighting prowess, but they are not strong with magic, and Lord Israel is." Hallow tapped absently on a map. "Depending on the size of Israel's company—"

"There were but a score of men with him," Idril murmured, her expression untroubled.

Hallow made a face, and my stomach balled up.

"That doesn't sound hopeful. Lord Israel is a proficient magister, but with such a small company up against the force of Jalas in his homeland…" Hallow stopped and shook his head.

"He needs reinforcements, then," I said, thinking aloud.

"Aye, but it would take a battalion of men several weeks to reach Ilam, and I don't know that Lord Israel has such time if Jalas is…"

"Unhinged?" I suggested.

Idril's lips thinned.

"Unreasonable? Deranged as a bumblepig in a vat of ale?"

Idril shot me a sharp look. I smiled at her, showing as many teeth as I could manage.

"Something is definitely wrong with him if he has left the Council, and he sees conspiracies everywhere," Hallow said with another tap of his fingers on the map. His gaze was still turned inward while he no doubt tried to come up with a plan.

I had a feeling he was planning how best to get Israel's army to him. "There's a much easier solution," I told him.

He looked up, his eyes troubled. "Than what?"

"Moving the Fireborn army."

"Oh?"

I pointed to where Quinn was examining Lord Israel's bookshelves. "We have a ship at our disposal."

Quinn turned to cock an eyebrow at me.

"We couldn't fit more than a small company on that ship—" Hallow started to object.

"There's nothing that another company of soldiers would do other than rile up Jalas," I pointed out, taking Hallow's hand and rubbing my thumb over his fingers. "Certainly they would not be as effective as a seriously impressive arcanist and a lightweaver. Assuming I still am one…no, you needn't reassure me again. Now is not the time for that. Also, there is the fact that Jalas knows us. Or at least, he knows you. He won't be suspicious if just the two of us arrive, but if we were to approach Ilam with a large contingent of men…" I let the sentence trail away, sure that he would picture Jalas's response.

"There is that," he agreed, his fingers tightening around mine. He lifted my hand and kissed my knuckles before grinning. "Very well, since an army of soldiers is out of the question, we'll bring an army of two."

"Three," Quinn said with a sigh, gesturing to the whistle, which he wore around his neck. "Unless you'd like to release me from my service?"

"Not yet," Hallow told him.

"I can help, too," Dexia said, shoving her doll into Idril's face. "I am very good with curses that make nipples fall off. How many nipples do you have, lady?"

Idril slid out of the chair, giving Dexia a little frown as she moved over to the window seat with a grace that I would never, no matter how hard I practiced, manage to achieve. "What an odd child you are—ow!"

Dexia smiled when Idril paused to glare at her. Behind the girl's back, Dexia held a long strand of white blond hair.

Idril continued with only a moment's pause. "You are welcome to go to Ilam, Hallow, but I warn you that although the Tribe of Jalas is not learned in the way of magisters or arcanists—"

I cleared my throat.

She gave a minute eye roll. "—or lightweavers, my father is not one to be taken advantage of easily. Especially not when he is in his stronghold."

"If you have any other suggestion, we would be willing to hear it," Hallow said with his usual patience.

Idril gestured toward Quinn. "The captain was telling me that he is lifebound, and that he has sailed to Eris. Why should we waste more time attempting to get the moonstone from my father when we can simply board the ship that even now sits in the harbor and sail there? It would take only a week, far less time than would be needed to make my father see reason... or to remove the stone from his possession."

"*We?*" I asked at the same time that Hallow said, "You have no idea just how perilous the journey to Eris is, Lady Idril."

"Of course *we*," Idril answered me, ignoring Hallow's protest. "Naturally, I will go with you."

"There's no naturally about it—" I started to say, but Hallow, always diplomatic, interrupted me.

"Even if we use the stones to open a portal to Eris, it is far too dangerous for you to accompany us," Hallow told her. "The land is crawling with Harborym and blood priests. Not to mention the captain of them all, Racin. I'm sure you wish to aid in the release of Deo and the queen, but you are not learned in the ways of either chaos magic, or arcany, as Allegria and I are."

Her lips thinned again. "It does not follow that I am useless and unversed in battle."

"Oh really," I blurted out, then heard how obnoxious I sounded. "My apologies, Lady Idril, I would never cast doubt upon anyone's abilities based on their appearance, but you certainly don't have the look of a warrior."

"And that is my most valuable skill," she said, idly brushing a bit of nothing from her gauze sleeve. "People underestimate me."

I glanced at Hallow. He gave Idril a piercing look, one I knew was tinged with a bit of arcane power, and which gave a boost to his ability to perceive what was hidden from normal view, but after doing so, he gave a little shake of his head. "It would be far too dangerous. We would have to assign a guard to protect you, and we will need to go with as small a force as is possible if we hope to avoid detection by the Harborym and Racin."

Idril was silent for a moment before saying in her calm, unhurried voice, "All my life I have been told to remain behind. First it was my father, telling me battle was no place for me; then later, when I was forced to wed Lord Israel, I was left behind again."

"You were forced to marry him?" I asked, surprised. I glanced at Hallow, but he was only giving her half of his attention, no doubt working out the best way to get the stone away from Jalas. "Why?"

She gestured the question away. "My father insisted. It was the only way Lord Israel could get him to commit to the Council of Four Armies. The why is unimportant—what *does* matter is the fact that I am tired of being told that I must remain behind while others fight. I am not a hindrance, as my father claimed. I do not need a contingent of guards to protect me, as Lord Israel—" she leveled Hallow a pointed look that he completely missed— "and others feel is necessary. I can protect myself. I can fight. I am my father's daughter."

"Jewel of the High Lands," I murmured, referring to one of the titles people used for her.

She dismissed that with another wave of her rose-tipped fingers. "Jewels can be just as deadly as blades."

"Huh?" I asked, trying to puzzle that out.

"Gems can be quite hard and sharp," she said, a tinge of annoyance edging her tone.

"Not as hard as a sword—"

"Regardless," she said loudly over my words, her golden gaze now filled with ire that was unfortunately directed at me. "This time, I will not be left behind. Either you agree to take me with you, or I will take actions into my own hands."

"Meaning what, exactly? Are you threatening us?" I asked, then nudged Hallow so he'd stop introspecting and pay attention to Idril's bizarre statements.

"I will not be left behind again," she repeated. Then with a swish of her silk and gauze gown, she spun around and glided out of the room.

"I think I'm in love," Quinn said as he watched her depart, his fingers twitching. "Do you suppose her husband allows her to have boyfriends, too?"

Dexia narrowed her eyes at him, then wound Idril's hair around the doll's neck a few times before smiling again, her sharp little teeth so very wrong in her child's face.

"What were you mulling over that had you ignoring Idril's obvious threats to us?" I asked Hallow, elbowing him gently in the ribs.

"Hmm?" He looked up from where he'd been frowning at the maps again. "I was wondering how difficult it would be to learn how to form arcany to take on the shape of another person. I haven't seen any reference to such a thing in the notes that Exodius left, but if Avas can learn to take on the shapes of animals, surely the same must be possible for people."

"Would Thorn be able to help with that?" I asked, a ripple of unease making the hairs on my arms stand on end. For some reason, the thought of Hallow donning the appearance of another made me very nervous.

"Possibly, but imbuing your spirit into an inanimate object after leaving the mortal world is a different matter from changing your form using arcany," he said, then smiled and wrapped an arm around me. "Don't look so unhappy, love. We'll have five days sailing to the High Lands to work out the best way to tackle Jalas."

"Five days?" I shook my head. "We should go by land. It will be quicker."

"The pass is treacherous this time of year," Hallow said. "Master Nix and I once tried to venture north through it, and it was nigh on impenetrable. We'll go up the River Sian as far as the town of Threshing and take the road east from there."

"The valley road is far easier when the pass is frozen over," Quinn agreed, pocketing a book from Lord Israel's shelves. He caught me watching him and grinned, his charm palpable despite his petty thievery. "It's slower going via the Sian than open water, but the Tempest is a light ship, and has a shallow draw, so she should get you to where you want to go."

With few other options open to us, we settled on that plan, and spent the rest of the day gathering supplies, soaking off the dust and salt of our last week of travel, and enduring Idril's frosty looks and frostier manner.

"You will at least allow me to travel with you to Ilam," she said the following morning when fresh water, a few barrels of dried meat, and a couple of milk goats were loaded onto Quinn's ship. I was in charge of making sure the supplies we'd bought were safely stowed and stood next to an odious individual named Rixius, once Deo's body servant, who had lately affixed himself to Lord Israel. Rixius was insufferably rude, no doubt because he harbored secret passions that even I didn't like to dwell on—I suspected he might be one of the turnip people—and was more or less a bane of my existence.

"I thought you were supposed to stay here because you made your father insane?" I asked her as I watched a crate of vegetables dropped into the hold. I turned to Rixius, and asked, "Did the barley get stowed?"

He made a face and shoved a board with several papers attached to it in my face. "Do you see the check mark? Yes? Then it means the barrel containing barley was placed aboard."

"Kiriah's shiny hair, man! You don't have to snap my head off just because I asked a question."

"That was ten days ago," Idril said smoothly, ignoring Rixius. To my surprise, rather than toadying up to her, he was obviously pretending she didn't exist. "By now Father must be over the worst of his fit—they normally last only a few weeks. And as you have made clear, Abet is not my home."

"Mmhmm." I watched as a couple of men staggered by with more barrels, one marked dried peas, the other flour. I couldn't think of any objection to Idril sailing with us to her homeland (other than the knowledge that she would continue to look utterly gorgeous even in the direst storm, while the second we set sail, my hair would twist itself into a mass of unruly curls, my clean tunic would somehow become stained, and I'd most likely acquire an unsightly muscle twitch on the side of my mouth) and said with as much grace as I could muster, "I don't see a problem unless Quinn says there isn't room for you."

Quinn, who had been up on a mast attending to rigging with one of his men, slid down it and immediately noticed Idril. He shimmied over to her side, taking her hand in his so he could slobber over it in a most ingratiating and blatant manner.

"He said last night that I might have his cabin," Idril said once she—with a smidgen of effort—managed to reclaim her hand. "Did you not, captain?"

"It would be my greatest honor for you to inhabit my personal cabin," he agreed with alacrity. "I can think of nothing I would enjoy more, short of you allowing me to spread your hair across my naked torso, while at the same time my hands were full of your—"

"Thank you," Idril said quickly, giving him a graceful nod of her head. "My handmaidens have my things. Would you please show me to my cabin so they might put them away?"

I pursed my lips when, mingled in between the tradespeople who were supplying the ship, a line of six women in the gold and amber colors that Idril favored, hauled aboard a number of satchels, bags, and even two wooden trunks. "I'm not sure if you're bringing enough," I told her as she turned to follow Quinn. "You never know how many gauzy, gossamer cobweb gowns you might need in the next five days."

Rixius gave a disgusted click of his tongue. "It will be good to have the keep back to its rightful inhabitants."

"I'm sure it will, although to be honest, I'm surprised to find you here. I thought you were Lord Israel's shadow, ever on his heels."

"High Lord Israel himself asked that I stay behind and monitor the business pertaining to the keep," Rixius answered in an officious manner.

"Oh, it's High Lord Israel now, is it?" I asked, nodding when one of the men carrying a large wicker crate full of fresh eggs called a greeting. I recognized him from the battle the previous year.

"As befitting one who leads the Fireborn and controls Aryia," Rixius said with smugness, just as if Lord Israel's glory covered him, as well. I thought of pointing out the error of his ways, but at that moment Hallow, surrounded by four magisters wearing the white gowns and red cloaks of their kind and all apparently talking to him at the same time, slowly made his way down the dock toward the gang plank.

"She is the most exquisite, loveliest creature I've ever seen," Quinn said when he emerged from the cabin that he'd handed over to Idril. He gazed back at the door to the cabin with eyes that could only be described as googly with infatuation. "Did you see her hair? I just want to rub myself all over that hair."

"I can arrange for that," Dexia said as she strolled over to us, a dead rabbit slung over one shoulder. Judging by its squashed, muddy appearance, I gathered it had been run over by a cart. "I bet I could find a perfectly good curse to cause baldness…"

Quinn heaved one last besotted sigh, and turned his attention to the crew, chivvying them to get the ship ready to sail.

"Baldness is good," I said thoughtfully. "I imagine that would evoke some sort of emotion from the icy block that is her heart."

Dexia looked thoughtful. "Ice floats."

"Yes, it does." I watched her, wondering what horrible things were going on in her mind.

She moved her gaze to the rail. "So if she went overboard, she wouldn't drown immediately. She'd just float there, being nibbled on by fishes. That might be better than baldness."

"You really have a dark, dark soul," I told her, more than a little disturbed by the way her mind worked.

"What soul would that be?" she asked, her childish eyes wide in question.

I backed away slowly. "Er…just so. Idril's heart isn't really made of ice, so why don't you pretend I never said that, and you never had the thought of throwing her overboard to be eaten by fish, all right?"

Dexia ignored my request and narrowed her eyes in thought. "Warts. How could I have forgotten about them? Warts are very easy to manifest. If she was covered in great, crusty warts, one with thick black hairs, perhaps a couple of which might ooze…yes, that is definitely something worth thinking about. I will need some toad leg ferns, but those are easy enough to come by. It's only the lark's tongues that are difficult…" She drifted off, her departure making me feel as if Kiriah had come out from behind a black cloud.

By the time Quinn shouted to Hallow to get a move on or we'd miss the tide, it was evident that my husband's ears had been filled by the few magisters who'd survived the Harborym's previous attacks.

"I'm surprised to see there were four magisters left," I told Hallow a short while later, when all the porters and Idril's handmaidens had departed the ship, and we made our slow way out of the harbor. "I thought most of them were consumed by chaos magic while trying to destroy the portals."

"Not quite all of them, thankfully," he answered, pulling me up against his side. As expected, my hair immediately whipped free of the ribbon with which I'd tied it back, and blew all over Hallow's face. He pulled a few strands of it out of his mouth and eyes and added, "None of them knew of ways to adopt the skin of another, let alone an animal. That surprises me. The grace of Alba which all magisters have learned is based in earth magic."

"Yes, but it is mostly used in the healing arts. Or at least so Sandor claimed whenever I begged her to teach me how to remove the toes of the butcher's son, who repeatedly tried to put his hands inside my robe."

Hallow looked startled, pulling yet another strand of my hair from his face before tucking it behind my ear. "The butcher's son tried to touch you?"

"Only once. Sandor said the grace of Alba was not to be used for such trivial things, though, so I never did learn how to wield it."

"Don't tell me," he said with a slow smile. "You discussed the matter with Kiriah and took care of him yourself?"

I grinned back at him. "I would have, except Sandor had already done it. She might have been unreasonable about giving up the moonstone, but she really did not tolerate men taking advantage of any of her priests. Did you see that Idril is on board?"

"I did. And can I say how proud I am of you for not referring to being blighted by her presence?"

"You may show me as many physical forms of appreciation as you please," I allowed, ignoring the guilty memory of the conversation with Dexia.

"And so I shall. Earlier today, I made a stop by a little shop which specializes in a form of restraint that I think you'll find...oh, no! No! He can't be back already!"

"Thorn? He can't be. You only sent him off a few days ago."

"Almost a week. He certainly should not have been able to fly to Ilam and then to Abet in that time. Kiriah's breath, he's already yammering... yes, we are naturally thrilled almost unto death to see you."

A shadow flickered overhead when Thorn flew low over us, swooping through the masts until he alighted on his accustomed perch of the black wooden staff on Hallow's back.

"We are surprised you're back so quickly, however—he's not! Did you get him out? Yes, we heard about that bear. No. No, we plan to go straight there. Yes, she is looking particularly fine. Allegria always looks fine. It's one of the many things I love about her. And I'm sure she's equally as fond of you. Why don't you stop talking for a few minutes so I can tell her? Yes, I know that was rude, and I apologize for my abruptness, but I can't think when you fill my head with chatter." Hallow made a face, and said quickly to me, "Thorn returned because there was nothing he could do in Ilam. Evidently Jalas's mood did not improve when Idril left, and he threw Israel and his company into the depths of his keep, where they are locked away in various unpleasant cells. I *will* tell her, but you have to be quiet. Thorn says Jalas's pet bear tried to eat him and patrols the passages outside the cells as a guard."

"That's just bizarre," I said.

"What part? Using a tamed animal as a guard?" he asked.

"All of it. Those aren't the actions of a sane man, Hallow. I begin to think that Idril was right and her father has lost his wits."

"Either way, now we have Lord Israel to rescue," he said with a sigh that I felt go right down to his toes.

I held him tight, wishing again that he wouldn't take on so much responsibility, but knowing that his sense of honor was as deeply ingrained in him as lightweaving was in me.

We'd just have to add Lord Israel to our list of chores to perform before we wrestled the moonstone away from Jalas.

Or his bear…

Chapter 8

"Does the she-witch travel with you?"

Idril folded her hands together, mindful as ever of the need to present a placid, unruffled demeanor, no matter how much she wished to yell at her father. And shout that she was innocent of all wrong doing.

Not to mention demanding that people stop treating her as if she was a doll made of fragile glass. She was Idril, Jewel of the High Lands, daughter of the most ruthless man alive in Poronne, and quite capable of taking care of herself, thank you.

If only others saw that fact.

"I am here, Father," she said, gazing with apparent serenity at her father, who stood before the entrance of his keep in Ilam, legs braced in battle stance, his arms crossed over his long red beard. Tucked away in an inner pocket of her gown, her fingers curled around the toad-sized rock that she had picked up on the ride to Ilam after docking at Threshing, the closest river town. It was a good rock, a solid rock, one that was smoothed by centuries of tidal currents in the estuary, and which fit perfectly in her hand. She thought lovingly of the rock even though her voice carried no emotion but that of the mildest interest. "I hope you have been well in my absence."

"Well! *Well?* If I have been any better, it's because you weren't here to pour poison down my throat at every opportunity! Why are you here, arcanist? Why did you bring the she-witch back? Is it part of your overlord's plan to destroy me? Kiriah's hairy wart, is that a Bane of Eris with you? I thought she was killed with the others…no, they didn't die, did they?" Jalas's golden eyes, so like Idril's, narrowed in suspicion. "That was part of Israel's devious plan to rid the High Lands of my tribe."

Idril considered him, her temper—which could be just as prodigious as her sire's—well in check. His face was red with fury, but he looked unchanged, no better or worse for her absence. She sensed something different about him, however, an aura of suppressed excitement that both surprised and baffled her. "No one wishes to rid Aryia of either you or the tribesmen," she said with her usual calmness. "Especially Lord Israel. You know that he has long viewed you as a valuable ally."

"Bah," Jalas said, waving away the idea. "That was nothing but sweet words to lull me into complacence."

"On the contrary, he did everything he could to prove to you just how much he valued the Tribe's membership in the Council of Four Armies," she pointed out, sighing mentally. She grew tired of always being the reasonable one. Just once she wanted to be as irrational and unreasonable as her father. She wanted to make dramatic statements, and storm around the keep making scenes and scattering servants and courtiers before her. She wanted, just once, for someone to realize that she was a volatile, dangerous person.

Just as Deo did. He alone knew the emotions that ran so hot under her cool exterior…and the passions that bound them both with sharp-edged ties.

"Name one thing he did that was not for his own purposes," Jalas demanded, waving his hand in a dramatic gesture, his voice ringing so that it would reach the maximum number of people clustered around them. "Name just one thing that was not simply a stratagem, intended to bring me and my Tribe to heel!"

"He wed me," she answered simply.

Jalas's jaw worked.

"When you told him that you would not lend your aid to ridding the world of the Harborym unless we were bound by ties of marriage, he wed me. Against both our desires, I will add. He did that solely to show you how much he honored and respected your wishes."

Deo's priestling gave a sharp intake of breath, sliding Idril an odd questioning look that she had no time to consider. She was aware of the spurt of jealousy that was always present whenever she met Allegria, but as with other emotions, she pushed it down, stifling it even as a little resentment bubbled out at the unfairness of life. That the priest could live her life the way she wanted, fighting at Deo's side, earning his admiration and affection while she, Idril, was bound to a life of bone-deep boredom and frustration…it was almost too much to bear, but Idril had long ago learned that emotional scenes were allowed only to her father.

"That was trickery," Jalas finally ground out, making a sharp gesture when Idril would have answered him. He turned to Hallow, his eyebrows bristling with anger. "For what purpose have you come to the High Lands if not to heed the command of your overlord?"

"I have no such lord," Hallow said calmly. "Although I have come to speak to you about Lord Israel's imprisonment, along with the whereabouts of the moonstone that Exodius left in your care."

Jalas's intake of breath was almost a hiss. "You speak of that which you do not know," he all but snarled. "As for your overlord—and as a member of that blasted council, you *are* beholden to him—I have nothing to say. He was found guilty of attempting to kill me and has been tried and sentenced to imprisonment. If that is all you wish, you may leave, and take the she-witch with you. I will have no more of her attempting to rid Alba of my presence."

"My lord Jalas, you misinterpret our intentions," Hallow said, spreading his hands in a gesture of innocence.

Idril had a flash of fore-knowledge at that moment, an insight that she had inherited from her mother. It was as if the events of the next few minutes were compressed, playing in her mind at a rapid speed. She saw Hallow trying to explain their presence, trying to reason with Jalas, and her father getting angrier and angrier until they were all thrown into the lowest level of the keep with Israel and his men. She knew with every iota of her being that unless she acted, the future that sped past her mind's eye would be cast in stone as solid as the one in her hand.

"And I do not wish to spend the rest of my days with Lord Israel in a cell," she said, brushing past Hallow and Allegria to approach her father. "I simply do not have the time, not with Deo in need of me."

Her father was in mid-rant, pausing to look at her in surprise when she stopped next to him, giving him a regretful, gentle smile before she brought down her rock-bearing hand directly on the side of his neck, where it was easiest to knock a man insensible.

Jalas dropped with a soft thump that was the only sound for a few seconds while their company—and Jalas's servants, a group of four men clustered together at the door of the hall, stared with disbelieving eyes at the prone figure at her feet.

"Well done, Lady Idril," Captain Quinn said, giving her a heated look that would have—if her heart did not already belong to Deo—given her much pleasure. As it was, his admiration pleased her, but only so far as it meant he would be more amenable to her plans. "I couldn't have done any better. Well, I could have taken off his head, but that's a far more permanent solution than simply knocking him out."

"How—" Allegria stared first at Jalas, then at Idril. "How did she do that?"

Idril smiled and showed her the rock. "My mother taught me about a spot just behind and below the ear where a very small blow can disable even the most enraged man."

"Your mother?" Allegria looked even more astonished, if that was possible. "Was she a warrior like Queen Dasa?"

"Blessed Kiriah, no," Idril said, knowing her mother would be scandalized at the very idea. "She was the most gentle of women, known far across Poronne for her skill with herbs, and her abilities to heal."

"But she taught you how to—" Allegria mimicked bashing a man on the side of the head with a rock.

"Of course." Idril opened her eyes wide. "Didn't your mother do the same?"

"Er...no."

"That's a pity. My mother said all maidens should know of such things, as they could be most beneficial." Idril tucked away her rock, giving it a fond pat as she did so. She would save this rock. It was effective, yet fit so well in her hand.

"Yes, but...you're so...*you*," Allegria protested, making a vague gesture. "You're so delicate and frail and ladylike."

"I am neither delicate nor frail, and you are not the only one who can take care of problem people, priest." Idril raised an eyebrow at the arcanist, who was looking amused. "Do you wish to free Lord Israel, or shall I?"

He was a smart man, she would give him that. He didn't ask her what she meant; he simply turned his head to look at the wooden bird that sat atop his staff. "Thorn, would you check the route to locate Lord Jalas's pet bear? No, it doesn't want to eat you. Bears in general don't care for animated wood. You *are* special and very valuable, but that doesn't alter the fact that no bear in its right mind would want to...well, that is a point, but we're going to have to assume the bear is sane. Just go, please, to make sure that it's safe for Lady Idril to release Israel and his company."

"What are we going to do with him?" Allegria asked, nodding toward Jalas.

"Mlarg," Jalas said, as if in answer to her question, and pushed himself up slightly from where he was face down in the mud. "Frang?"

Idril sighed and tossed the rock away. Evidently it wasn't as perfect as she'd first thought. "I suppose now he will claim I tried to kill him, when I only wanted him insensible for a bit." She turned to the servants, who now looked profoundly worried. "If you tell Jalas what happened, I will remove several of your respective body parts in an extremely unpleasant and very bloody manner."

Allegria gave a snort of laughter. "I'm sorry, I know you just said you're not frail or delicate, but if you need us to threaten your servants so that they listen to you, we will be happy to do so."

Idril gave Allegria a long look. "Do you think my servants do not heed my commands?"

"I'm sure they do, but you have to admit that you're not very..." She stopped, clearly trying to find words that weren't offensive. "You're not known for your fighting prowess. Hallow and I are, though, and we'd be happy to help you keep your people in line."

"There is no need for that." Idril pulled out the dagger that hung from her crystal and gold linked girdle, dusting off the jeweled hilt before restoring it to its sheath. "They know what I can do when I put my mind to it."

The servants, to a man, blanched. One looked like he might vomit.

Jalas, with a grunt, managed to roll onto his side, and was ineffectively trying to wipe mud from his face.

"Perhaps it would be best if I..." Hallow took Jalas by one arm, gesturing to Quinn to take the other.

"Lady Idril?" the captain asked her, his eyes filled with a besotted look of boundless admiration that both pleased and annoyed her.

"I suppose you'd better," she said, nodding.

Quinn and Hallow got her father to his feet, although he weaved and his legs buckled underneath him when they more or less hauled him up the stairs into the hall.

"I'm going to want you to show me the spot beneath the ear where you hit him," Allegria murmured when she followed Idril inside.

"I will show you if you promise to stop growling at me," Idril answered in just as soft a tone. "It makes me feel as if you are a dog worried that I will steal your supper."

Allegria's eyes widened, but Idril had more important things to worry about. By the time Jalas had been placed in the massive, heavily carved oak chair that was his version of a throne, he had started to sputter indignantly, demanding to know what had happened.

"Er..." Hallow glanced at Idril.

With yet another sigh to herself, she moved forward, taking a bit of cloth wrapped around the waist of one of the servants, and using it to wipe the worst of the mud from Jalas. "You had an attack, Father, and fell insensible for a few seconds. Have you had too much ale today?"

"An attack?" he asked groggily, wincing when he turned to look at Idril. "Ale?"

"He's still a bit rattled from the attack," she announced to the servants with meaningful glances. They all glanced at the dagger, turned even paler than before, and nodded eagerly. "Perhaps he should be put to bed. Would you like that, Father?"

"Hrn?" he asked, passing a hand over his eyes. "Head hurts."

"I'm sure it does," Idril said soothingly, gesturing at the servants, who hurried forward to more or less lift Jalas. "An overindulgence in ale always gives you pain in the head. Sleep will make you feel better, and when you wake, you will take a posset I will make with your favorite wine."

"Posset," he repeated as the servants bodily hoisted him and carried him toward the stairs. "Wine."

"We have about an hour," Idril said, turning to Hallow. "Less if he becomes angry about something. There's nothing that sharpens his mind like one of his rages. I will go down to see about Lord Israel if you will search for the moonstone."

Hallow nodded his agreement.

"I will assist Lady Idril as is right and proper and wholly wonderful," Quinn announced, bowing low to her.

"There's a possibly mad bear down there who may or may not have highly inappropriate thoughts about men," Allegria told him.

"On the other hand, perhaps I should see to securing the gates, lest any of Lord Jalas's men arrive unexpectedly," he said, doing an about-face and calling over his shoulder as he marched out the door, "Dex will go with you, Lady Idril. She's worth a dozen men, especially when she's hungry."

The odd, small girl with the disturbingly pointed teeth smacked her lips. "I haven't had a good meal of souls in ever so long."

Idril pursed her lips, thought of sending the worrisome child on her way, but decided, upon a moment's reflection, that if her father's men were foolish enough to object to her freeing Lord Israel, then they deserved to have their souls snacked on.

"Come, my heart," Hallow said to Allegria, holding out a hand for her. "Between your communing with Kiriah and a spell I've been working on, we should be able to find where Lord Jalas has secreted the stone."

Allegria didn't look convinced. "She's already mostly shunning me, Hallow. I'm not sure that Kiriah will agree this is worthy of her time, but I will try."

He lifted her hand to his lips. Idril felt a little bubble of sadness well inside her. Deo had once looked at her the way Hallow was looking at his priestess. It had been far too long since those days...

"Thorn will return as soon as he makes sure the passage is clear for Idril, and there isn't much we can't do when the three of us are together," Hallow said.

"You're better with Deo at your side," Idril pointed out, and lifting the hem of her gown so it wouldn't get filthy, headed for the narrow door that led to narrower stairs down into the bowels of the keep. If Boris, her father's bear, was indeed patrolling the dungeon, then she'd simply have him removed before convincing the guards that they had best heed her desires.

She would not tolerate being crossed. Not again.

Chapter 9

I could tell Hallow was beyond frustrated. He spun around the room into which we'd trekked—one of at least a dozen through which he'd led us—but it contained nothing but the usual bedchamber accoutrements. Not even the great wooden chest that lurked in a corner held anything but a family of startled mice.

"I don't know what's gone wrong with this spell," Hallow said, rubbing his chin in the abstracted way he had whenever his magic didn't go quite right. "I did exactly as was written on the script that Exodius hid behind the panel in the garderobe."

"I want badly to comment about the feasibility of any spell you find hidden in a toilet," I said gently, "But since I know you're distracted and out of sorts because we've been searching for almost an hour now, and haven't found the stone, I won't."

"You are a wise woman," he said, flashing a grin at me before squaring his shoulders, preparing to speak the words and draw the runes that comprised the spell of finding. "Right. Thorn, this time, I want you back on the staff. Maybe having you there will focus the arcany, and that will bring forward the stone's hiding place, and we can—"

A muffled sound arrested him. We looked at each other for a few seconds as the low notes of a battle horn faded away to nothing; then we were both running, racing down two flights of stairs until we emerged in the great hall. There was no one visible, but we didn't wait to see what was happening—we continued down a narrow, steep stone staircase into the depths of the keep. Long before we reached the lower level, we heard the sounds of battle.

A man screamed an oath, the sound quickly turning into a raspy burble that disappeared altogether. An ironbound door ahead of us was shut and locked, but Hallow took almost no time in working magic that opened it for us.

A mad cacophony of noise swirled around us when we ran down the central aisle of the lowest level of the keep. Doors leading to numerous storage rooms stretched out before us, rooms that were now being used as cells, all but two of them closed and locked, but it was the battle in front of us that had me mentally reaching for Kiriah, pulling hard on the heat of her sun at the same time Hallow's fingers began dancing as he drew spells on the air.

Once again, only a warm glow lit my hands. I pushed down the despair that Kiriah no longer found me worthy of her trust, and pulled out my swords, tackling the nearest clutch of attackers.

"This must be—Hallow, to your right!—an entire unit down here. Ack! Kiriah's blisters, you will pay for that!" I stumbled forward at the blow to my back, twisting when I fell so that I could slash at my attacker. The man was huge, almost as broad as he was tall, clad in skins and leather, and with a beard that reached halfway down his chest. He held a massive axe, which he'd raised in preparation of cleaving me in two, but even as I severed several tendons in one of his giant arms, Hallow had disabled the two men attacking him from the sides, and leaped forward with both hands held palm forward. A loud percussive blast echoed as my attacker was sent flying backward, crashing into a wall with the sound of breaking bones.

"Allegria?" Hallow asked, spinning to slash at an attacker's legs with the staff. Thorn, who had taken off the second we entered the area, flashed in and out of the melee of fighting bodies, spinning his own spells, and pecking at faces when he had the chance.

"I'm fine, just watch your right side. Idril! Do you need help?"

"With these men? Of course not," she answered, her white blond hair shimmering when she ducked before stabbing upward, sending an attacker staggering backward with a wet gurgle.

I'd had a few surprises come my way that day regarding Idril, but none more startling than the sight of her gauzy apricot and gold gown fluttering, her lithe and graceful form losing none of its charm while she slashed and stabbed. She held two daggers, both slightly curved, and both covered in blood that sprayed out as she dealt with one attacker and moved on to the next. Behind her, with his back to hers, Lord Israel fought another axe-wielding attacker. Beyond them, Quinn used a cutlass against a couple of smaller men, while Dexia leaped on the back of a third and pounded his head into the stone wall, biting off his ear in the process.

Just as I was helping Hallow deal with a group of four men, shouts could be heard from an influx of soldiers at the far end of the vast room, past where Quinn and Dexia fought.

"Hallow, there's another entrance," I panted, nodding toward the men who swarmed in on a wave of axes, swords, and pikes. Even as I watched, one of the newly arrived soldiers skewered Quinn on the pike, pinning him to a wooden door. "Kiriah's blood, no!" I yelled, and desperately fought my way forward, taking off legs and arms as I went, not waiting to finish off the attackers in my need to help Quinn. Hallow roared an oath, and above my head Thorn flew on a massive blast of arcane magic, knocking back the men who were still pouring in through the other door.

To my relief, Quinn, who had gone slack when his body was gutted, suddenly shook his head, and jerked himself forward, pulling the pike out of his chest, and tossing it aside with a growl.

The soldier nearest him watched in horror as he stood, the massive hole in his chest closing even as we watched.

"If that's what it's like being lifebound, then I'm very glad to have you with us," I told him as I separated one of Jalas's men from his head, dancing around a wounded man on the ground who still held an axe.

"Hurts like the fires of Kiriah herself, but it is a handy talent to possess," Quinn agreed, grinning when he twirled his cutlass before slamming the hilt down on the head of a man who had rushed past him to get to Idril.

"Allegria!" Hallow bellowed over the chaos of noise. "Seal the door!"

Thorn flitted over my head as I leaped over an armless man who scrambled backward as best he could when Dexia turned to look at him, smiling her extremely unpleasant smile. Even as I ducked, slid, and spun around the soldiers who had made it into the area, I chanted, calling on Kiriah to bless me with her power, my fingers moving in a rhythm that would weave the light into an unbreakable barrier, but there was nothing there to weave.

Kiriah had abandoned me, withdrawing when I needed her most. My heart sang a dirge, but I couldn't pause to grieve my loss. Just as the man nearest the entrance got to his feet, his sword raised, and a cry on his lips for the others to follow him, I slammed shut the door. Grabbing the pike that had skewered Quinn, I shoved it through the handles, effectively locking it. The barrier wouldn't last long, but it would buy us a few minutes to take care of the attackers already inside the dungeon.

It took only four minutes before we'd dealt with the guards and soldiers that remained in our area. We stacked the dead in one of the rooms that had held some of Lord Israel's men, now released to help us, while the wounded were placed in another room.

"That door won't stay in one piece for long," I warned Hallow, nodding toward the pike that served as a barrier. The door had rung with various blows, but it had been strangely silent for the last two minutes. "They're probably getting a battering ram."

"No doubt. We'll have to hope this way is clear." Just when we were about to go out the way Hallow and I had come in, the sound of men's voices and boots became audible; Jalas's men had obviously decided to come at us via the other end of the keep. We slammed shut the door, and Hallow drew several runes over it.

"How long will that hold?" Quinn asked, eyeing the door when the men on the other side realized we'd sealed it. The frame shook a little as they tried to open it, but Hallow's magic held.

"An hour if we're lucky," Hallow said, glancing around before turning to Lord Israel. "Did you have a chance to search for another exit?"

"Earlier, yes. There is none that we have found. Marston! Do another check for an exit." His men searched the rooms again while we paced the walls, looking for signs of a secret entrance cut into the stone walls.

"So now what do we do?" Quinn asked some three minutes later when we gathered together in the center again. "We're trapped good and proper."

Hallow glanced upward. "Only on the sides. Allegria, do you think Kiriah would answer your call?"

"No." I didn't meet his gaze when I spoke the word, feeling as if a shaft of glass had pierced my soul.

He cast me a questioning look, but didn't say more, just gave the ceiling an assessing look. "I'm pretty drained, and Bellias is sleeping, but I might be able to do what is needed."

"We could probably fight our way through the soldiers waiting for us," I pointed out, guilt swamping me. Guilt and a desperation to be useful, to find the value that I once held.

His lips gave a wry twist. "At what cost? Jalas did not harm Lord Israel and his company, after all, and to repay his restraint by destroying a full company of his men seems unwise."

"You might tell that to the fourteen men who lie dead in the room behind you," Quinn said with a cock of his eyebrow.

"Those men tried to kill us," Lord Israel said, pacing the length of the area. "They forfeited their rights when they attacked us."

Idril held out a hand and tsked. "Lovely. I chipped a nail."

I stared at her in disbelief for a moment before returning my attention to the man at my side. Hallow, I had discovered during my time with him, did not like killing unless it was unavoidable. On the whole, I agreed with that sentiment, but I was a little less nice in my feelings when people were trying to destroy us.

"I can try asking Kiriah," I said slowly. "But I don't think…she has not heeded any of my calls, and I begged her most penitently."

Hallow smiled, the love in his eyes serving as a balm to ease a bit of the pain that gripped my soul. "I'm sure Kiriah is saving her support for something more important. I think I can do this if I have a minute to gather sufficient arcany."

Although I wasn't a priestess in her order, I sent three prayers to Bellias, asking her to hear Hallow's call, thanking her in advance for her aid, and promising that we were doing her work in attempting to bring peace to her children on Alba.

For a few minutes, I didn't think she was going to heed me, but Hallow suddenly lit up with a blue light that sparked and crackled down his arms. He held the staff in front of him, Thorn now perched on top, his eyes closed as he focused. Suddenly he struck the staff on the ground, then thrust it upward at the same time that Thorn flapped his wings so rapidly they were a blur. A blue-white stream of light blasted from Thorn, slamming upward through floor after floor until the arcane light was suddenly gone, and cold air, dust, and tiny splinters of wood swirled down upon us.

I looked up along with everyone else and saw the pale grey sky.

"Damn me! Did he just blow a hole through the entire keep?" Quinn asked.

"He did," I said, full of pride and admiration. "I told you he's a powerful arcanist."

"And you think *my* talent is handy?" Quinn blew out a breath. "Having access to Bellias's power is a thousand times more amazing than being lifebound."

"It's all a matter of perspective," Hallow said modestly. "It's nothing any arcanist who had a good master couldn't do."

When Hallow wielded magic, it always got my gears turning, and now was no different. I had the worst urge to tear off all his clothing and have my womanly way with him, but managed to restrain myself, and simply told him, "I love you."

His eyes lit with a look of passion that told me he was thinking the same sorts of things I was thinking at that moment, and he moved toward me, stopping only when a voice cut through our mutual desire with the effect of ice cold water.

"Shall we get out of here before Lord Jalas regains his senses, or do you intend to bed the priest right here and now?" Lord Israel crossed his arms. "We can wait if you like. I won't say that it will be easy to escape a second time, but considering the look she's giving you—"

I ran a finger down one of the sword blades I'd finished cleaning a few minutes earlier.

Lord Israel cocked an unimpressed eyebrow, and I reminded my wounded pride that he had fought for and protected Aryia for many centuries, and that my sword held no fear for him.

"Escape is definitely the wisest plan," Hallow said, but not before he could send me a look that promised much just as soon as we were alone.

Luckily, the soldiers were still working on the door bearing the pike so that the hall, when we climbed up to it from our gaol, was empty of all but a few terrified servants who huddled together in a corner, weeping and calling upon Kiriah for protection.

Idril looked upward, where a circular hole about the width of a yard had been punched through three floors of the keep. Cold air flooded the hall with occasional minute snowflakes lazily drifting down upon us.

I cleared my throat when Idril turned an unreadable look upon Hallow. "Your father will probably want to get that hole in the roof fixed."

"Indeed," was all she said, and it was then I noticed that although she'd fought just as hard as the rest of us, the delicate material of her gown was unmarked by blood or entrails, unlike my own garments; her hair hung with its usual glossy sheen (my head was covered in the dust of incinerated stone and wood), and she looked as if she'd just stepped from her bedchamber after a long night's restful sleep.

There was a painful stitch in my side, one of my knuckles was grazed and bleeding profusely, and my nose itched terribly from all the dust.

"I think the first order of the day is to ascertain the whereabouts and status of Lord Jalas," Israel said, striding forward to the servants. "I have a few things to say to him about my incarceration. Er...where is the bear?"

"I had him removed to a pasture outside," Idril said, tsking again over the state of her chipped fingernail. "It was the servants leading him away that alerted the guards to the fact that I was freeing you."

"And you?" Israel turned to Hallow. "Do you come with a company, or alone?"

Hallow quickly detailed the last few weeks, how we'd found Quinn, and met Idril in Abet before journeying to Ilam.

"Your face is vaguely familiar. I believe we met a few centuries ago. And you are lifebound, eh?" Israel considered Quinn for a few moments. The latter bowed, but said nothing, looking wary.

Hallow frowned. I watched him, asking, "What do you think? Do we stay or go? It seems the sheerest folly to remain if Jalas sent men after us, and he clearly has issues with Lord Israel."

"We have to stay until I can locate the stone," Hallow said, rubbing his nose. "Much though my instinct is to get out while we can. Lady Idril, will your father's men listen to you if you give them orders?"

"As was witnessed below, not the soldiers, no." she answered him with an annoyed look. "The servants in the keep will, but my father has apparently turned the rest of the Tribe against me. And much though I wish to say a few things to my father, to remain is folly. We must leave now, before the men investigate the noise the arcanist made blowing holes through the keep."

"The stone—" Hallow started to say but was interrupted.

"Is not here," Lord Israel said, turning when the servants slipped away. Thorn flapped his wooden wings a few times before settling back into position on the staff.

I examined Lord Israel, noting that his face was drawn, as one would expect in a man who had been imprisoned. Although he looked tired and battered—unlike Idril, he had taken a few bloody blows during the battle—there was a light of retribution in his eyes that promised his spirit hadn't given up the cause.

"It's not?" I asked, annoyed on Hallow's behalf. "Where is it if it's not here where some insane bear can guard it?"

"The bear is not insane—" Israel paused, grimaced, and made a dismissive gesture when his men, who had taken up defensive positions at the entrances to the hall, murmured dissent. "Well, he has an odd attraction to one or two of my men, but once we figured that out, we were able to deal with his ways. And to answer your question, priest, Jalas took the stone away shortly after he had me imprisoned. He made sure to taunt me with the fact that even should you come to rescue me—not that I needed rescuing, mind you—you would not find it."

"Well…great big mounds of steaming dung," I swore. "Do you know where it is?"

"No, but I will find it." He thought for a moment, then turned to Idril, asking, "The guards in the keep who attacked…is that the extent of your father's force in Ilam?"

"More or less," she said with another graceful shrug and plucked a nonexistent bit of fluff from her embroidered sleeve. "There are a few who guard the roads, but he dismissed the army after the battle of the Fourth Age, save for the few soldiers who serve the keep. However, he can summon more should he have need. The Tribes are ever quick to provide men when called upon to do so."

"That is not my concern. We can see to it that he does not have the opportunity to get a message out of the keep, assuming we can lock away the remainder of his company. Marston?"

Hallow shook his head even as Lord Israel's right hand man moved over to confer with him. "If you are thinking what I'm thinking," Hallow said somewhat confusingly, "it won't serve."

"What are you thinking?" I asked.

"Lord Israel wishes for us to go to Eris without him, while he remains behind to locate the stone, at which point he will use it with the other two in order to open a portal through which he can join us."

"That is exactly what we will do," Israel said, interrupting his conversation to answer Hallow. "There is no reason it won't serve us extremely well. I realize you wish to be the one to find the stone, but you must set aside petty desires in order to do what is best for us all."

"You make it sound like it's just a matter of pride that Hallow find the stone," I said, a little annoyed. Lord Israel's high-handed manner always seemed to rankle. I wholly understood Deo's frustration with his father. "But Hallow is a very skilled arcanist, one learned in the ways of things like hidden stones."

"He is not the only one who commands a knowledge of magic," Israel said, dismissing me. "I am just as capable as he is of finding the stone. More so, since I have more experience with Jalas."

"Oh? Would that the same experience that landed you in a cell in the lowest level of the keep?" I asked, ignoring the little voice in my head that warned it was not wise to prick his temper.

His jaw tightened. "That was an unfortunate reaction that no one could have predicted," he finally answered when he got his jaw unclenched. "Jalas was being irrational in his insistence that I sought to remove him from power."

"But, you do," I couldn't help but point out.

"Now I do, of course," Israel said, looking as annoyed as I felt. "But I didn't previously. If you are done pestering me with petty comments and unhelpful remarks, I would like to get Jalas's soldiers confined."

I ground my teeth a little and would have argued more but Hallow stopped me. Instead, we crept down one of the flights of stairs, and took the soldiers by surprise, herding them into the recently vacated cells. The second force on the other side was smaller, and they capitulated easily enough once we showed them their compatriots locked into cells. Once the servants had taken away the wounded and dead, we met outside Jalas's chambers.

"I will deal with him," Israel said, nodding toward the door. "You two must go to Eris ahead of my forces. We have waited too long as is, and I fear that any longer delay will leave us unable to save the queen and Deo."

"Do you have some reason to believe that they are in danger now? They've been imprisoned for almost a year, and unless there is a pressing reason to rush to Eris, I would prefer we go in a manner that will ensure success," Hallow said, frowning a little.

"You must go now. We can wait no longer lest we risk the unthinkable." Israel said no more, turning toward the double doors that led into Jalas's bedchamber.

"You have news from Eris?" I asked, surprised. How had he managed that when even Hallow's most talented arcanists couldn't penetrate the mist that seemed to hide the land from their magic?

"I have...feelings. The queen is in danger, and Deo..."

"He lives still," Idril said softly, just as if it was a point of minor interest, but I was starting to believe Hallow when he said there was more to her than what appeared on the surface.

"But we don't know what state he's in," Israel said, his scowl prodigious. "Why do you argue with me, arcanist? You and the priest must be the ones to go. There is no one else I can spare who has the power to free Deo."

"And the queen?" I asked, taking Hallow's hand just because I liked the way his fingers rubbed on mine.

A muscle in Israel's jaw twitched. "I will see to her release once I have the stone from Jalas. Marston, a word with you before we tackle Jalas..." They moved off a little way to converse privately.

The urge to argue, to point out the flaws in his thinking was strong, but stronger still was my need to be doing something, *anything*. We'd spent long months doing nothing but tracking down the location of the stones, and now, at last we were moving forward. A little kernel of defiance bit into me, saying softly in my head that even though Kiriah might have spurned me, I wasn't going to give up. So instead of arguing with Lord Israel, I nodded and looked at Quinn.

He leaned against the paneled wall, his eyes filled with regret and sadness that was almost painful to witness. "I am unable to deny your request," he told us, "but I urge you again to find another way. I can't guarantee that my ship will make it through the storms surrounding Eris, let alone ensure that you will survive if it does. To attempt this is the sheerest folly, and almost certainly a death warrant."

I looked at Hallow. He hesitated, taking both my hands in his.

"My heart, the last thing in this world or the next I want is to risk your life—"

I stopped him by pressing a gentle kiss to his lips, whispering against them, "We don't have a choice, though, do we?"

"Yes, we do." His eyes were bright with admiration that made me feel as if Kiriah herself was blessing me. "We can stay until we get the stone from Jalas."

"And risk Deo and the queen?" I shook my head. "It's my fault they are in Eris. I'm not going to leave them there, and if they are in danger now, then I most certainly am not going to put my own safety above theirs. I'd tell you that you could stay, but—"

He laughed, and pulled me against him, kissing me with enough heat to steam an entire field of cabbage. "But you won't because you know full well that I will never leave your side."

"I'm counting on that," I said, nipping his lower lip before releasing him and turning to face Quinn. "We'll put our faith in the fact that Kiriah and Bellias have blessed us and must want to see us right the injustices done to their children."

Quinn sighed, but pushed himself off the wall and with a little shake of his head, said he would go see to the stocking of the ship. He paused at the end of the hallway, looking back to say, "I won't risk my crew, though. I have enough deaths staining my soul, and I don't believe either of you want any more on yours either."

"Will we be able to sail with just the four of us?" Hallow asked, his brow wrinkling. "Allegria and I are more than happy to do what is needed, but neither of us are experienced sailors."

"No, the *Tempest* needs eight hands." A little smile curled the corners of his mouth. "But we will be able to sail nonetheless. Come, Dex. You have a lot of work to do if we expect to be able to sail at Bellias' light."

Dexia smiled, and hopped up and down, clapping her hands. "Can we have a blood sacrifice? I will need a blood sacrifice. Maybe two. Three to be absolutely certain."

"You may sacrifice the chicken that I intend to have for supper," Quinn told her as the two left.

Since Lord Israel was still in deep conference with his lieutenant, that left us with Idril, whose gaze rested on Hallow. "You will, naturally, allow me to come with you."

"Oh, no, my lady, not this time," Hallow said firmly, his gaze holding hers. I moved to his side so that we presented a solid front. "The journey to Eris with Quinn will likely end up with us dead or worse."

I frowned, wondering what was worse than death.

"If there was any way under Kiriah's gaze that I could possibly keep Allegria from going, I would," he added, which just earned him an elbow to the side. "But I can, and will, keep you from journeying with us."

"Deo is there, and thus, so must I go." Her gaze crawled over me for a few seconds. "Despite the fact that the priest reportedly did everything she could to ensnare him with her wiles, he is *my* beloved, not hers."

"Oh!" I gasped, outraged at the slander. "I never tried to ensnare—wait a minute, if he's so beloved, why did you marry his father?"

"That was a political gesture, nothing more," she said haughtily. "The marriage contract was broken a few months later."

"Convenient, that," I said, and would have gone on with more opinions about women who professed love for a man, and then married his father, but there was much we needed to do before we sailed, and I didn't want to waste any more time arguing with her. I lifted a hand when she was about to object and said, "My apologies, that was rude, and the last thing I want is to be rude. That said, Hallow is right that it's far too dangerous for you to accompany us. If you insist on going to Eris, you must wait for Lord Israel to convince your father to hand over the third stone. Who knows, perhaps you might even help him instead of standing around looking perfect. Come on, Hallow. Let's go find a private room so I can make sure you're fit for a trip to Eris."

Taking his hand, I pulled him past where Idril stood with a murderous look in her eye, one of her hands caressing the hilt of the dagger stuck into her golden girdle.

"Ah, my heart, the day you stop trying to be rude to Lady Idril will be the end of me," Hallow said with a laugh, but at the look I sent him, he swung me up into his arms and carried me up a flight of stairs to one of the many unoccupied rooms we'd visited earlier.

Chapter 10

"My lord."

The whispered words drifted through the red haze of pain that wound around Deo so tightly he was mildly surprised to find he could still draw air into his lungs.

"My lord, you must listen to me."

The words were as soft as a caress. Deo's mind spun off for a few minutes, remembering the feel of pale silver blond hair brushing against his naked, sated flesh. The memory pierced him with the agony of molten metal. Damn Idril. How could thoughts of her still have the power to hurt him when his entire body was locked in a world of agony?

"Lord Deo? It is I, Mayam. Please, my lord, you must listen to me."

Deo frowned to himself at the voice that he thought at first must have been manufactured by the madness that every now and then gripped him. Idly, he wondered what had happened to his friend Goat. The last he'd seen of his companion in exile, he was confined to a garden at his father's keep, eating all the shrubs, flowers, plants, trees, buckets, small pieces of cloth, and pretty much anything else the creature could fit into his mouth.

"You must focus, my lord. There is a great need of you. The Speaker…" The voice broke in a sob.

"What is Racin doing now?" Deo's voice came out as a croak, but with the sound of it, he opened his eyes, pushing aside the rush of pain that came with his heightened awareness. Deep inside of him, the chaos magic stirred, sensing the quick rise of anger.

"Oh, thank the gods, you are sensible at last," the serving woman cried, her voice catching as she stood before him. She had the long bronze hair of the Shadowborn, but unlike the blood priests who had bound him to the torture device that stretched his limbs to their fullest extension, her skin was tinged with the red that came from exposure to chaos power, indicating that she had been born after the arrival of the Harborym. "I prayed to Nezu that your wits would remain despite the ceremony, although I don't see how..." Her face was a mask of horror as her gaze traversed the chains and spikes that bound Deo to the wall.

"What has happened that you must disturb me?" Deo asked, fighting the rise of chaos within. Kiriah damn it, must the power always fight him?

Not fight. Assist. Guide. Enhance, it whispered.

He ignored the voice just as he ignored the pain that laced every inch of his skin. The blood priests had learned their art well, knowing exactly what parts of the body could be pierced to cause maximum pain without actually killing him, but they had underestimated Deo. He hadn't fought to become a Bane of Eris only to give in to a little torture.

"Lord Racin is combing the land, capturing as many Shadowborn as would be able to survive the journey to Skystead. He has killed most of the blood priests by subjecting them to what he calls trials, and now is decimating my people. My lord, you must aid us. We cannot face him, but you can."

Fury possessed Deo, instantly releasing the chaos.

Mayam gasped and leaped back as the stone walls began to groan and crack.

Quickly Deo leashed the power, every ounce of his will focused on controlling the need to lash out and destroy those who would harm the innocents of this land. The pain of his bondage intensified with his struggles, and for a few seconds, he thought that he might finally have reached the point where he would lose control once and for all, but at last the magic yielded to his will and subsided.

Although not without a whispered, *You grow weak fighting your true nature.*

"My lord?" Mayam crept forward, her hands fluttering gently along his arms and chest as if to reassure herself that he still lived.

"Where is Racin now?" he managed to ask.

"In Skystead, but the Harborym crawl over the land, herding Shadowborn men and women before them, dooming them all. Please, my lord, you must do something," she answered.

Deo turned his head and looked out of the high, narrow slit in the cell. The light outside was that of a gloomy dusk, meaning it was probably morning. He coughed up a bit of blood, his lips dried and cracked, wondering how long it had been since anyone had fed him. Had he been nailed to the wall three days ago? Three weeks? Time had ceased to have meaning to him. Mayam exclaimed to herself and hurriedly pulled a small gourd from a basket, from which she poured out a liquid, offering it to Deo's lips. He drank, both relishing the feeling of the wine burning a path to his belly and wincing as it seemed to wake his body up to the fact that he was impaled, bound, and laden with various confining runes. "I have brought food, too, only we thought you might not want that until you are set free," Mayam told him.

"We?" He pounced on the most important word. One part of his mind welcomed the idea of respite from his torture, while the other wondered suspiciously if this was not a trap that Racin had set for him.

"My brother is one of Queen Deva's serving men. He is most devoted to her, and since he was once a priest in the Order of the Red Hand he is learned in the ways of blood magic. He can undo what has been done to you."

"Dasa," Deo said without thinking.

"My lord?" Mayam clutched the gourd, confusion writ upon her face.

"My mother—the queen—her name is Dasa, not Deva. That is *his* name for her."

She blinked at him, casting one hand to the side. "I don't see—"

"Never mind." Deo took a deep breath, wincing at the pain. He needed to will his mind back to the state of insensibility that he'd embraced since he had been bound to the wall. "It matters not. Go, little maid, before the priests find you here."

"But my lord, we must free you! My people will die if you do not stop Racin!"

Deo closed his eyes against the need to rush out and protect the innocent people of this dark place, to destroy the one who ravished the land and decimated its inhabitants, but as Dasa had pointed out, he had to look beyond his own needs and remember the plan. "Some will survive. Racin is not stupid enough to kill all of you."

"But..." Mayam clearly was at a loss for words. "But we could free you—"

"Kiriah blast you, woman!" he roared, opening his eyes to glare at her.

She leaped back, one hand over her mouth, her own eyes wide with horror even as tears rolled down her face.

"Do you think I don't want to be free? Do you think I don't want to let the blood of those priests who did this to me stain the stones of this building before I turn it to dust? Do you think I embrace the thought of Racin destroying innocents?"

Yes, yes, destroy him before he can hurt others, the chaos inside him said with a siren's lure.

"Please," she said, the word a whimper, and in it, Deo heard the cries of thousands whose voices were being systematically silenced.

Deo closed his eyes for a moment, his struggle with the magic for once not the sole focus of his attention. He hated what was happening. Every instinct railed against inactivity.

You can do something about it, came the whisper in his mind.

It was too much. What Dasa asked of him was too much, he told himself with an anger that fed the magic inside him. How could he remain here, passive, doing nothing while all around him people died because of Racin's insane thirst for power?

"No! I was born to bring peace to Alba, and I will stand by idle no longer! Dasa's plans be damned!" He narrowed his eyes, searching the face of the cowering woman, intent on finding any signs of deceit, coming to a sudden decision that he prayed he wouldn't regret. "Fetch your brother, and any others who will fight for your people. Blast my father for scattering my Banes…I need them now more than ever."

"Banes?" she asked, getting to her feet, her face caught between a wary expression, and exultation.

"My army." He eyed her, thinking hard. Was there any reason he could not duplicate the Banes of Eris he had created the previous year? It was true that the Shadowborn were more used to chaos magic than the men and women of Aryia who had joined him before, but would that not mean they had a better chance of mastering it?

The decision was made. While Mayam scurried off to fetch her brother so that he might be freed, Deo made plans. First, he'd destroy this temple so no other prisoners could be held here. Then he would gather unto him a force of volunteers who were willing to become a new order of Banes… and then once and for all, he would destroy Racin.

Deo smiled. His mother would no doubt protest the change of plans, but she couldn't object to it if his actions achieved their goals.

He just hoped he could stay in control of the chaos magic inside him long enough to see Racin destroyed. He had a horrible suspicion it was getting stronger.

Oh, I am. I very much am.

Chapter 11

I think you're making a big mistake.

Hallow marched up the stairs from the lower levels of Jalas's keep filled with determination, grit, and the firmest of intentions. "Yes, you've made that abundantly clear."

You need me!

"I do, but sometimes, I need you to be my eyes and ears. This is one of those times."

I can't believe you'd go to Eris without me!

"My lord Hallow—"

He continued past Idril, his much lauded patience at an end where that woman—not to mention Thorn—was concerned.

You don't know what Eris is like! It's horrible! Truly horrible! Harborym so thick on the ground you'd trip over them, and chaos magic fair oozing out of the soil itself. It's no place for you without me to guide you.

"We'll be fine. It's much more important that you stay here and help Lord Israel with Jalas."

Faugh! If you get yourself killed and go to the spirit world, don't come crying to me. That's all I have to say!

"Oh, if only that were so," Hallow murmured, and strode across the hall toward the great curved wooden staircase that led up to Jalas's chambers. He'd have one last quick word with Lord Israel; then he would escape to Quinn's ship with Allegria, and finally be free of both Thorn's and Idril's persistent demands that they sail with him.

"My lord, I am just as tired as you are of these encounters," Idril said, hurrying up behind him. He made a note to tell Allegria that Idril sounded downright peeved. Allegria claimed Idril never expressed any emotion other than mild boredom, and she would be sure to appreciate that along with his own temper, Idril's had clearly been pushed to its limits.

On your own head be it, Thorn said dramatically, and with a rude gesture of his hindquarters, flew off, clearly in a snit.

"Gah!" Idril yelled and added something very rude indeed under her breath.

Hallow grinned to himself and merely said as he started up the stairs, "I'm glad to hear that you don't seek out these encounters any more than I do. We shall get along much better without them, don't you think?"

There was a brief noise that raised the hair on the back of his neck, and a sudden tugging of his sleeve. He stopped and stared in disbelief at the dagger that had skimmed his arm and pinned the edge of his cloak to the wood bannister.

He turned to look at Idril. She stood at the foot of the stairs, an expression on her face that he had last seen on his wife's stubborn mule. "You drove me to that," Idril said hurriedly when he plucked the dagger from where it was buried a good two inches into the wood. He gave the blade a curious look before handing it back to her. She moved around to block his advance up the stairs. "If you would cease these silly refusals of my most reasonable request—"

"No," he said, and bodily moved her to the steps behind him.

"I will be of use to you—" Idril started to say, but he was shaking his head even as he reached the top and headed to the right to Jalas's chambers.

"This is the fourteenth time I've said no. Nothing you can say will change my mind. You will have to wait for Lord Israel to persuade your father to give him the third stone."

He closed his ears to her protestations, trying to regain the equilibrium of mind that always amazed Allegria. By the time he reached Jalas's door, he felt much more in control of himself. He consulted with the guard outside the great double doors, then entered the antechamber. Lord Israel stood staring into a small fire, a nearby table littered with a meal that he hadn't touched.

"Is all at hand?" Israel asked him without shifting his gaze from the amber glow.

"Yes. The soldiers below are secure and have been fed. The men you left are settled, and I don't think—barring a catastrophe like the Tribesmen arriving—you will have any trouble keeping the denizens of Ilam under your control until you get the third stone. How is Lord Jalas?"

Israel grimaced. "He threatened to geld me, cut out my liver, and eat a stew made of both in front of me."

"So much as usual?" Hallow asked.

"Aye." A rare smile graced Israel's lips for a few seconds. "He doesn't seem to me to be in the least bit lacking in wits. He demanded I bring his pet bear into his rooms, and when I told him it had been banished to the stables because it had regrettable desires toward a couple of my men, he told me that they just needed to embrace the opportunity, and that he—the bear—meant no real harm. He simply had a taste for...er..."

"Regrettable desires," Hallow repeated, then felt that the less said about Jalas's bear, the better. "I take it Jalas was not forthcoming with information about where he's sent the stone?"

The look of amusement faded from Israel's face. He turned to meet Hallow's gaze with one of unwavering dark amber. "No. But he will."

Hallow knew well just how single-minded Lord Israel could be when he was focused on a plan of action. It was a trait that he admired, although he seldom had the luxury of being so inflexible. Still, in this instance, it was to the benefit of all Alba for the leader of the Fireborn to be so focused on a single goal. "You will call upon the grace of Alba to trick him into telling you the stone's location?" he asked, wondering if the magic that was bestowed upon the Fireborn race had the power to make Jalas speak the truth.

Israel smiled, and cracked the knuckles of one hand. For a moment, the look of strain, exhaustion, and desperation fled, leaving him a powerful king, one who was not afraid to fight for those he loved. "Better than that: I will speak to him on a level he understands."

"Jalas has a good five stone on you," Hallow pointed out. "And is a few inches taller."

"Nonetheless, this time, I will find the third moonstone's location. You have the others?"

"Yes." A strange sense of reluctance claimed Hallow as he dug out of the small leather bag that hung from his belt an object wrapped in blue silk and sealed with a number of runes that glowed silver on the fabric. "I need not tell you to guard these with your life. Exodius spent an entire day on our journey to Kelos telling me just how powerful these stones are, and that's why he split them up so they could not be used by someone who couldn't control their power."

Israel took the silk package and slipped it inside his jerkin. "You don't need to tell me, but I understand why you feel driven to do so. They will not be misused, at least not by me, and I will allow no other to possess them."

Hallow disliked letting the stones out of his possession, but knew if he was possibly going to his death, it was better that Israel have the opportunity to use them. If there was any chance of rescuing Deo and the queen, it would be worth the sacrifice.

"You are off now?" Israel asked, glancing out of an unshuttered window. "The moon is not yet up."

"Quinn promises that Bellias Starsong will bless our journey with her presence, and much as I am loath to start at such an inauspicious time, I have learned to trust his judgement."

"And yet you are half-Starborn," Lord Israel said, shaking his head in mock dismay.

Hallow's eyes widened in surprise. He could count on one finger the number of people who knew the truth about him, and yet here was Israel referring to his most well-kept secret. "I am, although I was unaware that truth was known except by one other."

"Your wife, I presume? No, do not scowl at me—she hasn't spilled your secrets." He made a face. "I doubt if she'd say anything to me of her own accord. She seems to dislike me."

"Do you wonder why?" Hallow asked, amused despite himself. "For almost a year she was under the impression you callously killed your son."

"I didn't."

"No, but you did wed his betrothed."

One of Israel's shoulders twitched. "Deo wasn't betrothed. He told me himself that he would wed if and when he chose, and he didn't choose to do so at that time. Besides, the marriage to Idril was a political maneuver that lasted all of six weeks before she formally conducted the ceremony of divorce."

"I simply offer you an explanation of why Allegria has trouble seeing you in any light but that of villain," Hallow said mildly.

"She can see me in any light she desires so long as she can help release Deo." Lord Israel's gaze was particularly piercing.

Hallow, who had been granted a seat at the Council of Four Armies when he had taken over as master of Kelos, could almost feel himself being judged. He resisted the urge to square his shoulders, and instead allowed one side of his mouth to curl up into a lop-sided smile. "The subject of my ancestry aside, we will do everything that's possible to save him. Assuming we survive the trip to Eris." His smile faded as he thought of the danger that faced his company.

Israel continued to watch him, and showing a moment of insight, said softly, "She would not let you go alone. She is not that type of woman."

"No, she is not," he said with a sigh, knowing full well that whether they lived or died, Allegria would be at his side. "But it's not devotion to me alone that drives her. She bears a burden of guilt that both Deo and the queen are in Eris."

"She is not to blame. Deo chose his own path. I do not say I would have chosen it for him, but I understand why he decided to join his mother." Lord Israel was looking past him again, staring sightlessly into the fire.

Hallow was silent for a few moments before saying, "I am leaving Thorn with you. He may not be able to talk to you, but he has powers of his own, and it is my hope he will be able to work some magic on Jalas that bends him to your will."

"Any help in that regard is welcome, although I thought only the Master of Kelos could use his powers."

"He likes to think that, but I've learned over the last eleven months that Thorn—annoying as he can be—is far more powerful than he lets on. Do not hesitate to ask him for assistance."

Israel murmured something about doing so.

Despite having one Fireborn parent, Hallow did not bear the grace of Alba, and lacked the ability some Fireborn had to sense circumstances surrounding those he loved, a trait that he knew Israel bore. "Is there anything you can tell us about the queen or Deo's situation? Are they still in peril?"

"Yes," Israel said, closing his eyes. His fingers fisted, the knuckles growing white. "But I have faith in Dasa's ability to protect herself. It is Deo you must concentrate on. He is too stubborn, too sure of his own abilities, and will run headlong into trouble rather than finessing his way out as any wise man would do."

"I have ample experience with Deo's insistence upon running, my lord," Hallow said dryly. "Should we make it to Eris, we will find him. It won't be easy to keep him from attacking the Harborym and their captain in order to free the queen, but we will do our best to keep him safe."

"That's all I ask." Israel slid a glance toward the closed door that led to Jalas's bedchamber. "It shouldn't take me longer than a week to get the stone from Jalas. If your journey lasts five days, that will give you time to locate Deo before I arrive."

It was on the tip of Hallow's tongue to ask how Lord Israel expected to do in a week what he had yet to accomplish, but decided he didn't want to go to his (possible) death with the idea of torture on his mind. He simply bowed and murmured that he had to find Allegria so that they could sail when Bellias was at her strongest. "You may need to placate Lady Idril some," he warned, pausing on the way out the door. "She is mightily annoyed with me at the moment, and I suspect will wish to vent her spleen on you."

Israel sighed. "What complaint does she have now?"

"The same one: we refuse to let her sail with us. She seems to feel that she will be left behind if she doesn't travel with us."

"There is nothing I would like more than to leave her here where she's safe, but she will insist that only she can control Deo, and thus must be included in my party." Israel's expression eased, and he looked a bit more cheerful. "She's welcome to vent whatever ire she has, but I'll redirect it to her father. Safe travels, arcanist."

Once in town, Hallow rounded up Allegria from the stable yard, where she was explaining to her mule that she couldn't take her on the ship to Eris because of the danger.

"Don't you give me that look," Allegria told Buttercup when the latter bared her teeth. "There's a very big chance we could be destroyed trying to get there, and I couldn't live with myself...er...couldn't rest easy in death knowing I had caused you to die as well."

She turned to tie Buttercup to a hitching post, but the rope slid from her hands when Buttercup first reared up, then rushed past her, hoof beats clattering on the cobblestones as the mule raced down the hill toward the harbor proper.

Allegria sighed. "Can mules swim?"

"I think we'd find out if we tried to sail without her," Hallow answered, putting his arm around Allegria to give her a squeeze. "I'm afraid, my heart, she's made up her own mind."

"Yes, and once Buttercup makes up her mind, there's no way on Alba to change it. What are we going to do?"

"Take her with us, I suppose. It seems to be her preference. Luckily, Penn is not so stubborn—" The second the words were out of his mouth, Hallow became aware of warm, moist breath on the back of his neck, followed shortly by a none-too-gentle nudge that sent him stumbling forward a few steps. He turned to glare at his horse, who gazed back at him with liquid brown eyes and a mute expression of expectation.

"No," he told Penn sternly. "Do not listen to what Buttercup told you. You do not need to come with us and risk your life. You are a smart horse. You value life. You may not be able to sire any foals, but you have a nice retirement in a sunny pasture to look forward to, should I perish. I have made arrangements with Lord Israel to take care of you, so you will cease looking at me like a puppy denied a walk and will return to the paddock."

Penn snorted and turned his head to look in the direction that Buttercup had disappeared.

"You wouldn't dare," Hallow told him, and reached for the horse's halter, but with a flick of his tail that caught Hallow dead in the face, the horse trotted off.

"You were saying?" Allegria asked when she emerged from a room in the stable used to hold tack. She held Buttercup's bridle, blanket, and saddle in her arms.

"Nothing," he said. After taking a moment to work through all the oaths he wanted to yell after his horse, he gave in to the inevitable by collecting Penn's tack and following Allegria down to the ship.

"You only have yourself to blame if you drown," he heard Allegria mutter to Buttercup, who was stationed at the narrow gangplank, scaring the porters attempt to bring supplies to the ship. "Don't you dare even think about biting me, you ungrateful beast. Come along then. No, you cannot be afraid of the water, nor is that a monster. It's Quinn, and he's going to be responsible for getting your motley hide safely to Eris, so you can just stop pretending you are a shy, delicate little flower. Up you go."

Allegria, having long experience with her mule, simply grabbed the lead and ran up the gangplank, giving Buttercup no chance to balk.

"At least you have better manners, even if you can be just as stubborn as the mule," Hallow told Penn and led the horse onto the ship and down into the hold.

By the time the animals were bedded down, fed, and watered, Hallow and Allegria emerged to the deck to find it empty of all but Quinn and Dexia. The latter was seated cross legged drawing runes upon a long narrow cloth of grubby linen.

"What are you magicking?" Allegria asked the vanth while Hallow proceeded to the upper deck, where Quinn stood before a small table. A couple of lanterns held down a dirty bit of map, their golden glow making Hallow suddenly yearn for a warm bed and his warmer wife. It wasn't that he feared death, but he very much wanted a long life during which he could explore all the quirkiness that made up Allegria.

"Surely you must know your way to Eris," Hallow said to Quinn, who lifted the map from beneath the lanterns, and held it at an angle, squinting at it. He pointed to the northwest. "It's that way."

"I know where it is, I just wanted to set a course for the Maquet Islands instead of trying to sail directly to Eris itself."

"Maquet Islands?" Hallow dug through his memories, but found only a faint fragment. "Where exactly are they?"

"Close enough to disrupt the charge of the storms," Quinn answered, pointing to a tiny blotch on the map. Hallow held it closer to the lamps, and noted the blotch was actually made up of a cluster of small rocky islands vaguely shaped like an arrow.

"How can a small group of islands disturb the storms that surround Eris?" Hallow asked, his curiosity pricked. If there was any chance of improving the odds of arriving in Eris safely, he wanted to explore it more fully.

"It's not the storms themselves that mean death to those who try to pass through them," Quinn answered, absently tossing the map back onto the table before striding down the few steps to the main deck, where he directed the stowing of the last supplies in the hold. "It's the electrical fluid charge contained therein. Make yourself useful, Dex, and check that the supplies are secure."

"I'm being useful," the small girl answered, not lifting her head from where she was now stitching what looked to Hallow's eyes like sigils into the narrow cloth that spilled from her lap down to her feet. "Let the priest do it."

"Where's the crew?" Allegria asked, looking around her. "Hallow said you didn't expect us to become sailors, not that I object to helping sail, but I know nothing about ships."

"The crew is here," Quinn said, making shooing motions toward Allegria, although Hallow couldn't help but notice that he managed to ogle her upper works at the same time.

"Where?" she asked, moving toward the steps that led down to the hold.

"Here," he said, and turned to Hallow, nodding toward the forward-most of two masts. "Shimmy up that mast and let down the upper jib, will you? Dex—"

"I'm busy!" the girl snarled and stabbed viciously into the cloth with a needle and thread that was a rusty brown, just the color of dried blood.

"This is more important," Quinn told her.

"Oh really?" She narrowed her eyes at him. "Do you want us to survive the trip?"

He thought for a moment, then gave a little bob of his head. "Point taken. Hallow, after you've set the jib, help me with the mainsail, and we'll get out of the harbor."

Hallow looked at the mast. He'd never had a head for heights, but now seemed like a poor time to point that out. Instead, he suffered through a hellish ten minutes during which he managed to pull himself up the rope-wrapped mast until he reached the spar. He kept his eyes firmly on the ropes while he released the small sail before gratefully—and breathlessly— making his way back to the deck.

He helped pull in the anchor, stood silently while Quinn called for the mooring lines to be released, and gazed back at the black silhouette that was the town with a mingled sense of excitement and regret. "May the blessed goddesses have mercy on us and not send us to our deaths," he murmured before going down below decks to find Allegria.

For some reason, he felt an overwhelming need to hold her.

Chapter 12

"Ghosts." I looked from Hallow to Quinn to the man who stood looking at me with pursed lips. "Your crew are ghosts. We have ghosts sailing the ship. Ghosts who, unless I'm mistaken, have limited amounts of time when they can interact with our world in a corporeal manner."

"We prefer the term lost mariners," the man told me in a voice that managed to be both ethereal and haughty at the same time.

"They are spirits, yes, but they are the spirits of sailors," Quinn pointed out. "And since I refuse to risk any lives—other than your own—on this misbegotten journey, that's what you're getting. If you object, we can go back to Abet, and I will be released from your service."

His gaze dropped to my breasts for a few seconds. I narrowed my eyes at him. "If the next words out of your mouth are that you would be very happy to service me, Hallow will turn you into a bumblepig. One with mange."

"I will?" Hallow's brows rose, but he must have seen the pointed look I shot his way, because he cleared his throat and tried his best to look menacing. "Er…I will. One with a particularly unpleasant chronic digestive problem, as well."

Quinn didn't look the least bit worried. The ghost, however—who went by the name Commander Ohare—eyed Hallow with respect. "Well? Do we turn around?"

"No, of course not," I snapped. "But if we die because your crew goes incorporeal at the worst possible moment, then I'm so going to haunt you. And I'm sure I could convince Buttercup to join me."

"Buttercup?"

"Her mule," Hallow murmured in his ear.

"Blessed Bellias and all her stars...that savage biting, kicking monstrosity has a name?" Quinn asked while absently rubbing a spot on his back. "It's your mount? I thought you brought it along as a weapon to unleash upon the Harborym."

In the end, my worries were for naught. The crew, it turned out, took turns being on duty, so that while one group wandered the ship in translucent, faintly blue tinted forms trimming sails, winding rope, and doing a hundred other things that were beyond the experience of Hallow and me, the others retreated to the spirit world and recharged their respective corporeal forms.

The next five days took on a fairly peaceful aspect, if the ever-present threat of making our way through the impenetrable storms of Eris was ignored. Hallow and I had a cabin to ourselves, which we made use of with such regularity that I heard Quinn ask Hallow if he'd cast some sort of spell on me.

"Yes," I called out from where I was feeding Buttercup and mucking out the small space that was her stall. "It's called Hallow."

"But that's his name," Quinn answered, his brows furrowed in confusion. "I meant the name of the spell."

"They're one and the same," I answered, wagging my own brows at Hallow, who just laughed and gave me a heated look that promised reward the next time we were alone.

That time was sooner in arriving than I expected. As soon as I had cleaned Buttercup's stall and done the same for Penn, I emerged onto the deck to a slap in the face from the salty sting of a windstorm. "Are we there already?" I asked, suddenly panicked. My palms pricked with sweat even as I reached for the light of Kiriah Sunbringer. Hallow and I had avoided talking about the possibilities of our potential deaths, preferring instead to spend our time enjoying each other. My own thought was that if I had to die now, I'd prefer doing so having been loved to the point of insensibility, rather than worried and fearful. "Kiriah's blessed bottom, I didn't know we'd reach our destination so quickly."

"These are not the storms of Eris, my heart," Hallow reassured me from where he stood with a spyglass, his grey cloak whipping around him with the power of the wind. I wove my way over to him, slipping twice as the deck grew slick with spray. "We're approaching Huw, the southern-most Maquet Island. Here, can you see it?"

He pulled me against his body, and I sagged in relief at the feel of him, so solid and warm. I nestled against him, grateful for the strength of his arm around me while I tried to hold the spyglass steady enough to look through it. A dark smear bobbed and disappeared in the lens, bobbed again, and then was gone. "Why are we going to an island? Are we stopping for supplies?"

"Not supplies," Quinn said, pausing next to us to call out an order to one of the ghosts. "Wren, go into the storeroom beneath my cabin and fetch up the small chest with the red seal binding it closed. The governor is said to be very exacting in the payment he requires."

"Payment for what?" I asked when the ghostly crewman hurried off to do Quinn's bidding.

Hallow took my hand. "Come, let us go into our cabin. I want to tell you about an idea Quinn had."

"If we go into our cabin, I'm going to strip off your cloak, leggings, and tunic, and lick every square inch of you," I told him.

"Are you absolutely certain you couldn't find room for another boyfriend?" Quinn asked, spreading his arms wide despite the fact that the wind was causing the ship to lurch from side to side. He, like Hallow, didn't seem to be bothered at all by the movement, whereas I stumbled and fell every few steps. "I have been told by two different ale wenches that I was quite lickable, and I'm willing to take a bath to make sure that there's no spilled ale or food in my chest hair."

"Ew," I answered, then punched him on the arm. "No. Stop asking. Besides, the licking offer was only open to Hallow. How about it, arcanist of my dreams?"

Hallow looked thoughtful for a few seconds, then with a sigh of pure regret shook his head. "No, tempting as the offer is, now is not the time for all the loving I wish to lavish upon your fair, nubile body."

"I'm known across three continents for the quality of loving I can perform on nubile bodies," Quinn murmured, looking hurt.

"You almost loved me to the point that I couldn't walk this morning," I whispered in Hallow's ear.

He slid a hand under my cloak and pinched my behind. "Likewise, my temptress. But this is something I think we should discuss. Quinn? Shall we explain your thoughts?"

Quinn started a leer, but aborted it immediately when he saw that Hallow held a ball of arcane light in his hand. "Very well. But it won't be as much fun as the discussion *I* want to have. Commander Ohare? Ah, there you are."

He gave a few more orders to the crew, then headed into the captain's cabin.

"What's this all about?" I asked Hallow, not liking the idea that he had been keeping things from me. We had an unspoken policy of sharing any information that was of major importance, and I didn't appreciate finding out he wasn't being as forthcoming as I'd desire. "Have you been making plans with Quinn?"

He hesitated for a few seconds. "Yes, but before you rail at me, it was only because I wasn't sure about them, myself, and wanted to wait until I had time to consult Exodius's journals before I asked you for your opinion."

I was mollified enough to bite his lower lip. "Is that why you've been closeted with those trunks of moldy books while I mucked out your horse's stall for the last few days?"

He smiled and kissed the tip of my nose, then turned me and gently pushed me toward the captain's quarters. "I told you that I would clean both stalls, but you insisted on doing it, if you recall."

"That's because I'm going mad with nothing to do on this ship," I said, grateful to be out of the storm. My hair was plastered to my head, some of it glued to my mouth, while the rest of me…well, mucking out stalls is never easy to do in the best of circumstances, and working in the hold of the pitching ship meant I hadn't escaped without some reminders of the experience. "But I am very interested to know just why we're stopping at an island south of Eris rather than fighting our way through the storms. Is there a portal here, by any chance?"

"Not that I've heard," Quinn said, glancing at Hallow. "You?"

Hallow shook his head. "It takes great power to open portals, the sort of powers belonging to the twin goddesses, not their mortal children. That, or an artifact of their power, like the queen's moonstones."

I had never thought about that, and was unable to keep from asking, "How did the Harborym open up so many portals if that's the case? They are most certainly not as powerful as Kiriah and Bellias."

"I'm guessing Racin drew upon the collective chaos magic held by his followers to open the portals. Exodius told me before he left that the Harborym found near the open portals were dead, depleted to the point of being empty husks of their former selves." Hallow gave a little shrug and pulled me down next to him on the edge of Quinn's bunk, while the captain seated himself at his desk. "We're going to Maquet instead of directly to Eris."

"Because the islands disrupt the storms. But that makes no sense," I scoffed.

"Not disrupt the storms so much as the charge—" The words stopped on Hallow's lips when the door to the cabin was thrown open, a blast of wind sending cold air and spray into the relative warmth of the space, followed by a figure in white and gold who was thrust into the room.

"Captain, I found a stowaway in the strong room!" the ghost at the door proclaimed.

I stared in complete surprise as the figure pulled herself from the grip of the sailor, who immediately faded into nothing, evidently having depleted all of his power. "Idril! By Kiriah's toenails, what were you thinking? We've told you how dangerous this journey is."

"And I told you—and your annoying husband—that I would not be left behind. Not again." She lifted her chin and I couldn't help but notice that despite the fact she'd evidently spent the last five days hiding in a small, stuffy strong room, her hair gleamed, her skin was flawless, and her white gown and cloak didn't have so much as a smudge on them. Before I could reflect—sourly—on the unfairness of life, she wrinkled her nose and asked me, "Did you bathe in shit? Your odor is unbearable."

I glared at her for a moment, then rose and pointed at her while demanding of Hallow, "Smite her!"

"Now, my heart—" he started to say in that annoyingly patient voice he so often used with me.

"Don't you *my heart* me! If you love me, you'll smite her. I'd do it myself, but not only do I have to go take a bath and throw these clothes overboard, but if I did end her life as she deserves, Kiriah would most definitely never bless me again. And Idril isn't worth risking that. Just punch a couple of large holes in her torso with the arcany you were using to warn Quinn. One or two holes. That's all I ask. I'm sure Bellias won't care."

Hallow laughed and pulled me back down next to him. "I think this time, I will refrain, and we will hear what Lady Idril has to say for herself."

"I have many things to say, not the least of which is that your wife is mad and is quite possibly a danger to herself and others. But since you have refused to listen to me about other, more important, issues, I doubt if you will do so now." With a fine look of distaste at me, Idril glided over to accept the chair that Quinn dragged forward for her. I thought for a moment he was going to throw himself at her feet, but he contented himself with pulling his own chair over to hers and staring at her with mingled lust and puppy dog hopefulness.

"You really are the most fickle of men," I couldn't help but point out.

He waved away my comment without taking his eyes off Idril. "You're taken. She's not. And her hair is beyond glorious, while yours is…less so."

"I like Allegria's hair," Hallow protested, twining a finger through one of my damp curls. "It is full of life, and doesn't like to be confined, rather like her spirit."

I kissed his cheek. "I love you, too."

"Lady Idril puts us in a difficult position," he continued, but pulled me closer against him. "I refuse to be responsible for her possible death. Therefore, we must put her ashore when we stop at Huw."

Idril looked at him as if he was a particularly uninteresting bug. "If you try, the mad priest will be a widow."

My eyes widened as I took in her threat. I thought of challenging her, or of calling on Kiriah to bless me one last time in order to call down the light of the sun onto Idril's fair head, and finally considered whether or not I could stuff her through one of the portholes that lined the back wall of Quinn's cabin.

Hallow didn't appear even remotely upset that she had just threatened his life. "Indeed," he said, looking thoughtful, stroking a finger across his chin in a way that normally made me pounce on him. Now I was too annoyed to allow myself anything but a moment to acknowledge just how sexy he was. "I think she means it," he said to me at last.

"Given that she killed at least six of her father's men without turning one of her perfect hairs, I suppose she does," I allowed. "That doesn't mean I have to like the fact that she hid away on the ship just to blight us."

"Your choice of words…" Idril shook her head, then addressed Hallow. "What is this island at which we are stopping, but which I will not be left upon? Why are we not sailing directly to Eris? Deo is in need of me. I do not wish for him to come to harm simply because you and the mad priest insist on dawdling."

"We are not dawdling!" I exclaimed. "And I highly doubt if Deo is so badly in need of you—the last time he saw you, he told you to leave."

Ire flashed in her eyes, but was gone almost instantly. "I grow tired of arguing with you. You are determined to think the worst of me, and I lack the desire to try to make you see the truth."

"Don't you dare make me look like the unreasonable one here," I said, annoyed at both the fact that she so irritated me, and that I couldn't seem to keep my opinions to myself whenever she was around. I caught the look Hallow sent my way, and said quietly, "Stop looking at me like that. You're supposed to be on my side."

"I am and always will be wholly and completely on both your sides, as well as your front and back, but you must admit that you have a slight sense of inferiority when it comes to Idril."

"She said I stink," I whispered furiously.

"My heart, you smell like sun warmed flowers on a grassy hilltop. Your clothing, however…"

"Right," I said, standing up. Pointing at Idril, I commanded, "No one say anything important. Feel free to lambaste her for stowing away on the ship, however."

Ten minutes later I'd had a quick wash, had indeed thrown my clothing (an old priest's robe that I used to wear when making soap) out the porthole, and returned to the captain's quarters, where I found Hallow, Quinn, and Idril all in possession of mugs of ale, laughing heartily at some joke as I entered.

"I'm back," I said unnecessarily, unreasonably prickly because Hallow was having a good time without me. As soon as I had the thought, I lectured myself that I was better than that, and instead of demanding to know what they all found so funny, took my seat next to Hallow and accepted a sip from the mug he proffered. "Now that I smell less like horse and mule, can we get on with the discussion of just how an island is supposed to help us get through the nigh impassable storms that surround Eris?"

"Ah, yes, as to that, I believe we'll let Quinn explain why the idea came to him," Hallow said.

Quinn, who was attempting to press more ale upon Idril, set down the ale jug, cleared his throat, and strode over to his desk, where he picked up a dagger and used it to point to a map on the wall. "It's less an idea, and more an experience. As I believe I mentioned, I have tried three times to sail to Eris, and only succeeded once. The first two times, all hands were lost, including myself. Only I returned to life almost immediately, and it took some time for me to make landfall clinging to a bit of the ship. I landed on one of the Maquet islands, as a matter of fact, although I had no idea what a unique role the islands play in the storms of Eris. The second time, I was in the company of two other ships, and once they saw mine break up as soon as we crossed into the storms, they fished the handful of survivors out of the water and returned to Aryia. The third time…" He paused when Dexia entered the cabin, trailing a long streamer of cloth, dirt-stained, and marked with rusty symbols. It had to be the length of the ship itself, but was no more than the width of a hand. She said nothing, just pulled the cloth in after her, now sodden from the wet decks, and plopped herself down next to a brazier that emitted feeble heat.

"The third time," Quinn continued, "I used the same crew we have now, and on the voyage to Eris I managed to keep the ship from sinking, although we did have to replace both masts, the bow, the rudder, and the entire port side. Leaving was another matter. The ship was laden with costly goods and six passengers, including the Regis and his family."

"Regis?" I asked Hallow in a whisper. "The king?"

"More or less, yes."

"Dexia was the only one of the family who survived, and then only because she was…different."

She grinned, showing all of her teeth.

"The ship sank, and Dex and I were rescued by the people of the northernmost island, Breakfront. And that's when I discovered that the islands disturb the magnetic properties of the storm."

"How can that be?" I asked at the same time Idril said, "That seems unbelievable."

"I could never lie to you, my sweet, silky one," Quinn told her in a voice that was borderline fawning.

Dexia made a face and gave her long streamer of stained cloth a quick jerk so that it slapped against the back of Idril's chair with a wet, nasty noise.

"As for your question—" Quinn's shoulders lifted. "I don't know the why of it, Lady Allegria. I simply know that the men of Breakfront said the reason we survived was because the storm blew us to the south, rather than to the east, where we had originally set course. In answer to your earlier question, the governor—for a fee—allows unwary captains to use his islands as a way to enter Eris."

"And?" I asked.

His lips thinned. "None have ever made it back but me."

We were all silent for a few minutes, taking in our doomed futures.

"I've consulted Exodius's journals during our voyage," Hallow said finally. "He had little to say about the Maquet Islands other than that the inhabitants were said to possess an uncanny ability to see in the dark, but there was a brief description of the islands, and the strange property of the iron that is found there. Exodius speculated that since iron was the antithesis of Nezu, the point where the island chain pierced the storms disrupted the protection he put in place to guard the Shadowborn."

"Nezu," I murmured, trying to remember where I'd heard that name.

"The god of the Shadowborn," Hallow told me.

"They have their own god? I assumed they must be Bellias's children, the same as the Starborn."

"I thought so, too, but Exodius had a brief note describing a tale he'd heard from a traveler about Nezu, stating that the god protects Eris by means of the storms. Supposedly, when Kiriah Sunbringer smote Alba with her fire, Nezu protected his people by casting them into perpetual shade, where Kiriah's rays could not reach."

I stared at him in horror, fear crawling up my arms and back. "You mean—you're not saying that Kiriah doesn't reach Eris?"

"My heart, do not look so stricken." Hallow turned to take me in his arms, his body a haven of peace in a world that was filled with fear and confusion. "You are Kiriah's chosen whether or not you believe she has turned her back on you. You have been favored by her in the past, and so you will be in the future. You will be fine in Eris."

"I hope so, because if not…"

I didn't complete the sentence since at that moment, a crewman alerted Quinn that the ship was approaching the harbor.

"It's up to you," Quinn said, looking at Hallow and me. "Should we take on supplies, then turn around to return to Aryia, or leave off Lady Idril—not that I wish to be parted from you, my beauteous one, but like the others, I would be loath to see your graceful and delicious form destroyed—and hand over a hefty fee to the governor in order to make a run for Eris?"

I peeled myself off Hallow's chest to meet his gaze. "What do you think?" he asked.

Idril sat stiffly, but her golden gaze was liquid with an inner fire. I bit back the demand that we put her ashore and gave Hallow a little nod. "I don't think there is any other path for us to try."

He smiled, the warmth and love in his eyes making me feel as if I was filled with Kiriah's fire. "To Eris, captain."

"You'll be wanting this, then," Dexia said, rising and dragging her soggy length of fabric with her. She plopped part of it on my lap.

"Your suman?" I asked, remembering the name she'd given the item she'd been working on for the last five days.

"It isn't mine, it's yours. Well, I'll use a bit of it, but the bulk of it is for you." She shot a sour look toward Idril. "I wasn't aware the white witch was going to need protection, too, but I suppose if you all stand close, it will work."

"What in the name of Bellias is that—" Hallow started to say, but I simply grabbed up the cloth, winding it in a tidy coil.

An hour later, after bleak declarations of our demise from the governor of the Maquet Islands, we received permission to sail close to shore along the chain of rocky islets.

"Right. Well, since your minds are made up, would you prefer to stay here, or join me on deck?" Quinn asked, his expression now black, without the slightest hint of humor.

"Deck," Hallow and I said at the same time; we were both tired of huddling together in Quinn's cabin.

"It's raining," Idril complained, but followed us when we all trooped out after Quinn.

"Where should we use your suman?" I asked Dexia before she scampered toward the tallest mast, no doubt heading to the crow's nest.

She pointed to the forward mast.

"Thank you," I told her, and drew a blessing on her. She shied just as I completed the blessing, leaving it floating on the air before it dissolved into nothing.

"Kiriah has no love for me," she told me, and started climbing upward.

I bit back the comment that I knew just how she felt.

"What exactly is a suman?" Hallow asked, an audible thread of worry in his voice. I know he was trying to remain calm for my benefit, but I was strangely at peace.

"Magic woven into cloth used to protect the wearer. Hold it for a minute, will you? I want to make sure Buttercup is comfortable before we hit the storm."

"I'll come with you," he said, and we spent a few minutes in the close, dimly lit hold, where a few goats, a handful of chickens and geese, and Buttercup and Penn were stabled.

"This is going to be rough," I told Buttercup, whispering into her ear as I risked a bite to give her a hug. "If the worst happens, I will see you in the spirit world. You may not be the best mule who ever lived, but you are my favorite."

She snorted snot on my back, clunking her head against mine when I released her, which I took as her way of telling me she loved me, too. I untied her lead, just in case that made it easier for her to maintain her balance, and found Hallow blinking back tears as he patted Penn.

"You're just as soft as I am when it comes to animals," I told him, my admiration for him going up yet another notch.

"More so, I fear. Are you ready for this?" he asked, taking my face in both of his hands. "We can change our course. We can wait for Lord Israel."

"And risk losing Deo and the queen?" I closed my eyes for a moment, then shook my head. "I can't, Hallow. I'm the reason they are there."

"You're not, but I will admire you to the end of time if for no other reason than you would risk everything to save them." He kissed me on my nose and then pulled me up the stairs to the upper deck.

I don't know how long it took us to sail past the small clutch of islands that made up Maquet and reach the storms, I only know that by that time we were wet, cold, and tired of being tied together, the three of us bound to the base of the mast by the suman that Dexia had created.

All the ghosts had come up to watch as we sailed so close to the shore of the northernmost island of Breakfront that we almost came to grief twice. Ahead of us, an ebony miasma blotted the sky, dark storm clouds hanging over it, flashes of light, and occasional branches of lightning illuminating what appeared to be a solid bank of wind, water, and the fury of Alba herself.

And we were sailing right into it.

"This nasty cloth is supposed to save us how?" Idril yelled over the howl of the wind. We stood on either side of Hallow, both of us clinging to him, Idril with her cloak hood up to protect her delicate self, while my cloak had wrapped itself back around the mast, leaving me exposed to the rain that lashed us like whips.

"It's magic." I pulled a thick clump of hair from my mouth and shouted across Hallow's Adam's apple. "Dexia says it will protect us."

"It's disintegrating as we speak," Idril argued, turning to snuggle tighter into Hallow.

I made a face, but couldn't blame her. He was strong and warm despite being soaked to the skin by the storm flying around us, and just being plastered up against him made me feel infinitely better.

"From what I understand of such things, that's the magic working," Hallow said, his eyes so narrowed they were only slits of dark blue as he stared into the oncoming storm. "It is consumed by the act of protecting us. Which means, my heart, I'm going to need my right hand free."

"Why?" I asked his wet, salty neck, pressing a kiss to it, and sending a little prayer to the twin goddesses to please help see us through this trial.

"Because that's the hand I draw protection bubbles with. If you would just move slightly—no, not away from me. Here, across my chest. That's better." He shifted slightly, pulling me into position. Despite the storm, despite our almost certain imminent deaths, I managed to shoot a look of pure cattiness across him to Idril. She made a face in return and tugged her hood down so that it completely covered her head.

Quinn shouted orders from the ship's wheel that were almost immediately lost in the wind. But his cry of, "We're for it now, my lovelies! Brace yourselves, and may the goddesses have mercy upon us all!" reached us just as the ship, sailing parallel to the island, turned slightly and pointed toward the tip of a long spit of land that stretched across the storm barrier. The bow pierced the thick miasma of wind, rain, and magnetic charge, and we were slammed back against the mast.

A wall of needle-like points hit me, screaming in my ears and eyes and body, until it tore away bits of me, sending the shredded pieces of flesh flying into the chaos, leaving nothing but bleached white bone and misery.

Chapter 13

It was the voices that poked little holes of awareness through the thick layers of cotton wool that seemed to envelope Hallow in a warm, slightly rocking embrace. He nuzzled his face into the warmth, the scent found within tantalizingly just out of reach of his memory. It was something pleasant, something that he associated with the top of a cliff, one with a green field filled with yellow flowers that bowed and waved under the afternoon amber light of Kiriah.

Allegria. The scent was Allegria, and he smiled into the cotton wool, pleased that if he had passed into the spirit world with her, at least the scent that clung to her physical form had gone with them.

"—don't appreciate you touching him. He's not yours to touch." The woman who spoke was as familiar as the scent, but as his mind was at that moment consumed with considering just how much he enjoyed Allegria, how he planned to greet her, and what suggestions he'd make for their life together in the spirit world, he didn't give it too much of his attention.

"He saved us with that bubble thing he did. I owe him my gratitude." That was the voice of another woman, also known to him. Less pleasing that the first, but familiar nonetheless.

"That doesn't give you the right to put your hands all over him. And stop trying to take off his jerkin! If anyone gets to touch his naked chest, I do. He's mine."

"Your what? You know, I think it's quite telling that you married him, and yet you don't ever refer to him as your husband."

"That's because husbands can be refuted and divorced, as you well know, whereas what Hallow and I have will never be sundered."

Hallow smiled at the acid archness in the last sentence. "Never, my heart. You are as vital to me as breathing is. Or was, rather."

"Hallow! You're awake at last! Does anything hurt? You have a big bump on the back of your head, but all the rest of you seems unharmed."

"I helped check," Idril said indignantly. It had to be Idril to make Allegria growl softly to herself. "As much as the mad priest let me."

He opened his eyes to find Allegria bending down over him, her nose bumping against his, those lovely black eyes with the gold flecks filled with concern. "I don't hurt anywhere but my head, and you, my darling wife, are the very best thing in this new world of ours."

"New world?" Her nose scrunched up in a wholly delightful manner. She pulled back so she could gently feel the back of his head. "Kiriah's ten blessed toes, that blow scrambled your brain."

"That's just perfect. Here we are trapped on Eris with no boat—"

"It's a ship, love," Quinn said as he stumbled past Hallow, dragging a waterlogged chest behind him.

"Ship," Idril continued without pause. "And now both the priest and the arcanist are mentally unhinged. I see I shall have to take charge of this journey. Luckily, I am quite excellent at making plans. Now, let me see... if we leave Hallow and his wife here, Quinn, you and I should be able to make quick work of finding the queen."

"Find the queen?" Allegria asked, frowning. "Why would we do that— not that you are taking charge of this expedition. Hallow and I will decide what is to be done. Stowaways have no say in plan-making."

"The queen is the answer to it all," Idril said with lofty disregard for Allegria's statement. "Where she is, Deo is sure to be."

Hallow felt as if he was about five minutes behind everyone else, conversationally speaking. "We're on Eris?" He sat up, wincing as his head throbbed at the movement, and glanced around, his eyes widening at the sight of lush, broadleaf plants that bobbed in the breeze. The light was strange here, reminding him of the times when Kiriah and Bellias drew together for the briefest of moments, leaving the land in varying shades of darkness. "We didn't die?"

Allegria brushed a strand of hair back from his forehead in a gentle caress. "We're very much alive, thanks to your fast thinking, Dexia's suman, and Quinn's cleverness in hugging the shore."

"You could have put me first on that list," Quinn said, staggering past them in the opposite direction from which he'd come.

"I said you were clever," Allegria yelled after him, getting to her feet.

Hallow carefully turned his head, noting through the odd twilight that he was located on a sandy beach that glittered a dull gold, deepening to brown where the waves lapped it. Beyond the shore, he could just barely make out a dense line of storm on the horizon. "By the goddesses, we made it!" he exclaimed. "I hate to admit that I didn't think it was possible, but... well, I was wrong. Wonderfully so."

"Stay there and let your head rest," Allegria said, shooting Idril a warning look before she hurried off after Quinn. Hallow turned his body so that he could see the sharp, black shapes that stabbed upward into the dusky sky. It took him a moment before he realized that they were what remained of the ship.

"She's very jealous," Idril said in a conversational voice, and eyed him thoughtfully. "I must admit I don't see why. You're certainly talented, and I'm extremely grateful that you are as learned as you are, because despite what Quinn said, I don't think we would have survived simply by sailing close to an island—"

Quinn, who had been approaching with an armful of wet gowns that Hallow assumed belonged to Idril, stopped, looked indignant, and dropped the gowns onto the sand before spinning on his heel and marching back to the ship.

"—so I can see that she values you for those abilities, but judging by the noises that emerged with regularity from your cabin, there must be more to you than meets the eye." Her gaze dropped to where his jerkin covered his groin. "Much, much more. Perhaps, since the mad priest didn't bother to check your lower limbs for injury, I should do so now."

With the knowledge that Allegria would again be likely to make references to gelding should she find Idril attempting to examine him for supposed hurts, Hallow managed to scramble to his feet just as his wife emerged from the ship's watery shadow. He stumbled toward her, calling, "Penn! And Buttercup! I am mightily pleased to see you both."

"Stay away from Buttercup," Allegria warned, releasing the lead rope on Penn so that the horse could go to him. "She's a bit annoyed about the ship sinking while she was still on it—stop that! Don't you even think of lifting a hoof to me, you monstrous beast. You're not harmed in the least bit, and Quinn has already found your grain barrel, so you can stop pretending that you're a heroine who starves to death in a tragic tale."

Hallow ran his hands quickly over Penn, suffered the horse to snuffle his hair and bump him several times in the chest before he led him close to where Allegria had tethered Buttercup.

By the time they had pulled from the wreckage all that was salvageable and lit a fire to both give them warmth and light as the dusk turned to inky blackness, Hallow's head felt much clearer.

"So the bubble spell worked," he said some time later, when they were all clustered around the fire clutching cups of warmed, spiced wine. Hallow sat on a driftwood log, while Allegria made herself comfortable on the sand, leaning back against both him and the log. "I wasn't sure if it could protect us against the magnetic elements of the storm. I'm pleased to know it did, though, and will need to take notes about our experiences so I may share them with other arcanists."

"Are we to stay the night here?" Idril asked, looking around with distaste. She'd managed to spread her garments upon all the broadleaf shrubs that marked the boundary between what appeared to be particularly fertile ground and the beach. "If Bellias graces us with a moon, we should be able to start our journey to Skystead."

"Skystead?" Allegria asked just as Hallow slid a hand into his jerkin to reassure himself that the oiled silk envelope he'd placed there prior to sailing into the storm was safe. He was loath to lose the few sheets of information arcanists had gathered about Eris.

"That is the Shadowborn capital city, where Dasa and Deo are likely being kept," Hallow told her, then addressed Idril's statement with a little shake of his head. "Bellias may send a full moon to the zenith point in the night sky, but we wouldn't see it any more than we will be blessed by Kiriah Sunbringer. I am not a fearful man, but even I would hesitate to set off in a dangerous land filled with Harborym with only a few lanterns to light our path. We will wait until morning for what light the god Nezu grants us before we proceed."

"We must leave now," Idril argued, getting to her feet. "You heard Lord Israel say that he could feel the clouds drawing over Dasa. The danger to her and Deo might already be upon them. We have no time to sleep."

She gave the last word a full serving of contempt, but Hallow remained unmoved. "It would be folly to go without some light. We have no idea where Skystead is. We will likely find small settlements and towns before we reach the capital, and I do not relish running headlong into Harborym camps."

"Why do you want to reach the queen so badly?" Allegria asked. "You claim it's Deo you're worried about, so why go to the queen first?"

"Because she is the reason he is here," Idril said with a note of impatience in her voice.

"And if they aren't together?" Allegria asked.

Idril gave a slight shrug. "It matters not. We must find her. Deo will be most intractable unless the queen is with us."

Hallow had his own opinion about that, but kept it to himself.

Allegria, on the other hand, nodded. "He can be stupidly stubborn about things."

"And that is why we must move now. There is no time to waste," Idril said with a derisive yet ladylike snort. She turned to Quinn. "You agree with me, surely."

"I'm afraid, my glorious one, that in this, I am with Hallow and Allegria. A night's rest will give us the strength to tackle whatever we find in the light that is granted to us with dawn."

Idril made a disgusted noise, and turning, snatched up some of her gowns, rolling them and stuffing them into a satchel.

"Which brings up the question, Quinn, of whether or not the crew will accompany us. Will we just have Dexia and you?" Allegria asked him, smothering a yawn.

The captain, who was reclining on one of the few dry blankets that he'd seen fit to thrust into a barrel and seal before the ship passed into the storm, waved his wooden goblet in the air, his gaze firmly affixed to Idril's back as she gathered her things. "The crew has returned to the spirit world."

"Blast. They would have been useful," she answered.

"And to that point...now that I've brought you safely to Eris, my obligation to you is fulfilled, and thus, I am no longer at your beck and call. In other words, I'm all yours, sweetheart." The last sentence was spoken to Idril, who turned to look back at him, but said nothing.

"Well...we're grateful you got us here, of course," Allegria said, slanting a look up at Hallow before leaning into his leg. "But I assumed you were with us for the whole thing. Finding Deo and Dasa, that is. Your abilities—and Dexia's, even if she is a bit scary—would be very welcome to us."

Hallow's gaze rose to the crotch of a short, stunted tree where Dexia had curled up. Only the occasional glint of firelight reflecting in her dark eyes could be seen in the blackness that had swallowed the land. He made a mental note to have a long talk with the vanth about the history and creation of the suman.

Quinn sent Idril another look of mingled adoration and blatant lust. "That depends on what she who holds my heart decrees."

"Indeed," Idril took the blanket Quinn had placed on a barrel for her, and said, "Since I am once again being forbidden to do as I desire, I will remove to a location further down the beach. I expect that a dawn start is agreeable to all."

"Let me help you make a comfortable bed," Quinn called after her, quickly scrambling to his feet and picking up his own blanket.

"I'd rather sleep with that repulsive wad of seaweed," Idril told him in a scathing tone, turning and marching off to settle herself a little way down the beach.

Quinn sighed to himself, then drained his goblet. "She's just a bit prickly, and will no doubt be more agreeable in the morning. Since I can see you two want to be alone—although again, I'm happy to share in the action should your tastes swing that way—I will go make my bed in what remains of my cabin."

He snatched up the jug of wine and hurried off whistling tunelessly, disappearing into the blackness that lurked outside the circle of their fire.

"And so we are alone," Hallow told Allegria, sliding off the log to sit on the sand next to her. "Shall we make use of the two blankets that the captain has kindly provided us?"

Allegria said nothing for several seconds, her brow furrowed in thought. He leaned over to nibble on her ear. "Wife?"

"Hmm? Oh, no, I don't think so. Not with Dexia there, and who knows how long it will take before Quinn realizes that Idril has no interest in him. He might come wandering back just as we were enjoying ourselves. Plus, I don't have a lot of faith in two blankets keeping prying eyes from seeing me ravish you the way I wish to. I didn't feel Kiriah, Hallow. When we landed. Not at all."

He told his libido to take the night off, and gravely considered her obvious distress, taking her hand to rub a thumb over her fingers. They were calloused and had occasional faded marks of old scars, but he loved her hands almost as much as she claimed she loved his crow's feet. Her hands could dance in the air, weaving together the most complex patterns of light, and a moment later wield swords and bow with deadly accuracy. "You fill my heart, my soul, my life," he said, overcome with emotion, no doubt due to their close brush with death. "And if you never again feel Kiriah's touch, you will continue to do so, but it is deep night here. More than deep night, yet I can barely feel Bellias's presence."

"But to not feel Kiriah here at all..." She stopped for a few seconds, her voice thick when she continued. "Hallow, what if I never again feel her presence? What if she is done with me? Utterly, completely done with me?"

"I doubt that would happen."

"But what if it does?" Her lovely dark eyes searched his, and he felt the depths of her pain.

He could have assured her that she would never be stripped of Kiriah's blessing, but he disliked lying, especially to her. So he said the only thing he could. "There is time enough to worry when we know that Kiriah is utterly out of your reach. In the meantime, you have your swords and bow. You are not helpless, my heart—far from it. You are an able and deadly warrior even without your magic."

"But if we have no magic, how are we to fight the Harborym?" she asked, her gaze still searching his, looking for answers he feared he did not have. "You know how powerful they are, and here, surrounded as they are by chaos magic...I shudder to think how much stronger they will have become."

"We, too, have grown stronger since the battle of Starfall City," he pointed out. "You have practiced swordplay, and I have learned much from the arcanists and Thorn, not to mention the documents that Exodius obviously left behind for my edification. We are a formidable pair, Allegria. The Harborym will not best us."

Allegria was silent again, obviously working through her doubts and worries. He held her, breathing in the pleasant combination of her flowery scent and that of the ocean, until she relaxed against him, her breathing deepening as she slipped into sleep.

Without wakening her, he lifted one hand and tried to summon a ball of arcany, pulling from the sky the light he knew glittered from star to star.

His palm remained empty.

Chapter 14

"In general," I told Buttercup as I ran a somewhat bent currycomb over her glossy hide, "I am not the sort of person who keeps her feelings to herself. I don't suffer in silence, something that used to get me in a lot of trouble back at the temple, but that's not really of concern now. What *does* matter is the fact that it's evidently dawn, and I can't feel Kiriah Sunbringer."

Buttercup, chomping happily from a battered tin bucket, swished her tail. I looked into the distance, not seeing the dense foliage that ran along the shore, my gaze turned inward as once again, I reached for the familiar warmth that always filled me with its golden presence.

I stretched out a hand, trying to summon Kiriah's strength. Heat tickled my palm, and I opened my eyes in delight, only to feel my joy fade.

"This is disappointing," I said, cupping my hand around where Buttercup was breathing on it. "I can't even summon up so much as a small light rabbit, and never, since the time I was six summers old, have I been unable to summon up light animals. This is a dire warning of what lies ahead for me, indeed."

I looked over Buttercup's bobbing head. Hallow had gone to fetch Idril while Quinn and Dexia gathered up their packs. By our best guess, the sun had risen beyond the dense cloud cover, and we needed to be on our way. After expressing my concerns the night before, I didn't want to beat Hallow over the head with my worry, but it sat within me like a hard kernel of pain and sorrow.

"And I dislike keeping anything from him…but on the other hand, he'll just tell me how able I am without my lightweaving, and that's frustrating on all levels. Here. Eat this." I dumped another handful of grain into

Buttercup's bucket, and before she could protest, had a saddle on her back, and the cinch tightened as far as she'd let it go.

"Are you ready?" Quinn asked, approaching a few minutes later. He gave Buttercup's rear quarters a wide berth, eyeing her in a manner that bespoke someone who'd been within range of her back hooves. "Dexia has gone off to feed, but she will return any minute."

"Feed? Feed on what?" I asked, then immediately regretted the question when I remembered her sharp little teeth. "Never mind. Pretend I didn't ask."

"It's really better if you don't." He nodded his agreement, his gaze straying down over my chest, but for once the leer that he usually seemed to wear whenever he looked at those parts was not present. He looked confused by my old black Bane of Eris tunic embroidered with gold and silver. "You bear a sun and moon insignia, and yet I know of no one else who has both the blessing of Kiriah and Bellias."

"That's because you haven't met Deo." I traced the symbol, the memory of my time as a Bane of Eris strong in my mind. "I was so hopeful then," I murmured, feeling as if I'd aged a hundred years instead of just one. "I was so sure that with Deo, I could bring peace to Alba, and yet all that we did was slow down the Harborym…"

"That is no small feat," Quinn said lightly.

I shook away the shadows that accompanied memories of that time and busied myself strapping my bow and what remained of my possessions to Buttercup's saddle. "It came at a great cost, though," I answered, and slid my swords into place, crossed over my back.

Quinn said nothing, just turned when Hallow called out a question while running toward us along the beach.

"Not since last night," Quinn answered. "When I went to check that she was comfortable, she told me that she preferred her own company, so I left her. I thought it might be her woman's time," he added in a confiding voice as Hallow, breathless, stopped in front of us. "My third wife—or was it the fourth?—one of them turned into a demon when it was her woman's time unless I brought her plentiful sweets and the syrup of the moonflower. That made her sleep, but it was a blessing considering the way she could tear the hide off a man with just her tongue."

Hallow, panting, caught his breath enough to stop Quinn's reminiscences. He turned to me. "Have you seen Idril?"

"No. Is she not at her camp?"

"She is not. And her things are gone." He closed his eyes for a moment. "Again, I find myself wishing I had Thorn…or a spell to find a missing woman. Kiriah blast her, she's gone off alone to find Deo. Or the queen. Or both."

"She wouldn't be that foolish, would she?" I asked, watching as he hurriedly filled his saddlebags, one with the book that had made it through the ship's breakup, while the other was stuffed with clothing and a few weapons. "We told her how dangerous it was to try to make her way while it was dark, and we had no knowledge of where we were."

He cocked an eyebrow at me. "Do you honestly think that would stop her from doing exactly what she wanted to do?"

I had to admit he had a point. Which was why, ten minutes later, we set out following what tracks Hallow could discover. Her footprints led inland, as we expected, along a game trail that wound through dense foliage for a good mile before the path started to climb, and the squat, broadleaf plants became sparser and sparser, replaced by thick-trunked short trees with short, stabbing needles.

Dexia caught up to us shortly after we set off, but said nothing, although at one point when I glanced behind me, I saw her talking with great animation to Quinn, her little hands flying as she spoke.

A few hours later we reached what had once clearly been a road. It had been paved, but was now nothing but broken stones pushed up and aside by clumps of grass and weeds.

"And here ends Idril's trail. Which way do you think she would have gone? Dexia, do you know this area?" Hallow asked, looking up and down the road. "I don't see any signs of her passing."

Dexia shook her head. "I'm a vanth. My home is in the Bleeding Woods in the far north. I haven't been anywhere in the south except Skystead itself."

I wanted to ask her what bled in the woods of her homeland, but decided it was better not to know. Instead, I dismounted and handed Hallow Buttercup's reins. For a short while I followed the road that curved southward, my eyes on the weeds and grass. Shaking my head, I retraced my steps and went in the opposite direction, where the road twisted around to the northwest. "There," I said, pointing where a small weed had been crushed. "And there. It may have been someone else, but this looks like a fairly fresh break. Someone went this way."

"I can't imagine there are many travelers here," Hallow said, his voice soft. The vegetation had given way to a few trees, many of which appeared to be scorched, and scrubby shrubs and grasses that clearly had undergone a long drought. The whole area had a hushed feel to it, as if the land itself was holding its breath to see who we were, and what we intended to do.

"Which doesn't explain the feeling I have that we're being watched."
I rubbed the back of my neck, searching the horizon, but saw no reason
for the unwelcome sensation. I took the reins and proceeded to lead
Buttercup, letting her have a break from the task of carrying me around.
Since Quinn and Dexia had no mount, I felt somewhat guilty riding while
they trudged behind us.

But it was the sense of something about to happen that kept my bow
within reach. I was painfully aware of just how quickly the Harborym could
attack, and we knew nothing about how the native Shadowborn people
would view our intrusion. We walked for another hour before cresting
a hill. Below us lay what must have once been a fertile valley, but now
appeared brown and yellow in the dim light. A town spilled down the foot
of the hill...or what remained of it.

"That looks abandoned," I said, quickly scanning the twisted and burned
remains of buildings. Only a few walls stood upright, and those were badly
damaged. "I wonder what happened here. An attack, do you think?"

"Possibly. Probably. Does that...is that what I think it is?" He pointed at
the base of the largest building. We approached it, my eyes first narrowing,
then widening as I saw the red stain that seemed to leach through the one
standing wall.

I recognized it immediately. Hallow clutched a long, wickedly sharp
dagger while I pulled my swords from the sheaths.

"Why are you arming yourselves?" Quinn asked in a harsh whisper,
glancing around us wildly. One hand was on the scimitar that was always
at his side. "Do you see someone?"

"Something," I said, pointing at the red seeping through the wall
of the building.

"Blood?" he asked, looking around nervously. "Are we about to be
attacked? Does the arcanist have more of those protective bubbles? Because
my death going through the storm was prolonged and painful, and just
once I'd like to live through a death without it hurting so much."

"Not blood, chaos magic," I corrected, and quickly tied Buttercup's reins
to Penn's saddlebags. Penn, unlike my obstinate mule, was well trained,
and would not budge from a spot where Hallow let the reins drop. "Maybe
you should stay here," I told Dexia when Quinn and Hallow disappeared
around the standing wall.

"Why?" she asked, looking curious.

I was about to tell her that she was too small to fight in case there were
Harborym within the destroyed village, but the memory of her attacking
soldiers in Jalas's keep rose to mind. "To protect the animals and our

things," I said quickly, and before she could protest, hurried off after the two men, my swords gripped tightly.

I found Hallow squatting on a bit of floor that was still intact, touching a stain on the floor with one finger. He snatched his hand back as soon as he'd done so, muttering an oath under his breath. "It's definitely chaos magic. And it's still very potent."

All three of us turned to examine the blackened remains of the buildings. This had evidently been a small village, with a cluster of four houses, one larger structure that must have been a mill since it straddled a broad stream, and another two-storey building that was now utterly reduced to rubble. There were no sounds but the crying of a few distant gulls.

"There are no chickens, no dogs, nothing," I said softly. "Everyone must have been killed."

"Not everyone," Hallow said in a pleasantly bland tone, turning to face the left. "There are at least two people behind the last building on the right. No, don't look. We'll stroll this way and see if we can't lure them into the open. Put away your swords, my heart. Whoever it is would have to be insane to approach you armed, and I very much want to talk to them."

"Not Harborym, then," Quinn said, but with a studied air of nonchalance, sheathed his sword, and puffing out his cheeks in a tuneless whistle, sauntered to the left toward a fallow field.

"No. I only had a quick glimpse, but it looked like two women."

Hallow and I followed Quinn, pausing to examine the burned houses just as if we were only mildly interested in what had happened. By the time we reached the last structure, we disappeared behind a blackened bit of wall that stuck upward as if it was an accusatory finger pointing to the twin goddesses.

Two minutes later, a shadow fell across us, and before the woman had a chance to do more than gasp, Hallow grasped one of her arms, pulling her forward. A smaller form followed, and Quinn grabbed her as well, but quickly released her when the woman cried out.

"It's all right, no one is going to hurt you or… your daughter?" Hallow asked, keeping a firm grip on the woman lest she run away. She'd shrunk against the wall, clutching the slighter form of a girl of about twelve. Both females had the bronze hair that Hallow had told me was common to the Shadowborn, but while the older female had skin so pale it was almost bluish, her child's complexion had a reddish tint that reminded me of the Harborym.

"You're not…you're not priests?" the woman gasped, her eyes dilated with fear as she looked from Hallow to me.

"A priest?" Hallow's brows pulled together. "You have priests here? For the god Nezu?"

"No, blood priests. They honor the old magic. You're not priests?" the woman asked again.

"I'm a priest, but I honor the goddess Kiriah Sunbringer," I said in a soothing voice, smiling in order to show them we meant no harm. "My name is Allegria. This is Hallow, who leads a group of arcanists, and the other man is Quinn, the captain who brought us here."

"Captain?" The woman's look of fear turned to amazement. "You sailed here? To Eris?"

"Quinn is a very capable man, and Hallow has many skills," I said, giving her another friendly smile.

The woman turned from me to Hallow, studying him for a minute; then she nodded. "I can see now you have not been tainted by the red magic. You look...different."

"We are from other lands," Hallow told her. "Allegria and I come from Aryia, while Quinn hails from Genora, land of the Starborn."

"There are other lands?" She was back to looking amazed again, then shook her head, and said softly to herself, "I thought I must have imagined the other."

"The other? You've seen someone like us?" I asked, hopeful that Idril had stopped here.

"Not like you," she said, eyeing me, her gaze resting for a moment on my forehead before nodding to Hallow. "But there was a woman at dawn with hair the same color as yours. Old Gerald said she asked for directions to Skystead, but I thought he was wandering again." She tapped her head. "In his mind."

"Old Gerald has many fancies." The girl spoke for the first time. "He sees faces in the trees, and says that one day, the blood on the moon will bring salvation. I've never seen the moon. Mama says she saw it once a long time past, when she was very small, before the coming of...them."

"The blood priests?" Hallow asked, letting go of the woman's arm in order to make notes in a small notebook.

"Harborym," the girl whispered, her worried gaze on her mother.

"Is Old Gerald about the place?" Quinn asked, glancing around. "The woman you saw was a friend of ours. A very lovely, if extremely stubborn, friend, and we'd very much like to make sure she hasn't been harmed by going off on her own."

"He is likely drunk, sleeping it off in the old mill," the woman said, jerking her head toward the remains of a once large structure. "Ave, run home while I escort this lady and the men to the mill."

"You live here?" I asked when the girl hesitated. "It looks like the whole village was burned to the ground."

"Aye." The lines in the woman's face stood out starkly despite her pale skin. "They came hunting for us."

"For what purpose? An army?" Hallow asked, tucking away his notebook.

The woman shook her head and moved past him toward the stream. A narrow plank had been thrown across the sluggish, brown water, which she quickly crossed. "It is said Lord Racin sought men and women for a special honor, to become part of an elite fighting force, but no one has ever remembered seeing such a force. When the men of our village objected, Racin's forces attacked, destroying everything. Ave and I escaped by hiding in the root cellar, but my husband…"

Without thinking about it, I drew a blessing over her when her voice choked to a halt, but despite knowing Kiriah was above the dense clouds that blocked her from us, the blessing refused to materialize.

"I'm so sorry," I said, frowning at Hallow when he made another note in his book. He looked guilty and stuffed it back inside his jerkin. "That must have been horrible to witness. The Harborym have killed many in our lands, as well, including Hallow's family. How long ago was the attack? The chaos magic appears to be recent."

She paused, glancing back at us. "You know about the evil ones' magic?"

"Very much so."

Hallow added, "We helped drive them from our lands, and we both have experience of just how…potent…chaos magic can be."

She shook her head sadly. "It is almost as bad as the blood magic of the Old Ones. This way. There is a cellar where Old Gerald has made his home."

We half slid down a muddy slope into the broken remains of a cellar. The stone cogs that once turned the mill still remained, but the rest of the building had been destroyed, leaving only shattered beams, crumbled stone, and dust everywhere. In the middle of it, propped up against the biggest cog, an old man lay snoring, an empty skin once most likely containing wine or ale still clutched in his hand.

It took us a while to wake him, and longer still before we got news of Idril.

"Gone north, she has," Old Gerald said, absentmindedly scratching his privates.

We took notes on the route Gerald said he'd told Idril to follow, then Hallow asked, "We seek the whereabouts of two other friends—a woman named Dasa, and a man named Deo. Have you heard of them, too?" Gerald's rheumy eyes were focused on the skin of wine that Hallow casually let dangle from his fingers. Gerald licked his lips and said, "The one who destroyed half of the keep in Skystead? Aye, the men of the village talked of him. Taken away to the red hand temple to the west, he was. Er...a fellow gets powerful thirsty recalling such things. Powerful thirsty. You wouldn't be willing to share that skin, now, would you?"

Hallow handed over the skin without protest, and a short time later we left Gerald guzzling happily from it.

"Idril's going to be annoyed when she finds out Deo was banished to a temple, and isn't in Skystead," I commented as we headed back toward where we'd left Dexia and the animals.

"That's assuming she is in Skystead," Hallow pointed out. "I wish Gerald had more information, but I suppose we were lucky to get what we did out of him."

We'd worked out a plan by the time we returned to Dexia.

"I regret we can't give you a mount," Hallow told Quinn. "But Penn doesn't like carrying two, and I doubt if Buttercup would allow herself to be parted from Allegria."

"Goddesses forbid the very thought of that monster coming with us," Quinn said, shouldering his pack. "Dex and I don't mind walking, do we?"

"Depends," the girl said, wiping her nose with the back of her hand, her uncanny eyes assessing him. "Where are we walking?"

"We are going after Lady Idril. I told Hallow and Allegria that since they were urgently needed to rescue Lord Deo, we will find Lady Idril and make sure no harm befalls her."

Dexia made the exact face that I expected, looking mildly disgusted. "All right, but if we see any Harborym, I get to feed on them."

"And have you ingesting their chaos magic?" Quinn gently buffeted her head. "Not on my unbreakable life. You can kill them, but no feeding." He looked up, meeting Hallow's eyes. "May the twin goddesses grant you favor, arcanist. I fear you're going to need it."

"And the same to you," Hallow said politely while I once again tried to draw a blessing, this time on Quinn. It refused to be drawn just as the other had, leaving me feeling as if I had been shut away in a dark room.

Quinn and Dexia headed off to the north, following the directions the old man had given us.

"Do you think he was telling us the truth?" I asked Hallow as we rode along a narrow track that led due west.

"Old Gerald? Aye. Once you dumped that leather of cold water on him, he seemed to come out of his wine stupor. I just hope that Quinn can reach Idril before she runs into trouble."

The memory of how the Harborym had treated the people of the village was all too fresh in my mind. "She's only had a few hours' headstart on him, and since he can survive anything he finds, he should reach her before the day passes."

We rode until the shadows that clung to the land started to grow thicker and darker.

"We should probably look for a safe place to stay the night," Hallow called back to me. We were riding single file along a narrow track that wound beside an old river bed.

I was about to agree when a flash of light caught the edge of my vision. Before I had a chance to shout a warning, two black shadows rose up and knocked me off Buttercup. I heard Hallow yell something, and the scream of a horse, but it all faded away as pain burst through the side of my head, dazing me for a minute.

"Hal…" I fought the pain, trying to gather my wits and make my body respond. Hands grabbed at me, yanking me upward with fingers that felt like they were made of steel. "Hallow."

My voice came out a whisper even though I wanted to scream his name to the sky. Something was wrong with my eyes; my vision was blurry, but I desperately tried to gather power from Kiriah. If I could weave light, I could stop my attackers and find Hallow.

The seconds seem to crawl by while I was yanked forward, stumbling over rocks despite the cruel hands holding me. But with each step, slowly, my mind cleared, and although my head hurt abominably, at last my eyes focused, and I was able to look around.

My attackers weren't Harborym, as I'd expected. The two men who held me were dressed in the linen robes of priests, reddish, rusty black with a symbol of a red hand on the chest. "Who are you? Where's Hallow?" I asked, struggling against the men. I kicked out at one of my captors, twisting my body around to incapacitate him, but the man on my other side simply growled something in a voice that seemed to rake against my skin with little barbs, and my body went limp, unable to respond to my demands.

"Stop fighting," a woman's voice said from behind me. The two men were now dragging me along the riverbed, my feet colliding painfully with the rocks. "You will only hurt yourself. Not that you deserve to be unharmed, but since *he* will wish to question you, it is better if you are awake and without too much damage."

"Is this a spell?" I asked groggily, my body feeling as if I was in a vat of molasses. "What have you done to me? Who wants to question me? Where's Hallow?"

"The man who was with you? His horse spooked and ran off. But have no fear, the brothers will find him."

Panic rose within me at the thought of Hallow on his own, fighting the goddesses only knew how many men. "Brothers? Are you priests, then? Priests of..." I tried to remember what the woman at the village had said. "Blood?"

"Bring her to the tent," the woman said, striding off into the gloom. I caught only a glimpse of her silhouette before she disappeared out of view. My two captors hauled my unresisting body up the bank and through some bushes before tossing me down in front of a make-shift tent. When I managed to roll on my side, my vision filled with a brightly burning campfire, beyond which I could barely make out the dark forms of several people moving about. Dusk had changed to near night now, and if I rolled my head back, I could see the blackness seeping across the canopy of clouds.

Where was Hallow? Was he hurt? I knew he would come looking for me, no matter what his state, but would that lead him to fight with these blood priests? And if he did, would he defeat them, or was he even now in the same position as I, utterly helpless, with a head that ached, and a heart that felt incomplete because we were apart?

Chapter 15

Hallow didn't know until much later what made Penn bolt, but he assumed—rightly, as it turned out—that some magic had touched the horse, maddening him and awakening his flight instinct.

All Hallow knew was that he had been taken by surprise at both the ambush and his mount's running off into the short scrub that crept up the sloped sides of the riverbed. He had tried to turn Penn in his wild dash, but to no avail. He called to the horse, hoping his voice would calm him, but it seemed to take eons before Penn at last slowed down and allowed himself to be guided. Immediately, Hallow turned him back in the direction they'd come and sent him into another gallop, this one controlled. But either he was confused by the featureless, flat surface of the land surrounding the deep cut of the dry riverbed, or Penn had run farther than he estimated, for when he pulled up at the top of the sharp slope that led to the channel, there was no one to be seen.

"No, no, no," he said aloud, panic filling him as he urged Penn forward along the crest of the riverbed. "She can't be gone. Allegria!"

His voice seemed to lift with the wind, evaporating into nothing. Swearing to himself and growing more worried with each passing second, he searched both the riverbed and the land above it, desperate for signs of his beloved, or the group of marauders who had sprung out of the shadows. Due to the dim light, he wasn't able to see far into the distance, but heavier shadows on the land to the north hinted at other channels like the one he had been following.

"She could be in any one of them," he said, his heart sick. Which direction would she have gone? Was she captured, or pursuing their attackers? "There's no doubting her bravery," he said aloud, looking first in one direction, then another. "But she's not foolish, and she wouldn't chase attackers on her own. No, Penn, something happened to her while you were running like a deranged fool. The attackers must have taken her somewhere, to a settlement or camp. We're just going to have to search all the possible locations."

Thus started what turned out to be a fruitless night, one spent in frustration, anguish, and a quiet, simmering fury at anyone who dared touch his Allegria. At least he had no fear that Allegria had been taken by Harborym.

"Those were men," he told Penn some four hours later, as he dismounted to examine what turned out to be the dried blood of an animal. "Harborym are bigger. Much bigger. And they would have destroyed her on the spot, not taken her away. Bellias blast whoever they are! Where have they gone?"

Penn, who had been shaking his head and snorting once or twice, suddenly reared, almost knocking Hallow over. The horse's nostrils went wide as he scented the air.

"What is it you—" The words came to an abrupt halt when a massive form appeared at the top of the riverbank, the silhouette pausing for a moment before calling out in a guttural, harsh voice.

"Harborym," Hallow gasped and desperately clawed the air in an attempt to gather arcany. But the light from the stars could not penetrate the dense clouds of Eris, leaving him with nothing but a pale, weak ball.

Without waiting to think about it, he flung the ball of arcane light at the Harborym, then swung up into the saddle, this time not protesting when Penn leaped forward. He turned the horse so that he headed straight at the Harborym, yanking a long dagger from his boot as the horse screamed. The Harborym, a twisted parody of a man who stood a good two heads taller than most mortals, sneered, his skin glistening even in the dull light. He reached for a sword, but Penn had been trained by Lord Israel himself, and was no stranger to battle. The horse spun when he reached the Harborym soldier, slashing out with his back hooves even as Hallow twisted in the saddle, stabbing his dagger into the attacker's neck. Blood as black as Allegria's glossy hair sprayed out while the monster gargled horribly, the sword dropping from his hand. Hallow might prefer negotiations to battle, but this monstrosity would kill him—or Allegria—without a moment's hesitation, so he felt nothing but satisfacation when he snatched back the dagger and plunged it into the creature's chest where he assumed its heart was.

The Harborym gurgled a few more times, then fell over backward. Hallow, his breath ragged and rough, stared for a moment to make sure his attacker was really dead, then with a shaking hand patted Penn's neck. "You really are as brave as Allegria, my friend. Let's get out of here before we see if this thing had companions."

The area of the riverbed he was in seemed to twist and turn every few hundred feet, so he turned Penn and rode quickly up the opposite side of the bank, relief filling him at the sight of a flat, empty plain before him. "That must have been a scout on his own. Thank the goddesses, we won't have to fight any more of them without mag—"

A noise behind him had him glancing back.

Three Harborym were bearing down on him, at least a dozen more following.

Penn leaped forward in response to his yell and the pressure of his heels, while Hallow swore in a profane stream as he bent low over the horse's neck, once again desperately trying to pull arcane light down from Bellias and her stars.

The riverbed turned north just ahead of them, and Hallow, deciding that he was too exposed on the upper plain, directed Penn down into the gulley again. If the going wasn't nearly as easy for them, it would likewise slow down the Harborym.

The horse half slid down a slope of loose dirt and shale, and just as they reached the ground, another massive shape emerged from the deep shadows on the far side.

His heart gave a cry of pain at the thought of his imminent destruction at the hands of the invaders. What was he to say to Allegria when she discovered he'd died and gone to the spirit realm without her? She'd be furious, and he'd just decided to haunt her simply so they could be together when the figure paused a few feet from him, and a voice rumbled out one word. "Arcanist?"

Hallow stared, his mind unable to believe what he'd heard. "Deo?"

The shape moved forward until the dim light fell upon it. With much relief Hallow scanned the face that scowled down at him. Deo was every bit as big as the Harborym, having consumed the very same magic that gave them their power, but where their skin was red as chaos itself, Deo's had grown dusky just like Allegria's. His hair was as dark as midnight, as were his eyes, although now they glinted with ominous reddish-gold lights. Just as Hallow remembered the year before, Deo's chest was crossed in a silver harness inscribed with powerful runes. Silver cuffs were clamped on his wrists and ankles, also runed; the power in those protective devices allowing Deo to control what was for most, impossible to master.

"What are you doing here?" Deo's expression was filled with suspicion before it twisted into annoyance. "You came with my father, didn't you? I might have known he would try to ruin everything."

"No, I—"

He didn't finish the sentence, since at that moment the Harborym appeared at the top of the riverbank and paused for a minute.

Deo roared out an oath, a look of pleasure flitting across his face when he pulled a massive sword from the scabbard on his back. "Harborym! To battle!"

To Hallow's amazement, several other shadows broke free of the darkness that embraced the opposite side of the river bank. Several men clad in dark reddish-black tunics rushed past him to follow Deo when he charged the oncoming Harborym.

Hallow made a mental note as he ordered Penn out of the way of danger that each of the four men with Deo bore the symbol of a red hand. According to Exodius's notes, that implied they wielded the old magic.

But what did it mean that blood priests were working with Deo?

Hallow fought as best he could, armed only with a dagger and no arcany. One of the four men went down with a cry when the Harborym nearest him skewered him on a curved sword. Hallow and one of the others leaped at the attacker, but it was Deo who destroyed the monstrous creature.

At first Hallow didn't think Deo was using chaos magic since the runes on his harness hadn't lit up the way they used to—red or black, depending on the situation—but then Hallow realized that the soft reddish-gold glow that surrounded Deo *was* his magic…and he saw the exact second when Deo gave in to it.

The main force of the Harborym had isolated him, clearly recognizing Deo as the most dangerous of the small company, leaving two others to take care of the men in the red tunics. But when one of the men fell, Deo stiffened for a moment, then suddenly, an inhuman cry tore through the gathering darkness, and the pale gold light that glowed around him gathered for a few seconds before bursting out in a cone of dazzling brightness. The color seemed to turn white, blinding Hallow for a few seconds, but when he blinked the white blotches from his eyes, he beheld Deo standing, head down, panting, his hands fisted.

Surrounding him in a circle were the bodies of the Harborym. It was as if they'd dropped where they stood.

"What in the name of Kiriah did you do?" Hallow asked, stumbling forward as the other men stood looking as dumbfounded as Hallow felt. "That wasn't chaos."

Deo stood silent, his body language telling Hallow just how hard he was fighting to control his magic. His runes, oddly, were now so pale as to be almost white.

"Deo?" Hallow said, approaching cautiously.

"I did what needed to be done," Deo answered after another few seconds of silence. "No. No more. He is a friend. It doesn't matter—you got what you wanted. They're dead. Does it matter how they died? Stop inciting me! I will perform no more violence at your will!"

Hallow eyed Deo, remembering that just as Thorn could speak directly to him, so Deo's magic had an awareness that allowed it to speak…much to Deo's dismay. "The chaos still talks to you?" he asked.

"Aye." Deo finally lifted his head, his face showing the strain of controlling the magic within him. "It's worse now, though."

"Worse? You said that it was urging you to take revenge on everyone who ever slighted you. How could it be worse?"

"It wants me to kill every living thing." Deo turned and marched over to where his fallen soldier was being wrapped up in a cloak by the three surviving men. "That was Barnit? We will grieve for him later. Take him back to the temple, so that the priests might say their prayers for his spirit. Heath, you and Fian will come with me. It's not safe here."

"Safe," Hallow said with a snort, whistling for Penn when Deo walked toward the deepest shadows across the riverbed. "The way you killed those Harborym? I don't think any of us have anything to worry about from them."

"The danger is not from the Harborym," Deo said grimly. "It is the magic within me that is not to be trusted. Where is my father?"

"The last I saw, threatening to do heinous things to Lord Jalas unless the third moonstone was delivered to him."

Deo stopped in the act of gathering up items from what was obviously a hastily made camp. He frowned at Hallow. "He's threatening Jalas? Has he lost his wits?"

"Jalas? It's hard to say. Your father was very much in possession of his, if that's what you were implying. Jalas was being…difficult. But Lord Israel was determined to prevail."

"How did you get here if you didn't use the moonstones to open a portal?" Deo demanded. His scowl was intimidating, but Hallow, despite his worry about Allegria, was at ease. Deo might bluster, and he might have a sometimes less than reassuring grasp on his magic, but Hallow knew he had nothing to fear from the man who had embraced chaos and mastered it…most of the time.

Quickly he explained the happenings of the recent months, editing the middle part to leave out the fact that Idril had come with them since he knew if Deo found out Idril was wandering alone in Eris, he would charge off to rescue her and not focus on helping Hallow find Allegria.

"Several men attacked you? Shadowborn men?" Deo asked. "Was there a woman with them?"

Hallow was silent while he dug back through his impressions, fleeting as they were. "I don't...perhaps. There may have been a woman's voice in all the noise, but Penn can be very fast when he chooses."

"Ah." Deo waved away Hallow's concern. "That would be Mayam, then."

"And she is?"

"A serving woman from the temple where I was held prisoner. She is searching villages for my company."

"You already have a company?" Hallow couldn't believe what he was hearing, and for a moment, felt himself all sorts of irritated that he had risked Allegria's life to rescue Deo when his friend clearly needed no such help.

"Not yet, no. But I will. Mayam and her brother search for Shadowborn who have knowledge of blood magic. With them, my Banes of Eris will rise from the ashes of the Battle of the Fourth Age and destroy the Harborym and Racin once and for all." Deo eyed Hallow in a manner that made him uncomfortable. "If your arcany is useless here, you might as well be a Bane. Then at least you will be able to defend yourself."

"I don't think so," Hallow said, dismissing the idea immediately.

Deo cocked an eyebrow. "Can it be that you are afraid of chaos power while Allegria embraced it?"

"No." He tried to pick out a reason that would placate Deo without irritating him to the point that he refused to help find Allegria. He settled on the truth as being the most effective. "I am an arcanist by birth as well as by training. My mother was Starborn, just as yours was."

"Then you should handle the chaos as I do," Deo said, looking thoughtful. "You will be my lieutenant."

"An honor, I'm sure," Hallow said hurriedly before continuing, "but not possible. Not with chaos power. I'm an arcanist, Deo. I've given my life over to it. It's as much a part of my blood as chaos magic is yours. And I don't think the two would mix."

"Allegria had no issues in that regard," Deo pointed out.

"That's because as a priest she was blessed in Kiriah's eyes, so much so that she ended up channeling the goddess. I have no such protection. Bellias may gaze upon the arcanists with a benevolent eye, but we are bound to the night. Chaos is as different from the source of arcany as you are from me."

"We are more alike than you think if we both have Starborn mothers," Deo said drily, then obviously giving up the idea, called out a few orders to the other two men who were scrambling to collect the last of their gear.

Hallow stood thinking for a few moments when Deo moved off to gather his belongings. His first instinct was to go after Allegria, but he could not even protect himself, let alone her. And if her power was as adversely affected as his was, then they would have only her skills with the bow and swords to protect them both.

"Bellias damn me if I will allow it to come to that," he said grimly and reconsidered Deo's proposal.

Would the chaos power mix with the arcany that ran in his veins, or would it bring about a battle that would end in his destruction?

Deo handled it...but Deo was not an arcanist. Idly, Hallow watched one of the blood priests when the latter packed up a saddlebag, musing over the fact that the Shadowborn and Starborn were so much alike, yet the two races had progressed along very different paths. It was a shame that their blood magic was so different from that embraced by the Starborn, because he was desperate enough that he would have welcomed it if he could only find and save Allegria.

Blood magic...the words echoed in Hallow's head as he watched one of the priests.

Deo strode by, saying, "You would do better to join me, arcanist, than worry about Allegria."

"My wife matters more to me than anything in this world, or the next," Hallow said, nonetheless mounting Penn when Deo got upon a tired-looking black horse.

"Finally wed her, did you? Is she with child yet?" Deo asked in what Hallow knew was his conversational tone of voice. In any other man, it would be considered a growl.

"I did, and she is not, at least not that I know, and she would tell me if she was. Deo, much as I am pleased to see that you are not imprisoned or in any danger that I can see, I am not joining your company. I must find Allegria. You say you know the woman who captured her? Why would a serving woman abduct her?"

"I told you that Mayam is combing the nearby villages to find Shadowborn candidates. She won't kill Allegria." He thought for a moment. "Well, she might try if she thinks Allegria means me harm. She has a tenderness for me," he added.

"Allegria?" Hallow felt as if his head was whirling.

"Mayam. She wishes to become my woman." Deo rode up the side of the riverbank and turned his horse to the northwest.

"Does she know you at all?" Hallow asked before he could stop himself.

Deo's lips twitched. "Not very well."

"Deo, stop," Hallow said, pulling Penn to a halt. To his surprise—because Deo was a lot like Buttercup in that he didn't like to be given commands—Deo halted as well.

"Are there more Harborym?" Deo asked, glancing around. "If so, we will have to leave them. My magic gets obnoxiously pleased when it goads me into killing things, and I'd rather keep it under my control. Things tend to get destroyed when my control slips."

"Where is Allegria?" Hallow asked, curbing the need to shake Deo.

"I have no idea." Deo looked annoyed. "Is that why you are slowing me down?"

"Yes. You have to help me find her. I don't like admitting I'm weak, but if that will drive home how important it is that you go with me to find her, I will shout it from the highest cliff. It's the truth. If I hadn't come across you, those Harborym would have finished me."

Deo made a face and started forward. "Allegria has more power than you. She'll be fine. I'm almost certain that Mayam wouldn't kill her outright."

It took an effort, but Hallow managed to keep from leaping onto Deo and throttling him, as he badly wanted to do. "I agree that she—my wife, my heart, my everything—is stronger than you and me both, but she is not so on Eris. She does not feel the sun here just as I do not feel the arcany of the stars. We have to help her. *You* have to help her. Deo, you owe her."

It was the last sentence that did it. Deo stopped his horse and looked back at Hallow again. "How so?"

Penn walked forward until he was level with Deo's mount. "When you went through the portal in Abet…Allegria channeled Kiriah Sunbringer herself. She burned out the chaos magic within herself…and did something to you at the same time. She changed your magic."

Deo touched one of the bands of silver that crisscrossed his chest, his expression thoughtful. "I have long wondered if that was what happened. I thought at first it was the act of crossing through the portal, but if her lightweaving touched me as I went through…yes, that could explain everything."

"You have to help me find her," Hallow said, daring to hope.

Deo thought about that for a moment, then shook his head, pressing his heels to the horse's sides. "There's no time. We are going to Skystead.

The army that Mayam is raising will join me, and with my Banes once again at my side, I will destroy Racin and his Harborym, thereby saving the Shadowborn from destruction."

Hallow wondered if Allegria would still find him attractive if he pulled out all of his hair in frustration. He decided he'd better not risk it, and instead, did the only thing he could. He threw a weak ball of arcane magic at the back of Deo's head, and turned back to talk to one of the priests.

Chapter 16

Israel heard the whispered rasp of metal just a second before the cold touch of steel pricked the side of his neck. He froze in the act of brushing aside a leafy frond.

"You make enough noise to wake the dead," a voice whispered. "I'm surprised the whole of Skystead hasn't come out to see what you are doing."

He relaxed at the breath that brushed his cheek, pushing aside the tree branch before turning to note the mocking silver eyes that shone out from the shadows. "As I was relieving myself, I doubt if they would have found much to entertain them."

The woman jerked her head toward the low canvas structure that sat hidden by the copse of trees. "I assume that's yours?"

"It is." He made Dasa, queen of the Starborn, a formal bow, and gestured toward the tent. "And I assume you wish to parlay?"

"That's one way of putting it." She slipped in and out of the shadows so quickly that if Israel hadn't been watching, he'd never have known she'd passed by. He followed, pausing at the flap of the tent to call softly to Marston. "Double the guards. And send a few up into the trees to watch for movement from Skystead."

"I've already done so. My lord, that…thing. It's gone."

"I expected Thorn would leave as soon as we were through the portal," he answered, not in the least bit surprised by the disappearance of the former master of Kelos. In his experience, all arcanists were a few carrots short of a stew, and Thorn had done nothing to disabuse him of that opinion.

Marston looked nervously over his shoulder. "What if he flies into the city? Racin is sure to recognize him from the battle of Starfall and will assume that you have managed to bring a force here."

"It's doubtful Thorn would have any reason to visit Skystead unless Hallow is there, and if he is, then Racin must already be on alert. Do not disturb me unless attack is imminent."

Marston raised his eyebrows, but said nothing when Israel entered the tent. Dasa had lit one of the lamps, and stood next to his leather trunk, holding in her hand a small enameled case opened to display two miniatures: One of a woman, and the other a child. Dasa touched a finger to the woman's painted black hair. "So much time has been lost since you had this made. No, not lost...wasted. Spent in battle, and suffering, and in waiting. And now here we are again while time slips inexorably past us. Waiting. Suffering."

"Fighting," Israel said, taking the miniatures from her and studying them for a minute. How many centuries had past since he'd had the miniature of Dasa made? He'd been a young man then, young and idealistic, and head over arse in love with a woman who was his greatest enemy. And yet, despite the centuries of battling both his emotions and the Starborn army, they had come together to bring an end to the war that had bound Alba for so long. "Deo is well?"

"Would I be here now with you if he wasn't?" Dasa's voice, Israel was relieved to note, warmed as she turned away, one hand making an abrupt but still graceful gesture. "He is being held a few hours' ride to the south at the temple of the blood brotherhood. Priests, they call themselves, but they are not any kind of priest that I've ever seen. What I wish to know is why are you here? And how did you manage such a feat?"

"You didn't think I'd let the monster take you off without so much as a word of protest?" Israel asked lightly.

She wrinkled her nose. "No, I didn't. But I wouldn't be surprised to find that you had moved an army through the portal, which naturally would have alerted Racin to your presence, and then there would be a massive battle in which most likely I, and you definitely, would die, leaving Deo to run amok without supervision. Still, I hoped you had enough common sense to keep from making such a foolish mistake."

"I am not so reckless," he said mildly, amused despite himself. "My company is small enough that it should escape Racin's notice."

"But how is it you came to Eris? Racin has opened no portal. He does not have the Harborym needed to sacrifice to do so."

"I used your moonstones, the ones Exodius found."

She frowned and tsked. "I thought I had hidden them better than that."

"You hid them quite sufficiently. It took him some time to find them. I used them to send Deo to safety when Jalas would have killed him." He thought for a moment. "After Deo was banished, Exodius said he would hide the stones again because they were too powerful to be used, but I had no idea that he had split them up until Hallow, the current Master of Kelos, told me he had no idea where they were. Once we realized that Jalas held the last one, it took the combined magic of a former Master of Kelos joined with my grace of Alba to force Jalas into revealing his stone's hiding place. Afterward, he was not...rational...but that is a matter for another day."

"And so you came to Eris." She tipped her head to the side as she considered him. "If I didn't know better, I would say you came here to rescue me, but you are not so ignorant of my ability to handle myself."

"I am here to end Racin," he said simply.

She was silent for the count of seven. "Do not attack him, Israel. He has more power than either of us imagined. Your small company would not survive."

Israel was of that mind, as well, but a question that had been nagging at him took precedence over his plans to rescue Dasa and defeat Racin. "When have you last had news of Deo?"

Dasa unbuckled the scabbard strapped around her waist, setting it on the camp stool that sat next to Israel's pallet of furs. "About ten days ago. He was bored, and obstinate, and unreasonable."

"So, normal, then," Israel said, thinking hard. Israel had spent most of his life in the harness of battle, first caught in the millennia-long battle between Fireborn and Starborn, and in the last thirty or so years protecting the Fireborn from Harborym invasion, so he was no stranger to the weight of responsibility that sat on his shoulders. And yet now, he felt as if his entire body was gripped in a vise created by the vision he had of Dasa in danger...a feeling that spread to Deo. Perhaps the vision had been about Deo, instead?

She shrugged and gestured toward the pallet. "As normal as he can be, given the circumstances. Are you disrobing, or do you expect me to seduce you?"

Israel's dark thoughts were yanked to the woman who stood before him, his body responding to her as it always did. His smile was hidden when he pulled his tunic off over his head. "Even a few centuries ago when I saw you in battle, I had fantasies of you standing before me in nothing but that pair of silver scale boots that went halfway up your thighs."

Dasa paused in the middle of removing her own garments, carefully folding and placing them on the camp stool. She frowned for a few seconds before her brow cleared, and she gave a low, throaty chuckle that went straight to Israel's groin. "My dragon scale boots! I haven't thought of those for a very long time. Really? You wanted to see me in naught but them? They were the most uncomfortable things, but my sister had them made for me, so I felt obligated to wear them."

"They were very...arousing," Israel said, admiring her lush form as she slipped beneath the furs. It had been far too long since he'd been able to meet with Dasa privately, and as always, he yearned for more than just a few stolen moments.

But that could not be...at least, not until they had taken care of Racin and his Harborym.

"Well, why don't you join me, and I'll see what I can do about arousing you even though those boots have long been melted down," she said, patting the furs.

He hesitated, his body urging him to do as she requested, but his heart cautious. "Does it matter so little to you that you've come from your lover's bed to mine?"

"My lover?" She looked genuinely confused for a moment. "Who—Racin?"

"He called you his queen. He said you had a new name—Deva." Israel was silent for a moment, trying to read the emotion in her eyes, but she was never one to let him in to her private thoughts unless she desired for him to know. "He wouldn't have done so if he hadn't bedded you."

"Oh, that." Dasa waved his words away as if they were nothing but annoying gnats. "He used my body, yes. But we both know there is a difference between that and desiring someone. Wanting to be with them, touching them...tasting them. I very much want to be with you now, Israel. I wouldn't have risked being found here if I didn't."

He thought about that, decided that since he, himself, had not been celibate during their time apart, he had no right to complain if she hadn't been, either. It was a matter of moments before he had removed his boots, leggings, and small clothes, and his arms were full of warm, soft woman.

His woman. He smiled to himself even as Dasa moved over him, touching and tasting and teasing him almost past bearing. It had ever been thus between them: opponents—even at times enemies—during the day, and at night, the most passionate of lovers. And when she arched over him, her body tightening around him, he relished the knowledge that she chose him over the other men who had filled her life. Separate, they were formidable foes, but together...Israel smiled into her hair when she collapsed down on him, his body limp and sated, while for the moment, at least, his soul was at peace.

"I missed that," Dasa said some time later, pushing herself off his still-heaving chest. She bent back down to press a kiss to his lips, her mouth lingering on his with a sweetness that never failed to touch him. Dasa was a warrior first, a proud queen, a brilliant leader, but not someone who valued softness and romance. "It's been...three years? Four?"

"Four, I believe. We met at Kelos to talk about ways to deceive Racin. That's when you insisted that it would be more effective for you to appear to side with him, welcoming him to Starfall City rather than fighting his force." Israel tried to keep the bitter notes from his voice, but he suspected Dasa heard them nonetheless, for when she slid off his body, she rubbed a finger over his lower lip.

"And I was right to do so. He would have decimated the Starborn. Our army had suffered massive losses until that point, and when Racin himself suggested joining forces, I knew he would simply destroy us all if I said no."

"My army was at your service. I told you that you would not fight him alone," he couldn't help but remind her.

She made a face, and rolled onto her side, stroking a hand down his damp chest. "We didn't have the time it would have taken your forces to get to Genora, let alone Starfall. I made the only reasonable choice possible."

"And now?" He allowed his hands to do a little stroking of their own, the soft silkiness of her skin filling his mind with a hundred erotic thoughts.

Her hand stilled for a moment, then continued to trace an intricate design on his pectorals. "Now I adapt as best I can. I won't say it didn't almost ruin everything when you allowed Deo to go through the portal—"

"I assure you, I had nothing to do with that. The blasted arcanist had me trapped, and I couldn't stop Deo from his foolish act."

"—but I managed to convince Racin that it would be the purest folly to destroy our foolish son on the spot." She hesitated again, saying in a less sharp-edged tone, "What happened to Deo? When I saw him at Starfall, it appeared he was wielding the same chaos magic that Racin and his Harborym used. But when he came through the portal, he almost destroyed half of Racin's keep. The magic was...different. Far more destructive and seemed to be almost out of his control."

"I believe that has something to do with the destruction of the master portal that the monster used to return to Aryia. Allegria the priest channeled Kiriah Sunbringer herself in order to destroy it...that act must have affected Deo, as well."

"Kiriah? Yes, only the magic of a goddess would be able to do so. Interesting." Absently, Dasa tapped her fingertips on his breastbone, clearly considering this information. "That would explain much about why Deo seemed to be struggling with the magic…and why Racin can't duplicate it."

Israel allowed his eyebrows to rise in a silent question while he drew a few protective runes on Dasa's smooth back.

She sighed and gave a little roll of her eyes. "When Deo blasted half the keep to nothing in mere moments, Racin immediately wanted to know what he'd done to the chaos power to forge it into such a powerful state. And Deo was unwilling—or what's more likely, unable—to tell him, so at my urging, Racin imprisoned Deo while he experimented with changing chaos power into the type that Deo wields."

"He won't be able to do so," Israel replied with a wry twist of his lips. "Not without Kiriah's goodwill, and I doubt if he will manage that."

Dasa was silent for a moment. "That might not be as—"

"My lord!"

The urgency in Marston's voice had them both stiffening. "Yes?" Israel asked, reaching for the sword that was always nearby.

"Riders are leaving the city. They appear to be a search party."

Dasa swore under her breath, leaping to her feet and hurriedly pulling on her clothing. "Bellias blast that new maidservant. She must have reported to Racin that I slipped out of my rooms."

Israel was likewise donning his garments, quickly strapping on his sword as well as tucking the totem made of bone and feather into his belt. "You let a maid see you leave?" It was unlike Dasa to do anything so foolish, and as soon as he spoke the words, Israel knew she would take umbrage with them.

"Of course I did. I marched loudly through the halls proclaiming to everyone who would listen that I was going to see my lover, whose body I have not felt next to mine in many years." The look she shot him was filled with silver-tinted scorn. "I have a new maidservant. She claimed she was lost, without family, and needed protection, so foolishly, I took her in. She saw me when I was climbing out the window. I told her I simply wished to stroll the garden by myself and to say nothing, but clearly she reported me missing. And may Bellias singe her toes, for now we haven't time to discuss what is to be done about Racin."

Israel placed a hand on Dasa's arm to stop her from rushing out of the tent. "If you are in danger, then you should not return to the beast who uses your body. I have a small company, but Hallow and Allegria should be on Eris by now, and together with Deo, we will be able to remove the threat to the future of Alba."

Dasa was shaking her head even as he was talking, her long black hair sweeping across her back like spilled silk. She smiled quickly, leaned in to kiss him with enough passion that he pulled her hard against him, reveling in the feel and taste of her. "There is no time for that, Israel. If Racin has troops sweeping the area for me, he is already in a furious state. I will return by a secret path and calm his fury."

"I dislike the idea of you returning to that monster's arms," he growled.

"There is nothing he can do to me. I've convinced him he needs me to control Deo, and when he returns to Genora, I am to be hostage for the good behavior of the Starborn. Let me go, Israel. The sooner I get back, the easier it will be to appease his temper."

"If he harms you—" Israel warned.

She smiled and kissed him again, this time with a fleeting touch to his lips. "He'll concoct a little minor punishment, but it won't be anything that bothers me." Her smile turned grim. "It will certainly be nothing like what I will mete out to Idril for telling him that I'd left the keep. Farewell, my lord. Stay safe, and do not attack."

She was gone before he could register the words she'd spoken.

Idril? Idril was her maidservant? What madness was this? He shook his head. In the end it made no difference to his plans...unless she was responsible for bringing down Racin's wrath on Dasa's head.

Then he'd have a few things to say to his former wife.

Chapter 17

It took me the entirety of the night to shake off the effects of the magic the red hand priests had placed upon me, and even then, my steps were not as steady as I would have liked. I clutched Buttercup's bridle as I tried to adopt a confident expression, but Mayam looked less than impressed with me when I came to a halt in front of the spot where she squatted before a fire. "I want to find Hallow. You have to take off these ankle shackles."

The man who knelt next to her, her brother Jena, stopped speaking and slid me a look that was part hostility and part curiosity. "The arcanist who you said ran off? Why would you want such a one as he?"

"For one thing, he's my husband, and I love him more than anything on Alba. For another, he didn't run off. Mayam said his horse was spooked when your men attacked us, not that I believe such a thing was possible. Penn is the very best of horses, and never so much as bobbles his ears at attacks. And finally, I wasn't speaking to you." The last words were rude enough that I immediately felt guilty, and hastily sketched another unsuccessful benevolence ward over him.

Jena rose to his full height, which I assumed he was trying to use to intimidate me, but coming as I do from hearty peasant stock, I was not of a small, delicate make. "It would seem to me that prisoners who speak so unguardedly don't remain prisoners for long." He leaned closer to clarify, just in case I missed the warning in his voice. "They don't remain alive."

"I thought we had all this out earlier," I told him, pulling Buttercup's head back from where she was trying to nip his behind. "I don't know how you could have missed it since Mayam was shouting loud enough to rattle the birds in the trees, but evidently you did. She has stopped threatening to kill me, and I have ceased attempting to part her from her head. We understand each other. We are in agreement about all things except one—the need to find Hallow." I turned from Jena, who was making sputtering noises of protest, to where Mayam stared into the fire, absently poking it with a stick. "When you told me that you were working with Deo, I agreed to help you however possible, but I must find Hallow first, and I can't do that with these shackles on."

"You are a prisoner," Jena said stiffly. "You're lucky that you have been given the freedom to move and are not bound hand and foot."

"Take off the shackles," Mayam said without glancing toward us.

Jena turned an outraged face on his sister. "You are mad! You know nothing about her. Just because she is not Shadowborn does not mean she is *not* from Skystead."

I didn't even have to protest that. Mayam waved a hand toward me and simply repeated her request.

With a lot of muttering of things I felt it better to pretend not to have heard, Jena finally knelt and with an odd sort of cross-shaped device, unlocked the shackles that connected my feet. The shackles had allowed me to move at a shuffling pace, but not run or ride. I wiggled my ankles as each shackle fell away. "Thank you. Now, about some men to help me find Hallow—"

"Oh, this is ridiculous!" Jena threw away the shackles in disgust. "First she wants the freedom to attack us again, now she wants men to help her chase after a cowardly arcanist. Next she'll be asking for her weapons back."

"Well, actually, that *was* going to be my next request," I started to say, but at Jena's profane exclamation, I thought about allowing Buttercup to do her worst to him.

Luckily, I didn't need to.

"Cease, Jena," Mayam said, glancing up at her brother as he stormed around the fire, his hands gesticulating while he described how foolish it was to allow me freedom. "Get her weapons. No, do not argue with me. I know what I am about. The woman has the right of it. We have made our peace."

It took another two minutes of argument between the two of them, but at last Jena snorted very rude things under his breath and stomped off to gather my swords and bow.

"He spoke of you, you know," Mayam said, her gaze on the smoldering coals that were all that remained of the fire.

"Jena?"

"No. Lord Deo. When he was in a delirium, he would speak to people who were not there, holding long conversations with them. Most of the time he argued with a man who seemed to want to keep him from doing what he desired, but there were a few times he spoke to a priestess, one who both amused and annoyed him."

I made a little face, and admitted, "That sounds about right."

"He had much admiration for her. For you. It is why I agreed to accept your help. Jena doesn't understand because he does not understand Lord Deo. He doesn't know just how...powerful...Lord Deo is. Or how tortured." Her gaze lifted to mine at last, and I could see that she had eyes almost as black as the night. "But you do."

"Yes," I said quietly, remembering the scars Deo bore upon his back. "I know how he has struggled, both before he changed, and after."

"Who is..." She hesitated a moment, her expression clouding. "Idril?"

"That is a complicated question, one which I don't really have the time to go into fully if I want to start hunting for Hallow before much of the daylight is lost, but she is the woman to whom Deo once gave his heart. She betrayed that gift...or at least, I thought she did." I remembered the fire in Idril's eyes when she spoke of Deo and decided that it was quite likely I'd been mistaken about her feelings.

"So he is not heart-bound to her?" Mayam asked quickly.

I chose my words carefully, realizing that Mayam was harboring feelings of a tender nature for my old friend. I had a suspicion such emotions would not be reciprocated, but I didn't want to point that out lest she retaliate in anger. "So far as I know, they are not bound to each other. When they were last together, Deo ordered her from his presence."

"Ah," she said on a long sigh and looked pleased.

Now was clearly the time to press her. "Mayam, I understand that you feel it necessary to gather men for Deo—"

"Not just men," she interrupted, still poking the embers of the fire. "Shadowborn who haven't been taken by Lord Racin. So many people have gone to Skystead, never to be seen again; not many remain who meet Lord Deo's criteria. He said only a very particular type of person can fill his ranks."

"As I well know, having belonged to those ranks."

Mayam looked up at that, her eyes narrowed, and I realized with a start that she was jealous. "So you say, and I'm willing to admit that your bear his mark, which is the only reason you are alive now, but until I hear from Deo himself that you are who you say you are, you will remain with us."

"A prisoner still?" I asked, annoyed.

"One who has her freedom and weapons is not a prisoner. Consider yourself...our guest," she finished lamely, rising. "We have many miles to travel today before we rest. Are you ready to ride?"

"Yes," I said, considering my options. I could strike out on my own to find Hallow, but I had no idea where I was, let alone in what direction he had gone. Without assistance from those who knew the area, I was helpless. "Yes, I'm ready."

"Good. We are likely to meet with some Harborym while we travel. A scout returned during the night saying they, too, are scouring the villages in search of victims to take to Skystead."

I was still a bit confused about exactly why Racin wanted Shadowborn men and women rounded up, but it really didn't matter to me now. What *did* matter was reaching Deo. He, I was certain, would not refuse to help me find Hallow.

The first two villages we came upon were much like the one that Hallow and I first visited—burned and charred, with only one or two survivors clinging to once familiar landmarks. Mayam spoke with the clearly fearful individuals, returning to our party with a grim expression.

After the second such visit, I overheard her telling Jena, "The old woman said that the Harborym are now taking children."

"What madness is this?" Jena looked as if she'd struck him. "What use would they have for children? Harborym do not take prisoners."

"The rumors must be true. Racin is gathering young Shadowborn in hopes that they are resilient enough to survive his heinous experiments." Mayam mounted her horse, looking lost. "Are we too late, Jena? How can Lord Deo rescue us if we cannot raise more than a handful of priests?"

Jena bristled defensively. "My priests are worth an entire army of soldiers."

"Rescue us?" I said softly to myself, eyeing Mayam. When we'd worked out an accord, she had said simply that Deo had sent her out to find Shadowborn who would be willing to become new Banes of Eris...but what if her vision of Deo's goals was not the same as his? Or had he promised her that he would rid all of Eris of Racin and the Harborym? Even if Deo, Hallow and I were at our full powers, I wasn't sure if we would have the strength to do that, and with Kiriah shunning me, and Deo in who-knew-what sort of a state...the hard nut of worry in my belly grew larger.

We reached a village a few hours after that which hadn't been destroyed, although there were few enough people to see. Mayam and Jena met with the headman while I stretched my legs and allowed Buttercup a turn at the water trough next to a well in the center of a dusty square.

"I come from the savior of Genora and Aryia," Mayam said in a piercing voice, climbing onto the lip of the well before turning to face the few people who stood half-hidden inside doorways. "Lord Deo, bringer of the Fourth Age, was taken prisoner by the evil one, but he has escaped, and seeks worthy men and women to join his force to free Eris. Who amongst you has the bravery to fight to free your family from the destruction that has rained down upon us since the coming of the Speaker?"

There was a murmur of voices, but no one came forward.

"Are you content to cower in your shelters? Or will you protect that which you value!" she shouted, her voice echoing off the handful of buildings that dotted the square. "Other villagers have hidden away, and their homes and lives were destroyed because they would not stand up to fight. Is that what you want?"

"What you ask is impossible! We cannot win against the Harborym," one young man called out, stepping forward a few feet from a doorway. He looked around nervously, but no one else emerged to stand with him, either figuratively or literally. He licked his lips, then said in a less antagonistic tone, "They have come to our village before, and taken away the strongest of our kin. You speak of a savior of other lands, but what has he to do with us?"

"He has come to liberate Eris, just as he liberated the lands of the other born." She gestured toward me. "This is one of his kind, a Fireborn who traveled here with the Savior. See the marks upon her brow? Those came from the battles she fought at the side of Lord Deo, earned by the deaths of thousands of Harborym."

"Well, actually—" I started to correct the misinformation, but stopped when she continued with a sharp look flung my way.

"If a stranger can come to Eris and dedicate herself to saving us, then how can you refuse to stand beside her?"

"She doesn't look like a great warrior." That voice was female and came from behind me. "Those marks on her head could be from a pox."

"Aye, what proof do we have that this great savior of yours intends to help us?" another voice called, although the speaker remained within his house.

I sighed and tied Buttercup to a rail before getting onto the opposite side of the well. "I am Allegria, called Hopebringer, priestess of the goddess Kiriah, lightweaver, and once Bane of Eris. I may not be a great warrior, but I assure you that I have defeated Harborym in the past, and I will do so again."

There were a few murmurs of disbelief, but evidently my appearance was different enough from the Shadowborn to lend credence to my words, for slowly, one by one, a dozen of them emerged from their houses. Mayam went to meet them while I returned to Buttercup.

A short while later, Mayam announced that we would ride to the next village. We had two new recruits, the nervous young man, who was named Peter, and his younger sister, Ella. To my eye, the girl looked too young to become a Banesman, but I figured I'd talk to both her and Deo before she made a final decision. "Mount up. Peter, you and Ella will have to walk until we can find you suitable horses. The nearest village is about an hour's ride to the—"

A hoarse cry tore across her words, follow by shrieks. From behind one of the houses, four Harborym emerged, their skin, stained red by chaos power, glistening with oil as they charged forward, weapons held high.

I ran back to the well, leaping onto it even as I snatched my bow from Buttercup's saddle, and pulled arrows from the quiver at my side. I had an arrow nocked and sent flying as soon my foot touched the lip of the well, shooting the foremost Harborym in the left eye. He snarled, and yanked the arrow out without pausing his charge forward, but the second arrow I fired caught him in the throat, and he dropped with a wet gurgle.

"Get to safety," I yelled at Peter and Ella, who had frozen, clearly unsure of what they should be doing. Behind them, the dozen blood priests and Jena stood weaving spells, the air growing darker with chains of symbols that they'd drawn in the air. I emptied my quiver, taking down another Harborym before tossing away my bow and rushing forward with a sword in each hand.

Mayam was battling with one of the Harborym on her own, a two-handed sword in her hands, but she was in trouble. Three more Harborym emerged and spread out, clearly looking for villagers to snatch up, but seeing the two I had killed, and one that Jena's priests had bound so tightly with blood spells that he simply collapsed onto the ground twitching, they turned and started for us.

Just as the Harborym fighting Mayam raised a massive axe that I had no doubt would cleave her in two, a black shape flashed over his head, dipping and swooping in a way that had me blinking in surprise before letting out a cheer. "Thorn! Go for his eyes!"

Thorn did as I ordered, flashing past the Harborym in question while I rushed him, slashing at his thick neck with both swords.

He lunged at me, but Thorn was quicker, and the monster stumbled forward, black blood spurting in a thick arc that stained the earth seconds before his body hit the ground. I leaped out of the way and dashed to the far end of the village where one of the Harborym was dragging Ella by her hair.

Peter had leaped onto the beast's back in an attempt to free his sister, but with a twisting move—and a sickening sound of snapping bones—the Harborym jerked Peter forward, twisting his head in an unnatural position in the process. Ella screamed when Peter's now lifeless body fell to the ground at the same time the Harborym dragged her away, one massive hand tangled in her hair.

"Thorn, distract him!" I yelled and desperately tried to summon a bit of light, but Kiriah would not hear my entreaties, leaving me with nothing but my swords to rescue the girl. Thorn dipped and whirled in front of the Harborym's face at the same time I flung myself onto the creature's back. Unlike Peter, however, I didn't wait for the monster to grab me, but sliced off his hand, freeing Ella.

The Harborym roared, and flung himself to the side, his one remaining hand raised when Thorn attacked his face, which allowed me to stab my sword through his neck. He fell forward, his body twitching horribly for a few seconds before he went still, with me still on his back.

Panting, I pushed my hair out of my face and leaped up to check Ella. "Are you harmed?" I asked.

"No, but Peter—" She choked, tears mingling with dust and black blood to form streaks on her face.

"Stay here," I ordered, pressing her into the shadow of the nearest house. I didn't have time for words of comfort. "Thorn, protect the girl."

I spun on my heel and ran back to where Jena and his priests were wildly casting spells upon the remaining two Harborym. Just as I raised a sword to help, one of them dropped, revealing Mayam and one of the villagers struggling with the final Harborym.

Five minutes later the Harborym, strangled by blood magic, spewing oaths and curses, dissolved into a black puddle of viscous liquid, his flesh and bones melting away before our eyes.

Jena, panting loudly, his face covered in sweat, kicked a bit of dirt over the puddle, and turned to look at his sister. "Is that it? No more?"

Mayam shook her head. She was breathing so hard she had to double over for a moment, her hands on her knees as she filled her lungs.

The villagers were huddled around Peter's body, several of them wailing, while the others stared with pale, ghostly faces, numbness the only expression in their eyes. I moved past them to where Ella had collapsed onto the ground, her face white against the coppery red of her hair. Thorn, perched on a bit of the cottage's thatched roof, fluttered down, and flew a circle around me, clearly agitated.

"I'm sorry about your brother," I said, ignoring Thorn for a moment to kneel down next to Ella. "He did a very brave thing, tackling that Harborym on his own. He must have loved you very much."

She blinked rapidly for a few moments, but surprised me by getting to her feet, her eyes shiny, but not welling with tears. "He hated the monsters. He hated what they did to us, how every night, we would pray to Nezu to keep us safe from the blood thieves."

"Harborym?" I asked, not having heard that name for them.

She nodded. "They are corrupted, taking the magic Nezu sent to give us ease and twisting it to their own purposes, just as they corrupted the priests. Peter wanted the villages to form together into an army to fight them, but my Nan said that we were not strong enough. No one was." She eyed me curiously, her gaze softening a little as she reached out to wipe a splash of black blood off my face. "But Nan is wrong. You are strong enough. The others are strong enough. I want to help you. Will you show me how to fight like you?"

Something inside me felt an instant sense of kinship with this girl. I remembered all too well how I had yearned to be trained to fight, how once, as a child, I had begged Deo to convince his father to take me into his company. "The Harborym are not invincible, and if you truly wish to learn how to fight, I'm sure that Mayam and her people will see to it that you are taught."

"Thank you," she said with a relieved sigh, her gaze moving to where the villagers were carrying her brother's body into one of the cottages. She turned away, her forehead wrinkling when Thorn, evidently tired of not being the center of attention, alighted upon my head. "That...that's a..."

"It's a wooden bird, yes," I said with a little sigh. Thorn bobbed up in down. "It actually is the spirit of the Master of Kelos, a famous arcanist." Thorn bounced up and down on my head a couple of times until I plucked him off and held him on the palm of my hand. I had no doubt just what he had objected to. "Famous and very powerful. And he is the companion of Hallow, the current master. Thorn, have you come from Hallow?"

The bird tipped his head to look at me, but otherwise didn't move. I took that to be a negative. "Did you come from Lord Israel?"

Thorn hopped up and down and flapped his wings.

"He's here, then? In Eris? He got the last moonstone and opened a portal?"

Thorn took to the skies, circling around Ella, who watched with wide, unsure eyes.

"And you're searching for Hallow?"

Thorn dove and rose, then dove again before landing on Ella's shoulder.

"I don't know where he is. We were separated," I told the bird. "Can you feel his presence?"

Thorn remained still, his wooden eyes watching me without blinking. I knew that Thorn and Hallow were bound via arcany, and that somehow, Thorn sensed the magic that was particular to Hallow, guiding him to Hallow no matter where they were.

Although evidently that was not so on Eris. Worry gripped my heart, and I asked in a voice that sounded foreign to me, "Is it...do you feel no arcany at all, or just not Hallow's magic?"

Thorn bobbed his head.

"No arcany at all?"

He bobbed again. Relief filled me, giving me hope that Hallow was well and unharmed. "You must go find him. I don't know how you're going to do it, but it's important that you do. Make sure he's safe and well and not worried about me."

Thorn flapped his wings and would have leaped into the air to take flight but I caught him up, and said softly, "And when you find him, tell him...tell him I miss him. Greatly."

Thorn gave my wrist a little rub with the side of his beak. I pressed a kiss to his head and tossed him into the air.

He flew two fast circles around me in what I assumed was a promise he would do as I asked and disappeared into the dim horizon.

In the end, another of the villagers succumbed to the Harborym attack in addition to Peter. Two of Jena's blood priests deserted the company while we were burying the dead, leaving Jena to rant to Mayam about the circumstance.

"We don't need them," Mayam told her brother. "We need only those who are willing to do whatever it takes to bring an end to our torment."

"With me, we have ten, Mayam. *Ten.* And a girl and the Fireborn. She may have impressed the villagers by taking down two of the Harborym, but unless she is holding back some immense power, we do not have enough force to do more than tackle wandering bands. *Small* wandering bands."

"You have always looked only at the negative—" Mayam started to say, but I decided to intervene.

"Actually, about this I think Jena is right," I said, coming up with Buttercup, who I noticed had black blood on her hooves, indicating she had done her part to take down one of the Harborym. "We aren't strong enough with such a small company."

"Others will join us. We will continue to go to the villages and soon, our numbers will swell," Mayam told me, then turned away as if she was going to leave.

I stopped her by moving around to block her path. "Oh? Villages like this, you mean?" I gestured toward the people who were still clustered together. "According to what they said, all the able-bodied adults have been taken. Who do you expect to find left but the old, the infirm, and the young?"

Her jaw worked. Anger lit her eyes, but I had seen too much death today to be concerned about either her welfare or mine. I put a hand on her arm, saying softly, "Mayam, there is no army to raise. The Harborym have taken all those who could fight. The children like Ella who are left are not soldiers. They can be trained, but it will take time, and that is something we do not have."

I thought she was going to brush past me with a sharp word, but to my surprise her shoulders slumped. "What, then, would you have me do? Give up and return to my lord like a dog slinking home with its tail between its legs?"

"Return to Deo, yes. But not like a slinking dog. You have tried to do what he asked, but it's not possible. Deo will understand. He saw the devastation the Harborym wreaked upon the Starborn, and that was in thirty years. How long have they been on Eris?"

"Centuries," she said tiredly, her gaze slipping from mine. "Corrupting our land. Crushing it...crushing *us*."

"Let us rejoin Deo. Our forces combined with his—and once I find him, Hallow—will accomplish far more than we can, combing the country for volunteers."

It took her a few minutes, but at last she nodded. "What you say makes sense. If the Harborym are taking children now, it must mean there are no adults left. Jena! Tell the men to mount. We ride to rejoin Lord Deo."

"That's the first thing you've said today that makes any sense," Jena called back and went to organize the mounts.

"Do you know where he is?" I asked Mayam.

"Lord Deo?" She glanced upward at the sky. I could discern no difference in the perpetual gloom, but evidently the Shadowborn could read the different shades of clouds to determine time. "Aye. He is to the north, following the road to Skystead."

We set out shortly thereafter, Ella riding double with one of the smaller priests. I sent up a few fervent prayers to Kiriah to not only look after Hallow, but to help Thorn as well. We rode through the night, only stopping when it was necessary to let the horses rest, and by the following morning, my spirits were as dark as the woods through which we were riding. With the shadows cast by the tall, straight pines, it felt as if we were moving through a morass of blackness and might never see light again.

Buttercup clumped along, sleepily bobbing her head while following the priest's horse in front of us, unconcerned despite the fact that we had rear guard. Suddenly, the train of tired horses jerked to a ragged stop. I looked up from where I had been half dozing in the saddle, horrified that I was almost asleep when I should have been alert. I listened for a moment, recognizing the meaning of the screams and deep, grating cries.

"Harborym." I swore and slapped a hand on Buttercup's neck to wake her up. She leaped forward when I shouted the warning, my heels pressed into her sides.

Mayam was just in front of me when we broke through the trees. I tucked the reins under one knee and pulled forward my bow and a couple of arrows, nocking one even as Buttercup galloped after Mayam. Ahead of us, a solitary stone building stood, with people streaming out of its doors and glassless windows.

Beyond them, I could see at least a dozen Harborym, all of whom were fighting with men wearing familiar-looking rusty black tunics bearing red hands.

"—temple of Mudwallow—" Snatches of words carried to me when Mayam turned her head. I assumed she meant the temple was dedicated to blood priests, which gave me a spurt of hope.

That hope blossomed into a full-fledged whoop of joy when we grew close enough for me to recognize a figure almost as big as the Harborym he handily decapitated.

"Deo!" I screamed and pulled Buttercup to a fast stop, hastily apologizing under my breath before planting three arrows into the nearest Harborym.

Deo had turned at my call, but immediately turned back when two more Harborym rushed him. Behind Deo, to my left, a semicircle of priests in rusty tunics stood with heads down, their hands dancing in the air as they wove spells. I ignored them to rush forward into the battle, quickly exhausting my arrows and switching to my swords, fighting my way toward Deo. Just as I was about to reach his side, a word floated across the screams and oaths, causing me to stop and turn back toward the priests.

"Allegria? My heart!"

"Hallow!" I bellowed at the full capacity of my lungs. Ignoring the Harborym I'd been fighting, I dashed toward him. Above his head, Thorn flew before making a dive at the nearest monster.

"You're alive!" I shouted, throwing myself onto Hallow, kissing every inch of his face I could reach. "I knew you would be, but I'm so happy you are. Blessed Kiriah for keeping you safe."

"My love, you must stop—" Hallow's voice, rich with laughter breathed in my ear. "We are in the middle of taking down this company of Harborym."

"I know, but I'm just so happy to see you safe. I feared the worst."

"As did I, until Thorn found me and told me you were well. As, evidently, are Idril and Quinn, who are with the queen."

"Idril made it to the queen safely, then? Thank the goddesses for that." I pulled back, my eyes dewy with tears of happiness, about to ask him a hundred more questions when I noticed two things.

The first was that Hallow was clad in the same rusty black tunic as the other priests...and the second was that his eyes were no longer a glittering, pure blue. Now they shimmered a brilliant violet.

"What...what—" I stammered.

"No time now," he said, giving me a quick, hard kiss before moving me aside. "It takes all my concentration to be able to cast links in the chain. Evidently my Starborn half helps me control the blood magic, but it's so different from arcany..."

I stared for three seconds, my brain painfully slow in processing what he was saying, but as soon as it finally chugged through the fact that somehow, Hallow had become learned in blood magic, it pointed out that there was still a heated battle going on, and I needed to help destroy the Harborym.

With a shout, I ran past the line of priests and threw myself at the monster attacking Mayam. Jena and his priests had bound the Harborym with magic, but he was still able to swing a sword, and was coming dangerously close to Mayam.

Madness seemed to reign. Now that my heart was easy about Hallow's well-being, I could focus on fighting the large force that must have come upon Deo while he was camped at the temple. I slashed and hacked my way from Harborym to Harborym, knowing Deo was able to cope on his own. Mayam was beginning to flag, and I kept an eye on her to make sure she wasn't overwhelmed. Ella was at Jena's side, I was happy to note, as the priest wielded a short staff in between drawing spells in the air. I was behind the building, helping a small group of priests take down two Harborym, when I heard a faint shout from the front. It took some time before I could work my way around to the other side, but when I had hacked off the arms of the last Harborym, I dashed past the wounded and dead, wondering if more of the enemy had arrived.

Just the opposite. A small group of them rode away from the temple at great speed, coppery-red dust rising in their wake. I limped over to where Deo was shouting an order for his horse.

"I know you love a fight, Deo, but even you can't be crazy enough to want to chase down Harborym," I said, struggling to catch my breath and rubbing a spot on the side of my thigh where one of the monsters had kicked me. "Now that we're all together again, we'll take them down sooner or later."

Deo turned a face of fury to me. "They have a prisoner with them."

"Really? I didn't think they took prisoners." Idly, as I massaged my aching thigh, I looked around for Hallow. The line of priests was in disarray now as they clumped together in groups, tending the wounded and dead.

Deo took one of my arms, saying softly, "They did this time. They took Hallow."

Ice took hold of me, the frozen chill of complete, all-consuming rage, beginning at my heart and creeping outward along my veins with frosty fingers until my entire body felt as brittle as glass. "Then they will die," I swore, and turning, ran to find Buttercup.

Chapter 18

The darkness that held Hallow eased a little, awareness coming slowly to him. Something was not right with his body. For one thing, there was the pain that rippled down his arms and back. Then there was the fact that he couldn't feel his hands. And lastly, there was a voice in his head.

Did I tell you that she kissed me before I found you? Right on the head. You picked right there, lad. I didn't think at first you had, because a priest at Kelos...well, it just unsettles the spirits, but now I see that you were right. Allegria has substance, and you don't see that in many of the gormless fecks you seem to surround yourself with. She'll come after you, she and that demon lord you insist on befriending.

It took Hallow a few minutes to work through his confusion to the point that he realized the voice belonged to Thorn. And with that, memory returned in hazy little scenes, most notably a picture of himself kneeling as he received the rites of the blood priests, and later, trying to understand the ways of their magic.

"Chains," he mumbled. "The magic is performed in circles that link together to create chains."

You don't have any chains, although your hands are bound behind you. Would you like me to undo the binding? It's only rope, and my beak is quite sharp.

"Yes, please," he mumbled and struggled to open his eyes. The ground beneath him, which had been lurching and bumping, was not ground at all. He was in some sort of a covered cart, one that jounced across ruts in the road that made his head bang into the side. He rolled forward onto his belly, feeling Thorn perch on his arms as the bird worked to peck away the bonds. "Where are we?"

Heading for Skystead. The Harborym captured you. I didn't think I'd see the day when an apprentice of mine was taken by such puling monsters, but Eris is a strange land.

"I'm not your apprentice. Ah, thank you." Hallow tried to sit up and bring his hands around, but his arms seemed as lifeless and dead as lead weights. He pulled himself into a half-sitting, half reclining position, letting his hands rest on his legs until the blood returned to them.

No, but you were beholden to my apprentice, and that makes you bound to me. How did they capture you? I didn't see it; I was too busy checking on Allegria and making sure she wasn't in trouble, and then of course I had to blind as many Harborym as possible, although that's not as easy as you'd think since they seemed to anticipate my attacks, but still, as a former Master of Kelos, I feel it's important that I do what I can in this blighted land. I don't care for the place, myself. I don't like not being able to feel arcany. It's not right, lad. It's just not right.

"No, it isn't, but we have to deal with what we are given, and right now, I have to figure out why the Harborym took me. How many others did they take?"

None that I saw, not that I saw you taken, as I just said. The first I knew, four Harborym were riding away with you slung over one of their saddles, and the demon lord was yelling that they had you. I thought of telling your priest, but she doesn't always understand me, so I felt it was wiser to find you. They rode for about a league, then threw you into this cart.

Hallow could see nothing through the canvas hung over the cart. He winced when a sharp, stabbing sensation warned that feeling was coming back to his hands. He wanted badly to peer out to see where he was, and how heavily he was guarded. Instead, he asked, "There are four Harborym here?"

Only two now. The others rode back toward the temple.

Which meant Deo and Allegria would have to deal with them before they came after him. "I have to get free. I am too unlearned to do more than cast the most basic links. I don't even know if I could make a chain without the presence of the other priests to aid me. Here's what we'll do—"

He stopped when the cart gave a painful lurch, almost immediately smoothing out into a gently rattling movement. Hallow listened for a second, worry gripping him. "Thorn, look outside. Are we on a paved road?"

Thorn flew out the back of the cart.

Cobblestones. This must be Skystead. How interesting. I approve of the towers—there's nothing like a few well-built towers to give a town a dignified appearance. Oh, and there's a fountain in the middle of a big square. How odd. The water in it is red. It appears there is some scaffolding being built in the square, too. I wonder what that's for? You should really see these towers, Hallow. Now that you are Master, you can rebuild Kelos, and I think you should add one of this sort of tower. The old ones were well and fine a millennium ago, but clearly whoever built Skystead is very talented where towers are concerned.

Hallow flexed his fingers, the pain in them excruciating while the nerves recovered from the restraint. He tried calming his mind and recalling the brief instructions that he'd been given after his initiation. "Feel the blood that flows through the veins of all living things," he murmured, pushing down the pricking sensation in his fingers in order to spread them wide. "Use that energy to shape it into a link."

He summoned up a symbol that floated red in the air before him. "Now, shape another. And another."

Sounds swirled around them, threatening to distract him, but he hadn't lived in Kelos for almost a year without learning to ignore the constant chatter of the spirits who also resided there. He shut out everything but his intentions and the feel of the blood flowing through the people surrounding him. It was as if the blood was itself a living thing, an entity that could be molded into whatever shape Hallow wanted. He made link after link until they allowed themselves to be joined together, the individual symbols that hung in the air shifting into a new, more powerful form. "Now to escape and find Allegria and Deo."

A few minutes later, when the canvas covering the cart was yanked off, Hallow, who had been holding the chain in readiness, flung it on the Harborym standing there, quickly throwing himself off the cart in order to escape.

While the Harborym he'd bound with his weak chain struggled and shouted abuse, six others surrounded the cart.

One of them held Thorn, the bird's wooden wings snapped off, and while Hallow watched in horror, the Harborym threw Thorn and his wings to the ground. The one he'd bound with the chain shook off the magic, now so weakened it could hold him no longer, and with a grimace that Hallow took to be a smile, the monster ground Thorn's wooden shape into splinters.

"No!" Hallow leaped forward, gathering up the broken remains of Thorn before the Harborym jerked him upright.

"Did you think your familiar could help you?" The Harborym sneered, and shoved Hallow forward, sending him stumbling toward a large fountain, beyond which he could see a structure made of new wood. It wasn't a gallows, though. He wasn't entirely sure what it was. but the sight of it filled him with dread. "There is nothing to save you now, priest."

"What's this? Why do you return with only one subject?"

Hallow recognized the deep, grating voice that bellowed across the square. He swore under his breath, frantically trying to summon arcane magic, just a little, he pleaded to Bellias. Just enough to free himself from the Harborym gripping his shoulder.

"Master, you said to bring you any of the other born. This one wears the garb of a red hand, but he is not one. There is an aura about him," one of the Harborym answered, gesturing toward Hallow. Racin, who had ignored him, now turned to look, and Hallow saw the moment when he was recognized.

His spirits fell.

"You!" Racin roared, stomping forward, his long black hair swinging. "You tried to stop me on Genora along with the others! Kill him!"

Hallow squawked a protest, but just as the Harborym holding him grabbed his neck in massive hands, Racin shouted again.

"Stop! I have changed my mind." He stared intently at Hallow, circling him as if he was an object of curiosity. "Grenji spoke true. You do bear the sign of the red hand, and yet, you are not one of them." He sniffed the air, his lips curling. "You have the stink of Bellias about you. You are an arcanist, yet you embrace blood magic. Interesting. You might be useful to me. Perhaps it is Starborn blood that made my enemy stronger. Yes, it might be. Put him with the others until I can attend to him."

Hallow clutched the remains of Thorn as he was dragged off by two Harborym, followed by a couple of Shadowborn guards. As he expected, he was taken to the depths of the massive keep that sat atop Skystead and flung into a cell without a word from the Harborym.

The cell was dark, with no light except that which came through a barred window on the wooden door.

"Oh, Thorn," he said, picking himself up from a floor that seemed to consist of dirt and moldy straw, "what have we gotten into now?"

"A nightmare would be my definition," a light female voice said from the dark.

Hallow spun around, still holding the splintered bits of Thorn. "Who's there?"

"We are, although I must say, I'm disappointed to see you join us. You were supposed to save us." A pale shape glided toward him until the faint light from the door fell onto a familiar face. Idril gave him a look that said she expected better from him. "You promised that when you, Deo, and that priest got together, you would be unstoppable. If you are here, you cannot help Deo."

"Deo has no business doing anything but what he's told," another voice from the darkness said. This one was also female, but held a no nonsense tone that Hallow guessed belonged to the queen of the Starborn. When she strode into the pool of light, he saw he was correct. "As we discussed numerous times, I blame his father."

She slapped her hands on her legs and continued forward into the darkness. Hallow had a feeling she was pacing the length of the cell, much like a caged swamp cat he'd once seen in the south of Aryia.

"You blame Lord Israel for Deo's stubbornness, or the fact that you and Lady Idril have been imprisoned?" Hallow asked, drawing three links of magic in quick succession.

"And me! Don't forget about me," a male voice called out from the shadows.

"You, too, Quinn? I'm lucky there is room in the cell for me with all of you here. Shall we have a bit of light?" He added one last link of magic, strung them together, and twisted the chain into a symbol that absorbed the darkness, and gave forth a steady pale light. "That's better. Now I can see just what we're up against."

The cell wasn't very wide, but it was long. At the far end, a couple of disreputable pallets had been drawn together, one of which held a reclining and bare-chested Quinn. The queen was indeed pacing the length of the cell, her hands behind her back, and her expression one of concentration. Idril, making a soft little coo of pleasure, moved over to the light, carefully seating herself on what appeared to be Quinn's shirt and jerkin.

"You can start by telling us who you are, although I take it the lady knows you?" the queen said as she strode past him before turning and retracing her steps.

He made his best bow. "I am Hallow of Penhallow, now of Kelos."

"Kelos?" The queen stopped in mid-pace and spun around to glare at him. "Did Exodius send you?"

Hallow glanced at Idril. She was busy smoothing out the folds of her gown. "Er...not so much. Not in the manner you mean." Quickly, Hallow explained how he had been taken by Exodius to be Master of Kelos before the latter moved on to the spirit realm, finishing by holding out his hand to show the remains of Thorn. "And now Exodius's former master has been destroyed, which would be bad enough, but once I find him a new form to adopt, I will hear no end to his tale of woe."

The queen clicked her tongue in annoyance and resumed pacing. "Exodius always was too stubborn for his own good. Never would listen to advice. And now look where it's gotten us—Israel is here ruining all my plans, and now you, who should by rights be back in Kelos giving direction to that chaotic group of madmen who make up your order, are here getting in my way."

He bowed again, struggling a little to keep his expression sober. "You're welcome, your majesty."

"For what?" she snapped, glaring at him again as she passed by. "You've doubtless stirred up Racin with suspicions and outrageous ideas of invasion?"

"We came to rescue you. At great personal risk," he said, still amused despite the gravity of the situation. He was about to wish that Allegria were here to appreciate the irony of the queen being peeved with them for attempting to rescue her, but realized the foolishness of such an idea before it finished forming in his mind.

"Not to mention my ship," Quinn said from where he lay.

"And most of my clothing," Idril added.

"No one asked you to rescue me," Dasa said with enough force that Hallow felt himself duly chastised. "I was perfectly able to do that when I was ready, but Israel had to come riding up like he's a dashing hero and I'm a feeble maiden in need of a savior, not to mention Deo almost throwing away everything I've worked so hard for by showing up with the very same idea."

Hallow thought of pointing out to her that her loved ones' desire to rescue her was hardly a reason for mocking their actions, but reminded himself that she was, after all a queen, and that wisdom was often on the side of the man who kept his thoughts behind his tongue. Then he decided that if he had a choice between wisdom or sanity, he'd choose the latter any time. "According to what Deo told me, your entire plan was to wait for some unknown time when Racin was weak enough for you to destroy him. With all due respect, that doesn't seem like much of a plan to me. It relies too heavily on chance."

Dasa snorted and stormed over to Hallow, her silver eyes blazing. "You've seen Deo on Eris?"

"Yes." Hallow was silent for a moment, judging whether or not to tell the queen everything, and in the end deciding it was inevitable she should find out. He gave her a quick summary of his time on Eris, ending with, "The last I saw Deo, he had just killed more than a dozen Harborym."

The queen swore under her breath before demanding to know, "At which temple was this?"

"I don't know the name of it, but it was located at a crossroads. Deo said that one of the roads led to Skystead, while the other followed a dried river bed to the coast."

"The temple at Mudwallow," the queen said slowly, obviously considering this information. "What was Deo doing there? He agreed to stay at his prison on Blood Rock until I told him the time was ripe for attack! Bellias blast the boy! He's going to ruin everything."

Hallow felt his temper rise at the queen's comments. Although he was normally slow to anger, the blood magic that now flowed through him acted as an irritant, one that lacked the smooth, soothing power that came from wielding arcany. "And is being confined in the belly of this keep part of your plan? Because I don't see how Deo and Lord Israel have ruined anything. They—we all—are here to get you and Deo off Eris. Does it matter how we do so?"

"Of course it matters!" Dasa slapped her hands on her legs again, and marched past him before spinning on her heel and returning. "If I didn't want to be on Eris, I wouldn't have allowed Racin to bring me here in the first place."

"Why would you do that?" Idril asked, looking only mildly interested.

"I was wondering the very same thing," Quinn said, sitting up and scratching his bare chest. "It seems to me that the lady doesn't want to be rescued after all. So our whole journey here was for nothing."

"My plan—one that Israel agreed to—was always to find a way to destroy Racin. We both knew that driving the Harborym from Genora and Aryia was only a temporary fix. Once Racin had regrouped, he would return. As many times as was needed until he conquered the whole of Alba. Do you understand now, arcanist? Your so-called rescue plan has put at grave risk the plans I have been working on for years."

Hallow was silent for a few seconds while he considered this. "I agree that Racin needs to be destroyed, but now that we are all here—Deo, and Lord Israel, and Allegria and I—together, we can accomplish that. He is strong, yes, but not invulnerable, a fact that we saw in Abet when he retreated rather than face the three of us. No matter how much chaos magic he wields, he's still a man, and can be destroyed just as the Harborym can be destroyed."

The queen whirled, her long black hair flying out like an ebony curtain. "What makes you think he's a man?"

"What is he if not—" Hallow stopped speaking when a grinding sound came from the door. He spun around just in time to see one of the Shadowborn guards at the door before he tossed in a small figure.

"You lot can have this devil on two legs. She slaughtered almost half a dozen of my men! Now I have to tell Lord Racin, and he'll likely rip my head off..."

With a snarl, Dexia leaped at the guard, but he had the door closed before her teeth closed on his flesh. She stood muttering under her breath for a few seconds before turning to face the others.

"There you are," Quinn said, getting up with a stretch before strolling over to where a small bucket sat with a metal cup. He dipped the cup, sniffed at it, and made a face before dumping the contents on the floor. "You'd think they could give us some decent ale, not this watery mess the Shadowborn think is a real beverage. Well, Dex? What news do you have?"

"I was captured," the little vanth said, foregoing the cup to guzzle greedily straight from the pail. She belched, wiped her mouth on the back of her hand, then looked around. "Who's that?"

"I am Dasa, Queen of the Starborn. I assume you are also part of this blighted rescue party that I never asked for? How many more of you are there?" The last she demanded of Idril.

"She's a feisty one," Dexia told Quinn. "I like her. You should lust after her instead of the white haired one."

"My hair is blonde, very pale blonde, not white," Idril told Dexia before answering the queen. "That little girl belongs to Quinn, my lady, and has nothing to do with my plan."

"Your plan?" Hallow, feeling a bit drained by the events of the last twelve hours, sat on a three-legged chair. "Not to sound argumentative, but the plan to come here was made by Allegria, Lord Israel, and me. You simply stowed away."

"Because you left me behind!" Idril rose with a dramatic flare of her nostrils. "I told you that I would not be treated like some porcelain doll that must stay behind and look pretty!"

Hallow rubbed his forehead, feeling the beginnings of a headache form. "Shall we leave off that argument again? I really don't feel up to it, and I'd like to find out how the queen and you and Quinn ended up here."

Dexia strolled past him chewing on something. Hallow averted his eyes to avoid seeing just what it was she'd caught in the cell to consume. "And me. Don't forget about me. I'm here, too."

"And you," he agreed gravely. "Why don't we start with the queen and work our way through everyone?"

For a few seconds, Hallow wasn't sure if the queen would answer. She stood with her back to the rest of them, staring at nothing in particular, her arms crossed. She was clad not in the usual fluttering gowns in which Hallow had always seen her, but in a pair of leggings and short cloth jerkin.

"I am here because Israel was determined to prove to me that he is a bigger fool that I thought him."

"She was caught after leaving the keep to engage in carnal acts with Lord Israel," Idril told Hallow, retaking her seat. "Racin found she was gone, and grew quite unreasonably angry, in my opinion. After all, the queen has borne Lord Israel's child, and if she wishes to continue such illicit relations, that is her business."

"It didn't help matters that you let the guards into my chambers," Dasa snapped, shooting a glare at Idril.

The latter shrugged one delicate shoulder. "He threatened to break down the door if I did not do so. I didn't think you wished to have your door broken. I *did* think to distract the guard until you returned, but alas. Your carnal acts were evidently much more involved than I assumed."

Hallow glanced at the queen. She made an annoyed sound and turned to face them all. "The handmaid speaks the truth, much as it annoys me to admit. I thought she'd betrayed me to Racin, but evidently one of the guards patrolling the city saw me slip through the postern gate and tattled on me. If I hadn't gone to see Israel—not that my goal was carnal acts, although they were, in fact, quite satisfying—if I hadn't gone to see why the fool was all but banging on Skystead's gates, then I would never have drawn Racin's ire upon me."

"And me," Idril said with an injured sniff. "I don't see why he assumed that just because you were out having carnal acts, I was to be punished, but he said I was clearly aiding you, and thus, I am to die in the morning. I don't wish to die, in the morning or any other time. I wish to see Deo and tell him to stop being an idiot so that we, too, can enjoy the carnal acts that everyone else seems to be filling their nights with."

"I'm yours, my lovely one," Quinn protested, throwing wide his arms in a way that he clearly thought put his physique to an advantage. "Any time, any place. I will be happy to carnal you up one side and down the other."

Idril eyed him with an expression that had Hallow remembering just how efficiently she had killed Jalas's guards. "You were dallying with the kitchen maid last night. Don't deny it; I saw you with your tongue hanging out, and your hand down her bodice."

"That, my sweet one, was naught but a spot of research. I was simply grilling the girl as to the nature of the guards who sat on the ramparts watching the comings and goings of the keep. I deserve a reward for such a sacrifice of my time and better feelings than your scorn."

"That covers how we were caught," Idril said, dismissing Quinn's excuse. She studied Hallow for a moment, a little frown between her brows. "But why do you appear different than you did when I last saw you? Why are you wearing such a curious tunic?"

"He's a blood priest despite claiming he's the Master of Kelos," Dasa said, giving him a quick raking glance, but her eyes narrowed on his for a few seconds. "He is clearly learned in blood magic."

"Blood magic?" Idril smoothed a hand over a slight wrinkle in her otherwise pristine gown and looked puzzled. "I have not heard of this. What is it?"

Hallow struggled for a way to explain something he wasn't entirely certain he understood himself. "It's…well, I suppose it's best if you think of it this way: arcany is magic that comes from Bellias and the stars. It is the purest form of light, and thus, the purest form of magic."

"It is the strongest of all the magics," Dasa said, pacing past him. "It far outreaches the Grace of Alba."

Idril kept her gaze focused on Hallow, clearly waiting for him to continue.

"As the queen says—and yes, my lady, I *am* an arcanist. Or at least, I was before I was initiated into the brotherhood of blood. I don't know exactly what I am now other than sorely put upon—as the queen said, arcany is the strongest of the magics that we know. The grace of Alba, which all Fireborn are blessed with, is based in roots and earth, rock and sea. It is the magic of the elements. Its strengths lie in healing and magics based on the elements that make up Alba; thus, it does not have the range of possibilities that can be found in arcany."

"And your priestess?" Idril asked, raising one eyebrow. "Where do you place her lightweaving?"

He smiled. "Allegria is unique. I know of no other living lightweaver. Her magic is a blessing from Kiriah, and thus, on the same level as arcany, although of a different form. It is more…" He searched for a word that would encompass Allegria's power. "…benign. Which brings us to blood magic."

Idril pursed her lips. "Good. I was fearing you were going to recite some sort of liturgy of magics that would take hours."

He ignored the dig, again hesitating before he put into words the nature of blood magic. "Blood magic is unique to the Shadowborn. Where arcany is pure power, and the grace of Alba is about healing and the elements, blood magic is a vehicle for change. It takes an object from one state to another. Chaos magic is an extreme form of it, a corruption that draws its power from the act of destruction. Blood magic is about changing objects by binding them with long strings that move them from one state to another."

"Strings of magic?" Idril gave a little shake of her head. "How can magic form a string? It makes no sense."

"To be honest, I'm only just learning about it. It has a tie to arcany, as well, or I wouldn't understand the tiny bit I do."

Idril didn't reply to that. In fact, Hallow reflected a short time later as he tried to settle in a way that would allow him to doze while still remaining ready to leap up in case of attack, no one really had anything much to say. Idril curled up on the one pallet that didn't look as it if it had been home to many generations of rodents, while Quinn claimed the other one. Dexia stalked through the cell, occasionally diving at something, and much to Hallow's horror, eating whatever she found.

He had no sense of just how much time had passed since he'd been thrown into the cell. He was deep in a dream in which Allegria stood across a dry riverbed, which for some reason he was unable to cross. He had been trying to persuade her that she needed to come to him because the blood magic that he'd assimilated wouldn't allow him to leave the bank, but just as she was telling him that he was not to give up hope because she would save him, the door to the cell was thrown open with a violence that had him on his feet before he was even fully awake, one hand automatically trying to gather arcany. Two Shadowborn guards stood in the doorway, demanding to know which one was named Hallow.

"I am Hallow of Penhallow," he answered, trying to form links of magic out of sight of the guards. "May I ask why you wish to know?"

"Lord Racin has asked for you specifically," a Harborym said, shoving aside the two guards to grab Hallow's arm in a painful grip. The Harborym's lips split in what was no doubt intended to be a smile. "He has great hopes that you won't disappoint him."

Fear filled Hallow's belly as the Harborym started to drag him away, but it wasn't fear for his own life. He'd been an arcanist too long to fear moving on to the spirit world. But if he was killed by some torture that Racin had decided upon, what would become of Allegria? Who would protect her when she was focused on saving others? What of Deo and Idril and even Quinn and the queen?

"Why are you taking him?" Dasa leaped at the Harborym, but he backhanded her and sent her flying into the wall.

"Your time will come soon enough, Deva," the Harborym answered with a sneer. "It will come for all of you in just a few hours. But first, the master wishes to try the latest conversion magic on this one."

And without another word, he marched off, dragging a stumbling Hallow with him. The slamming closed of the cell door shut out not only the protests of those left inside, but also any hope Hallow had left to him.

Chapter 19

"Woman, you cannot do this. Stop! Your plan is ridiculous!" Deo had few occasions to be the voice of reason, but he'd found himself in that exact position when he'd stopped Allegria from riding off in the direction the retreating Harborym had gone.

"My plan? I have no plan," she'd snapped and tried to wrestle the reins out of Deo's grip.

"That is my point exactly," he'd growled, glaring at Allegria's mule when she swung her rear around in order to kick at him. "You do and I'll feed you to my dogs," he'd warned the animal.

"You don't have any dogs, you great big oaf," Allegria said, slapping at his hand at the same time she shoved the mule's hind end out of range. "Buttercup, don't you even think of acting up. We have avenging to do!"

"You do not. No, Allegria, *do not*." With a mental sigh at the obstinacy of women, Deo simply picked her up and removed her from the vicinity of her mount. "Stop struggling and listen to…by Bellias's glittering blue balls, if you bite me, I will bind your arms and legs and sling you over the back of your mule so you will cause no more trouble!"

The outrageous threat served its purpose, for Allegria stopped fighting him and gasped in outrage. "You wouldn't dare! And Bellias doesn't have balls. Have you been so long without a woman that you've forgotten that sort of thing?"

He ignored the taunt, knowing well that she was beyond distraught at the loss of the arcanist. He set her down but kept his hands on both her arms so she wouldn't try to escape. "I am not going to let you run after Hallow on your own."

"Then you'll come with me?" She glanced around. "I suppose it would take too long to get everyone ready to go. You and I can ride faster than the whole company anyway."

Deo found himself in another seldom encountered situation: he had to pick his words carefully. "We will follow the Harborym, yes. If, by some miracle, we come upon them with Hallow, we will rescue him."

She stood very still, her dark eyes watchful and filled with pain that shone like light glancing off dark water. "And if we don't find them?"

"We go to Skystead. That is, I am certain, where the Harborym are headed. They would have no other reason to take Hallow than to—" He stopped, remembering in time that Allegria knew nothing of the inhuman experiments Racin was performing.

"Than to what?" Her eyes narrowed, and he could see her fingers twitching.

Again, he was uncomfortably aware that he had little experience in being circumspect. "Racin is trying to make his Harborym...more."

"More what?"

He gestured vaguely toward nothing. "More like me, basically."

She frowned in thought, then her brow cleared as her eyes widened. "And you think Racin is going to try to make Hallow like you? He's going to make him a Bane of Eris?"

"Not exactly. He wishes to improve the Harborym so they are stronger than I am." Deo, still holding Allegria by the arms, yelled over his shoulder, ordering those who were not wounded, or caring for the wounded, to ready themselves for the ride to Skystead. "We will ride, priest, but we will do it together; there is strength in our numbers. All right?"

Reluctantly, Allegria had agreed, although Deo knew that she'd harbored suspicions that he didn't wish to admit were valid. While he would have happily rescued Hallow if it was possible, he had a more important task at hand: with or without an army of Banesmen, Racin must be destroyed.

Now several hours had passed, and just as the little light that marked daytime hours had started to fade, they caught sight of a lone rider in the distance, a man who had his back to them. Deo squinted into the distance, anger flaring to life when he recognized the white and gold tunic.

"Is that—" Allegria started to say, but at that moment the man turned his head, caught sight of them, and wheeling his mount, bolted into the dense shrubs that lined the rocky track.

Deo swore under his breath and put his heels to his horse, but Allegria was faster. Her mule evidently had a racing dam, because she charged past Deo with Allegria crouched low over her neck. The man didn't stand a chance, mostly because his mount was tired. Six minutes after spotting him, Allegria had him pinned to a tree with arrows through the cloth covering one arm.

"—will tell me know what I want to know, or it will go very badly with you. Have you seen Harborym pass by here with a prisoner, a Fireborn man wearing a black tunic with a red hand on it? Answer me, blast you, or I'll geld you so fast you won't know what hit you!"

"Allegria, cease threatening my father's scout. He won't tell you anything. He has sworn an oath to die before he does so."

Allegria growled, her eyes glittering dangerously.

Deo elbowed her aside, plucked the arrows out of the cloth pinning the man to the tree, and then as easily as if he was lifting a sack of potatoes, he hoisted the unfortunate man by the throat. "He will, however tell *me* everything. Where is my father?"

The man sputtered and turned red, his hands waving around as his feet kicked.

"Well, he's not going to be able to answer you if you throttle him to death," Allegria said with what Deo thought was an unbecoming amount of waspishness.

He told her so. "You become more outspoken with each passing day," he said, giving her a good glare which she summarily ignored, just as he knew she would. "It's not seemly in a priest."

"You pick the oddest times to lecture me. Let him down, Deo, or kill him outright, but don't strangle him slowly." She gestured toward the scout, who was now gurgling in an unpleasant manner.

Deo set him down, waiting until the man had gasped enough air into his lungs to demand again, "Where is my father?"

"My lord...I don't know if Lord Israel...if I should..."

"Goddess give me strength," Allegria said, turning when the rest of the company arrived breathless and full of questions. "Does anyone have a gelding knife?"

The scout spoke after that, giving Allegria quick, worried glances. "Lord Israel is on the Watcher's road. He rides to Skystead to rescue the queen."

Deo grunted an acknowledgement and gestured to Mayam, who hurried over to him. "Do you know this Watcher's road?"

"Aye," she said, her gaze touching the scout for a moment before returning to Deo. "It's to the east. It leads from the Forest of Eyes northward to Skystead."

"How far is it from where we are?" Deo was torn between taking the quickest route to Skystead so that he would be certain of getting there before his father, and putting aside the ever burning need to prove himself to his sire. If it took his force combined with the company from Aryia to destroy Racin, then he'd join together with Israel.

Mayam glanced at the sky, evidently judging their position despite the ever-present cloud cover. "About four hours."

He eyed Allegria, knowing she would refuse to accompany him unless he gave her a reason to do so.

"You had better not be thinking what I think you're thinking," she told him, as prescient as ever. He disliked that about her. "You are not abandoning Hallow just so you can join up with your father."

"I would not abandon one to whom I owe a debt of honor. Since you and Hallow saved me from certain insanity on the Isle of Enoch, I can't leave him to Racin's non-existent mercy."

"Good," she said, her shoulders relaxing a bit as she tucked away her bow and quiver.

"The Harborym who captured Hallow will already have arrived at Skystead. Therefore, it makes sense to join up with my father's company, and together we will attack Racin." Having thus made his pronouncement, he mounted his horse and turned in the direction Mayam indicated.

"What? Wait...Deo! No, that isn't what we should be doing! Kiriah blast you, Deo! Gah!"

Deo spent an uncomfortable half hour while Allegria—in the hearing of his company of blood priests—blistered him with tales of just what she'd do to him if the delay in getting to Skystead resulted in any harm to her beloved. But after silently marveling that she was far more inventive (and bloodthirsty) than her priestly upbringing would have led one to believe, he spent the remainder of the journey focused on what he would say when he found his father.

It took six hours in total to reach the camp that Israel had set up. Mayam and Jena had to lead the way once night had fallen, lanterns in hand while Deo and the others followed, single file in order to avoid any pitfalls.

A guard some distance from the camp challenged the procession, but at the sight of Deo, he backed down quickly, and a few minutes later, Deo faced his irate parent.

"You look in much fairer health than your mother indicated," Israel said, walking around Deo to examine him from head to foot. "She said you were being tortured, nailed to a wall in order to keep you from destroying the priests holding you prisoner, and yet, here you stand, looking as unmarked as a maiden's cheek."

Deo pushed down the complex mixture of emotions that never failed to rise when he saw his father. For one, he simply didn't have the energy to deal with them, but mostly, he contained his emotions in order to keep the chaos magic from waking. It had been silent since the battle at the temple, a fact for which he'd been grateful, and the last thing he wanted was for it to drive him into a berserk state in front of his father. "As a matter of fact," Deo said in what he thought was a perfectly calm, reasonable tone, "I *was* tortured, nailed to a wall, and tormented daily by the priests. I assume I need not ask why you are here, although I would have thought you'd know I would not let my mother suffer at the hands of Racin."

"I am here because my son foolishly took upon his shoulders a burden that should have been shared by several, myself included," Israel snapped, his gaze shifting to examine Deo's priests.

Deo felt an irritating need to defend the fact that he hadn't managed to convert any Shadowborn to Banesmen and had to rely upon the blood priests for strength.

"I see you have a small company," his father pointed out. "Is it with these few poor souls that you intend to challenge Racin?"

"I will back my company, small as it may be, against yours any day," Deo sputtered. "We took down several Harborym earlier today, and you see how fresh they all are despite that battle."

One of the priests fell off his horse with a groan, crawling to the side of the path before collapsing.

"Except that one," Deo said quickly, moving so he blocked his father's view of the rest of the men as they stiffly dismounted. "I doubt if you can say as much of your people."

"My people are, as always, prepared to follow whatever plans I put in motion, unlike your group which appears to be put together of outcasts and rebel priestesses."

Allegria sighed loudly and pushed her way between Deo and his father. "Everyone knows that I am the most tolerant of rebel priestesses—"

Both Deo and Israel both rolled their eyes.

"—but this is too much. Can you two posture at each other another time? Hallow has been taken by the Harborym, and I very much wish to get to him while he's still alive. So let us make a rescue plan before Racin does horrible things to him."

"What's this? The arcanist was taken?" Israel looked puzzled.

Quickly, Deo explained what had happened. As the men and horses were taken into the main camp, Deo and Allegria claimed three-legged stools at a small portable table that sat outside Israel's tent. Mayam stood behind Deo, evidently adopting the position of his lieutenant. Food and wine was placed before them, of which Mayam and Deo partook. Allegria did nothing more than crumble a bit of bread and take a few sips from a cup of wine.

After the tales of their various adventures had been related, Israel rubbed his chin, gazing out past Deo to the trees beyond. "It is interesting that the Harborym took the arcanist. What use do they expect to get out of him? You said yourself that he could not use his magic here, and yet, they sought him out."

"He's not just an arcanist now," Allegria said, her voice weary. "He evidently joined the blood priests."

"Is that possible?" Israel looked disbelieving.

She shrugged and poked Deo in the arm.

"Hmm?" Recalled from the contemplation of just what he was going to do to Racin when he caught him—and he'd incorporated a few of Allegria's more inventive punishments—he gave a shrug of his own. "Since he was able to master the magic, I assume it is possible. I did not have long conversations with him about it—he was initiated the night we found him and spent the rest of his time closeted with the priests, learning their ways. How do you plan to free the queen with just a score of men?"

"I had hoped to meet up with Allegria and Hallow, and together with you, thought we would attack Skystead as a unified force."

"That would seem to be the best choice."

"No, it's not!" Allegria slapped the table, making Deo look up from where he was tracing the spot on the folding camp table where, as a child, he'd carved his initials. "What about Hallow? For that matter, what about Idril and Quinn? If you attack, they, along with the queen, could be used as hostages."

"Idril?" Deo's blood seemed to turn to ice at the mention of the name. "What does Idril have to do with the siege of Skystead?"

His father suddenly became interested in a smudge on his boot. Deo turned to Allegria, piercing her with a look that she met with one of her own.

"She's here, Deo. On Eris, and evidently, according to what Thorn told Hallow, she's safe with the queen. And before you start yelling at me, neither Hallow nor I allowed her to come with us. She stowed away, and then when we were shipwrecked, she ran off in the night on her own. Our captain, Quinn, went after her."

Deo was hit with a pain unlike anything he'd endured at the hands of Racin and the blood priests. The thought of Idril within Racin's grasp was unbearable. His mother was a warrior, the greatest warrior of their time, and while he was prepared to move the heavens themselves to save her, he knew she could protect herself. But Idril...he closed his eyes against the pain her image brought. She had destroyed his heart when she'd married his father, but despite that, he would rather die himself than see her under Racin's control. He'd rescue her from the monster's grip, and then—when she was safe—he'd spurn her as she deserved. Yes, that was a good plan, a solid plan, one which no one could dispute.

He was on his feet and halfway to his horse before he realized he was even moving. Shouts followed him, and Mayam, clutching his arm, begged him to stop.

"You must stop, my lord. We cannot attack at night—to do so is the sheerest folly—and the priests are tired. They need rest. Please, Lord Deo, heed my words. We can do nothing more until the dawn brings light."

"Then stay and rest. I need no such pampering." He shook her off and stalked forward, intent on one thing: saving Idril.

"Deo! Don't be a fool! Come back, and let us make a sensible plan," his father shouted after him.

He ignored that command, his now frozen soul driving him on.

It was Allegria who stopped him when no one else could. Just as he reached the place where the horses were tethered, their heads hanging in exhaustion, Allegria rushed in front of him, spinning around to face him, slapping her hands on his chest to halt him. A gentle warmth permeated the icy cold that howled inside him. "Deo, don't you dare."

He blinked, focusing his gaze upon her face. To his surprise, her eyes were shiny with tears.

"I would dare much to save Idril from that monster," he said, his voice thick.

"As would I to save Hallow, but think." She slid her hands inside his tunic until the warmth of her fingers penetrated to the blood frozen in his veins, slowly bringing life back to him. "Just as you said I can't do this by myself, neither can you. We must join forces. You were right about that. We can't do this by ourselves."

It took two tries before he was able to say, in a voice pitched low so that only she would hear, "Idril does not have the powers Hallow has, nor is she a warrior like my mother. She is vulnerable where they are not."

A little smile curled Allegria's lips. "She may not be as great a fighter as the queen, but give her a dagger, and she can hold her own in a fight. Deo, my friend, I know the pain you feel. I bear it, too. Hallow means everything to me, but I was willing to listen to you when you pointed out what was reasonable and what wasn't. So you must now listen. We will save Idril, just as we will rescue Hallow and the queen and Quinn. But you must use your head rather than your heart."

He took a great, shuddering breath, placing his hands over hers, giving her fingers a squeeze of acknowledgement.

Behind him, he heard an intake of breath, but when he turned with Allegria, there was only Mayam looking worried. "Very well," he told them both. "We will make plans. We will allow the men and horses to rest until dawn. And then we will bring down Racin, or raze Skystead in the attempt."

Chapter 20

We sat next to a modest camp fire and made plans.

"A three-pronged attack seems to be the best strategy." Lord Israel tapped the small scrap of paper upon which Mayam had drawn a crude map of Skystead. "Racin will be sure to be drawn by the distraction that my men and I will make at the main gate. That will allow you, Deo, and your motley group of priests to slip into the city via the drainage tunnels." He stopped speaking and cocked an eyebrow at Mayam, who still stood behind Deo. "How sure of this map are you?"

"Tolerably sure, my lord," she answered, her hands clasped together in what I would have thought was a sign of humility but for the glint of anger in her eyes. The part of my mind that was not consumed with fear for Hallow wondered at that anger, but I lost my train of thought when she continued. "Before I was sent to attend Lord Deo, my mother and I served a noblewoman in Skystead. The drainage tunnel will be guarded, but not so heavily that Lord Deo will have difficulty entering the city."

"A full company of Harborym could be housed there, and they would not stop me," Deo said simply, and given his abilities, no one raised so much as an eyebrow over what would have been outright bragging in anyone else. "Once I have Idril and the queen safe, then I will destroy Racin once and for all."

Lord Israel was silent for a few moments, and I realized with some surprise that he was struggling with a strong emotion. At last he said, "So long as you make sure the women are safe, then I have no objection to that plan."

At that moment, I understood the depth of his emotions regarding the queen. I smiled to myself, touched that he would give up the need to be the one to rescue his beloved in order to see the end of Racin. Like Deo, I knew that accepting the fact that he must subjugate his own desires for the greater good must have cost him much.

He tapped another spot on the paper. "Then you, priestess, will go with this handmaiden to the Temple of Rebirth, which is located just outside the city walls."

"I would rather fight at your side, my lord," Mayam told Deo, an odd pleading note in her voice.

Deo shook his head even while she spoke. "Your skills are better suited elsewhere. Allegria will have need of your guidance around the city. Your brother and his priests will be all the help I need."

"I'm fine with leaving you two to fight Racin while I save Hallow, but I don't see why we should go to a blood priest temple," I said slowly. "Surely, they will hold Hallow in a gaol?"

"The Temple of Rebirth *is* a gaol," Mayam said with an air of resignation. She cast a few glances toward Deo, but he was moodily staring at the map, his fingers tracing the same shapes on the camp table over and over again. "Or rather, it is now. Once it was the center of learning for the Shadowborn, but with the coming of Racin, its high priests were turned into Harborym, and its stones ran black with despair. If Racin has your husband, he will be kept in the Temple with the others intended for the trials."

"What trials?" I asked suspiciously, my heart alternating between horror at the thought of Hallow in peril, and the need to snatch him from Racin's grasp. "How can he be tried when he has done no wrong?"

"The trials are what Racin calls the experiments he performs," Mayam told me, leaning over the map to touch a spot at the north edge of the city. "Here. When Jena first joined the brotherhood, he served at this temple. There is a way into it from the roof of the storehouse next door. We will be able to get inside without alerting any of Racin's men."

I closed my eyes for a few seconds against the horrible picture of just what Hallow might be enduring at that moment, but I couldn't let myself dwell on it. I had to keep focused on the one, bright shining hope in a world made of darkness: that Mayam and I would find Hallow, free him, and together, we would help destroy the one who was responsible for so much death and sorrow.

"Then once you have Hallow—assuming he's in a fit state to help fight—you two can join us and we will see an end to this threat at last," Lord Israel concluded.

I narrowed my eyes at the "fit state" comment, but nodded and rose. Deo and his father followed suit.

"A little rest will not hurt any of us," Lord Israel said, his gaze moving from me to Deo. "You both look as if you have been dragged behind your mounts rather than riding upon them. You and the handmaid may use my tent, Allegria. Deo, I'm sure, will find a pallet somewhere."

I wanted to demand we leave at that moment, but recognized the folly of my desire, and reluctantly, nodded and started toward the small tent behind us. I was stopped by a soft voice calling, "My lady?"

I turned back to find Ella standing at the edge of the tent, half-hidden in the shadows, the light of the fire flickering over her, making her hair seem as if it was made up of flames. "Ella, you should be sleeping. Did Jena not make a spot for you with the priests? You may join Mayam and me in the tent if you wish."

"I was given a pallet with the priests, but..." She hesitated, watching warily as Mayam followed Deo when he stalked off toward the area where Lord Israel's men were bedded down. "But I could not help hearing what you said."

I doubted if that was true, since Jena and the blood priests were resting next to the horses, but said nothing, suddenly too tired to argue. "And?"

"And I wanted to know...I wanted to offer myself..." She made a frustrated noise and said in a tumble of words, "My lady, I wish to go with you to Skystead. I want to help you free your husband. I know you think I have no skills yet, but I am willing to fight, and Peter always said that he could never best me when I put my mind to beating him at targets."

"Targets?" My mind was moving sluggishly. "You have experience with a bow?"

She nodded eagerly. "Aye, my lady. I can shoot faster and more accurately than Peter, and I'm quick to learn if you have another weapon—"

"Fine," I said, holding up a hand to stop her catalog of skills. There really was no other decision to be made. I couldn't leave her with Deo or Lord Israel, since both of their companies would be fighting Racin and the Harborym. Ella would be safest with me, where I could keep an eye on her. "Be ready to ride as soon as it's dawn."

"Oh, thank you, you won't regret this, I swear to you," she said, clasping my hand for a moment before releasing it to slip away into the darkness.

"I just hope *you* don't end up regretting it," I said softly, then entered the tent. Despite my worry and fears, I fell asleep immediately upon Lord Israel's cot.

A few hours later, Kiriah Sunbringer sent the sun to rise over the land of Eris, and if the clouds had not been obscuring her view, she would have seen Mayam, Ella, and me slipping from barrel to barrel outside the temple storehouse. There were a few guards set, but the only one we couldn't avoid was quickly dispatched by Mayam, who was particularly brutal with a very long, curved dagger.

"Upstairs," Mayam said as the guard whose throat she'd just cut slid to the ground with a gurgle. She stepped over his body and started up the stairs. "The passage leads from the roof to the upper rooms in the temple. We must be quick before anyone notices the absence of the guards."

I said a quick prayer over the fallen form of the guard as life left his body, calling on Kiriah to bless him and see him to the spirit world, more than a little troubled by the easy way Mayam removed any obstacles. My soul was not without the stains of the lives I had taken, but those had been in battle, and although I wouldn't hesitate to kill someone who posed a threat to Hallow, I preferred finding other ways to disable people who had done me no ill.

Behind me, Ella gagged and retched quietly before rejoining me, her face pale and damp with perspiration. She avoided looking at the body.

"Do you want to stay back?" I asked her softly. "We can find somewhere safe for you to hide—"

"No," she said quickly, one hand darting out to touch my arm briefly. "No, I'm…it's just that the noise he made—"

I nodded. "It's not pleasant, but I sent a special prayer to Kiriah to guide the man to his just reward, so at least he will not suffer there." It was small comfort, but all I could offer.

We hurried up the narrow wooden staircase as silently as possible, entering a series of attic rooms, one leading to another, some filled with barrels and crates, others with broken bits of furniture, and the last with bales of bound wool. Bits of loose fiber floated gently through the air, stirred by the passing of Mayam, who waited at a small freight door set into a wooden wall. The door came only to my waist, forcing us to crawl through a passage of rough planks until we emerged into a dark room of stone. I lifted the lantern I held and shone it around the room. It, too, appeared to be used only for storage. We made our way through it to the passage outside. We were faced with a stone stair that curved upward to the left, and down to the right.

"Which way?" I asked Mayam in a whisper.

She hesitated. "I'm not sure. I was never told where the prisoners were kept inside the temple. The ground floor is a barracks, with the priests' offices on the floor above that. I would say up."

I turned to follow her when she took a step toward the staircase leading upwards, but something kept my feet from moving. I came to an immediate decision. "You look upstairs. I'll go down. Ella—"

"I'll come with you," she said quickly, pulling an arrow from her borrowed quiver.

I decided it didn't matter which of us she went with. We were in danger the longer we stood and discussed the situation, so with a gesture for Mayam to go up, Ella and I crept down the stairs, pausing every few feet to listen for sounds of occupation.

We were making our way along a balcony, keeping well back from the priests we could glimpse below, when a horrible scream ripped through the air. I froze for a second, then, convinced its source was Hallow, raced across the balcony to the stairs that led down to an inner courtyard. A priest was coming in the door as I leaped down the stairs, but he had no time to say more than, "What are you—" before I slammed the hilt of my sword against the side of his head. He slumped to the ground without another sound, allowing me to jump over his form, yank the door open, and race through it.

The courtyard was filled with wooden crates, barrels, and a couple of empty carts. Ella and I dashed behind one of the latter, peering over it to get our bearings.

Three wooden pillars had been placed along one wall, two of which held the bound, squirming figures of two women. One of the women screamed again, a pinkish froth spewing from her mouth as she writhed in obvious pain. The massive form of Racin blocked the view of the third figure. Even as I eyed the target he made, trying to decide whether, if I leaped on his back, I could slice off his head with one or both of my swords, a Harborym lumbered into the courtyard, growling a warning. "There is an assault on the city's main gate, and a second in the tunnel leading from the sewers."

"Deva will pay in hide for this disturbance of her spawn," Racin growled, turning to gesture at the Harborym. "Has she been bound to the flogging post?"

"Aye, my lord, and the others have been brought forth as well. Even the vanth, although that one cost several men various fingers, ears, and in one case, an entire foot."

Racin gave an exaggerated sigh, but turned to march toward the Harborym. "Very well, we will attend to this display by the queen's spawn at the same time we teach her what behavior is expected of my consort."

"And the main gate?" the Harborym asked. "Should I send some of the company there?"

"Don't be a fool," Racin snapped. "That is a diversion only. The queen's spawn believes us to be as stupid as he is. Send some of the locals to delay the force at the gate. It won't matter if they die, and that will allow us to descend on the spawn with our full force. Rally the Harborym! We will bring back the spawn to die at the queen's feet."

"What of the trials?" the Harborym asked, hastily moving aside when Racin passed him and proceeded to the arched doorway that I assumed led to the north gates.

"By the time I am done taking care of the queen and her spawn, we should start seeing what effect the trial has on these three," he answered without pausing.

"Alas, my lord, one appears to have died already..." The Harborym's voice trailed off as he followed his master. I glanced over at the screaming woman, but indeed, she had stiffened with a horrible twist of her torso before she fell limp against the ropes binding her to the pillar.

I crept along the cart until I could see better. The second woman was retching and trying to claw at her bonds, a low keening sound coming from her mouth as she did so. But it was the slumped figure at the third pillar that had me throwing caution to the wind.

"Hallow!" I was across the courtyard before I had time to consider the best way to free him. He jerked at the sound of his name, but his head remained hanging down until I reached him. "My love! Are you hurt? I see no blood, but you don't look—"

He lifted his head to blink at me, confusion written across his face. "All'gria?"

"Yes, my darling, it's me. What...oh, Hallow, what has he done to you?"

The eyes that tried so hard to focus on me weren't the familiar blue of an arcanist, or even the glittering violet of his blood priest self. These eyes were as red as a garnet glowing in the light of Kiriah Sunbringer. "He tried...Harborym...chaos magic fought the arcany inside me." His words tumbled out in between soft little pants. He summoned half a smile, one side of his mouth curving upward. "Guess I know now how you felt when you became a Bane of Eris."

My heart sang a dirge for what had been done to him, but I didn't have time to bemoan the hell that I knew he was undergoing. I had to get him out of there before Racin or the guards returned. "If I help you, can you walk?" I asked while cutting him free of his bonds.

He fell to his knees with a grunt of pain.

"Get the other woman free," I told Ella, who was hovering next to the cart, looking unsure. "Can you find your way out of the temple?"

"Aye," she said, hurrying over to the woman to cut the ropes binding her to the pillar. "I think so."

I helped Hallow up to his feet, sliding one arm around his waist in order to help him walk, staggering a little when he stumbled, and I took the full brunt of his weight. "Take the woman and get her out of the temple. Go around the outskirts of the city to Lord Israel's camp."

"But...but what about you?" Ella shot Hallow an assessing look before putting an arm around the woman she'd just freed. "I could get this woman to safety, and then return to help you—"

"No, get her to our camp. I'll be there soon enough. Oh, Mayam, there you are. I feared something happened to you."

"I was eliminating the guards," she said, eyeing Hallow with an impersonal curiosity. "I saw you from an upper window freeing your husband. If you go out through that door, it's a short way to the postern door. There are only three guards there, so we should have no trouble getting past."

"Lead the way," I told her as Ella, with several backward glances, helped the other victim of Racin's foul plans out of the courtyard. "Come, Hallow, let us find a safe spot for you to sit for a few minutes."

"Feel horrible," he mumbled, but after we took a few steps, he leaned less on me. By the time we made our slow way through the side entrance to the temple—and I ignored the smears of blood and obvious signs Mayam had dragged bodies into a nearby room—he seemed to be doing better.

I propped him up against a wall while Mayam and I took care of the three guards...she killing one, while I hurriedly disarmed and struck unconscious the other two. The town itself appeared to be empty of inhabitants when we moved as quietly as possible down a rough cobblestone road.

I spotted the sign of an inn and made a snap judgement. "We're going to stop for a few minutes. Hallow needs some wine, and a few moments to catch his breath."

"We have no time to be taking refreshment," Mayam said impatiently, scowling back at me. "Can you not hear the crowd? The people are gathered in the great square to witness the flogging of the queen. Lord Deo is sure to stop that, and he will have need of me. Of us."

"Racin is going to flog the queen?" I asked in outright horror. "That must be what he meant by taking it out in her hide. Well, regardless of that, Hallow needs a few minutes."

"We have no time to wait," Mayam warned, stamping her foot in the manner of a petulant child. "Since Lord Deo has stated that he is more powerful with you and that one at his side, then you must be there."

"Deo has survived for almost a year without us; he will be able to hang on another ten minutes," I murmured, pushing Hallow into the inn and sending up a little prayer to Kiriah that she not only give Hallow any aid she saw fit, but that she keep Deo safe until we could get to him.

Mayam said something quite rude that I ignored, instead breaking open a locked door leading to the area containing barrels of ale and wine. A few minutes later Hallow, who had slumped onto a chair, was sputtering and coughing as I tried to pour spirits into him.

"What in the name of Bellias's shiny pink belly is that?" he asked once he was done coughing. His eyes were watering, but his voice was stronger, and color had returned to his face.

I tilted the bottle to catch the weak light streaming in through the door. "It says *Hammer of Rexus, a Cure For Chillblains, End to Catarrh, and Guaranteed Remover of All Stains Including Blood, Ink, and Rust From Soft Fabrics and Stone.* Have another sip."

"Not just now," he said with a little chuckle, pushing the glass away. "I feel like it's eating a hole in my insides as it is. My heart, I am beyond happy to see you again. When Racin forced the chaos magic down my throat, I feared—but we won't go into that. I am, however, going to be eternally grateful to you for getting me out of his clutches."

"We're not quite out of them yet, but on our way," I said, kneeling in front of him, allowing him to kiss my hands. I freed one and touched the crinkles that spread out from his eyes, which never failed to charm me. "Oh, Hallow, I'm so sorry. Does it hurt very much?"

He was silent for a moment while he obviously conducted a survey of his body. "Oddly enough, no, not now. It did at first. I thought I was going to burn up inside, but that was the arcany fighting with the chaos magic. Ultimately, I think it was the blood magic that kept me alive."

"How?" I asked, unable to keep from gently kissing him. I was torn between the need to get him to safety so he could recover and the deep, burning desire to see the end of Racin.

"It changed the damage the chaos was doing to me and allowed the blood magic to contain it. Now it is my turn to ask questions. Who was that woman with you, and why was she so upset about Deo? I assume he's here?"

"Of course he's here. Are you sure you're not in pain?"

"I feel a hundred times better now that you are with me." He kissed my knuckles and waggled his eyebrows in the way that always melted me. "A thousand times, but—"

He stopped speaking, and we both held our breath, listening. The dull rumble of what I assumed were the townspeople gathered together in the main square had stopped abruptly, and then the air was full of screams and the sound of metal against metal.

"Deo?" Hallow asked, leaping to his feet, and helping me to mine.

"Or his father." I put a hand on his arm, stopping him when he would have run out the door. Already, a few people were racing past the inn, their faces filled with fear as they took shelter in the safety of their homes. "Hallow, are you sure you're able to fight? I know what it's like to become a Bane, and you don't even have the runes that protected us—"

"I'm fine, my heart. The arcany and blood magic are acting as a control for the chaos," he reassured me, and taking my hand, pulled me after him as he surged out into the stream of maddened townspeople.

I had a feeling that Hallow was keeping something from me. There was a sense of something...other...about him that disquieted me, but now was not the time to press him for details.

We fought our way through the screaming, crying people until we caught a glimpse of a square ahead of us. On the other side of it, a keep rose, a behemoth of black stone and sharp, pointed spires. In front of it stood a scaffold where a woman with her back to us hung by her hands. Beyond her, four Harborym stood in a line, their heads turned to the side as they watched a battle that raged across the square.

"Look," Hallow said softly, pulling me back to stand in the shadow of a building that lined the square. "Idril and the captain are behind those Harborym guards. They're still alive."

"And may blessed Kiriah keep them safe," I murmured, edging forward to peer around the side of the building. Positioned as we were, we couldn't see what was happening on the other side of the square.

"Don't go any further," Hallow warned. "We can do no good if we are captured with the others. If we go behind that small shop to the left and climb onto the roof of the house behind it, we should be able to drop down on the Harborym and free—"

At that moment, the clattering sounds of many men moving filled the now empty square as a phalanx of Harborym entered, Racin at their head.

But it was the man they dragged with him, bleeding and bound with chains that seemed to dig into his flesh, that had me gasping in horror. "Deo! Hallow, Racin has captured him!"

Chapter 21

Hallow swore profanely under his breath at the sight of Deo, one hand on my arm when I instinctively started to move forward to help my old friend. "No, wait, Allegria. We must think. Deo would die before he'd let Racin capture him. Therefore, he must have allowed himself to be taken prisoner. He must have a plan."

"Well, if he does, it's a stupid one," I said sharply, both furious and terrified for Deo. "How can he do whatever he plans to do—which I assume includes destroying Racin—if he's bound like a chicken heading for market?"

Hallow grinned at me, and for a moment, I saw beyond the strange eyes to the man who filled my life with such joy. "Looks like it's up to us to save the day, my heart. Shall we?"

"I love it when you're cocksure," I said, gently biting his chin.

He pinched my behind. "You're going to love it a lot more later, when we are alone. But now, let us go hide ourselves behind that pushcart and see if we can determine what Deo's plan is."

We scuttled our way over to a fruit cart that had been overturned, crouching behind it to watch. The Harborym guard, seeing their captain enter the square, hurried over to their brethren and called out vile comments as Deo was dragged forward to where the queen hung. He was flung onto the ground before her.

"Ah, my queen, I see you are ready and awaiting my attentions," Racin said, strolling forward. He paused to stop and put a foot on Deo's head, shoving it to the ground. "And here is your spawn, whom I found attempting to breech the city's defenses, no doubt to come to your rescue."

"I need no rescue," the queen said, her voice as brittle as glass. "Whatever plans my son has made, he has done so without my approval."

The emphasis on the last few words was impossible to miss, but Racin seemed not to notice them, or if he did, he didn't heed them. Instead, he lifted his foot, and gestured for his men to lift Deo.

I glanced at Deo's face, but other than a sharp look of hatred in his eyes, his expression was impassive. I wondered about that. Deo was not, generally speaking, a man who embraced serenity and calm. For him to remain impassive now when his most hated enemy stood before him was bizarre. I could only conclude that Hallow was correct—Deo must have some plan in mind, one that he really should have mentioned to someone.

Namely me.

"He would do well to learn from you," Racin said, circling slowly around the queen. "Sad that he won't have the chance. But perhaps, before I kill him, he may share in your learning."

The queen swayed gently, her fingers flexing against the ropes that strung her up, no doubt in a fruitless attempt to get blood back into them. "What learning? My lord, I have told you a hundred times that I have not betrayed you—"

"Silence!" Racin roared and held out a hand. The man nearest gave him a short lash tipped with barbs. Beyond the queen, the Harborym formed a semicircle, their ill-favored faces expressing delight.

Idril, Quinn, and Dexia stood together. Idril watched Deo, who ignored her even though she had to be in his line of sight, while Quinn stood protectively in front of Idril and Dexia.

Dexia watched Hallow and me. I gestured for her to keep quiet about our hiding spot. She wrinkled her nose, but said nothing.

Racin circled the queen again, slowly, speaking as he went. "You were caught outside the city gates when you had no business being there. Is it a coincidence that your spawn escaped his prison? Did you help him in a misguided attempt to save him from my wrath? These are the questions I intend to have answered." With a quick movement, he tore the back of the queen's tunic down to her waist, exposing her bare flesh. "You, Deva, queen of the Harborym, must pay the price of your perfidy."

The sound of the lash striking her flesh made me feel ill. I clutched Hallow's arm, wordlessly telling him we needed to be doing something.

"I know, my heart, I know. But watch Deo. Look at his face. He is biding his time. He would not thank us for ruining whatever plan he has made by charging out and being captured."

"But the queen—" I flinched as the lash struck a second time, drawing blood. The queen made no sound but a slight intake of breath. "Hallow, I can't take this."

"Don't look at her. Watch Deo," he said. His voice filled with despair, but his fingers were moving even as he spoke, drawing symbols in the air which he flicked toward the queen as soon as they were drawn.

Her body twitched and she half turned her head toward us for a second, then resumed staring straight ahead as Racin lifted his arm again. I closed my eyes, but heard the sound of the lash nonetheless. It was one that would remain with me for many decades, haunting my sleep.

"Your spawn is unmoved by your punishment," Racin told the queen, pausing for a moment to consider this fact. He walked around to touch Deo's lips with the bloody straps of the lash, leaving a smear of crimson behind. "It is odd, do you not think, for a son to go to all the trouble of coming to Eris to save his mother, and yet, there he stands, impassive, while her flesh is flayed from her body. It makes me wonder."

Hallow continued to draw short little symbols and send them to the queen. I blocked out the scene in front of me as much as possible, and began a communion with Kiriah, pleading with her to work a miracle and clear the clouds so that I could receive her blessing. A slight warmth gathered in my palms as I recited the prayers I'd been taught from childhood, but I was unsure if the heat came from Kiriah, or my own tightly clenched fingers.

"My son is a fool about many things, but he knows that I am strong," Dasa replied, her voice cracking slightly. "You desire to punish me, and I am willing to accept it, but you will not break me, my lord. You will not break my son."

"No?" Racin lifted her chin and peered down into her face. "Perhaps, then, there is someone who has a stronger hold over him." He turned and pointed at Idril with the lash. "You, hiding behind the pirate—come forward."

Several things happened at the same time: Idril charged past Quinn, a dagger in her hand, which she stabbed into Racin's chest. The latter just looked down in mild surprise, then up at her, at which point he laughed. "Did you think to hurt me with this little trinket? String her up!"

A roar echoed off the walls, one that made every hair on my arms stand up. Deo lunged forward, slashing out with his legs and shackled hands, taking down several of the Harborym who had been nearest. Then the chains were gone, torn from his body, which now glowed with a rich reddish-gold light, almost as if Kiriah was giving him her blessing directly. But it was not the power of the sun that surrounded him—it was something sickly hot that prickled my flesh.

Hallow and I stood at the same time, as if we were of one mind, his hands dancing in the air while he wove spells. I nocked an arrow and sent it flying. It hit Racin in the face, causing him to bellow in pain, but he merely plucked out the arrow, leaving a wound on one of his cheeks. Several Harborym rushed toward us just as a horn sounded behind us, and a clatter of hooves on stone heralded the arrival of Lord Israel.

I snatched my swords off my back, my gaze quickly going over the oncoming rush of Harborym, trying to pick my first target, but before I could, Hallow started flinging long strands of magic in front of him, building up a barrier that crisscrossed like a net. Harborym rushed in from behind us, and I made a snap decision. Without my lightweaving, I was limited, and Hallow was far better suited to deal with the larger group. "You take them down," I told him, spinning around and standing with my back to his. "I'll keep them off you."

"Have I told you today how much I love you?" he said somewhat breathlessly while his hands, moving so fast they were almost a blur, danced in the air.

I laughed and picked off the first few Harborym with arrows to the head before they were too close.

The fight that followed remains in my mind in brief flashes, little moments that seem to have been frozen in time: Lord Israel cutting down the queen, and handing her his sword while he spun around and incinerated a group of Harborym with one wave of his hand. Evidently the Grace of Alba had no problem working in Eris, because with a small bone talisman in one hand, and a sigil in the other, he leaped into battle, Harborym melting before him.

Quinn and Dexia are frozen in another moment in my memory, with Quinn in the act of beheading a Harborym while Dex attacked the face of another…with gruesome results.

But it was Hallow and Deo that I remember the best. Deo and I had once, under the influence of chaos magic, run berserk against another mass of Harborym. I knew I was seeing him in the same state when he ripped limbs from Harborym, slashing and hacking with a sword he'd picked up from one of the men he'd destroyed. His eyes were on Racin, however, as he plowed ever forward, blood spraying, and entrails spilling while he headed toward the monster who was responsible for all the ills of our world.

At first I thought all was well with Hallow, but once the last of the Harborym who had tried to take us from the rear were destroyed, I turned to see how he was doing and realized something was very wrong.

"Hallow, stop!" I grabbed at his arm, trying to stop his hands, which were moving far faster than was humanly possible. His eyes positively glowed red, and his lips were pulled back in a snarl as magic poured from his hands onto the Harborym who remained.

The chaos had him, and I knew from experience that it was almost impossible to come back from its grip once it had control.

"Hallow, listen to me." I threw myself onto his chest, blocking his view of the Harborym fighting with Lord Israel, Dasa, Quinn, and Deo. I grabbed his head so that he couldn't peer around me, forcing him to look into my eyes. His pupils were huge, his eyes unfocused. "My darling husband, hear me. You must fight the chaos. I know that it gives you power, so much power, but you can't let it have the upper hand. Hallow, think of the stars and the moon and the cool, silver light of Bellias. Feel the stars beyond the protection of Eris. Use that strength to force the chaos back down."

Slowly, his eyes refocused and lost their glowing appearance. I continued to talk, babbling, really, pleading with him and trying to ground him, until at last his hands dropped, and he blinked a couple of times, as if he'd woken up from a long sleep. "What did…was that what you felt when you were a Bane? That surge of …" His voice trailed off as he shook his head, rubbing one shaking hand through his hair. "I felt like I was a god, like I could do anything."

"That's the chaos magic. It lies," I told him. I would have kissed him but at that moment, I heard my name shouted, and spun around. Quinn pointed to the other side of the square, where there were now only a handful of Harborym circled around Racin.

"Do you think you can—"

"Yes," Hallow answered before I could even finish. He took my hand and we ran across the square. "The three of us together should be able to do it."

"The two of you," I said sadly, holding up my lightless hand.

"You can help keep me in control," he answered.

"This show will do you no good," Racin sneered to Deo. The former was unarmed, but I had a feeling he didn't need a weapon to destroy us all. "In the end, you will fall to me as all else has. It was so prophesized centuries ago."

Deo checked himself for a moment; Idril stood at his side. She held a short sword, one that was black to the hilt with Harborym blood. And yet, the ironic side of my brain pointed out, there wasn't so much as a smear on her pristine white and gold gown.

I peeked down at myself. I was covered in blood, bits of flesh and tissue, a few blobs of brain matter, other assorted gore, dirt, and mud from the tips of my boots to the quiver band that cut under my arms.

"That prophesy is false," Dasa declared, panting, her long hair splattered with blood, but the look on her face not that of a woman who was giving up. "It was so proven with Deo's birth, and the coming of the Fourth Age."

Racin laughed, a horrible sound that rolled around the square. Deo, who was still in his berserker state, said nothing, just leaped at the circle of Harborym protecting Racin at the same time Hallow flung a wide net of blood magic. I held onto the back of Hallow's jerkin, prepared to help him overcome the chaos if it once again took hold of him.

But it didn't. Racin simply brushed off the magic as if it was a biting gnat, and with an imperious gesture, held out his hand. "You think that the birth of your spawn can undo a millennium of my plans? I have not suffered in the shadows all this time to be banished by that creature," he said, and without turning his head, demanded, "Where are the stones?"

"My lord, they are here." It was a woman's voice that spoke, and a woman's form that slipped through the circle of Harborym to where Racin stood. I stared in stark surprise at Mayam as she handed Racin the three moonstones. "Lord Israel had them hidden well, but I found them. Take me with you, my lord. Please take me with you. There is nothing left for me here, and as you have seen, I can be of much use to—"

Deo roared again, this time in frustration as Racin, with a curl of his lip, said simply, "And now the world is mine, thanks to your folly," before holding up the stones and disappearing into a shadowy portal.

"Mayam," I said, shaking my head, unable to believe what I'd seen. "You betrayed us?"

She snarled something rude, but before anyone could do anything, slipped through the quickly closing portal after Racin.

For a moment, silence reigned in the square, then Deo, in another mad rage, flew from Harborym to Harborym, tearing the remaining dozen of them to pieces with his bare hands.

And when he was done, he stood in the center of a grisly circle of red chaos magic, black Harborym blood, and strewn body parts, his head hanging as he panted.

"I don't..." I let go of Hallow's jerkin and moved forward, the words that I sought eluding my bemused brain. "I don't understand what just happened. What prophesy was he talking about? Why did Mayam—"

It was at that moment that Deo lifted his head to answer me, but his gaze focused behind me, where Hallow stood, and for a moment, he froze, then he snarled, "Harborym," and rushed toward Hallow, grabbing him by the neck.

I knew it was the chaos magic he was feeling in Hallow, and in his berserker state, he mistook Hallow for another Harborym, but that didn't stop me from wanting to brain him. I leaped on his back as the two men fell to the ground, Hallow desperately drawing spells around himself while Deo snarled and tried to throttle the life from my beloved.

"Deo, let go of him! It's Hallow, not a Harborym! Let go of his throat. He's turning bright red. Blast you, Deo, I don't want to hurt you but so help me, I will cleave your arms off your body if you don't let go of him!"

Deo just growled and continued to throttle Hallow. The latter's eyes started to roll up, his hands moving slower and slower, and I looked around desperately for a weapon, something heavy which I could use to hit Deo on the head, but at that moment a calm, cool voice pierced Deo's snarls of rage.

"Deo, release the arcanist. He does not deserve to die, and if you kill him, we will be saddled with the care of the priest until the end of our days, and I do not wish to be saddled with her. Deo, let him go."

Idril glided over in her perfectly clean dress, and with a hand that looked as if it had never seen a day's strife, reached down to tap one of Deo's massive hands.

He twitched, then released Hallow's neck.

"You great big oaf!" I yelled, shoving Deo aside to kneel next to Hallow. "I swear by Kiriah's toes that if you ever touch him again with the intention of harming him…my darling, are you all right? Here, let us get you up so you can catch your breath again. Deo, seriously, you were this close to being smited as you have never been smited before. Don't you give me that look. I will smite you still if Hallow has been hurt by you!"

Idril, with a slight roll of her eyes, guided Deo off to the other side of the square, murmuring softly to him as she led him to a barrel, where as if by magic, one of Lord Israel's men ran up with soft cloths and bandages with which she could tend Deo's wounds.

"It's enough to give me a complex," I growled to myself. With Quinn's help, I got Hallow to his feet.

"What is?" Quinn asked.

"You don't want to know," Hallow croaked, then with an arm around me, limped over to where Lord Israel was watching a healer attend to the queen's back.

"—the arcanist did something to allay the pain, although I could have told him that wasn't necessary," Dasa was telling Lord Israel when we drew closer. "I was pleased that you treated me as a proper warrior, and not some helpless woman simply because I'd endured a little flogging."

I averted my eyes from the state of her back. I couldn't imagine standing and talking with that sort of damage, let alone insisting that she didn't need the magic Hallow had used to help her through the experience. "I don't understand any of what just happened," I announced in a loud, aggrieved voice. "Why did Mayam betray us when she helped us get here? What did Racin mean about a prophesy having to do with Deo? And where did he go with the stones? To Aryia? Genora? Some other land? Because if we have to go back there and start the whole battle with him over again, I'm going to need a bath. A long bath. And time with Hallow. He needs some help controlling his chaos magic."

Deo looked up at that. I was relieved to see that the golden glow around him had faded, leaving him looking exhausted, but in possession of his wits once again. "You are a Bane?"

"No," Hallow said, shaking his head. He looked puzzled for a moment, then slowly nodded. "Or perhaps yes. I don't know what I am other than an arcanist, a blood priest, and now a wielder of chaos magic."

Deo looked incensed, and despite Idril's soft protests, got to his feet, marching over to us to share his ire. "Is it your plan to consume *all* the magic of Alba, Hallow? Can you not be content with just one type of magic that now you must learn them all in order to lord your abilities over me? *I* was the first one to master chaos magic, and I refuse to allow you to best me at it."

Hallow laughed at that, but it was a short-lived laughter. "Oh, yes, I endured Racin's attentions simply so I could challenge you to a magic competition."

"You see?" Deo turned back to Idril "He admitted it! I was correct, and you are wrong."

"No, you're paranoid, overly competitive, and stubborn as the day is long, but now is not the time to discuss those particular traits," Idril said smoothly as she glided over to put a possessive hand on Deo's arm.

I cocked an eyebrow at the hand, and the fact that Deo wasn't spurning her as I expected him to do. I would have said something to that effect, but Dasa, clearly impatient at the time it was taking to treat and bandage her back, waved away the healer, answering my earlier questions by saying, "This is not over, priest. Now that Racin has the stones…" She closed her eyes for a moment, shaking her head. "It was foolishness to bring them here."

"I had no other choice," Lord Israel said stiffly in response to the censure in her voice.

"Of course, you did. You simply chose to follow your desire to free me." She shook her head again, looking at each of us in turn. "Do you not see what you have done? All of you, together? You have freed that which was bound to Eris, and for that, all of Alba will pay the price."

"Racin?" Hallow asked slowly, his brow furrowed. "He wasn't bound here, was he? He resided in Genora for more than a dozen years, after all."

"Racin is the name he took for the form that was bound to Alba," the queen answered, squaring her shoulders. "But he has another."

Hallow drew in his breath, pulling me close to his side. "You can't mean—"

The queen gestured to the sky. We all looked upward. The clouds, ever present, dense and protective over the entire land of Eris, were starting to thin. Here and there, faint beams of sunlight could be glimpsed. I stretched and lifted my hands to Kiriah, feeling a slight tingling of warmth. It wasn't much, but it was more than I'd felt in a long time, and my soul sang a song of pure joy as I embraced it.

The joy of that moment faded with Hallow's next words.

"Nezu," he said, his expression thoughtful. "Racin is Nezu."

Dasa look furious enough to challenge us all. Instead, she said with a grim finality that chilled me despite the joy of being once again within Kiriah Sunbringer's sight, "Lord of the shadows, brother to the twin goddesses, they who forced him into the form of Racin when they bound him to Eris. They gave him this land as his domain so that the rest of Alba would be safe…and you six have released him back to the domain of the gods, where he is sure to rain down death and destruction over all our lands."

Chapter 22

"There are several things I wish to know."

Hallow smiled at his wife. She sat cross-legged next to a coil of rope, the wind lifting her dark curls as she used a delicate set of tools to etch runes onto a narrow silver hinged cuff. Although he always received pleasure in looking at her, the sight of her had become even more precious since he was convinced he would die at the hands of Racin.

"I would be surprised if there weren't," he told her, blowing her a kiss that she caught with one hand without looking up. "I'm sure most, if not all, will be answered shortly."

"They'd better be," she said darkly, squinting in concentration as she etched another rune on the cuff.

He proceeded past where Dexia was telling the young woman named Ella the blood-curdling tale of just how Quinn had rescued her from the former Shadowborn regent when she was a young vanth and climbed the short flight of stairs to the quarterdeck. Deo stood frowning at a map, while Quinn explained the route they would take back to Aryia.

"I don't see why we can't just sail straight there," Deo said, shoving a finger at a point on the east coast of Aryia. "Why do we have to go south to some islands that no one cares about?"

"Because your mother is a queen, and very persuasive when she waves a sword around, which I have to admit seems to be a disturbing amount of time." Quinn shot Deo a disgruntled look that the latter ignored, simply staring at the captain. Quinn, obviously realizing he'd met his match in Deo's obstinate refusal to have his way gainsaid, added, "The queen wishes to consult with the abjurors there to determine what they know of the prophesy mentioned by Racin. Or I should say Nezu."

"Abjurors? Who are they?" Deo asked.

Quinn shrugged. "Former priests."

"They're a bit more than that, if they are who Exodius referred to as unmakers of magic," Hallow said, wishing he had the books that had been lost in the journey to Eris. Somewhere in one of them was sure to be information about the secretive cult of former wielders of magic who had made it their life's purpose to unmake the effects brought about by conjurors, magisters, and arcanists such as he.

"And before you demand that I sail you in a ship that isn't strictly speaking mine—although Hallow swears Allegria and he didn't use force to convince the fisherman to relinquish this ship to us—I will remind you that your mother is a queen, and you are not. Thus, I will heed her commands, and not yours," Quinn added when it was clear Deo was about to do just that.

Hallow adopted an expression that would befit a man innocent of such a charge as forcibly encouraging a fisherman to part with the only ship big enough to sail to Aryia.

Deo did not argue Quinn's point, instead turning to consider Hallow before saying, "I don't sense chaos about you, and your eyes aren't as disturbing as normal. I assume that means the cuffs are working?"

Hallow held out his wrists so that Deo could see the runes that had been etched upon the silver bands. The intricate symbols glowed with a faint blue light. "They help a tremendous amount. I can barely feel the chaos and the blood magic, and with the clearing of the skies after Racin was freed, I am once again aligned with Bellias Starsong. Allegria, however, is convinced that the chaos magic will surge to control me the next time I'm in battle and is in the process of making me a pair of ankle cuffs to add further protection. I've told her that the cuffs you made me are enough, but she worries about me." He smiled when he said the last few words, touched to the depths of his soul that she cared so much for his well-being.

Deo didn't smile at the folly of an overly cautious woman, however. He eyed Hallow as if he was an engorged tick about to explode. "She is likely correct. Chaos magic loves nothing more than strong emotions. It feeds off them, and the twin goddesses alone know how Racin corrupted and changed the chaos magic he fed you. You could go off at any time."

"What a very reassuring thought that is." Hallow studied Deo's face for a few seconds. "You appear to be your usual self, too, despite the strange appearance of your chaos magic yesterday. Was that due to Racin being present, or something else?"

Deo waved a hand in a vague gesture of dismissal. "My magic is ever changing. With the removal of Racin, its voice has been silenced, and I no longer have the urge to destroy everything and everyone indiscriminately simply to appease its hunger."

Hallow's eyes widened at the words. He'd had an idea that Deo's control of the magic that tormented him was not as strong as it had been in the past, but it appeared it had been tenuous at best. "Let us pray to both goddesses, then, that the new runes you've added to your harness will continue to give you such protection. And Lady Idril?"

"What of her?" Deo's countenance took on its normal moody expression.

"I ask only because I know Allegria will want to know, and I am nothing if not an obliging husband. I assume, judging by the fact that she was pressing herself against you in a way that indicated a good dozen children in your future that you have come to an accord?"

"If by accord you mean she has apologized for wedding my father simply to torment me, yes," Deo answered with a slight pursing of his lips. "Also, she said she refused to go back to Aryia unless I agreed to bed her and threatened to take up with some son of a sea witch that she met coming out here."

"Hey!" Quinn said, looking up from a logbook where he'd been reading past entries. "That's the basest of rumors, and I defy you to prove that my mother had anything to do with the bewitching of the Ravenfall Fleet."

Deo ignored him to don a noble expression. "I suppose I'll have to wed her just to show my father that although he may have married her first, I'm the one she wanted all along."

Hallow, with wisdom that he suspected Allegria would not appreciate, decided not to get into a discussion about Lord Israel's true motives in wedding Idril, feeling that was up to the pertinent parties to work out. Instead, he said, "I am bidden to tell you that your parents wish to discuss what is to be done once we get to Aryia. We are meeting in Quinn's cabin, since he took the only quarters large enough to hold more than a single person."

Quinn smirked, his gaze drifting down to the main deck, where Ella had managed to escape Dexia's tales, and was now speaking with one of the ghostly crew Quinn had summoned. "I am captain, after all."

"And I could rip your head off with less effort than it takes to scratch my arse," Deo said in what for him was a pleasant tone.

"You could, but it wouldn't stop me from inhabiting the cabin," Quinn said, moving slightly to keep Ella in view when she wandered over to lean over the rail. "Ah, yes. Not a substantial upper story, but one ample enough to frolic upon..."

Hallow was about to warn the captain that Allegria had taken it upon herself to guard the girl who followed her with the devotion of a family dog, but decided he'd let Quinn find that out for himself. Instead, he trotted down the stairs, following the flutter of white and gold fabric. "Lady Idril, you look well," he said, bowing politely.

She pinned him with a pointed amber gaze. "I would look far better if the cabin we had was bigger than a mouse's hole. We hardly have room to copulate on the extremely insufficient bed provided for us, let alone enjoy variations on that activity on other pieces of furniture, of which there are none but a trunk, and I defy anyone to copulate successfully on a trunk."

"Er...yes, well, we all have small cabins," Hallow said with as much diplomacy as he could muster given the situation. "Allegria and I don't have a wide variety of lovemaking choices in our cabin, either, although I suppose if she bent over the trunk, and I stood behind..." He stopped at the narrow-eyed look from Idril.

"I am very well aware that you and the priest get up to no end of variations upon that particular theme, having heard your nightly, and very frequently daily, activities on the way out here. I do not need any further explanation, thank you."

"My apologies," he said gravely, keeping the twitching of his lips to a minimum as he bowed again. "Are you on your way to the captain's cabin? I've just been telling Deo that he has been summoned."

"I am, although what Lord Israel and the queen expect us to do to control a god is beyond me."

"Having been unwittingly the cause of said god's release, I fear we must at least try to do what we can to fix things. Ah, and here is the light in my eyes, the heat in my groin, and the joy in all that life brings to me."

Idril rolled her eyes and shoved him aside in order to enter the captain's cabin. Allegria hurried up, one of the cuffs in her hand. "I think this one should offer excellent protection. I don't know if you want to wear just one, or wait until I get them both done. What are you grinning about?"

"Nothing but how much pleasure I take in you," he answered, giving her a swift kiss. He wished he could escort her back to their miniscule cabin and bend her over the trunk there, but he had duty to think about.

"Mmhmm," she said, then suddenly smiled, and pinched his ass. "You certainly took a lot of pleasure last night despite still recovering from everything you've been through the last few days. Hallow, do you think we can do it?"

He was about to make a risque jest, but the worry in her eyes sobered him immediately. He took her in his arms, relishing the pleasure to be found in her scent, in the feel of her softness against him. "My heart, we've done the impossible. Twice, if you consider sailing to Eris. We helped defeat Racin and his forces...or at least freed the Shadowborn from his abuse... and we survived situations that would have destroyed others. I have every confidence that we, with the queen and Lord Israel's counsel, and yes, even that of your boyfriend, will come up with a plan to stop Racin from striking back at Alba."

She nestled into him, her arms hard around his waist. "And Thorn?" she asked in a muffled voice.

"We will create for him a new form just as soon as we have the materials. You needn't fret over him; his spirit can't be destroyed even if his physical form can."

Hallow didn't mention the concern that tinged all his thoughts: that when they returned to Kelos, he might no longer be recognized as Master. For that matter, he didn't know if he was still technically an arcanist. His magic felt a little different, as if even the arcany that bound him to the universe had changed when Racin poured chaos magic into his body.

"No one is going to want to talk about this..." Allegria pulled back, her lower lip caught for a moment between her teeth before she continued. "But I have to know why Mayam betrayed us the way she did. I trusted her, Hallow. Deo trusted her. How could she fool both of us so completely? Both Deo and I are able to judge the truthfulness of a person, and yet, neither of us saw the deception in her. She seemed to me to be nothing more than a worshipful acolyte who believed Kiriah Sunbringer herself rose and set with Deo. I thought for a time she was jealous of me, but I see now that was just an act intended to throw me off."

He was silent for a moment. "I don't think it was. She had no way of knowing that Lord Israel had the moonstones until Deo and you joined forces with him. And she would have had no reason to bring Deo to Skystead unless she was helping him...at least, initially. No, my heart, I think your instinct was correct: she was jealous of first you, and then Idril. Jena said she was almost fanatical about Deo, and you said that you were able to stop him when she could not. Seeing his reaction when he heard Idril was here must have been the final straw for Mayam. She saw she could never gain such status in Deo's eyes, and at that moment...well, we won't know for certain, but I suspect she chose the lesser of two evils. She probably pledged herself to Racin while ostensibly helping you, knowing it would not interfere with her new plans. It took her next to no time to search Israel's things and take the moonstones while we were watching the happenings in the square. She knew that giving Racin the stones would grant her favor in his eyes."

"No doubt intending to spite Deo while she was at it."

"I don't doubt that at all."

Allegria touched a finger to the crow's feet that spread from the corners of his eyes. He had been relieved to note earlier that morning that by donning the cuffs Deo had given him the day before, his eye color had returned to the blue of arcanists.

"I'd never call Racin the lesser of any evil. What he did to you…but I suppose we are doing all we can to make sure that the chaos inside you doesn't take hold again. You're sure it's not doing anything…odd? It's not talking to you? Deo says it taunts him."

He laughed, and with his arm around her, escorted her toward the cabin. "Thorn talking in my head is enough for me. Stop worrying, wife. I feel like myself again, and with your help—and that of Deo—I have all the various and sundry magics inside me under control. Now, after the meeting with the others, I'd like to have a discussion with you in our cabin."

She giggled a little as he caressed her rear. "About what?"

"There's a trunk in our cabin that I think poses some very interesting possibilities…"

Epilogue

"The first thing I want to do when we get to Deacon's Cross—"

"—is take a bath. Yes, my heart, I know. You've mentioned it several times. I wish we'd been able to stay at the inn in Sanmael for a few days to rest, but I can't shake this feeling that I need to be back at Kelos."

I let go of the complaint I was about to make regarding the fast pace Hallow had set for us, realizing that although he appeared his normal adorable, handsome, sunny self, worry had settled on him in a way that no amount of amorous attentions could defuse. "If you promise me that you'll take a bath with me when we get to Kelos, we can sail as soon as we get to Deacon's Cross."

He said nothing, just looked distracted. I wanted badly to ask him if he was worried about finding Thorn a replacement body, or the arcanists in general, but didn't like discussing such private concerns in front of the others.

We rode along silently while ahead of us Deo and Idril argued loudly over some slight that Deo had perceived when Idril greeted her former husband in what Deo claimed was an overly warm manner. Behind us in a long line that straggled at the end, Lord Israel, his men, the queen, and Deo's company followed.

Buttercup had fared much better on the trip returning to Aryia, and she trotted almost happily along the packed dirt road that ran from the west coast eastward through Sanmael, and on northward until it reached Abet. Deo and I would take the fork that led us to the port town of Deacon's Cross while the others proceeded northward.

"Will you have trouble gathering the arcanists?" I asked Hallow in a quiet voice, not wishing to be overheard. We'd all agreed to return to our respective homes to assess the strength of our armies, but although it was easy for Lord Israel and the queen to gather their troops and get them whipped into fighting shape, Hallow had a harder task ahead of him. Arcanists were notoriously solitary, and shied away from being led, but still, we'd agreed that it would take the full strength of all the armies of Genora and Aryia combined to defeat Nezu.

"Hmm?" He came to with a slight jerk that had Penn dancing beneath him. "Sorry, Allegria, I was lost in thought. Will I have trouble doing what?"

"The arcanists," I prompted him.

He sighed and looked nobly martyred. "Probably. But they'll just have to get over themselves. Do you think your head priestess will allow you to gather fighters from your temple?"

"Yes, well…" I made a face. "That's a question that we'll have to wait to see answered. I think I can convince Lady Sandor that those priests who have the ability and desire to fight will be of use to us in the coming battle, but you know how she is."

"Circumspect," he said, nodding.

"Stubborn," I corrected.

We rode along in silence after that, a silence broken only by the occasional bickering of Deo and Idril ahead, but even that stopped as we approached the town of Temple's Vale, where my home temple was located. To my surprise, no children ran out to greet us when we entered the town's limits.

"Where is everyone?" Hallow asked in a hushed voice.

"I don't know." I looked around, puzzled. Beyond the town, I could see the walls that marked the temple grounds, but even the fields there were devoid of the figures of priests out tending the garden and animals and going about their daily business.

"Is it normally this quiet? Is everyone at the temple in prayer?" he asked.

I shook my head. "Only a handful of townspeople come to the temple. Most have little altars to Kiriah in their homes—" The words dried up on my lips as Deo held up his hand, halting our dusty, weary train. He slid off his horse and pulled down a bit of parchment that had been nailed to the side of the well in the center of town.

"What is it?" Hallow was at his side before I could swing a leg over Buttercup and slide off her, but after a moment spent silently swearing at all the muscles used in riding that were now screaming a protest, I hobbled over to see what the men were looking at. Lord Israel and the queen joined us.

We all looked at the ragged bit of parchment, then as one, turned to look at Idril.

"Is there a dipper?" she asked, getting off her horse and eyeing the well. "I'm parched, and if the water is cool, I would be grateful for a cup...why are you all looking at me like that?"

No one moved. I took the parchment and marched it over to her, holding it up so she, too, could read it. Her lips twitched as she read the declaration at the top.

LORD ISRAEL HAS BECOME THE ENEMY, SIDING WITH THE INVADER RACIN AND HIS ARMY OF HARBORYM. I, JALAS OF THE HIGH LANDS OF PORONNE, DECLARE THAT ISRAEL LANGTON, ONCE STYLED LORD OF ARYIA, IS NOW NAMED TRAITOR. THE TRIBES OF JALAS WILL RULE IN HIS STEAD. All able-bodied men, women, and children are summoned to Abet to witness the ceremony of blessing as Jalas takes the throne. Those who refuse to acknowledge his right to rule will be driven from the lands, their property confiscated, and their families exiled.

"Now I know your father is insane," I told Idril.

"I..." She frowned. "I never thought he would be so brash. To claim that Israel is a traitor...but why?"

"He's trying to take over, clearly. I bet he's been jealous of Lord Israel's leadership all along," I answered.

"It's worse than that."

It was a woman's voice that spoke, a familiar woman's voice. I turned to see Sandor, the head of my temple, emerge from behind a building. Her face was just as I had known it all my life, but there were now strands of white in her brown hair, and lines around her mouth that I could have sworn were not there when I'd last seen her. She studied each of us in turn before continuing, saying to the queen, "Darius has crowned himself king of the Starborn."

Dasa clicked her tongue and made a curt gesture. "So Lord Israel has already warned me. He will not remain king for long."

Sandor inclined her head at that, then turned to Lord Israel. "The northern half of Aryia is overrun with Tribesmen. Those of us from the southern climes were summoned north on pain of exile...or worse. Most of the people have gone to witness Jalas's coronation."

A muscle twitched in Israel's jaw, but he said simply, "Then it is my duty to be there, as well."

Sandor smiled a brief smile. "I would very much like to be there to witness that, but someone needs to remain behind to protect the temple and the priests." She turned her gaze to Deo. "It is said that three men bearing your mark have been seen in Jalas's company. They are most prodigious fighters and have at their control a strange magic that defeats even the strongest of foes."

"The Banes," Deo said, his gaze narrowing on his father. "Did you not say they were in a safe place?"

"They were," Lord Israel said slowly. "I sent them to Doom's End. Jalas must have tracked them down."

"If they are siding with him against me, I will have their heads," Deo said simply. Idril made an annoyed sound and moved to his side. "We will stop in Abet and fetch my birthright."

"The boon I brought you?" I asked, pretending not to see the narrow-eyed look Sandor turned on me. Clearly, she hadn't forgotten the fact that like the moonstone, I had liberated Deo's boon from her keeping.

Deo nodded. "It will be useful in the fight ahead."

It was on the tip of my tongue to ask just what it was, but Sandor turned to face Hallow. She was silent for a moment, studying him.

"Go ahead," he said with a sigh, his shoulders slumping. "Tell me the worst. Has the captain of the guard incited the spirits of Kelos to rebellion? Has Thorn haunted the ruins in spectral form, driving everyone insane? Has my previous apprentice returned with a demand to take him in?"

Sandor didn't so much as bat an eyelash as she said, her gaze now moving to me, "I fear it is far worse. The Eidolon who have slept for so long beneath the ruins of Kelos have risen. One of the three kings who once ruled Alba before the coming of the blessed goddesses is now amongst us again...and he is not of a mind to share Genora with the living. I fear you have an extraordinarily difficult task ahead of you, arcanist, for they have claimed Kelos for their own."

I looked at Hallow. He looked at me. "I have a feeling our bath is going to be delayed," I told him.

He said nothing, but wrapped an arm around me, holding me against his body. I didn't know what the future would hold—how we would deal with the Racin, Eidolon, Jalas, and even Darius, not to mention the fact that I was now well and truly out of Kiriah's favor, but at least I had Hallow at my side.

We would face the future together.

Made in the USA
Coppell, TX
24 November 2020

42061744R00132